ALL
THE BEST
LIES

Also by Joanna Schaffhausen and available from Titan Books

The Vanishing Season
No Mercy

ALL
THE BEST
LIES

JOANNA
SCHAFFHAUSEN

TITAN BOOKS

All the Best Lies
Print edition ISBN: 9781789090581
E-book edition ISBN: 9781789090598

Published by Titan Books
A division of Titan Publishing Group Ltd
144 Southwark Street, London SE1 0UP
www.titanbooks.com

First Titan edition: February 2020
10 9 8 7 6 5 4 3 2 1

A CIP catalogue record for this title is available from the British Library.

Printed and bound in Great Britain by CPI Group Ltd.

Did you enjoy this book?
We love to hear from our readers. Please email us at
readerfeedback@titanemail.com or write to us at Reader Feedback
at the above address. To receive advance information, news, competitions,
and exclusive offers online, please sign up for the
Titan newsletter on our website:
TITAN BOOKS.COM

ALL
THE BEST
LIES

Las Vegas, 1974

Camilla Flores had always been in the wrong place at the wrong time, starting with the day she was born, six weeks early, in Puerto Rico, before her mother could cross the ocean and land on continental American shores. If Cammie had just stayed in the womb a few more days, people would understand she's an ordinary citizen with as much right to this country as anyone else. Instead, she'd had to move to Las Vegas eighteen years later to make her own kind of luck. So far, she had a crappy "garden" apartment with a view of some faded pink rocks and dented aluminum garbage cans, a rusted-out electric stove that only worked on one side, and a seven-year-old car with a broken alternator. Cammie's checking account currently had twenty-two dollars in it, and the repair bill for the car totaled almost a hundred. This time, though, maybe she had caught a break.

"You sure they won't care it's me and not you?" she said

to Angela as she shimmied into the tight skirt with its flashy gold sequins.

Across the room in bed, Angie paused her shivering long enough to look Cammie over from head to high-heeled toe. "Are you kidding? Look at you. I wish I had your ass. Besides, they probably won't even notice the difference. You know how it is—brown's the only color they ever see."

Cammie briefly met Angie's eyes in the full-length mirror, and she had to smile. The chills and 102-degree fever hadn't dulled her friend's acerbic wit. Cammie was born in Puerto Rico and Angie in Colombia, but in Vegas everyone assumed they were both Mexican, the nearest source of brown people. Mr. Crocker, their creepy landlord, hung around pretending to do maintenance work whenever Cammie and Angie had a few moments to lie out in the sun. He always got their names mixed up, and he didn't care if they corrected him. "One chalupa's as good as another," he liked to say.

Cammie slathered on the foundation and eye shadow like they were war paint, as though she were going into battle. The false eyelashes, rouged cheeks, and teased-up hair all made her look like a first-class hooker, and she said a brief prayer of thanksgiving that her mother wasn't alive to see her now. She wouldn't recognize her. Probably even the girls down at her usual job, waiting tables at the Howard Johnson's, wouldn't know her, either. That was the idea, after all. Tonight, she wasn't Cammie. She was going to be Angie, and she would make three hundred dollars.

A frisson of excitement went through her at the thought,

making her bare shoulders shiver. "Tell me again what I have to do," she said to the reflection in the mirror.

Angie coughed, a rickety, wheezing sound that vaguely alarmed Cammie whenever she heard it. Maybe she could use some of that three hundred dollars to make Angie see a doctor. "You go to room 611," Angie said from amid the pile of pillows. "You knock on the door. Mark will be there with the others. It's past ten already, so they'll be drunk off their asses. Just put on some music and wiggle around in your underwear. Maybe, if you feel like it, grind on 'em a little. You get more money that way."

Cammie made a face at herself, considering it. "But no going all the way, right? I don't have to get naked or . . ." She left the most distasteful part hanging there in the room.

Angie raised up her head. "No! Jeez, Cammie—you think I'm turning tricks now? I'm a dancer, not a hooker. The most they get is a little feel. Mark knows the routine. I've done this for him many times."

"Great. I'm glad somebody knows what they're doing," Cammie muttered, tugging at her short skirt, forcing it toward her knees. Like it mattered how much she was showing now when she was going to have to take the whole thing off soon.

"You'd better get going."

As if on cue, the cab honked outside. Cammie wiped her damp palms on her hips. No one wanted a clammy stripper. With a last look in the mirror, she raised her chin and forced herself into a confidence she didn't feel. In two hours, it

9

would be over and she'd have three hundred bucks in her pocket. *Eyes on the prize, chica,* she told herself. "Get some sleep," she said to Angie, tucking the blankets around her friend. Angie snuggled in, her eyes already closed.

Cammie climbed into the waiting cab and ordered the driver to the new crown jewel of The Strip, the MGM Grand Hotel and Casino. Her stomach did a little flip of excitement at the thought of going inside. After Caesars opened almost a decade ago, it had seemed like there would be no more big, brash hotels. Now the newly opened MGM towered over everything, the biggest of all, with its enormous stack of suites and the pyramid-like entrance on Las Vegas Boulevard. Cammie had read that celebrities were flocking to stay there. She felt like a movie star herself as she entered the lush, dazzling lobby. Crystal chandeliers glittered overhead and gleaming white statues gave an ambience of total class. She could almost smell the money.

By the time she reached room 611, she had her smile in place, ready to do business. "Hey, it's about time," said the man who opened the door. Angie had said Mark was a fifty-something banker with thick glasses and a beer gut, but this guy was younger, dressed in a powder-blue leisure suit, with a Rolex watch sticking out at the end of one sleeve. "Come on in, honey."

Cammie's smile faltered at the hungry look in his eyes, but he ushered her forcefully across the threshold.

"Gather round, gentlemen," he announced from behind her. "It's showtime!"

Cammie froze at the sight of them, the half-dozen men in various shapes and sizes who all turned to look at her. The room lived up to every bit of her imagination, with its rich tapestry drapes, thick rug, and plush chairs. There was a big TV console and a low coffee table that held a mix of alcohol and half-eaten shrimp cocktails. "Are you Mark?" she asked the nearest one.

The man behind her touched her naked back, making her jump. "Mark's not here tonight, honey. He let us have the suite instead. You can call me Rob."

From the way the other men chuckled, she knew Rob wasn't his real name. She didn't care, really, as long as his money was green. "I'm Angie."

"Well then, Angie . . . the floor is yours."

He turned on the music—some big-band number with lots of horn blaring from the expensive stereo—and Cammie got down to business. She shimmied. She swayed. She got almost close enough to touch and then spirited away again. The men grinned and hooted and howled through her act. It was easy to pretend she was someone else because none of them looked at her face. If they wanted to pay her fat money for gyrating her ass at them for a few minutes, well, that would be the easiest cash she'd made in her lifetime.

Maybe, she thought as she twisted away from Rob's groping hand, *I should think about joining up with Angie full-time.*

She did three songs for a total of twenty minutes, just like Angie had told her, ending dewy and breathless, with little more to cover her than a G-string and a demi bra. "Thank you," she said, reaching down for her skirt. "It's been a real pleasure, gentlemen, but I've got to be going now." She hoped fervently that this would be enough to prompt payment; Angie hadn't explained the details of how to collect the fee.

Relief washed over her when she saw Rob reaching for his wallet. "Let me walk you out," he said, slurring noticeably, sweeping his hand toward the door.

She followed him until they stood alone in the narrow alcove just inside the door. Just a few more feet and she would be free on the other side.

"Mark didn't tell me you were so pretty," he said as he touched her cheek with the back of his knuckles.

She willed herself not to flinch. "Thank you. I've really got to get going . . ."

He lurched forward unsteadily, and she could smell the liquor on his breath. "Aw, what's your hurry? Stay awhile. Have some fun."

"I can't. I'm sorry, but—"

"Butt," he breathed, reaching around to grab hers. "Yeah, you got a real nice one. Mmm."

Cammie tried to sidestep him, but he'd backed her up against the wall. "Rob," she said, trying to sound reasonable instead of desperate. "I'm on the clock here. It's business, mmm? I don't show for my next gig and the boss will come looking for me."

"Yeah? He wants the money, does he? I've got lots of money. Here, look." He pulled a wad of cash out of his pocket and sprinkled it over her head like a shower. "What'll this buy me?"

He pawed at her breast, squeezing hard, and she yelped, "Stop!" She raised her voice, hoping the men would hear her over the music still blaring from the other room. "Let me go!"

"In a minute." He started fumbling under her skirt. "I just want a taste, honey. Just a sweet little taste."

Cammie screwed her eyes shut and screamed at the top of her lungs, "Help! Stop it!"

"Shut up!" He slammed her so hard into the wall she saw stars. "If you quit fightin' me, this would be done by now!" She kept yelling, pushing at him, but the struggle only seemed to excite him more. His fingers bit into the soft flesh of her thigh as he wrestled for her underwear. "Hold still, dammit."

"Get off of me!"

She heard pounding and it took her a moment to realize it wasn't inside her head. Someone was beating at the door. *Thank you, Jesus.* She wilted as Rob backed away, wiping his mouth with his sleeve. He yanked open the door and another man immediately appeared inside, this one big and angry looking. Only he wasn't angry at her. He took one look at her torn skirt and the tears in her eyes and he pinned Rob up against the closet door, an arm to his throat. "What the hell are you doing?"

"N—nothing," Rob wheezed.

"You okay, darlin'?" Her rescuer had a Southern accent.

"I'm fine." She scrambled around, picking up the money that was owed her and then some.

"We can call security. Have them get the cops."

"No! Ah, no, thank you." She eased past the men on wobbly legs and gasped out a breath when she found herself at last in the safety of the hallway. "I just want to go home."

Her savior gave Rob another shove, pushing him deeper into the hotel room. "You're lucky this time," he said. "Next time, maybe I've got a gun with me."

He stalked into the hall and she could see him clearly now that the fear had receded its grip on her sight. He had broad shoulders and thick arms that strained at the cloth of his rolled-up shirtsleeves. His blue eyes were dark with concern. "Are you all right?"

She nodded, still clutching a fistful of cash. "How did you know I was in trouble?"

"I heard you screaming," he said with a touch of a smile. "That's my suite right over there. You want to come in—sit down for a minute? You still look a little shaken."

"Oh. I don't think I'd better . . ."

He raised his palms in a gesture of surrender. "No funny stuff—scout's honor. I just thought you might care for a drink of water."

Her free hand went to her throat. It did feel raw on the inside. All of her did.

"My name is Angus Markham, by the way," he said, and this time she believed it was the truth.

"Camilla," she told him. "Cammie."

"It's a pleasure to meet you, Cammie. You're sure I can't offer you that water?"

14

"What I need is a cigarette," she confessed in a single breath, and he answered with a grin.

"I've got that, too. Come this way."

So she allowed herself to be led along to his suite, which was a mirror image of the one she'd been in earlier. The place was neat, with only his shoes on the floor. He'd rushed to her aid in his stocking feet. "What brings you to town?" she asked automatically, because it was her lifeblood. Talk up the customers, make them like you, and they'll give you more money.

"Fund-raiser," he told her from over by the bar.

She drifted over to the window, where partially open drapes revealed the lights of the neighboring casinos down below. The repeated flashing was almost hypnotic. He touched her lightly on the arm, and she turned to find him holding a tumbler of ice water and an unlit cigarette. He waited at attention while she drank a liberal few swallows before he handed her the cigarette. "Fund-raiser for what?" she asked.

He smiled and handed her the cigarette. "If I may?" He withdrew a silver lighter from his trousers that looked like it probably cost a week's worth of her rent. She nodded and slipped the cigarette between her lips. When he leaned in to light it, she caught the scent of sandalwood on his skin.

"You're from the South," she observed as she blew out the smoke.

He lit a cigarette for himself and tucked away the lighter. "Virginia, born and raised. And you? Where are you originally from? No, wait. Let me guess." He looked at her appraisingly and she waited for the inevitable guess of Mexico. "Puerto Rico," he decided finally, giving an emphatic nod. "Am I right?"

"Yes," she said as her cheeks warmed with pleasure. "How did you know?"

"I'm good at reading people." Then he leaned into her personal space and dropped his voice in a conspiratorial manner. "Also, it's well known that all the prettiest girls come from Puerto Rico."

"Stop," she told him, but this time she didn't mean it. She checked his left hand: no wedding ring, and he had a nicer manicure than she did. "You didn't tell me what you were here raising all these funds for."

"Politics," he told her as he crossed back to the bar and began making himself a drink. "Boring old politics. You sure I can't get you something stronger?"

She evaluated the water in her hand, admiring the heavy crystal. *Imagine having all your drinks served this way.* "Maybe just one," she told him. "Vodka rocks, if you have it."

"Darlin', I've got some of everything," he drawled, and her insides thrilled at the rise and fall of his voice. He touched her again when he brought her a fresh drink—just a brush of his warm fingers on her arm. Nothing untoward. "Shall we?" he asked, indicating the couch.

She decided to sit with him, just for a few moments. She could pretend this was her room, too, that she wasn't wearing a cheap skirt and carrying a wad of sweaty cash in her purse.

Angus Markham sat a respectable eighteen inches away, his body angled toward hers.

"I'm sorry about that Neanderthal next door," he said after a beat.

Her face flamed. "Forget it; it's over." She didn't want him to think she was total trash. "I don't usually do this, you know. I'm filling in for a friend. She's sick tonight."

"You might want to tell your friend to find a safer line of work. What do you usually do?"

She hesitated, knowing the truth probably wouldn't be much better in his eyes. "I'm a waitress." She forced a bright smile. "I can prove it to you and go freshen up your drink." She nodded at his glass. "Really, it's the least I could do."

"No, ma'am," he said with a slow smile. "You sit just where you are and tell me how you got that set of lungs on you."

She looked down at her chest, and his gaze followed hers.

"I mean all the yelling," he clarified with a chuckle. "I expect they could hear you in Texas."

"Oh," she said, blushing again. "That. I did always want to be a singer . . ." Somehow, she got to telling him all about her early life in Florida and how then her mother died of ovarian cancer and with her loss went all of Cammie's hopes and dreams. This man didn't interrupt her when she talked. He watched her face and not her boobs. She felt him drawing closer, saw herself reflected in the endless blue of his eyes. "Who are you?" she murmured, reaching out to touch his face.

"I'm going to rule the world one day," he said, not breaking her gaze. "But tonight, darlin', I'm all yours."

17

Later, when his large hand crept under her skirt, past the bruises, and up to the place where her underwear hung together in tatters, Cammie didn't stop him, didn't move away. The protest died on her lips when he kissed her. It was easier like this, to believe it had been her idea all along.

1

The Internal Affairs investigator, a bald man with an egg-shaped head, regarded Reed over the rim of his glasses as he asked the question. "Agent Markham, you were positioned next to the victim when Ms. Hathaway shot him. How far away?"

How close had he been? Close enough that Reed could still taste the gunpowder. They all sat around a conference table in a windowless room in Boston, deep in the middle of frozen February, but the questions put Reed squarely back in the humid farmhouse, splinters like razors in his hands and William Willett dead at his feet.

"I was very close," he said, sitting up straighter. "Mr. Willett, your victim, had been recently engaged in the act of trying to murder me."

The police commissioner himself coughed at this, and Reed's interrogator pursed his lips. "Yes, thanks, we've all read your statement."

"Then why are you asking me these questions?"

"For context. We want to make sure that we fully understand Ms. Hathaway's actions before we make any judgment."

Reed glanced at Ellery, who slouched in her chair next to her union rep, looking disaffected and disinterested in the outcome of the proceedings, despite the fact that her career hung in the balance. "The fact that we're here at all signifies judgment," Reed said, while Ellery studied her fingernails. She was the only woman in the room, he noticed, taking in the frowning members of the shooting review board and Internal Affairs who ringed the room—men with lines on their faces and stripes on their sleeves. "As for context . . ." He reached down into his briefcase and pulled out his carefully prepared eight-by-ten glossy photographs from last summer's crime scenes. The bodies, or what was left of them, spilled out across the table. "Here you are. Have as much as you want."

"Agent Markham—"

"Context," Reed cut in sharply. "That's why I'm here. You don't encounter these kinds of men very often—in fact probably never before—but I have. I've made a career out of it, as I think you're aware, so please feel the weight of all that experience behind me when I tell you: Willett was a killing machine. He murdered four people and that could have easily been five or even six. I think if that had happened, if the search teams had shown up just a little later, we'd all be looking at a different sort of narrative—one where

Officer Hathaway was a victim and a hero, the only one to recognize the work of a serial murderer operating for years under everyone's noses. She raised the concern repeatedly to her superiors. No one believed her."

Ellery shifted to look at him, her attention obvious for the first time. She might have even smiled. The IA investigator's eggshell head stained a vivid shade of pink. "She stopped him," he allowed tightly, "and we're all grateful. She also put a bullet in his head at an angle that suggests he was on the ground at the time."

"I told you, we were tussling."

"So she could have just as easily shot you." He rapped out the words like bullets. "That's the question we're facing here, Mr. Markham. No one is talking about charges. No one wants to punish Ms. Hathaway for what happened. But we have to be assured that she is fit for duty, that she can be relied upon not to endanger herself or anyone else in future investigations."

Ellery glared in his direction. Reed opened his mouth to object, but the IA guy held up his hand to forestall him.

"We're undergoing this review for Ms. Hathaway's protection," he said. "Hers and the citizens she would be sworn to safeguard. If she's unable to handle the demands of the job, then it's best for her to find more suitable employment elsewhere."

His pronouncement sat heavy over the room. The men looked to Ellery, who looked steadily at the wall. Reed imagined she was about two minutes away from giving them both her middle fingers and telling them exactly what they could do with the job. This was partly why he was here, to save her from herself. In return, he hoped maybe she'd do the same for him.

He fanned out the photos until he found the pictures of the victims from last summer, photos taken before the murders, back when they'd all had their hands attached. "These people died," he said slowly, "because the Woodbury Police Department took more than three years to admit they had a serial offender operating in their borders. Ellery sounded the alarm early, when several of these people were still alive." He plucked their smiling photographs from the pile to show them off to the group. "I'd say she's handling the job just fine. I'm wondering when you'll be launching the investigation into the many officers who ignored her. Perhaps they're the ones who are struggling with the demands of police work."

Not surprisingly, Reed was dismissed soon after this, banished to the corridor. He hung around anyway, like a schoolboy waiting at her locker. The men exited first, heads down, muttering to one another, and none of them spared a glance at Reed. Ellery, when she appeared, spotted him immediately. She looked up and down the now-empty hallway and approached him slowly. "You know," she said when she came to stop in front of him. "You could've just sent a letter."

He tilted his head as he considered. "I don't think a letter would have had the same impact. What was the verdict?"

She shrugged. "This was about fact-finding today. They have to meet again to make a final decision. I think they want to delay as long as possible so people forget what happened last summer."

"Ah. Well, I wish them luck on that score."

She shoved her hands into her pockets and looked down at the compact wheeled carry-on he had with him. "You're getting back on a plane, I take it?"

"Not just yet. I thought you might like to have dinner."

"With you?" She hesitated just long enough for him to know he'd messed up. He hadn't replied to her last few texts or emails, and that was partly why he'd made the trip up to Boston to see her—to explain. The problem was he couldn't find the words to explain it to himself yet, so he had no idea how to start the conversation with her.

"You. Me. That would be the guest list, yes."

She fixed him with a clear gray stare. "Seems I recall that didn't work out so well the last time."

He felt a flush go up the back of his neck at the memory of his hands on her body, at how he'd been so distracted by the instant heat between them that he hadn't seen the end coming. "This would be different," he said, and she thinned her lips, looking almost disappointed. He reached out to touch her arm but stopped short when she froze. "I—I could use your advice about something. About a case, actually."

Wry amusement returned to her gaze. "You're asking my advice? About work? I don't know if you were paying attention in there, Reed, but popular wisdom says I'm unfit."

"I don't know about that." He eyed her purposefully, taking in her long legs, full hips, and thick tangle of dark hair. Just because he was here on business didn't mean he couldn't admire the scenery a little. "You look plenty fit to me."

She smacked his arm. "Okay, dinner then. But this time, I'm buying."

She took him to her apartment, an old foundry building that had been converted to modern-style lofts with high ceilings, big windows, and no closets. Reed had spent a bunch of days camped on her couch a few months ago, so he felt at home the moment they stepped through the door. The sixty pounds of canine that came barreling at him, ears akimbo, was familiar, too. "Yes, hello again," Reed said, trying to maneuver around the worst of the slobber. Speed Bump the basset hound ran his considerable nose back and forth across Reed's Italian leather shoes while Ellery looked on with a grin.

"He's missed you," she said. "You left a sock here last time and he carried it around with him for three straight weeks."

"I'd wondered where that sock had got to."

"I have it around here someplace. You're welcome to it back."

Reed made a face. "No, thank you. He—he can keep it."

She leaned down and clipped on the dog's leash. "I'm going to take him out for a walk. You can order pizza if you want. The number's on the fridge."

Normally, he'd offer to cook, but given his nerves, he'd probably end up slicing off a finger or two. He called in the pizza order and then paced the length of her living room, watching for her out of first one window and then the next. She caught him looking and hunched deeper into her leather jacket, turning away from him. He smiled reflexively and touched his fingertips to the cold glass. Ellery had tried to escape her past by changing her name, dyeing her hair, and moving seventeen hundred miles from home, but she was constitutively unable to be anyone other than herself. He would know her anywhere.

"Boston again," his ex-wife, Sarit, had observed lightly when Reed dropped off their six-year-old daughter, Tula. "I assume it's that girl?"

To Sarit, Ellery was still the shattered fourteen-year-old from their bestselling book, the girl he'd rescued from a serial killer's closet during his first few weeks on the job. "It's not what you think," he'd told Sarit.

Sarit, who already had a steady new romantic partner—a sensible single dad of one of Tula's classmates—had made a tsking noise in reply. "It doesn't matter what I think, Reed. I realize I no longer have say in what or who you do."

"But . . . ?" He'd put his hands on his hips and waited for the zinger.

"But whenever you go up there to see her, you end up getting shot at. She's still suspended, right? They think she's unstable?"

"Ellery saved my life."

"Yes, and you saved hers. Perhaps the both of you should quit while you're ahead."

Ellery returned twenty minutes later with a burst of

wintry air, interrupting his thoughts. Speed Bump's nails danced across the hardwood floor as he raced over to greet Reed anew, as though they'd been separated for years instead of only minutes. Ellery lingered by the door, steeped in purple shadow, where the leather jacket, boots, and unruly hair combined to make her look like a fallen angel. "I'd give you the tour, but it's a one-bedroom apartment and you've seen it plenty by now."

"The sofa, at least," Reed replied, glancing at the place that had been his bed for several days in December when Ellery had decided to take on a serial rapist as a side project during her suspension.

"Yeah? You can keep it as far as I'm concerned. I'm tired of the damn sofa. Bump would lie on it all day, but to me, it's becoming a prison."

At the sound of his name, the hound nosed his food bowl out into the living room, leaving it pointedly at Reed's feet. He looked up expectantly and gave a boisterous woof. "I've got nothing but airline crackers," Reed told him as he patted his pockets.

Ellery picked up the bowl. "Well? Are you going to tell me the story now?" she asked over her shoulder as she went to retrieve the kibble. "The one you came all this way to get my advice on?"

The buzzer rang, signaling their pizza arrival. He glanced at his briefcase. The dead woman he had hidden inside had been gone for forty years; she could wait another hour. "Let's eat first."

He and Ellery ate on tall stools at her kitchen island, with only the pendant lamps illuminating the whole apartment. The glow created an intimate feeling as the pizza bones piled up between them. "What will you do?" he asked as he refilled their wineglasses with a blackberry merlot. "If they don't give you your job back?"

"Don't know. Maybe I'll move to Saskatchewan and raise otters."

His brow furrowed. "Do they have a lot of otters in Saskatchewan?"

"They would after I moved in."

"I think the department will see reason," he told her. "No need to go rounding up the wildlife."

She shrugged and sipped her wine. "Maybe then I'll quit. It'd be nice to tell them where to shove it after all the B.S. they've put me through. What about you? Still waiting on that promotion?"

"Ah, no," he admitted, leaning back. "McGreevy took an early retirement at the start of the year. I'm running the unit now—nothing official yet because they still want to do an outside search for candidates. I'll be in the unusual position of interviewing for a job I already have."

"Wow, congratulations. They'll pick you. Of course they will."

Reed ducked his head. At one time, he'd been sure of it, too, but he and Ellery had a hand in forcing McGreevy to step down. Then there was his current dilemma. If he was going to act, it had to be soon, before he lost the opportunity.

"As head of the unit," he told her, "I get to pick my cases."

"Aha," she said with satisfaction. "That must be where I come in."

He fetched his briefcase and returned to the island. "I can't talk to anyone else about this, for reasons that will soon become clear." His heart rate accelerated as he reached in to retrieve the folder. Right now, the secret was his alone, but once he said the words to her, the whole thing would become real. He couldn't take it back. He laid out three separate black-and-white photos from an old crime scene, each showing the same bloodied, broken young woman lying on the floor. Her face had been beaten beyond recognition, and there was a knife sticking out of her chest. "This is Camilla Flores," he said. "On December 11, 1975, someone broke into her Las Vegas apartment and stabbed her to death. Whoever it was, she fought him hard—there was blood all over the apartment, and the coroner counted more than twenty separate wounds to her body."

Ellery picked up the closest picture and studied it. "How awful," she murmured.

Reed took out another picture. "Her friend and neighbor, Angela Rivera, called it in. The responding officers found stereo equipment, a jewelry box, and a bunch of albums stacked at the front door. They decided Camilla must have arrived home and surprised a burglar. I don't think that's so."

"Why not?" Ellery was still frowning at the photographs, rearranging them like tarot cards.

"For one thing, she had an unusually expensive watch for someone in her circumstances—see it here on her left wrist? Why didn't he take it? Also, there's a pocketbook sitting in plain view on the kitchen counter." He tapped his finger on the photo to point out the white leather bag, easily missed amid the chaos. Camilla Flores had not been much of a housekeeper. "The purse was quick money. The thief could have grabbed it on his way out the door."

"Maybe he panicked after the murder and fled without taking any property."

"That was the theory, yes." He cleared his throat twice, trying to ease the lump there. "The local detectives pressed that angle hard to no avail. But you see, there was another anomaly at the scene. Camilla's baby, her four-month-old son, was asleep in his crib in the bedroom at the time of her murder. How did he get there if she'd just walked in to surprise an intruder?"

"Baby," Ellery said slowly, angling the picture so she could see it better. Her head jerked up, and her eyes went wide. "This is your mother," she said. "You were the baby."

He dropped his chin to his chest, acknowledging the truth that he'd told her in the past. His birth mother had been murdered in her own apartment at age nineteen. "After she was killed, the Markhams stepped in and adopted me. Her murder, as you know, is unsolved."

"And you finally want to take a whack at it," she guessed. "Now that you're in charge." She picked up one of the gruesome photos and studied it a moment. "I don't blame

29

you. I'd want the truth, too. But Reed . . . it's been more than forty years."

"I'm aware of the math," he said, his voice hoarse.

She looked him over searchingly, her gaze full of sympathy, and she didn't yet know the worst of it. "You said you'd looked into it before and the trail had gone too cold."

His father had presented him with the bare facts on Reed's eighteenth birthday. When he'd signed on with the FBI, he had enough clout to ask to see the murder book, which appeared complete, if unsatisfying with its lack of conclusion. At the time, he figured there was nothing more to be done. "I know what I said."

"You've had twenty years on the job to investigate this formally and you never did," Ellery said softly. "Why now?"

Reed clenched and unclenched his fist. "Because I . . ." He stopped and started again, his heart hammering in his throat. "Because it's possible my father may have murdered her."

2

"Your father?" Ellery asked, confused. "You mean your biological father? Does that mean you've found him, too?"

"Oh, yes, I found him all right," Reed replied. "Turns out he was right there all along."

"I'm not sure what you mean."

"Do you remember that little DNA project my sister had going at Christmas?" He bent down and retrieved his laptop.

Ellery nodded. One of Reed's many sisters had decided that the whole family should get DNA tests as some sort of genealogy project for their father. The sister asked Reed to get tested, too, even though he was the only one in the family who was adopted, a twist that had struck Ellery as a cruel joke. Reed had insisted that his sister meant no harm and that she was hoping they might even find they had a common ancestor, someone way back on the family tree who would finally link them all by blood. "You said you weren't sure about going through with the genetic analysis," she said to Reed.

"I wasn't, not at all. I sent in the DNA swab and got the results, but then it took several weeks before I could make myself look at them. Finally, I thought maybe it would be better to know. That I should find out anything I could about my background for my daughter's sake. So, I looked." He turned around the laptop so that she could see the screen. It had a lot of information on it, with numbers and bar graphs, but what jumped out at Ellery immediately were the three names listed under Reed's: Kimberly, Suzanne, and Lynette—Reed's three older sisters. Probable match, it said next to each one: 99 percent. Probable relationship: half sibling.

Ellery leaned in closer. "I'm not sure I'm reading this right," she said. "Does this mean the DNA test shows you're related after all?"

"All four of us," Reed replied grimly. "It seems we're siblings by blood as well as circumstance. And since I've seen enough family photos taken around the time that I was born to know for sure that my mother wasn't pregnant at that time, that means that the DNA link has to come from my father." He punched a few keys and called up a picture of Virginia State Senator Angus Markham, an aging lion complete with a full head of white hair. "Meet my dear old dad."

Ellery looked from the picture to Reed's face and back again. "What? How? I mean, I know how, but—Why would your own father have to go through the charade of adopting you?"

"Because he obviously didn't want anyone to know he was my father." Reed's voice took on a hard edge. "You've seen the crime scene photos, so I'm betting you can guess why. What was he supposed to do—swoop in and say, 'The child is mine from some random Latina waitress I impregnated on a trip to Vegas'? You think my mother would have stood for that? You think the voters in Virginia would have?"

"He could have told you the truth. He owed you that much."

"He plucked me out of foster care and set me up in a sprawling mansion," Reed said darkly. "He probably thought he'd done enough. Besides, do you think he could have shared this little bombshell with me alone? It would have detonated the whole family."

"You're saying your mother doesn't know," Ellery realized. "You think she's been kept in the dark just like you have."

Reed scrubbed his face with both hands. "I don't know. I don't know anything right now. I can't see how she could've known and kept up the good face all these years. Dad's always been the showman, not her. But maybe I'm the one lying now, lying to myself. Maybe I just don't want to believe it."

Ellery stretched her hand across the countertop, almost but not quite touching him. "I'm so sorry," she murmured. "It's terrible that he lied to you all those years. Still, he must have loved you, must've wanted you . . ." She let her voice trail off. Her own father had skipped out on her family when Ellery was ten, and he hadn't looked back—not when she was kidnapped and brutalized by Francis Coben, not when her brother, Daniel, had died of leukemia. Ellery had spent weeks and months waiting by the phone or at the window, hoping for some sign that John Hathaway remembered the family he'd left behind. She'd designed a million scenarios to explain why he might not have been in contact. Maybe he was secretly an American spy who'd had to abandon his children to keep them safe. Maybe he'd been kidnapped himself, held prisoner by some crazy person like Coben. At fifteen, she'd floated this idea past her mother, that maybe her father was trapped somewhere, needing their help, and that they should look for him. She must have picked a bad day, one where her mother had worked since dawn cooking, cleaning, and looking after deathly ill Daniel, because her mother's answer was uncharacteristically flat and direct: *Your father left because he wanted a different life. One that didn't include us. If he wants us, he knows damn well where to find us. Meantime, we're not going chasing after him.*

So, they didn't chase, and he hadn't come around again. Not for fifteen years. Then a few weeks ago, Ellery had received a letter forwarded from the Woodbury Police Department with a return address of John Hathaway in Franklin, Michigan. She'd put it directly in a drawer. During her growing-up years, she'd made up every excuse in the world to justify his behavior. Now she knew—there was nothing he could say to make it right.

"What did your father say when you told him what you've found out?" she asked Reed.

"I haven't asked him about it yet." He frowned at his father's image on the screen.

"What?" Ellery would've taken the DNA results and shoved them in Angus's face. "You have the proof. It's not like he can deny it."

"Yes, he'd have to acknowledge the truth about my paternity, but that's not enough for me anymore. All these years, I thought I knew who he was—I thought I knew myself. Now it turns out everything I thought I knew was based on a huge lie. I don't want a little bit of the truth; I want the whole thing. All right, I can prove he's my biological father—that's great, fine. I want to know who he was when he slept with this girl. I want to know why he didn't step up right away. I want to know . . ." He broke off and swallowed hard. "I want to know if he could've done this to her."

Ellery's gaze drifted to the horrific crime scene photos. "You really think he's capable of something like this?"

"I don't want to think it." He touched the pointed edge of one photo. "Camilla's killer stabbed her twenty-seven times. She fought him hard. The autopsy shows numerous defensive wounds on her hands and forearms." He raised his arms as if to protect his face. "The knife kept coming at her over and over again until she was on the floor bleeding to death. But her attacker didn't stop there. He stabbed her at least six more times and then left the knife like that, stuck inside her body. Even that wasn't enough to satisfy his rage, because then he grabbed a metal horse head bookend from Camilla's shelves." Reed sifted through the photographs until he came across one that showed a heavy metal horse head. "He used this bookend to bash her face in. He didn't

35

just want to kill her. He wanted to obliterate her entire existence."

His words sent a prickle over Ellery, making her mouth go dry. She'd once been the girl on the other end of that white-hot rage. Coben had derived his power from seizing young women at will, feeding on their fear, and keeping pieces of them where only he could see. He'd cut off their hands and dumped the rest like trash in the street. Ellery had escaped with her life, with her hands intact, but Coben had kept her fear and nothing would ever change that. She pushed the pictures of Reed's mother out of her line of sight. "Your father had an affair," she said. "But it's a big leap from illicit sex to . . . this."

Reed turned his head so it was half in shadow. "I know that; of course I do. But back when it happened in 1975 no one understood that much about these kinds of murders—or any kind of murder, for that matter. My job didn't even exist yet. The cops at the scene saw the pile of valuables at the door and they made an easy call that Camilla had surprised a burglar. But a burglar just wants to get in and out with the goods—he's not looking for confrontation. At most, if surprised, he might fight long enough to get away. He's not going to hang around and stab a woman twenty-seven times. He's not going to pick up a bookend and smash her in the head. He's a stranger who doesn't care one way or another about the people he's stealing from—he just wants to make a quick buck and get out of there. The person who did this to Camilla knew her and hated her."

There was a beat of silence as Ellery let this sink in. "And you think he hated her," she said softly. "Your father."

"I think . . . I think he had an enormously dangerous secret and she was the one who knew it. She had a lot of power over him back then. She was a waitress, a struggling single mom who was strapped for cash. Maybe she saw my father as her meal ticket." A pained look crossed his face, and he shut his eyes tight. "I certainly don't want to believe it. But everything in my training tells me it could be true. When a woman is murdered like this in her own home, there is a ninety percent chance that her intimate partner is responsible. I can't ignore those odds. Could you?"

Ellery bit her lip, her role in this conversation becoming suddenly clear. Reed knew very well that she always leaped when she should've looked. "What are you going to do about it?"

Reed stretched back in his seat, diffident now that he had to say the words out loud. "The case is inactive. The last detective assigned to it gave up about eight years ago, after decades with no new leads. He gave me a courtesy call to let me know the case was closing. It's not like there would be some turf war over whose investigation it is. If I want it, it's mine. The way I see it, I've got the first new suspect in more than forty years."

"What about the old suspects?" she asked. "Did the cops have any at the time?"

"A few. Cops back in 1975 weren't totally ignorant— they checked up on her current boyfriend, a guy named

37

David Owens. But I'm not sure how hard they looked at him because it turns out that Owens was himself a cop."

"You're kidding."

"Nope. I guess it was a meet-cute story for the time. He stopped in every night after his shift at the restaurant where Camilla was working and they got to talking. I gather from the notes that their relationship was getting serious at the time she was murdered. His statement says he'd been looking to buy her a ring. Near as I can tell, the cops did a cursory check into his relationship with Camilla and everyone said they got along fine. But what sealed the deal was that Owens was working a beat across town on the afternoon Camilla was killed. Absent both motive and opportunity, David Owens dropped off the suspect list pretty quickly."

"I guess I can understand that, but you do have to wonder how carefully they checked his whereabouts."

"The cops liked this guy," Reed said, pulling out a new photo, this one a black-and-white mugshot. It depicted a white male in his twenties with receding hair and narrowed eyes. "His name is Billy Thorndike, and he sold drugs out of the basement of the house next door to where Camilla lived. She dropped a dime on him to the cops and they showed up to bust him. Needless to say, Billy wasn't happy about it."

"Alibi?" Ellery asked as she studied Thorndike's mugshot. There was a hard, angry demeanor about him despite his scruffy appearance, as though he'd stood in front of the cops' cameras before and knew this wouldn't be the last time, either.

"Yeah," Reed replied laconically. "His mom."

Ellery snorted. "We all know how much that's worth," she said, and Reed nodded.

"Less than the paper it's printed on."

"So then what's your plan?" Ellery wanted to know.

Reed shrugged. "Go to Vegas. See if I can find Angie Rivera or Billy Thorndike, or any of the other witnesses. See what they might have known about my father, if anything."

Ellery glanced at the horrible photos and imagined walking in on a friend slaughtered like that, lifeless with a knife in her chest. "You would think Angie would have known the truth, right? Her best friend. If she'd suspected your father at the time, then she might have said something to the cops."

Reed thought for a moment and then punched a few keys on his laptop. A video of Angus Markham delivering a campaign speech began to play. Broad-shouldered and attired in a vibrant blue suit, he might have been a ringmaster or an actor seizing the stage. "You know," he said, his voice at once friendly and booming from the podium, "sometimes a candidate for public office, if he has an admirable track record, might be tempted to rest on those laurels. He might say, 'Look at my long list of good deeds and consider them when casting your vote.' But, my friends, past good deeds are just that: in the past. They're not enough. They do not help us now. Our people are always looking forward—this is a go-ahead country; we in Virginia want to lead the way. However good things are today, we want them better tomorrow, for ourselves and for our children."

He paused for the roar of the crowd, and Ellery let out a shuddering breath. "He's good," she admitted as Reed stopped the video.

"You should see him in person," he said. "He walks into a room and he doesn't even have to say anything. It's like the energy changes—like the charge in the air before a lightning storm. You're drawn to him. You forget whatever you were talking about because you want to hear whatever he has to say." He shook his head. "So yes, I can definitely see why a young woman might've gone to bed with him. I can also see why another young woman—if she thought he had done this to her best friend—might've wanted to keep her mouth shut."

Ellery dragged one of the pictures toward her and she made herself look. At the end of this quest, no matter where it led, was a person capable of butchering another human being. "So, when do we leave?" she asked, and Reed's eyebrows lifted.

"We?" he echoed.

"Of course we. That's why you're here, right? That's why you told me all of this. I'm the only person you know who's crazy enough to go chasing after a killer whose trail is forty years cold by now."

"I wanted a sounding board, and I couldn't tell my family—not yet, anyway. You're smart and you're a cop. I figured if I was a making mistake, you'd let me know."

For the first time since he'd brought out the pictures, Ellery smiled. "Bullshit," she said. "You told me 'cause you knew I'd say go for it."

An answering smile played at Reed's lips. "I didn't expect you to volunteer to go with me. I'm touched, by the way."

She gave an exaggerated shrug. "What else have I got to do? You've got a badge behind you, but I don't. Seems like each one has its own advantages."

"Meaning?"

"You have to play by the rules. I don't."

Some of the color drained from Reed's face, like maybe he was remembering what had happened the last time she hadn't played by the rules. Either way, she always got results. He knew that, too. She collected the last of their dishes and took them to the sink.

"I have a flight booked for Monday," he admitted finally.

Amused, she turned around to look at him. "Oh, I see— and you still want to stick with that story about how I was going to talk you out of it?"

Reed ambled over to the sink and leaned against the counter next to her, six feet of warm, sleek male. He was an amazing leaner—casual but authoritative. She envied the comfortable way he occupied space in the world. "I could've canceled the ticket," he told her.

"You could still cancel tomorrow's," she replied. He had a nine A.M. flight home to Virginia.

She felt him stiffen, felt his intake of breath. Her bold invitation vibrated the air between them. Ellery had taken men to bed before, but never her bed, never in her private space, and never for pleasure. After all the years, Reed was still the only man who had seen her all the way naked, back

41

when she was fourteen and there wasn't much to see except a skinny girl covered in cuts and bruises. Her body seemed to remember him, enough that she'd broken her own rules a couple of times and let him touch her. As a result, she'd awoken in the dark with the memory of his hot mouth on her bare shoulder, throbbing in places she usually tried not to think about.

"Ah, I . . ." He backed away infinitesimally, just enough for her to get her answer.

"Forget it. Forget I said anything." She pushed off from the sink and fled to the shadows in the living room. Reed trailed after her, but she kept her back to him, searching around in the shadows for his overnight bag. Ever helpful, Speed Bump snuffled around with her. "Do you need a ride to the hotel?" she asked, her voice echoing to the high ceiling. "Or I could call you a ride if that's easier."

"Ellery . . ."

"Oh, here it is," she said, her hands closing around the plastic handle. "You should be all set now. What flight are you taking to Las Vegas? Let me know so I can book one for about the same time."

"I'll book you one myself," he said, his voice gentle.

Her chin rose up. "I can pay my own way."

"I know, but I insist." He was standing close to her again, near enough that she could smell his aftershave. "You're the one doing me the favor this time."

She kept her eyes trained on the floor. "I haven't done anything yet."

42

"Yes, you have." He touched her chin, urging her upward until she had to look at him again. The intensity in his dark gaze made her catch her breath, but she didn't move away. They watched each other as he brushed his fingertips over the curve of her cheek like a blind man reading Braille. "I want to stay," he murmured, his voice thick. "So much. But you don't know how crazy I've felt these past few weeks, ever since I found out the truth about my paternity. Like I'm going out of my skin."

A shiver went over her at the word "skin." She never let anyone touch her like this, but with Reed she couldn't seem to stop. "Reed, I—"

His fingers landed on her lips, shushing her. "There's a chance I'm making a terrible decision with all of this. I—I don't want to make more than one of them. Not now. Not with you."

Shame washed over her, hot and quick, and she pulled back. She was always someone else's mistake. "It's okay. I get it. Let's just forget the whole thing."

Reed shook his head slowly. "No," he replied. "You're distinctly unforgettable."

She hugged her arms around her middle and regarded him in the low light. Speed Bump leaned against her legs. "Why did you really come up here to see me?"

He took a long time with his answer. "Because," he said finally. "I always know who I am when I'm with you."

3

Reed strolled aimlessly around the baggage claim area of McCarran Airport, waiting for Ellery's plane to arrive. Airports and casinos had a similar buzzy, dizzy atmosphere— swirling with activity and yet totally isolated from the outside world, filled with people who had no idea what time zone they were in. Reed had awoken at the cold inky dawn on the other side of the country and now found himself just steps away from the desert sunshine where, by the peculiarities of east– west travel, it was still morning outside. McCarran wasn't crowded, so Reed had plenty of space to amble and reconsider his potentially foolish undertaking. Already it seemed like Vegas was mocking him. The omnipresent slot machines flashed twinkling lights and beeped out cheery songs, while overhead large electronic billboards advertised illusion shows that promised to astonish and mystify. Vegas, Reed knew, was all about keeping your attention at the front door while the truth slipped out the back. He'd come seeking the kind of answers that the city might not care to give.

Las Vegas didn't care what you were before—here you could be bigger, brighter, new again. Immense casinos were imploded in a matter of seconds. Old glitzy signs, once grand, were dismantled and hauled off in pieces to the Neon Boneyard. Vegas history lived only in faded black-and-white pictures, in the dust of the desert. His mother, too, had gone that way. He'd glimpsed her only in scant pictures, and her body had been cremated years ago, the ashes spread he knew not where.

Reed's cell phone rang, and he fished it out, thinking the call might be from Ellery, but the ID said it was his sister Kimberly. He hesitated, the phone buzzing in his hand. He had been avoiding his family ever since he found out the truth about his genetic origins. Kimberly, Suzanne, and Lynette had clearly done nothing wrong, and he didn't want to punish them with the bad news about their father—not until he knew the whole story. His sisters, however, were starting to suspect that something was amiss. "Hi, Kimmy," he said cautiously as he clicked on the phone.

"Finally!" she said on the other end. "I've been trying to get ahold of you for three days. Are you and Tula coming to Max's party next Saturday or not?"

"Uh, I'm not sure," Reed replied hazily as he glanced around. Ellery's flight had landed and passengers were starting to pour into the baggage claim area. He didn't want to disappoint his ten-year-old nephew on his birthday, but he also couldn't imagine standing around with his family faking a jocularity he did not feel. "Are Mama and Daddy going to be there?"

"Depending on Daddy's schedule. They said they'd try to make it, but you know how it goes."

Their father's constituents always came first. Senator Markham had visited local public schools almost monthly while his children were growing up, and yet he had managed to miss most of their recitals, concerts, and athletic games. He loved his kids but had to fit them into the margins of his demanding public schedule. Sundays, Reed had learned early on, were a good bet for Daddy's attention—those few golden hours between the end of church and the start of the football game. His father would throw a ball around in the yard with Reed or listen to the latest piece Reed was practicing on the piano. Angus was an active music listener, closing his eyes, swaying with the notes like he was taking the melody right into his heart. He'd always been Reed's favorite audience. In return, Reed had played the dutiful son, standing on the campaign stage next to his lily-white sisters, pretending he never heard the mutterings from the crowd. *That one's adopted.*

Reed felt the steam rise up in him at the memory. His father had certainly heard the comments, too, and he'd never said a thing. "I don't think I'm going to be able to make it," he said to Kimmy. "I'm busy working on a case out of town."

"Oh, that's a shame! Max will be so sad that Tula isn't there. What case are you working? Not a bad one, I hope."

"They're all bad," Reed said shortly. He saw Ellery appear across the room, but she hadn't spotted him yet.

"I know, I know. It's just . . . the ones with the little kids seem worse, that's all I'm saying. I hope it isn't kids this time."

Reed gripped the phone tighter. "It's a baby," he told his sister, his tone harder than he'd intended. "A baby whose mother was murdered while he slept in his crib in the next room." Joey Flores, a name Reed knew had once been his but which felt completely alien. All these years, it had been easier to pretend the horror belonged to someone else—some baby barely out of his mama's womb who didn't get the chance to know everything he'd lost that day.

Kimmy's breathing deepened on the other end. "Oh my God, that's horrible . . ." Reed had never discussed the specifics of Camilla's death with any of his sisters, and they'd never asked. Now he found himself wondering just how much they'd really known.

"I've got to go," he said. Across the room, Ellery stopped short as her gaze locked on to his. At one point, she'd had to shed her old identity like a snakeskin, becoming someone entirely new, a trick Reed would have to pull off if he was to find the truth. He counted on her to show him the way. As a start, he hung up on Kimmy without saying goodbye.

"I hope you haven't been waiting long," Ellery said as she came to stand in front of him.

Reed smiled faintly. "Only about forty years."

He'd rented a black SUV, something suitable for his secret ops mission, and Ellery fit the tableau just fine. She wore her usual black leather jacket, boots, and no-nonsense expression. In the car, she rolled down the passenger-side window and let the breeze ruffle her hair as she watched the passing scenery. "You think of Vegas as glitzy neon lights," she said. "But from up in the air, it looked mostly dirt brown."

"Wait until the sun goes down."

Ellery turned her head to look at him. "So what's your first move?" she asked.

"We're meeting the sheriff down at LV Metro headquarters," he replied, and Ellery's expression reflected surprise.

"The sheriff," she repeated, settling back into her seat. "Boy, they sure roll out the red carpet for the FBI, don't they? I'd have thought the sheriff would be too busy to take a meeting on a forty-year-old cold case."

This thought had occurred to Reed as well. "I assume it's a professional courtesy as well as a personal one. He's got to know by now that I'm the baby from the crime scene." No doubt he also knew Reed's father was running for governor in Virginia.

Ellery was quiet a moment. "If they know your personal connection," she said, "it's kind of a surprise they let you take the case."

"Who else wants it? It's dead as far as they're concerned."

Reed had worked with the Las Vegas Metropolitan Police Department in the past, so he found their headquarters with no trouble. It was a large, modern complex of sandy-colored buildings four stories high. The pale brown bricks blended in with the surrounding desert, while the large windows reflected a big blue sky. The impressive structure hadn't existed at the time Reed's mother was murdered; in fact, the LVMPD was an infant barely older than Reed at the time. It came into being when the Las Vegas Police Department merged with the Clark County Sheriff's Office in 1973, forming one of the largest police agencies in the United States. Since then, the Flores murder had passed from one cop to another, sitting idle on the shelf, until the sheriff had finally ordered it closed.

A group of tall waving palm trees beckoned at the entrance, and Reed turned into the large parking lot. After a quick check-in at the front desk, Reed and Ellery received a uniformed escort up to Sheriff Brad Ramsey's office. Ramsey stood up and came around from behind his desk to greet them. "Come in, come in," he urged as he shook their hands in turn. "Please have a seat." Trim and compact, he had a head of silver hair but a surprisingly unlined face for a man in his sixties, especially one who had spent his adult years presiding over the city's yellow underbelly. He moved with quick efficiency, no wasted effort as he pulled out a chair for each of them. Reed noted the panoramic view from the corner office included more palm trees and sprawling city streets. In the distance, the casinos on The Strip formed their own kind of mountain range, shimmering in the sun.

"Thanks for seeing us," Reed said, and Sheriff Ramsey spread his hands in a magnanimous gesture.

"Of course. I wanted to take the opportunity to express my personal condolences to you for the loss of your mother and to offer my sincere regret for our inability to solve her case. If we had unlimited resources, I'd leave the case open indefinitely—no one wants to see a killer go free—but you know how the numbers are. The taxpayers have their current concerns, and sometimes we have to make hard decisions."

"I understand," Reed replied. The sheriff reminded him somewhat of his father, with his relaxed but authoritative tone and the direct eye contact and open body posture. *I'm in charge, but I want you to like me anyway,* his demeanor said, and Reed remembered that sheriff was an elected position in Las Vegas.

"We'll cooperate in any way we can, of course. It's just that I can't devote any more man-hours to the case."

"What if we found a new lead?" Ellery wanted to know, and the sheriff's gaze fell on her.

"If you found new evidence that substantially changes the picture of this case then we'd certainly revisit our position, Ms. . . . I'm sorry, but I didn't catch your name."

"Ellery Hathaway."

Reed watched as the sheriff leaned back in his seat and tried to place the name. The murders last summer had blown up Coben's story again, this time with Ellery's real identity attached. He jumped in before the sheriff could make the connection. "She's helping me with the investigation," he said smoothly, hoping no one would ask to see Ellery's official credentials. It was a closed case anyway, so what did it matter who took a look at it?

"Well, you're welcome to look over whatever we have. I

had Sergeant Don Price bring it all up to room three for your perusal. The murder book and its contents are yours to keep if you'd like them. As for the rest, you're welcome to take photos, but the physical evidence has to remain on the property. I hope you understand."

"Of course," Reed replied.

"Do you mind my asking what exactly you're looking for? I appreciate your personal investment, but I'm surprised the FBI would take on a case this old."

"As it happens," Reed said, reaching down to withdraw a folder of his own, "your office requested our help with the case back in 1988—a Sergeant Lewis McGinley wrote the letter." Reed handed the typewritten document across the desk so the sheriff could take a look. "So, you could say I'm only following up."

The sheriff gave a little frown as he read it over, and then forced a smile as he returned the letter to Reed. "You FBI guys sure keep long records." He gestured toward the door. "Shall we go take a look?"

Reed and Ellery followed the sheriff down the hall to where he knocked on the door and opened it without waiting for an acknowledgment. "Don? You have a minute? Our guests have arrived."

Don Price turned out to be a large man in a cotton uniform that strained his shoulders and whose reddened ears suggested he'd recently spent too much time in the sun. "Sure thing," he said, digging out a set of keys. "I've got everything locked up in room three right down yonder."

They followed him to the locked room where Reed rolled his neck and braced himself for what was on the other side of the door. He could feel Ellery's eyes on him but did not turn to meet her gaze. "Ah, here we go," Price said as the door came free. He stood to the side and let Reed pass through first.

The first thing Reed noticed was the smell—old and warped cardboard boxes covered in a faint film of dust. There were three of them lined up on the table, next to two fat black binders marked with Camilla Flores's name and several aging manila envelopes that were faded and threatening to tear. The others hung back as Reed slowly approached the table, hesitant as he was to begin the historical autopsy. He had been through this process enough times with other cases to know what he was likely to find in the boxes—bloodied clothes, the knife, and other physical items from the scene. He instead concentrated first on the murder book, flipping it open to the first page. The abbreviated reports he'd received earlier had not included any statement from the first responding officer. Reed wanted the story right from the beginning, especially since the rookie at the scene was likely to still be alive today. He passed through the first few pages and did not see what he was looking for, so he sped up his search until he reached the back of the first book. When that proved fruitless, he started on the second one.

Ramsey stepped forward and cleared his throat. "Are you looking for something in particular? Maybe I can help."

"There's no statement from the first officer at the scene,"

Reed said, and Ellery came to look, too.

"No?" Ramsey scratched the back of his neck and shook his head. "I guess with forty years piled up, sometimes things go astray. But I can assure you he's got nothing of value to add. He was a beat cop who just happened to be closest to the scene when the call came in."

"I'd still like to talk to him, if possible," Reed said.

Ramsey spread his hands and smiled. "Ask away," he replied. "First murder I ever saw, and it still stands as one of the worst ones all these years later."

"You?" Ellery asked with surprise. "You got the call?"

"It was my regular patrol. I was three blocks away when dispatch got the call just shy of seventeen hundred hours. By the time I rolled up, neighbors had already started to gather on the street. They got to watch me lose my lunch about two minutes later once I got a look inside. The apartment door was open, but I could see that the lock had not been obviously tampered with. The victim was as she's described in the reports—lying on her back near the kitchen area, with a knife sticking out of her ribs. Someone had beaten her about the head and face as well. I checked for vitals, but there were none, and then I went outside to call it in." He shrugged. "I stayed at the scene long enough for the big boys to arrive, and then I got out of their way."

Reed pulled out his own notes and consulted them briefly. "Her friend and neighbor Angela Rivera called it in. Did you talk to her at all?"

"Angie," the sheriff replied, as if the name was strange on

his tongue after all these years. "Yeah, I saw her. She made the call from her apartment next door. She'd been out shopping and came home to find Camilla's door standing partway open, just like I found it. She heard the baby crying, so she pushed the door all the way open, and that's when she found Cammie. According to her statement, she, uh, she grabbed the baby and ran to her own apartment to phone it in. We have the recording if you'd like to hear it."

Reed felt his skin grow tight as Ramsey described Angie removing the baby from the crime scene. Him. He was the baby. So much blood in the apartment that day, and somehow he'd escaped clean. "Yes, sure," he said, keeping his voice as neutral as he could. "Let's hear it." He told himself it was just a bunch of words, spoken more than forty years ago. He'd heard at least a hundred distress calls in his career, and this would be just one more. The sheriff nodded at Don Price, who produced a tape recorder and slipped in the cassette.

They stood around the table as it began to play. First there was a loud crackle and then a sharp click, followed by a calm, male voice. "This is Emergency. How can we assist you?"

"Help; she's dead! Come quick; I need help!" A young female voice, trembling and steeped in fear, filled the narrow room. "Please, she's not breathing and there is blood all over . . ."

"Ma'am, where are you? Who's been hurt?"

Reed heard a long moan, followed by a baby's cry. The noise made the hair on the back of his neck stand up. "Cammie. My neighbor. She's dead, she's dead. He killed

54

her! There's blood everywhere. Please, please come."

The dispatcher eventually got Angie to reveal the address. "We have help on the way, ma'am. Are you someplace safe?"

Angie's hiccupping cries echoed back through the ages. "She's stabbed with a knife in her. I told her . . . I told her he'd come. Shh, *niño*, shh . . ." She said something in Spanish that Reed could not translate. He wondered if his baby self had known the words.

"Who would come? Ma'am, do you know who did this?"

There was static on the line, like Angie was juggling the phone. Reed heard himself again, wailing now along with Angie. She muttered something incomprehensible. He caught the word "mama" and it chilled him to the bone. The baby kept screaming inconsolably. Reed wondered about the killer. *Did I see him? Did he even know I was there?*

Sirens came through on the line. "They're here." Angie snuffled close to the receiver, her harsh breathing overwhelming the small room, and then the call went dead.

Reed stood stock-still as the tape player continued to hiss. He gripped the back of the chair as the sound of Angela's sobs and his own infant terror continued to wash over him. *I was there,* he thought, his ears buzzing. *I heard her die.* He had seen enough of the crime scene photos to know his mother had not gone quietly. He could imagine her screams and the sounds of the death blows, metal against bone.

"Reed?" Ellery touched his arm and he jumped. He whirled to face her, but his eyes couldn't make her come into focus.

Dimly, he saw her waving toward the door. "You guys want to give us a second here, please?" she said to the others.

Sheriff Ramsey and Sergeant Price cleared out of the room, and the sound of the door clicking shut jolted Reed from his nightmare memories. Ellery was looking up at him, filled with concern. "Reed, are you okay? You want to sit down?"

He forced himself to take a slow, deep breath. "No, I'm fine."

Ellery looked him over, assessing. "That 911 call was intense."

He paced away from her, but she followed after him. He could see the cardboard boxes in his peripheral vision and turned to look at Ellery instead. He cleared his throat. "On the phone, Angie said 'he' did it. It sounds like she believes she knew the killer."

"Reed. You don't have to be the one to do this. You don't have to be the one to work this case."

"I do have to do it. There's no one else."

"No, I absolutely get it. You, you're a fixer." She paused to give him a coaxing smile. "Believe me, I should know. I'm your biggest reclamation project. You fly all over the world trying to make it a better place, and I'll admit it's one of your more amazing qualities." He checked to make sure she wasn't rolling her eyes as she said it, but she seemed sincere. "But you don't have to fix this," she continued softly. "Not— not if it's going to hurt this much. You were just a baby when it happened, and it wasn't your fault. I'm betting if your mother were alive and standing here, she would tell you the same thing."

If your mother were alive and standing here . . . Reed sagged against the chair at the thought of his mother, the only one he'd known. Marianne Markham wouldn't be pleased to see him paging through Camilla's murder book, not at all. She kept a tidy house and a tidy life to go with it. He didn't doubt she loved him. She just wouldn't understand. Neither, of course, would his sisters. On occasion, Reed had heard one or the other relative make a comment—*We love Reed just as much as if he were our own*—and the words always set a quiver in his belly because he himself had no comparison. The Markhams were all he'd ever had, all he'd ever known. "I need to find out the truth," he told Ellery quietly. "No matter what it is."

She searched his face for a moment and then nodded reluctantly. "Okay. You know I'll back your play no matter what. I just felt like someone ought to give you an out."

He smiled a little and nudged her. "Thanks for being that someone," he said, and she ducked her head and looked at the floor. Reed crossed to reopen the door and admit the sheriff and Sergeant Price, who had been milling in the hall.

"Everything okay?" Sheriff Ramsey asked.

Reed ignored the question and nodded in the direction of the tape player. "On the call, Angela Rivera certainly acted like she knew the killer's identity. I presume your office followed up."

"Yeah, because of what she said, the investigating officers

initially thought this one would be easy to wrap up. Angie named Billy Thorndike as the killer, but under questioning it became apparent she had no direct knowledge of the case. She was speculating based on prior threats Thorndike had made against Camilla Flores."

Reed had read the summary of her statement. "Camilla turned him in for running drugs."

"That's right. Broke up his whole operation for a while. But the inciting incident actually didn't even involve drugs. Thorndike had a violent disagreement with one of his runners—the guy ripped him off for six hundred bucks, I think it was—and so Thorndike pistol-whipped the guy in an alleyway. Cammie just happened to be walking by that night after work and saw the assault."

"Pretty brazen to be disciplining your people out in the open like that," Ellery remarked.

"Yeah, well, brazen was Thorndike's style. He kept people in line with violence, and it worked. Of course, we all knew he was bad news, but we could never convince anyone to testify against him. The whole neighborhood was spooked. Camilla, though, she'd had enough. She said she didn't want to be raising her baby in that kind of neighborhood."

The whole room fell silent as they all realized they were standing in the presence of that baby. Reed felt his cheeks go hot.

Sheriff Ramsey coughed before continuing. "Cammie was a little bit of a thing and Thorndike was built like a boxer, so all of us were surprised that she wanted to take him on. But I remember, she said something like: 'There's more of us out there than there are of him. So he doesn't get to make the rules for everyone.'" He smiled as he said it, remembering. "That wasn't my case, either, of course—I didn't do any investigating back then—but I admired her guts."

"What happened with the case against Thorndike? The one for the beating?" Reed asked.

"It got dropped after her death," Ramsey answered with obvious disgust. "The SOB walked. The victim had always refused to testify, so without Cammie around to provide context to his injuries, Thorndike could've easily argued the guy slipped on a banana peel and smashed his face in. The D.A. wouldn't go forward with charges."

"You think he did it," Reed said, eyeing the sheriff. "You think he killed her."

"I don't know how it works at the FBI, but around here, when a guy says he's going to kill someone and then that someone ends up dead, odds are good that he's the one that done it."

Ellery had started leafing through one of the binders. "It says here that the cops served a search warrant on Thorndike's house. What were they looking for?"

"Billy had a recent cut on his right hand, just about here." The sheriff indicated the flap of skin connecting the thumb and forefinger. "Detectives figured he got it when he was stabbing her." Reed agreed with their logic. It was common for assailants to sustain cuts during a knife attack because the hilt often became slippery with blood. "The search warrant was looking for anything that would tie Thorndike to the knife, any sort of property he might have stolen from the apartment, and anything that would disprove his story that he got the injury working on a motorcycle at his house."

"And?" Ellery asked with interest. "Did they find anything?"

The sheriff shook his head, dismayed. "Naw. No property linking him to the crime, and all knives from the house appeared to be accounted for. The only item of interest was a rag with blood on it found in the trash in Thorndike's garage. He said the location of the rag backed up his story, but we always wondered if maybe we could test it somehow and find out if some of that blood belonged to Cammie Flores. We finally got that chance about ten years ago when the state agreed to pay for DNA testing, but it came back empty—no sign of anyone else's blood on that rag but Thorndike's. Of course, that doesn't prove he didn't do it, but it was our last bite of the apple, so to speak. We'd run out of leads to follow."

"Do you know where Billy Thorndike is now?" Reed asked.

"Eventually, his luck ran out, thanks in part to the advent of security cameras, and we busted him. He was in and out of prison during the eighties and nineties on a combination of assault, drug, and weapons convictions. He was paroled for good around 2002, I believe. Last I heard he was working up in Summerlin at a gas station, but I have no idea whether he's even still alive."

Reed gave a thin smile. "You can be sure I will find out. What about the other suspect? David Owens."

Sheriff Ramsey lifted his eyebrows. "Owens? He wasn't a suspect. He was a cop—a straight shooter from the sound of things. They ruled him out right away."

"Nonetheless, I'd like to talk to him if I could," Reed replied mildly.

"That'll be easy to do. He lives right in town over on Faulkner Avenue with his wife, Amy. He's been helping her run her catering business ever since he retired about five years ago. I imagine he'd welcome the chance to help you in any way he could. Camilla's death tore him up good, and I think he always felt like he should've been there, you know? Like he could've stopped it. He knew same as we did that Thorndike was scum, and he knew that Cammie was afraid of him. I guess he just figured Thorndike would never dare go after her—not when David had his unit parked in front of her apartment every other night."

The sheriff had painted a picture of a distraught boyfriend who'd mistakenly believed his badge could keep his girlfriend safe, but what Reed heard was that David Owens knew Thorndike had threatened Camilla. "Thanks," he said aloud. "We'll definitely want to talk to him."

"Well, sure," the sheriff replied with sympathy. "He knew your mom. Maybe better than anyone." He hesitated a beat and then made an officious noise as he drew himself up to full height. "Look, I'm sorry to run out on you like this, but I've got to get to another meeting. Don will help you with anything you need. I sure hope you find the answers you're looking for."

He shook Reed's hand again before he left, and then Reed felt the others' eyes on him as they awaited his next move. He would usually want to see the crime scene, ideally as close as possible to the way it was when the murder occurred, but he knew Camilla's apartment had been torn down years ago. Reed had looked it up, and there was now in the same place a mini-mart and a nail salon, probably one that employed young women around the age Camilla had been when she died. People walked by every day and had no idea a woman had been murdered right where they stood. What happens in Vegas stays in Vegas, or so the saying went, but to Reed, it seemed like the city had no memory. Camilla had disappeared into the history books, and he was determined to find his way back to her.

He looked across the table at the artifacts of his mother's murder. Plenty of other detectives had looked at these same files, the same boxes of evidence, and come up empty. As much as Reed wanted to catalog the story for himself, he suspected he wouldn't find any easy answers by covering the same trodden path. "Is it okay to leave this for now and then come back?" he asked Sergeant Price.

Price's expression was a mixture of surprise and irritation, as though he'd performed this large an excavation for nothing. "Well, sure, I guess so. I'll keep it under lock and key for you 'til we close up at six. Thought you'd want more than a quick look-see."

"Thank you," Reed replied, ignoring the sergeant and heading for the door. Ellery fell into step beside him.

"Where are we going?" she asked as they hit the hallway.

"I want to talk to David Owens."

Ellery seemed to ponder this as they walked back out into the warm sunshine. Once inside the car she shifted to look at him. "You're not buying Billy Thorndike as the prime suspect, are you?"

Reed reached into his briefcase and withdrew a sheaf of crime scene photographs, the ones he'd shown her before. "What kind of murder does that look like to you?"

Ellery flipped through the black-and-white pictures one by one. "Messy," she said finally. "The struggle obviously went on for quite some time."

"Exactly. Thorndike was a big man, over six feet according to his vitals, and apparently quite practiced with dispensing violence to keep people in line. Camilla Flores stood five foot four and weighed a hundred and fifteen pounds. She should've been no match for him. It's possible she put up much more of a fight than he anticipated, but it's much more likely her killer was an amateur—maybe someone who snapped just this once, who went insane inside that small apartment and then slipped out the door and back into regular life, where he's been hiding in plain sight ever since."

Ellery turned over the pictures in her lap so they were facedown. "Someone like her boyfriend you mean."

"Yes." Reed started the car and put on his sunglasses, hiding his eyes from her gaze. "Or someone like my father."

4

Ellery rode to the Owens house with the car window down
and her hand stuck out to feel the passing breeze. She'd
been raised in Chicago, where the winter wind came
screaming off the lake, and then moved to Massachusetts,
where spring didn't arrive until mid-June some years. Mild
temperatures in February felt like an exotic novelty to her.
She stretched out her fingers to catch the sun, and the big,
leafy palm trees seemed to be waving back at her. It was
difficult to imagine anything horrible happening in such a
warm and lovely place.

"I think this is the house," Reed said as he rolled the car
to a stop in front of a well-manicured two-story home. It,
too, boasted a welcoming palm tree that stood as high as
the house itself. Half the lawn was decorated in a rocky
hardscape, while the other half shone a brilliant emerald
green that Ellery had only glimpsed on golf courses in the
summertime.

She turned and squinted at Reed. "So how do you want to play this?"

"I just want to get a feel for his story, see what he remembers. As we've noted, forty years is a long time. If he's been holding on to some kind of secret, he might be willing to let go."

Ellery looked at Reed with a touch of surprise. "You think you can go in there and just have him confess, just like that?"

Reed shrugged. "Stranger things have happened. That's probably the only way this case is getting solved—if someone who wasn't willing to talk forty years ago finally comes forward." He leaned into her personal space to study the house. "If you can, I'd like you to separate the wife, Amy, and chat her up a bit. Find out what she knew of Camilla's death back then, and what, if anything, David has said about it in the intervening years. If he's confessed to anybody, it would probably be her."

Ellery remained skeptical that it could ever be that easy, but she cracked a smile in his direction. "So what you're saying is that you want me to use my feminine touch."

"I don't know," Reed replied. "Are you quite sure you have one?"

She shoved him lightly before exiting the car. "Isolate the wife. Make her squeal. Got it."

She meant the words ironically, but Reed tilted his head in a quizzical manner as they headed for the house. "You might find she has an interesting perspective of her own," he said. "David and Amy Owens will be celebrating their forty-third wedding anniversary this fall."

Ellery did some quick math in her head. "Married forty-three years. That's a quick rebound for young David after his intended fiancée was murdered."

"Yes," Reed replied through a fixed smile as he reached for the doorbell. "In some circles it might even be referred to as motive."

The door opened to reveal a pleasantly plump woman in her early sixties, tanned, with bleach-blond hair and wide-set blue eyes. "Can I help you?" she asked with a genuine, friendly smile that suggested she sincerely did want to be of service.

Ellery hung back as Reed pulled out his FBI credentials. "Reed Markham, ma'am," he said, his voice low and gruff. "This is my associate Ellery Hathaway. We were hoping to speak with you and your husband for a few minutes, if you can spare the time." Her eyes grew even wider as he spoke, and she put a hand to her mouth.

"Oh, my heavens! Brad Ramsey told us you might be coming by, but he didn't say it would be today. I'm Amy Owens. Please, please come in." She stepped aside and let them into the home.

Ellery looked around with interest at the neat, new-construction home. She'd grown up in a brick walk-up—thick and sturdy, built by people who remembered the great fire. Her apartment in Boston had once been a factory that had manufactured everything from soap to salt. By contrast, the Owens home dated to perhaps 2010—clean and new, with bright white walls and shiny white tile on the floor. The rooms had curved archways instead of the hard right angles Ellery was used to, and watercolor paintings in beachy tones hung on the walls.

Amy had turned to yell up the stairs for her husband. "David! David, the man from the FBI is here!"

Ellery heard footfalls and turned so she could see the shadow coming into view, curious as to what he might look like, the man who might have hacked his petite girlfriend to death and then resumed a normal, ordinary life. "Hello, I'm David Owens," he said as he ducked to avoid hitting his head on the arch as he entered the room. His baritone greeting was pleasant, but there was an alertness in his gaze and tension in his handshake that belied his relaxed demeanor. He had broad shoulders and a toned physique atypical for a man his age. Ellery had no trouble imagining the authoritative figure he must have looked like in uniform, armed with a gun. "Welcome," he said, clapping his hands together. "Did Amy offer you something to drink? She's also rustled up some fresh-baked cherry chocolate chip cookies that are not to be missed."

"No thank you," Reed said at the same time Ellery replied, "That sounds delicious."

She smiled at Amy. "I'm starved. They don't even serve peanuts on the plane anymore."

Amy flashed a return smile, seeming grateful for the break in tension. "Don't I know it. We fly to Seattle to see our daughter and grandkids three times a year, and I swear the airplane food gets worse every time. Be right back—I'll fix you up in a jiff."

David became uncertain as his wife whisked out of the room. "I guess we ought to take a seat. Knowing Amy, she's whipping up a three-course meal."

They followed him into the sunny front room with its matching pale green chairs and floral sofa. Ellery noted a family portrait on the wall that seemed to date back at least twenty years, judging from the poufy hairstyles on the women. It depicted a proud and smiling David and Amy surrounded by their teenage daughters, the oldest of whom was about the same age Camilla Flores was when she died.

David Owens shook his head, bemused. He glanced in Reed's direction and then away again. "I would've known it was you even if the sheriff hadn't told me why you're here. You look just like her."

Ellery watched a pink stain appear on Reed's cheeks, and his gaze slid to the floor. Whatever he'd been expecting, this clearly wasn't it. She had become used to strangers approaching her out of nowhere thinking they knew everything about her life since they'd read a book or seen a movie that told Coben's story. But she and Coben had been the only two people there on the farm during those awful three days—the only two who knew the real story—and so she could turn those strangers away unsatisfied. The ordeal was horrible, but it was hers. In Reed's case, here was a stranger who knew something about him that Reed did not. Reed had to either live with the gaps in his own narrative or sit there and grope for pieces of it from someone else.

"I remember I asked the detective on the case what was going to happen to you," Owens continued. "Can't recollect his name after all these years."

"Dobson," Reed supplied immediately. "Lou Dobson."

"Dobson. That's right. He asked me why was I asking and did I want to take you?" Even now, Owens looked uncomfortable at the thought. "I was twenty-four and living in a run-down one-bedroom apartment, working ten-hour shifts. How was I supposed to take care of a baby?"

His tone was half apology, half-defensive, as though he wanted Reed to offer him absolution for this long-ago human frailty. Ever the people pleaser, Reed obliged. "I understand," he said. "It would have been a lot to ask of anyone."

Owens gave a wry smile. "You may look like her, but you don't sound like her at all. Camilla still had traces of her Puerto Rican accent, and let me tell you, she could swear a blue streak in Spanish. I didn't know half the words she said, but Lord, I confess they made me blush on her behalf. You—you're a Southern man, isn't that right?"

"Virginia."

"Yeah, the sheriff told me. Your father's in politics there or something."

At the mention of his father, Reed looked up sharply. "Did you know my father?"

"No, sir." Owens looked puzzled. "Why would I? I've never been to Virginia."

"As it turns out, my father had made some trips out here

in the early seventies, entertaining some donors. I just thought maybe you'd crossed paths at one time."

"No," Owens said firmly. "Never met the man."

Amy returned to the room with a tray filled with tall glasses of iced tea and a plate of thick, delicious-looking cookies. Ellery helped herself to two and stifled a groan of pleasure as the combination of sweet chocolate and tart cherries hit her tongue. At the other end of the couch, Reed accepted a glass of tea, took a perfunctory sip, and set it aside with a tight smile. "That's very nice, thank you." He shifted his attention back to Owens. "What can you tell me about Camilla's death?"

Owens, who had been shoving cookies into his own mouth, faltered in surprise at the direct question. He put the latest cookie down, half-uneaten. "Not a lot," he admitted. "I wasn't there. Always felt bad about that, knowing she'd been worried someone was after her."

"And who was that?" Reed asked, although Ellery knew they already had the answer.

"A street punk named Billy Thorndike. Cammie caught him disciplining one of his boys in the alley one night, and unlike most in the neighborhood, she didn't look the other way."

"What was your theory of the murder?" Reed asked, and Ellery watched with interest for the answer. Owens took a deep breath and rubbed his palms on his knees as he considered his reply.

"Dobson thought it might have been a burglar. That

never made sense to me, even at the time. Camilla barely had two nickels to rub together—who'd want to steal from her? Even her stereo was bought secondhand, ten years old. I could never make the pieces of that story fit together, either. How was it supposed to have gone down—he was piling the stuff by the door when she came home and surprised him? But then you were in your crib. So this guy's got his knife at the ready when she comes through the door, but he says, 'Okay, go put the baby down before I kill you'? Doesn't make any sense."

Ellery supposed it was possible that the burglar had panicked when he'd heard Cammie's key in the door, grabbed the knife, and lain in wait for her to enter the room. Perhaps when he saw the baby he'd remained in his hiding spot until Cammie had put Reed in the crib.

"So then you liked Billy Thorndike," Reed concluded, and Owens pointed at him.

"Now there's a real suspect. Cammie squealed on him and he'd threatened to make her pay for it. He was trying to intimidate her—you know, scare her so she wouldn't testify. She got some weird hang-ups on the phone, like heavy breathing and then no reply. One morning, she got up and found all four of her tires slashed. I was worried enough that I'd started sleeping over her place most nights that I wasn't working."

"Who would like more tea?" Amy interrupted, leaping to her feet.

Ellery glanced at Reed, who nodded at her. She repressed

a sigh because Owens's story was just starting to get interesting and now she had to go follow the wife into the kitchen. "I'd love some," she said to Amy. "Please let me help."

"Oh, it's no bother," Amy replied, but she allowed Ellery to follow her to the kitchen. Ellery's first thought when she saw the room was that Reed would be right at home there. It was a chef's dream, with a six-burner stove, a wide granite island that had its own deep sink, and a plethora of hanging pots and pans. Amy tugged open the door on the enormous Sub-Zero stainless-steel refrigerator, and Ellery glimpsed a veritable bounty of food in all shapes and colors. Her own refrigerator growing up had often been bare, especially in the few days leading up to her mother's payday. They'd eaten mostly out of cans—gray peas and sickly-sweet peaches or oranges that had a metallic aftertaste. Fresh fruits and vegetables that rotted in under a few days were a luxury that the Hathaway household had not been able to afford.

Amy must've caught her staring, because she smiled and pulled out a large bowl of fruit salad. "I whipped this up last night, but David barely touched it this morning. Would you like some?"

"It looks amazing," Ellery admitted, and Amy got out two white porcelain bowls. As Amy served up the fruit, Ellery searched around for a way to begin the awkward conversation. "It must've been a surprise when the sheriff called and said we were coming to ask about Camilla Flores. The case has been inactive for a long time."

Amy shrugged and did not look up from her fruit.

"Maybe. But it's not like it ever went away, either. People talk. Of course, some of them thought David might've done it." She paused to see how Ellery took this possibility, but Ellery just stabbed a plump strawberry with her fork.

"That must have been hard, living with other people's suspicions."

Amy pursed her mouth. "No one who knows David ever believed a word of it. I could tell it bothered him, though, especially in the months right after it happened when everyone was still spooked. And since no one ever got caught for it, the talk never stopped entirely. You get a long look from someone when you're out at a restaurant or hear a whisper in the line after church. People love to gossip."

"Did you know her? Camilla, I mean."

"No, I only heard the stories."

"What kind of stories?"

Amy's big blue eyes grew wary. "I don't like to talk ill about the dead. God rest her soul."

"Ill? About Camilla?" The sheriff had spoken like he'd wanted to pin a medal on her for standing up to Billy Thorndike.

"Well, it's not like she had much of a choice, I s'pose." Amy pushed the fruit around in her bowl. "She had a baby to care for, and waitressing doesn't pay all that much."

"What are you saying?"

Amy gave a heavy sigh. "Probably more than I ought to. It's just . . . there was some talk at the time that Camilla and her friend Angie used to entertain guys for money."

Ellery put her fork down and glanced in the direction of the living room. "You're saying they were prostitutes?" Reed had not mentioned anything of this possibility, which probably meant he hadn't seen it in any of the reports.

"I don't know the particulars. Maybe. They were young girls, and good looking, too, I saw from the pictures they ran in the papers. Las Vegas always has its share of working girls. Men come here, far away from their wives with a lot of money to spend . . . if you needed quick and easy cash, that's one way to get it."

The sweet taste of the fruit on Ellery's tongue suddenly turned bitter. She was going to have to report the details of this conversation to Reed, and she wasn't sure how she was supposed to raise the possibility that his conception might have involved a cash transaction. Amy, as it turned out, had no such qualms.

"I mean, the girl did get herself knocked up somehow."

"She wasn't with David at the time?" Ellery was still trying to get the timeline straight.

"No, she was already pregnant when they started seeing each other. He felt sorry for her being all alone and having to work on her feet all day."

"What about the father? He wasn't in the picture?"

Amy gave her a pointed look. "That's what I'm trying to tell you," she said. "I don't think he wanted to be in the picture. Probably he already had kids of his own somewhere in Los Angeles or Houston or Bloomington, Indiana."

This acute truth made Ellery shift uncomfortably on her

stool, and she tried to steer the conversation back to the place Reed had wanted it to go. "When you say David felt like he was under suspicion, is that because the detectives investigated him?"

"Sure, they had to at least check. But he was across town on the job."

"You sound very sure of that."

Amy regarded her with a note of surprise. "Sure I'm sure. I was there."

"I'm sorry—what?" Ellery's head started to spin. She didn't have the case files, hadn't memorized the details the way Reed had. Keeping track of everyone's relationships now and back in the 1970s made her brain hurt. David and Cammie. Cammie and Angus Markham. Amy and David. She remembered that Reed wondered about the romantic overlap.

"David and I worked together—that's how we met. We didn't ride together all the time, but that day, I remember it well. We had car sixty-seven and we were working in my old neighborhood near Spring Valley."

"You were a cop?" Ellery tried to imagine this curvy platinum-blond woman with the deep laugh lines and soft hands dressed up in uniform and walking a beat.

Amy grinned as she started clearing away the dishes. "Don't look so surprised. I was young like you once—I ran an eight-minute mile and could bench-press my body weight." She stopped to pat her round stomach. "Of course, that was before I discovered Brie and jam sandwiches."

"So you're his alibi, then."

Amy made a face. "You make it sound tawdry when you put it like that," she replied with a touch of irritation. "But yes, I suppose so. It was a pretty quiet day up until we got the call to report back early. We had a fender bender, a fight at the grocery store because the manager accused one of the cashiers of helping himself to the till, and the alarm went off again at Martinelli Liquors—the fourth time that week— but it turned out to be another false alarm. We told them to get it fixed up or we'd be writing them a citation for wasting our time. I got to thinking about that later, how we were investigating a whole lot of nothing right at the time she got killed. You join up because you think you're going to make a big difference, you're going to keep the peace, but it turns out you're almost never in the right place at the right time to do any damn good." She shook her head sadly and reached for her tea. "I turned in my shield the day I found out I was pregnant with Mallory, but David stuck it out the full thirty. He's a good man."

Ellery had a flash of her own murky future and wondered whether she would have a job back in Boston or she would have to reinvent herself yet again. "Who do you think killed Camilla Flores?" she asked Amy.

Amy blinked those wide-set eyes for a long moment. "You know, no one's ever asked me that before. I'd guess that Billy Thorndike would top my list, too. But . . ."

"Yes?" Ellery leaned forward encouragingly.

"There was another girl cut up, about a year before

Camilla. Didn't get as much attention because she was definitely a working girl. Supposedly, the guy was waiting for her in her bedroom one night. He raped her and stabbed her and left her for dead. As far as I know, they never got the guy who did it."

"You remember her name?"

Amy squinted. "Giselle? Danielle? I don't know. It's been a long time." Ellery caught an undertone of warning, maybe even reproach, in the comment. Then Amy brightened again. "We should be getting back to the boys, don't you think? They'll have wondered where we wandered off to."

When they got back to the living area, Reed was in the process of asking David Owens about Camilla's friend and neighbor, Angie Rivera. "Angie, yeah," Owens was saying. "She was a pistol—always with the big plans. She wanted to be a singer and a dancer. Cammie dragged me to some hole-in-the-wall joint once to hear her perform, practically in the middle of the night. It's not like she was headlining the show, if you get my drift. But when Angie got up and did her numbers, I thought she wasn't half-bad. But then again, what do I know about singing?"

"I'd like to talk to her if I could," Reed said.

Owens snorted. "Good luck with that. Angie split right after the murder. Didn't even come to the funeral."

"Huh. Why was that?"

"I don't know. Word was she was real shook up, finding Cammie murdered like that. Can't really blame her for that one. Some knife-wielding maniac is on the loose and kills your best friend right next door to you—maybe you start thinking you'll be next."

"Do you think Angie might have had a specific reason to fear for her life?" Reed asked.

"Well, Thorndike hated Cammie, and Angie was Cammie's best friend. Plus, he was the kind of guy who liked to beat up people just for the hell of it. Anyway, Angie took off—I think she was headed for L.A.—a couple of days after the murder. I haven't seen her since."

Reed made a couple of notes, keeping his eyes down as he asked the next question. "About Cammie's baby—did Angie know who the father was?"

Ellery noticed Reed's careful, distancing language. *Cammie's baby. The father.*

Owens must have noticed it, too, because he cleared his throat twice before answering. "I think so," he said finally. "Only because I know Angie was bugging Cammie to try to get money out of the guy. I remember one night Cammie was searching through the pockets of her clothes, looking for loose change so she could buy some more diapers. I said I'd pick 'em up, no problem, and Angie blew her stack. 'You-Know-Who should be paying for them,' she said to Cammie. 'I don't care what other priorities he's got. He helped make a kid, he can help pay for it.' Cammie told her to knock it off."

"I see." Reed made some more notes, and Ellery felt a pang looking at him, watching him catalog his father's indifference. "Do you know if Cammie ever did get in touch with him? If she asked for money?"

"Can't say one way or another. Sorry."

"Right." Reed took a deep breath and folded up his notepad. "I guess that's all my questions for right now. Unless there's anything else you want to add—anything you think is important that I might have missed."

Owens spread out his massive hands in bewilderment. "Like what?"

"Like anything else unusual that happened in the days before or the days after she died."

"I already told you about the hang-up calls and her busted tires." He stroked his chin as he thought back. "A couple of times, Cammie thought someone might've been following her when she drove home from the restaurant. We both thought it was Thorndike or one of his goons. She started taking different routes and she put in for a day shift. It came through three days before she died."

He sounded at a loss. Silence stretched out across the room, across the ages, as they all sat there imagining a frightened young woman driving home alone at night, blinded by the headlights from a car that was following too close behind.

"We'll be going then," Reed said, preparing to stand, but Owens shot out a hand to stop him.

"Wait. There was just one more weird thing. It happened two, maybe three weeks before she died." He sat back and marveled at himself. "I haven't thought about this in years."

"What? What is it?"

"I was working the overnight shift and her restaurant

wasn't on my route, but I'd swing by occasionally during the slow times, just to check on her on account of all the crap going on with Thorndike. This one night, I saw her outside in the parking lot, arguing with a tall, skinny guy with red hair. She was yelling at him pretty good and I would've stopped the car, but she didn't seem scared and I got a radio call. Later, I asked her about it and she said he was a customer who tried to skip out on the bill." He hesitated. "But I didn't believe her."

"Why not?" Reed asked.

"The guy was wearing a nice suit. They were standing near a shiny Cadillac, which I presumed was his car. Why's a guy like that going to skip out on a five-dollar bill?"

"This man with the red hair, would you recognize him if you saw him again?"

"After all this time? No way. I didn't get a close look on account of I never got out of the car, and I only saw him the one time."

But Reed had pulled out his cell phone, and they all waited while he fiddled around, tapping the screen. "What about this man?" he asked as he showed the phone to Owens. "Do you think it could have been him?"

Owens squinted at the phone and then brought it close to his face. He shook his head. "Hang on. Let me get my glasses." Glasses procured, he took the phone and tried again. "Well," he said after a long look. "Maybe. The body shape looks about right. But maybe not. Like I told you, I can't really say for sure."

"Okay, thank you." Reed tucked away his phone, and both members of the Owens family walked them to the door. "I appreciate you taking the time to talk to us. I may be back in touch if I have more questions."

"We're not going anyplace. Right, honey?" David put an arm around his wife and hugged her to his side. "I hope . . . well, maybe it's selfish of me, but I hope you get some answers, because then I'll have them, too."

Ellery could barely wait for the door to close before their backs were turned to the house. "Care to let me in?" she asked as they walked down the path to the car. "Who's the man with the red hair?"

Reed's mouth was set in a grim line as he held out the phone so she could look at the image he had shown to David Owens. "His name is Rufus Guthrie," he replied. "He's my father's campaign manager."

5

When he thought of his father, Reed pictured the Angus Markham of today, the broad-shouldered, white-haired orator with the quick tongue and ready smile. A lion in winter, he could still command a rally of hundreds as easily as he held sway over the long Markham family dinner table. The Markham household had a distinctive energy when the senator was home, fierce and funny and competitive as the children all angled for a slice of his attention, but there was no question the family breathed easier when he was away. Reed recalled the long amber days of his childhood, when he was still in short pants and his older sisters went off to school, leaving him behind in the care of sometimes their mother but more often the nanny, Lucille, and the house-keeper, Betsy. The big house took on an air of waiting. Reed would linger by the windows with his toy cars in the after-noon, rolling them slowly up and down the wooden sill, all the while watching the circular drive for that moment when the burgundy Caddy would pull up and disgorge his three sparkling blond sisters. They would burst through the front door in a cacophony of sounds, shoving and giggling and swooping him up into their slender arms as though he were a beloved family pet. Reed would clutch them around their necks, exhilarated at their loving fervor but afraid they would drop him. They never did. They did once lose him right inside the family home, and to this day it was as angry as Reed had ever seen his father.

Reed had loved to play hide-and-seek because he was a master at finding anything and anyone. He won every game. Until one drizzly afternoon when it was his turn to hide and he climbed the creaky stairs to the family attic, where he found an old toy chest. It had a painting of Goldilocks and the Three Bears half chipped away on the lid and easily contained a four-year-old boy. He'd grinned in marvel at his ingenuity, not even minding the dust or the dark as he secreted himself inside the chest. The minutes had passed into an hour and his sisters hadn't come to find him. Reed grew restless, then bored, his elbows and tailbone hard against the wooden box. He'd decided to out himself and crow about his victory, but when he pressed against the lid it did not open. The hook-and-eye closure had apparently slipped into place when he'd shut the lid on top of himself, and he lay trapped in his own little coffin. He'd pushed and pushed, then kicked frantically at the lid, pounding the toy box so hard it jumped in place on the attic floor. "Help!" he had hollered, panic rising. "Come find me!"

Long after Reed had lapsed into silent tears of terror and self-pity, he heard thundering footsteps on the stairs. The latch had opened and there his father appeared looming over him, his face ashen with fear. He'd snatched Reed high up into his arms, holding him strong and tight so Reed knew he would never fall. "Girls!" his father had bellowed with a force that shook the walls. "Get up here right now and apologize to your brother!"

Reed learned they had gotten caught up in some TV program and forgotten about him entirely. Kimberly, Suzanne, and Lynette all sincerely and contritely offered their apologies, but that was not enough to satisfy their fuming father. Angus whipped them each with his belt while Reed looked on, the mean nugget of anger inside him glad to see their pale faces echo some of the fear he had felt, even as his heart squeezed with every crack of the belt. His sisters had sat stone silent at dinner, but that night Kimmy, the youngest, had let him crawl in bed with her.

"I'm sorry," he'd whispered, although he wasn't sure what for. He'd only cared that she let him hug her again.

"Me too," she had whispered back, and they'd never spoken of it again.

There was no more hide-and-seek after that. His treasured game was done. It was Reed's first lesson on the fragility of family life, how one small act could alter the whole interwoven tapestry and you could sew it back up, but it would never look quite the same.

Back in the colorless room inside LVMPD headquarters,

Reed surveyed once more the collection of boxes and folders that contained all that remained of his mother's life and death. He could smell the years on them, from the sagging cardboard covers to the brittle yellow pages, steeped in dust and decades of neglect. These files were elderly by investigation standards, having passed through three generations of detectives, yet his mother had been young and girlish when she died, not even out of her teens and less than half the age that Reed was now. He needed to find that girl, to know her better, if he was to hunt her killer, but he wasn't sure how to find her by studying these slim paper bones.

At his side, Ellery opened one of the original murder books and started leafing through it. "Sure enough, here it is," she said after a moment, tilting the file so he could see. "A statement from Officer Amy Conway verifying that David Owens was on duty with her at the approximate time of the murder. Of course, back then, no one knew she'd end up married to him."

"Even if they knew, I'm not sure it would have mattered. I'll bet Owens's colleagues were extremely eager to cross him off the suspect list."

"You haven't, though," she observed.

"I'm reserving judgment." David Owens had been forthright and cooperative, answering Reed's questions about Camilla Flores and the day of the murder to the best of his ability as far as Reed could discern. Still, Reed wasn't ready to exonerate Cammie's cop boyfriend just yet. The long pauses and searching quality to some of Owens's replies might have been due to the intervening decades, but they were also the hallmark of someone spinning circles around the truth. Reed had long outgrown hide-and-seek, but he retained a keen sense for the unseen and unspoken, and his gut told him David Owens was holding something back.

"Amy mentioned something else," Ellery said as she continued to page through the files. "She said there was another young woman attacked in her apartment by a knife-wielding stranger around the time Camilla was killed. Have you seen anything in here about that?"

"No," Reed replied, only half paying attention. The box that held the murder weapon sat in front of him, daring him to crack the lid.

"Giselle or Danielle something, she said the name was. We could ask the sheriff about it."

Reed didn't reply. He snapped on a pair of latex gloves and took a deep breath, mentally steeling himself for what he would find inside the box. He reached inside blindly and his hands met a large heavy metal object encased in a plastic bag. When he lifted it free, he saw it was the horse head bookend that the killer had used to beat Camilla's head and face as she lay bleeding out on the living room floor. Carefully, he removed the bag and set the horse head on top of it for study. He bent low, putting his own face only inches from the cast-iron surface. He could see dried blood and even a few dark hairs stuck to the side of the horse's face. There were also the gray remnants of fingerprint powder—a test Reed knew already had failed to yield any useful information.

He raised up to reach into the box again, and this time he discovered an old manila envelope with no markings on the outside. He untied the string that held the flap closed and tilted the contents into his hand. Polaroid photographs. About a dozen of them. He held his breath as he started perusing through faded images. One picture showed Camilla decked out in heels and a sequined minidress and smiling with another dark-haired woman about her own height and age, who Reed guessed would probably be Angie Rivera. Reed lingered over his mother, searching her face for traces of his own. All the pictures he'd seen of her were from the crime scene, where she was barely recognizable as a human, let alone his kin.

Ellery leaned in so she could see, too. "David was right," she murmured. "You do look a lot like her. Look, even your hair is parted in the same spot."

Reed touched his head gently with one hand. "I guess it is."

He moved on to the next picture, another shot of Camilla and Angie again, this time dressed in T-shirts and jeans, posing near a Route 66 road sign. On a whim, he flipped it over, and it read: *Getting' our kicks, 1973.* Camilla's handwriting? Maybe. He flipped to the next picture, and Ellery inhaled sharply at the sight.

"Oh, wow."

Camilla sat on the cement steps with a baby boy in her arms, his expression blank and bewildered. She squinted in the sun, her hair held back in a bandana, but her thousand-watt smile shone back through the ages. Reed's chest tightened as he turned over the photo. *Me and Joey,* it said, and she'd drawn a little heart next to his name, rather like Tula liked to do when she fashioned Reed a homemade card. His throat thickened and he swallowed painfully as he righted the picture once more so he could see Camilla's beaming pride. Love. He'd been loved at the start. This precious knowledge burst joy in his heart that quickly flared into an old, familiar shame, like this longing was a betrayal of his second family. He hurried to tuck the picture away.

"Who's that?" Ellery asked as he brought forth the next picture. Angie and Camilla had been joined by a blonder, stouter woman with cowboy boots and a halter top. Reed checked the back. *Angie, me, and Wanda,* it read. "Okay, so who's Wanda?" Ellery amended her question.

"I don't know. I don't recall reading anything about her in the reports I've seen."

Ellery took out her cell phone and made a note of the name. "We can ask the sheriff about her, too. What else have you got?"

"Looks like the rest are more of the same. Here's one with David." He showed her the snapshot of what appeared to be a happy couple, petite Camilla perched on the lap of a grinning, shaggy-haired Owens. They both had cans of beer in their hands. Reed checked the back, but he found no notation of the time or place.

The last picture was himself in the crib, all fat legs and chubby cheeks, dressed in a white onesie and cooing for the camera. *Joey, four months,* it read on the back. Reed imagined that if he looked close enough he might see his mother's reflection in the light of his eyes. He carefully slid the photographs back into the envelope and set it aside. They didn't provide any evidence of anything, except perhaps that Camilla herself had been loved, had been happy before she died.

Inside the box, Reed found more bagged items from Camilla's apartment: her clothes, which included a diamond-patterned blouse and blue jeans that were both soaked in dried blood and riddled with slashes; her Hamilton watch, also coated in a fine film of blood; a pair of brown flats almost worn through on the bottoms, which about broke Reed's heart. He forced himself to keep going until he reached the bottom of the box, where the knife lay inside a plastic evidence bag, tagged and numbered.

Gingerly, he removed it for study but kept it inside the bag. Ellery joined him in a sober appraisal of the bloodied seven-inch blade. "I read that they couldn't match it to her kitchen set," she said as they stared at the knife.

"No, but her utensils were made up of a bunch of odds and ends, not some fancy Wüsthof set. This is your basic butcher knife that could have been purchased at hundreds of different places. It was never clear whether the killer brought the knife to the scene or not." Privately, Reed suspected the killer had come prepared. If the motive wasn't burglary and Camilla had not been sexually assaulted, that meant her attacker had entered the apartment with one intent only. He picked up the bag and held it up so he could see the handle. "Just as I thought," he said. "There's blood here by the hilt."

"There's blood everywhere," Ellery replied.

"Yes, but in knife assaults, especially where there are repeated stabbings like in this case, the offender often cuts him- or herself during the attack. Blood from the victim makes the weapon slippery, and so you'll often see assailants with injuries here or here." He indicated the webbing of his hand and the fleshy part of the palm below his fingers. "There's so much blood from this attack that it's impossible to test it all. But we could justify a more limited analysis, and my recommendation would be to start here, at the base of the knife handle."

Ellery looked down at the knife again. "Do you think it could be that easy?"

"Remember it was DNA that provided the first new information in this case in forty years. I don't know that testing the knife will reveal anything, but it's a shot. Maybe the best one we've got."

They cataloged the remaining physical evidence before retreating to the hotel. Reed had scored a deal on a penthouse suite in a smaller luxury hotel just off The Strip. It boasted nearly as many square feet as his Virginia condo, with two master bedroom suites, each with its own rain shower and soaking tub. In between the two bedrooms sat an expansive living area with low-lying leather furniture designed in modern curves. The kitchenette featured a dishwasher, full-size refrigerator, and granite peninsula, illuminated by golden pendant lights. Most important to Reed, the dining area contained a long conference-style table that would be perfect for setting up a mission control for the case. He took the files they had brought from the sheriff's office and began spreading out and sorting the information while Ellery did a slow study of the entire suite.

"I think you could do laps in this tub," she called from the one bedroom. A few moments later, she stuck her head out and waved a miniature bottle of red wine. "This came with a note that says: 'Welcome and please enjoy with our compliments.' There's also a small box of painted chocolate truffles. Did you set this stuff up ahead of time or what?"

Reed gave a tired smile and shook his head. "No, that sort of token is often customary at these sorts of resorts."

"Yeah? At the Motel Six all you got was little soaps in individual wrappers." She regarded the wine in her hand. "This is better."

"Pour yourself a glass and we can order in dinner."

"Or I could just run out and pick something up."

He waved her off, returning his attention to his laptop. "This will be quicker and less hassle. Not to mention less greasy."

"So I can pick you up a salad. I know it's a desert, but they've got to have kale around here someplace."

He took off his reading glasses and turned around in his chair to look at her fully. "You're awfully keen to run out again considering we just got here."

"No. But room service has got to cost a lot of money, right?" She spread her arms. "And this place, Reed . . . it's gorgeous, but it's also just a bit much."

"I'm paying for it. It's not a problem."

"Maybe it's a problem for me."

Reed rubbed the side of his face with one hand. Ellery, he knew, had grown up searching for soda cans in the trash to redeem for meager pocket money. She didn't like to waste a nickel. "This is my fool's errand we're investigating, so I don't think you should have to worry about incurring any expenses. I picked this spot because it seemed convenient and comfortable, but if it's not okay for you, we can look for someplace else tomorrow. For tonight, though, let's just order dinner and get some rest, hmm? I've been up since five A.M. on the other side of the country."

"Fine," she said with a sigh. "I'll have the burger." She disappeared with the wine back into her bedroom, and Reed went to place the order. He selected a salmon steak with a side of braised asparagus for himself. A virtuous choice, yes, but he had to admit he was already contemplating those truffles.

He heard the shower switch on in Ellery's suite as he returned to peck at his laptop. The initial search results he'd requested were in, and his heart sank as he read the tally: there were at least 247 women named Angela Rivera living in Los Angeles—and that number ballooned to more than four hundred when he included the surrounding territory. Some names he could discard easily by their age, but that still left more than forty Angela Riveras to run down. Wearily, he closed the laptop and sat back in his chair. The FBI had granted him leeway in taking on this ancient case, but he didn't have carte blanche to fiddle around endlessly in the desert. He had to be able to show progress within a week or so, or the assistant director would start to get antsy. He could almost hear her now: *Run all the DNA tests you want, but do it from the office. There are other, more recent cases that demand attention.*

He ambled over to the balcony, slid open the glass doors, and stepped out into the cool night air. Las Vegas had come alive with light, a carnival of flashing neon that stretched up and down The Strip. Reed leaned on the hard rail and contemplated this electronic landscape, from the faux glittering skyscrapers at New York–New York to the bold green MGM that seemed the size of a small Emerald City. In the distance, the Stratosphere tower blinked its watchful red eye, while the intense beam from the Luxor shone high into the night sky—steady, not searching, a signal to all around that this was the place. From his vantage point, Reed could see cars moving slowly along the boulevard, but he couldn't pick out individual humans. The glitz outshone them all.

He tried to imagine his other life and wondered if he had grown up here as Joey Flores, if he would look at the ten-foot blinking signs and think, *I am home.* He was half-white or half-brown, depending on who was looking and what time of year it was. Raised as he was in a ten-room mansion by a state senator and his wholesome wife, alongside their three blond daughters, most times the white side won out. Reed examined his own hand in the dim evening light. His fair sisters might as well have been carved from ivory. The household staff had run to more colorful hues, from Lucille with her wide, welcoming bosom and soft ochre skin to Hector the groundskeeper, whose umber face lit up with pride come rose-blossom season. They'd each had their own kids, children matching their own skin with whom Reed had played the odd game of ball or tag in the expansive Markham yard. Privately, he'd sometimes envied them. Reed's skin was in-between. Neither here nor there. He got a seat at the family table almost by accident, or so he'd been raised to believe.

A lump formed in his throat as he thought of Camilla, a mother so young, with no family around, who was barely scratching out a living for herself. Her son had gone on to hit the family lottery, leapfrogging social strata Cammie herself never would have had a chance at attaining. Everything he had, everything he was, traced back to her violent death. He wondered, if she could see him now, whether she would know him. Whether she would be proud or repulsed at all he had become.

The doors slid open behind Reed, startling him from his thoughts. He turned to see Ellery, barefoot and wrapped in a voluminous white robe, padding out onto the balcony. She'd pinned her hair up and he could smell the lingering scent of the hotel's body wash, an aspirational mix of vanilla and coconut no doubt orchestrated to recall the beach. "Sorry. Didn't mean to scare you," she said as she joined him at the balcony's edge.

He considered just how many times she'd scared the

ever-loving crap out of him, starting with the night they first met. "It seems to be something of a vocation of yours."

"More like a side hobby." She looked out across the brilliant skyline.

"Well? What do you think?"

"It's something. Like a totally different city. All the colors and the lights, you hardly know what to look at first. But I guess that's the point, right? You're supposed to be paying attention to the blinking signs and the dancing girls and the booze or what have you. All this constant movement and distraction so you forget."

"Forget what?"

She looked at him. "The house always wins."

He held her gaze for a long moment. *Not always,* he thought. That she lived would always feel miraculous to him. He had been one of a hundred law enforcement officials working her kidnapping, and most of them had figured by day three that they were looking for a body. Reed had trembled when he'd pried open the closet door and found her lying there, bloody but breathing. Later, with Coben captured and his last victim recovering in the hospital, Reed had been eager to play to the cameras. He and Sarit had even written a bestselling book about the case. Only in reuniting with Ellery all these years later did he see the truth: yes, he had rescued her, and yes, he had stopped a vicious killer, but from her vantage point, he was already too late. He'd re-entered her life expecting gratitude and instead found himself hoping for forgiveness. Only when he realized that she owed him neither did they reach an understanding. He would treat her like a regular person, and in return, she would do the same for him.

She broke eye contact with him and stared hard toward the glimmering casinos. "I finally noticed back in the bedroom," she said after a minute, still not looking at him. "There are no closets."

Their hotel suite had a small coat closet, but the bedrooms used wardrobes instead. He'd made sure to check before making the reservation. "That does seem to be the case."

She gave a small nod, acknowledging his kindness. "You sure do think of everything."

He thought about her more than he liked to admit. She'd been a fourteen-year-old girl alone on the Chicago streets the night of her birthday, which, even if Reed hadn't later sketched in the rest of her biography, told him all he needed to understand how she grew up: with not enough. Not enough food. Not enough attention. Not enough love. She'd had just the barest essentials to keep her alive, until the night she'd nearly lost that, too. He could put her up in luxury hotels to the end of her days and it wouldn't make up for all she'd done without.

"That robe suits you," he said, changing the subject.

She rewarded him with a grin. "It's like wearing a cloud," she confessed. "I may sneak it into my suitcase when we leave."

He would gladly pay the fee. "We can stay then, I take it?"

Back inside, room service knocked loudly on the front

door. Ellery turned at the sound, and he could swear he heard her stomach grumble. "Yeah, we can stay."

A sudden sound jerked Reed awake in the middle of the night, and he sat straight up in bed, momentarily confused by his surroundings. *Vegas,* he remembered. He wondered if he'd heard Ellery prowling around in her usual insomnia, but then his cell phone buzzed again on the nightstand and he realized what had awoken him. He groped for the phone and saw the glowing caller ID gave the caller as Angus Markham.

Reed waited until the last second before the voice mail kicked in. "Hello."

"Reed!" His father's normally hearty voice sounded strained and hoarse. "I know it's late as hell, but I've been making speeches and glad-handing donors all day and just got in. The streets are slippery tonight, so Kenny drove like he had a newborn baby in the back."

Reed could hear the clinking of ice hitting the glass tumbler as his father made his customary bedtime bourbon. "What is it that couldn't wait until morning?"

"God, morning. I've got a radio interview at seven, followed by an elementary-school visit, a meeting with the rep from AFSCME, and then we have that 'GO Virginia' vote in the afternoon. I'm lucky if they've scheduled me time to take a piss somewhere."

"Ah, the life of the public servant," Reed remarked flatly.

His father chuckled. "Yes, and I surely do love it, even when I'm dead on my feet. Or at least I'll love it again by morning. But that's not why I called."

"Yes, why did you call?" Reed hadn't turned on any lights, so his father's voice seemed to float out of the darkness at him.

"I feel like we haven't talked much. When did I last see you? Christmas, wasn't it? You should come to dinner, you and Tula. Your mother misses you."

"You didn't call me at three in the morning to tell me Mama misses me."

"Three," his father repeated with a grunt. "So, then it's true."

"What's true?"

"Kimmy called me this morning and said you were out working a case in Las Vegas."

The hairs on Reed's neck stood up and he got out of bed. "That's right." He paced the floor as though he could somehow outrun this conversation.

"Kimmy said . . ." His father took a drink and started over. "Oh, hell, Reed, she said you were looking into a woman murdered while her baby boy was right there in his crib."

Reed halted, his heart in his throat. "I never said it was a boy."

Angus's breathing grew deeper, unsteady. "You're chasing your mother's case," he said finally. "That's what you're doing out there."

Reed said nothing. His tongue felt too large for his mouth.

His father cursed and took another drink. "Reed, we talked about this, remember? I told you what happened. I showed you the reports. You said you agreed with the detectives—the case was too old, too cold, to warrant new investigation."

Reed forced himself to swallow. "That was before I found a new lead," he replied.

"Yeah? What's that?"

"The father of Camilla's baby—my father—he was married with children. My conception and subsequent birth would have been very messy for him."

Angus coughed, long and deep. "Seems like the police figured he was married, even back then," he wheezed when he'd recovered.

"Yes," Reed said, his voice growing stronger again as he remembered his anger. How many years had this man looked him straight in the face and lied? "But I've confirmed it, you see. He was married for ten years at the time, with three daughters, and what was worse—he was running for public office. Imagine how it would look if the truth had come out. His family, his career—all of it down the shitter just because he knocked up some floozy while on a bender in the desert."

"God." His father sounded strangled. "You—you . . ."

"I know," Reed cut in coldly. "I know everything—Dad."

"Jesus, keep your voice down," he said, even though

Reed wasn't in the room, even though he wasn't yelling at all. "Your mother is sleeping."

"Did she know, too? Did you all know?" Maybe they'd all been laughing behind his back all these years.

"No, no," his father rushed to assure him. "Nothing like that. I just—I didn't tell anyone, okay? All I did was point the lawyers in the right direction and they did the rest. Your mother didn't know anything about it."

"My mother was dead," Reed said, carefully enunciating each horrible word.

There was a shocked silence on the other end of the line. "Okay," Angus cut in finally. "You feel better now that you've got that out of your system? Because you can be furious with me all you want—I've earned it—but your mother has done nothing but love you since the day she took you in her arms."

Reed thought of the picture where Camilla held him, smiling for the camera, and he went straight for the truth. "Did you kill her?" He felt dizzy, nauseated, but he had to know.

"What? For God's sake, Reed!"

"Did you?"

"No, I didn't kill her! That's what you're out there investigating? Jesus. You didn't even have the decency to come talk to me first? What if your mother had found out, or your sisters?"

Or the press, Reed supplied mentally. He resumed his pacing in the dark. "You mean, why I didn't come to you with this life-changing development? Why didn't I tell you the truth? Gee, Dad, I wonder."

"Okay," his father said, relenting. "You're damn pissed. I get it. But you have to understand, I did it to protect you."

"Bullshit. You were protecting your own ass."

"Now, you listen here—I didn't have to come get you. When I found out Cammie was killed, you were the first thing I worried about, my top priority. Were you okay? Who was taking care of you? I would've hopped a plane right that day if I could."

"Yeah? What was stopping you? Planes stopped running that day?"

"I had to do it legally. Make sure it was kosher."

"Make sure no one found out you were my real father."

"Damn straight I'm your real father!" Angus roared. "I'm the only one you'll ever have, and you'd do well to remember that fact."

"You couldn't go swooping in and announce yourself," Reed continued steadily. "Because if you gave away your real interest in the case, everyone would see you had motive."

"Will you listen to me? I didn't want to kill her. I wanted to help her. I just . . . needed to find the right way."

"Yeah, you helped her all right. You left her poor and pregnant and then she ended up slaughtered in her own living room."

There was a heavy silence. "And you think I could do that." Angus sounded dazed and defeated now, like the old man he really was. "I've seen the pictures from Cammie's apartment that day. I know what happened to her. You think I waited with a butcher knife and then carved her up while you, my son, slept in the next room. That's what you believe, that I'm some sort of monster."

"All I know," Reed said, his voice shaking with anger, "is that you lied. You lied to me my entire life."

"And that has killed me a little bit every day."

Reed shook his head, denying it. "So easy to say now, isn't it, now that I know the truth."

"I would have loved to tell you the truth, honest to God— you think I didn't bust my chest with pride every time you won some sort of genius prize or solved a big case or presented me with that precious little granddaughter of mine?"

"You leave Tula out of it." He didn't want to hear his daughter's name on Angus's lips.

"I loved you. I love you." Angus sounded mournful; whether for Reed or for himself Reed couldn't say. "You can call me a liar, but you can't deny that. You can't."

"Where were you on December 11, 1975?"

"You're asking me for my alibi?"

"I'm telling you you're going to need one."

His father took a long time with his answer. "I did not kill Camilla Flores. If you can't believe that, after all the years you've known me—if you really think I'm capable of something so vile and disgusting—then you can come ask me for my alibi for the record. I'll make sure to have my lawyer present for the conversation."

Reed ran a hand through his hair. "I've been doing this

job a long time, Dad, and that's the answer of a man with something to hide."

"If you want to come ask me about your mother, face-to-face, and you want to know how we met and what kind of person she was—those questions I will be happy to answer for you. The rest of it . . . well, I'd ask you to think long and hard before you torpedo my career and our entire family. I can't stop you. I won't. But neither will I participate in some sort of revenge campaign to smear my name."

"I only want the truth."

"And I gave it to you. I guess that means we're done."

"Not hardly," Reed warned.

They hung up without saying goodbye, and Reed threw his phone at the bed. *I love you,* his father had said, as though that justified four decades of self-serving lies, as though that absolved him of any sin. Reed had seen plenty of horrors committed in the name of love. He stood there, replaying the conversation, thinking of new rebuttals and accusations, but he knew he'd have to come with actual hard evidence if he wanted to budge his father from his story.

Gradually, his shoulders unclenched and he could breathe again. He crawled back in bed beside his phone and placed it like a stone upon his chest. It was only then that he remembered a key part of the conversation, one he'd been too riled to hear when his father let it slip. Reed picked up the phone and hesitated just a moment before dialing. His father answered right away.

"What?"

Reed didn't pussyfoot. "You said I was your top priority when you learned that Cammie was killed. How did you even find out?" If they'd kept the affair a secret and Cammie was dead, no one should have been the wiser.

His father apparently weighed the question and decided to answer. "Rufus told me," he said gruffly.

"Rufus told you. And how did Rufus find out?"

His father's silence stretched so long that Reed thought he might not answer. "You know," he said finally, "I'm not sure. I don't believe I ever asked."

6

Ellery twitched herself awake just before dawn, momentarily on high alert until she remembered where she was. When the shadowed hotel room came into focus, she wriggled around under the whisper-soft cotton sheets in unadulterated corporal pleasure. The high, cushioned bed was so vast she felt like she could swim laps in it. Her phone buzzed on the nightstand, and she retrieved it to see she had a text from Liz Simmons, her neighbor back in Boston. Ellery smiled when she saw the picture Liz had attached: Speed Bump, his muzzle covered in snow, frolicked at the local park with a perky-tailed dachshund in the background. *The boys are having a great time together!* Liz wrote.

Ellery texted back her renewed thanks for Liz's kindness in taking Speed Bump as a boarder while Ellery was away. Ellery had rescued Bump from an animal shelter where he'd been well treated but long-faced and palpably sad, shut in a cage most of the day. *Never again,* she had vowed when she took him in her arms that first day. No more locks. No more cages. She wasn't about to board him in a kennel while she followed Reed across the country. Instead, she could rest easy knowing Speed Bump was having the time of his life with his little buddy from the apartment next door—even if he might have preferred to be flopped out with Ellery on the king-size bed with its Egyptian cotton sheets.

She forced herself out from under the warm duvet and reluctantly put on her running clothes. The fancy hotel Reed had picked no doubt had a state-of-the-art workout facility somewhere on the premises, but Ellery avoided gyms whenever possible. They always featured floor-to-ceiling mirrors so you could watch yourself huffing and puffing. Ellery maintained a perfunctory relationship with mirrors, glancing once per day to make sure her hair was properly combed and that she hadn't left toothpaste on her chin. It had taken her more than a month to look at herself after Reed had yanked her free from Coben's closet, and the image of that sunken-eyed girl with her raised scars and ragged scarecrow hair had haunted her ever since.

That girl, that helpless little wraith, she was the reason Ellery took up running. Running, jumping, throwing, and shooting—she racked up as many physical skills as she could because they let her make friends with her body again. Her hands, the ones with the scars on them, they shot free throws with 91 percent accuracy on her high-school team. They passed the Handgun Qualification Standard with top marks on the first try. Finally, last summer, those once-broken hands had stopped a murderer dead in his tracks. She couldn't resent her body anymore for what Coben did to it; she no longer pretended it had happened to someone else. Her body, it turned out, was strong enough to carry the weight.

She slipped silently from her bedroom into the living area and saw across the suite that the door to Reed's room remained shut. The pink light of dawn shone in through the large balcony doors, the sun just beginning to climb over the hills. She crept up to the long dining table, which now sat littered from end to end with files and notes, proving Reed had continued working the case long after she'd retired for the night. He had sketched out the murder scene and created a timeline of known events leading up to Camilla's death, including the new detail that someone had slashed Camilla's tires. She flipped through some pages and found an outline of Camilla's apartment building, with neighbors identified and cross-referenced with the statements they gave at the time of the homicide. She set the notepad down gently and trailed her fingers over Reed's handwriting on the top page, feeling the indent of every painful word. He'd sorted stacks of folders and photographs into some sort of attempt at ordering the chaos. She hoped the organization gave him some comfort, because what she saw was a life blown to smithereens and a man convinced he could somehow piece it back together.

Outside, the brisk winter air hit her harder than she expected and a nearby bank clock advertised the temperature as a chilly thirty-nine degrees. *Still warmer than Boston,* she encouraged herself as she started her jog. As much as she loved music, Ellery refused to wear earbuds while running because they cut off one of her senses. She always cast a dubious eye at joggers and pedestrians lost to their electronic worlds, totally vulnerable to someone wishing them harm in the earthly terrain. The downside of her decision was that it often made running a deathly boring activity, with the repetitive slap, slap of her sneakers against the pavement and the same scenery every single day, so the novel Las Vegas landscape provided a welcome distraction.

She ran up East Flamingo Road toward the casinos, which had flicked off most of their overpowering neon shells to greet the light of day. At this hour, they looked like peculiar temples from another world, hulking relics with no signs of human life. Ellery wondered what it would be like to live every day in a city known for its sin. Did you just ignore the blazing lights after a while? Did you snicker at the gullible tourists coming with their suitcases full of dollars, thinking it's true that a fool and his money are soon parted? Or maybe you were someone like Camilla, who came here hoping to cash in on that blinding financial promise and then got stuck living on the outside of the city, close enough to see the cash but with no way to grab it for herself.

Ellery's run took her past the backsides of several casinos, which revealed less glamorous concrete parking structures and half-mile-high hotels. She admired the pink-and-white Flamingo and glimpsed the enormity of the High Roller Ferris wheel. Interspersed were signs of ordinary city life: a sub sandwich shop, coffeehouses, a UPS store. Still, The Strip promised the good life, with big winnings and lots of expensive stores to spend them in. There was no sign here of what happened to people when the money ran out.

She turned around and ran back to the hotel where Reed's money kept them ensconced with the glitterati. Reed was awake when she returned, wearing one of those amazing robes and holding a cup of coffee as he studied his notes from the night before. He looked up as she entered and indicated the mug in his hands. "I'd offer to make you a cup, but I know how you feel about such things," he said.

Ellery's body, already humming from the exercise, grew a little warmer at the sight of his naked legs, and she ducked her head into the refrigerator in search of a cold bottle of water. She had a more intimate relationship with Reed than any other man she'd ever known, and yet they had barely touched. Maybe this disparity explained her constant physical reaction to his presence. "What's your plan for the day?" she asked when she'd unscrewed the top of the bottle and taken a long drink.

"I want to visit the sheriff again and initiate that DNA test we talked about. We can also ask him about the blond woman in the picture with Angie and Camilla. Maybe he knows who she is."

"What about that other murder Amy mentioned? The one with the girl who got stabbed in her own apartment the year before Camilla was attacked."

Reed frowned, an indication he didn't think much of her

lead, but he said, "Sure, we can ask him about that, too." He set the mug on the only empty corner of the table and regarded her with a serious gaze. "I should warn you that the secret's out—my sister told my father that I'm in Vegas working a cold case, and he didn't have to think very hard to figure out which one."

Ellery pulled out one of the heavy chairs from the table and took a seat next to Reed. "Since we're in Vegas, I'm going to make a bet. I wager he wasn't happy with the news." She glanced at Reed for confirmation.

"That's safe money," Reed agreed. He leaned back in his seat and let out a weary breath. "He denies killing her, of course. Says he only ever wanted to protect me."

"What do you think?" Ellery asked him softly.

Reed took a long time with his answer. "I want to believe him. I want to believe him almost more than anything I've ever wanted." He paused. "So that's why I can't. Not yet."

Ellery nodded, trying to figure out how she could be most useful in this situation. Maybe she could be the believer. "I won't tell you," she said slowly, "that keeping the truth from you all these years is okay, because it's not. But I speak from experience that once you decide to keep a secret, once you've architected your whole life around it, it's hard to let it go. It can seem like its own kind of truth." She wondered sometimes if she had come forth with her true identity back in Woodbury when the disappearances first started she might have been able to stop the killer sooner.

"Yes, I gather that's the story Angus told himself. He was

already my father, so it didn't matter how he got that way, whether by birth or by some sort of legal documentation. He claims he acted immediately to start the adoption process as soon as he heard what had happened to Cammie. I can't even imagine what he told my mother to get her to sign on."

"Did you ask him?"

Reed replied with a curt shake of his head. "No, it was your average, run-of-the-mill late-night conversation between father and son. I accused him of murder. He proclaimed his innocence. The usual stuff."

Before Ellery could answer, her cell phone buzzed in the pocket of her fleece pullover. She took it out and saw the caller ID gave an unfamiliar number and no name. Her mother and Reed were the only ones who ever called her, outside of the occasional hungry reporter who somehow managed to dredge up her unlisted phone number. She accepted the call, ready to tell off the latest media hack. "Yes?"

The odd beat of silence on the other end, rather than the usual hearty, pleading sales push, made her blood run instantly cold. "Abby? It's Dad."

He got no further because Ellery immediately ended the call. She shoved the phone back in her pocket and out of sight.

"Who was that?" Reed asked.

"Wrong number," Ellery muttered as she jumped up from the table, moving around so he couldn't see her shaking. "Is there anything to eat in this place?" She opened and closed the barren cabinets one after another while Reed looked on.

"There's a coffee shop in the lobby. I thought we might stop there on our way out to see the sheriff, but I figured you might want to shower first."

Shower, yes. A perfect escape. "Okay, I'll do that." Heart pounding, she fled to her bedroom and stripped the clothes from her clammy skin. She had learned long ago not to make noise in her distress, and the roar of the shower covered her turmoil. Who the hell did John Hathaway think he was, stalking back into her life twenty years later—like he could just call her up and just say, *Hi, how's it going?* Apparently, he hadn't taken the hint when she failed to reply to his letter. Didn't he understand that silence meant no? Ellery sure got that message when he'd walked out and never said a word, not when she was abducted and tortured, not even when Daniel had died. Her brother went to his grave thinking his father no longer gave a damn about him. Daniel wasn't around to forgive him, so hell would freeze before Ellery ever would.

The water ran down her face like tears, and she banged her fist on the tiled wall until her hand hurt and she collapsed in the corner, curling her arms over her head. Maybe she wasn't the best person to stand up for Angus Markham and his chosen narrative after all. In the best version of the story, Angus was a loving father who moved heaven and earth to rescue his baby boy, risking family and career just to be with him. *I want to believe,* Reed had said, and this was Ellery's problem: she wanted it, too, maybe more than she'd realized. Because if your father was a piece of shit, what did that make you?

* * *

The desert warmed up with the rising sun, and Ellery seized on the brightening sky as the opportunity to hide her red-rimmed eyes behind a pair of dark shades. She could feel Reed's curious gaze on her as he started the car, but he kept any remarks to himself. At LV Metro headquarters, Sheriff Ramsey gave them a cordial welcome, although he seemed more distracted and hurried than the day before.

"I'm afraid I've got a nine A.M. meeting today, Agent Markham. I trust that Don Price should be able to help you with any remaining questions you might have. He told me that you've already made copies of all the available files, and, though it pains me to say it, that is pretty much the sum total of our information on your mother's case."

"I appreciate that, Sheriff, and won't take up much of your time. First off, I'd like to run a DNA analysis on the knife—specifically the hilt. If the killer injured himself in the attack, he may have left a sample behind."

Sheriff Ramsey leaned back in his chair with a frown. "That was a theory at the time, which is why Thorndike's cut got everyone so interested. Sure, a DNA test is possible. Why not? Maybe we'll get lucky. I'll put in the request myself today."

"Great, thank you," Reed replied. "I was also wondering if you might be able to identify the young woman in this picture with Camilla and Angela." He took out the photograph and handed it across the desk. "I'd ask Sergeant Price about it, except I think he was probably in nursery school at the time it was taken."

The sheriff grinned and took up the picture. "Boy, you're right about that. The new recruits look younger every year." He put on his reading glasses and studied the photograph for a moment. "She doesn't look familiar to me. I'm sorry, but as I've mentioned, my role in the investigation was limited to discovery of the body. Her name isn't in the murder book?"

"It may well be. We just can't tell. There must be a hundred names in there."

Ramsey nodded and leaned back in his chair. "We beat every bush we could think of and then came around to whack 'em again. If this woman isn't easily identified in the records, it's probably because the initial investigation didn't suggest she was of any importance. Why the interest? Do you have reason to think she knows something?"

Reed took the picture back and tucked it away. "Just covering all the bases. Speaking of, I'd like to talk to Billy Thorndike if possible. Do you have a current address for him?"

Ramsey held up one finger. "I had a feeling you were going to ask me that, so I had my boys look him up for you. Last we heard from him, Thorndike was living out in Summerlin with his daughter, drinking her hard-earned money. I'm amazed he hasn't drunk himself into the grave by now. I'll give you the address for his daughter if you'd like it."

"Thank you."

Ellery glanced at Reed while the sheriff wrote out the information on a slip of paper. Reed made no mention of the lead she'd uncovered, so she raised the issue herself. "Sheriff, was there another woman stabbed to death around the same time Camilla Flores was attacked? Maybe a year or so earlier? The name we heard was Giselle or Danielle."

The sheriff looked up, pen still in hand. "Giselle Hardiman, yes. What about her?"

"Well, it's just that we heard that case was also unsolved. Two young women, murdered in a similar way . . ."

"They weren't that similar. Yes, it's true that the Hardiman girl died from a stabbing attack that took place in her bedroom, but that's almost the extent of the similarities." He held up his hand to tick off the differences. "Giselle Hardiman was sexually assaulted, but Camilla Flores was not. The Flores apartment was either the scene of a burglary or staged to look like one, but we found nothing missing or out of place at Hardiman's apartment. Flores was attacked with two weapons, the knife and the metal bookend. Furthermore, the two victims lived at opposite ends of the city and there was no evidence that they knew each other or that their lives otherwise intersected."

"Still," Reed said, "we'd like to see the case."

Ellery nodded, pleased he was backing her up, at least. "Yes. What could it hurt just to take another look?"

Sheriff Ramsey shook his head. "I'm afraid I can't do that. You have to trust me that we've looked into this possibility before and come up empty. I appreciate your personal interest in the Flores case, and I stand by my offer of full cooperation on that score. But I can't have you digging around willy-nilly in all of our old cases. Sergeant Price has actual work to do and can't be trucking boxes back and forth from storage all day. Besides, we have rules and procedures to follow."

Reed sat forward, mounting a rebuttal. "Yes, but if the two cases could be related—"

"They're not," Ramsey cut in.

"With all due respect, Sheriff, the FBI likes to make those kinds of decisions for itself."

"Then the FBI can petition for jurisdiction," the sheriff answered with a new trace of steel in his voice. "And if you go down that road, I'd advise you to make sure she isn't the one signing the forms." He pointed at Ellery. "Because I looked it up, and she's not FBI. She's not even on the job."

Ellery felt her face flame hot, but Reed didn't flinch. "I never said she was. She's here at my discretion as a consultant."

"Call it whatever you like, we both know it ain't exactly kosher. Like I said, we've been cooperative with you on account of your personal interest in this case, and because we're officially deactivating our own investigation. Whatever leads you find that pertain to Camilla Flores, you have my blessing to follow them however you see fit." He glanced at Ellery as if deeply skeptical and then shook his head to clear it. "Now I'm sorry, but I've got to run to that meeting. Good luck tracking down Thorndike. I hope he has something useful for you. Hell, maybe the SOB will shock us all by up and confessing after all these years." He gave them a tight smile as he rose to his feet and gestured toward the door.

Ellery and Reed took the hint and showed themselves out. In the hall, they stood and watched Sheriff Ramsey stride away toward his meeting. "Well, that took a strange turn," Ellery murmured as he disappeared from sight.

"Here's your hat, what's your hurry?" Reed agreed, his gaze thoughtful. "If we're getting any information on Giselle Hardiman's case, it won't be from Sheriff Ramsey."

"Reed . . ."

He returned his attention to her. "Hmm?"

She hesitated, unsure of how to phrase her concern. "I'm not getting you into trouble, am I? By being here with you on this case?"

"I brought you here because you know how to make trouble." He touched her arm briefly and smiled. "Teach me your ways, Secret Agent Hathaway. I'm here to learn."

She ducked away, warm from his touch. "My ways usually end up in front of a disciplinary committee," she warned him. "If I were doing this on my own, I'd probably use Ramsey's meeting as a convenient cover to convince Sergeant Price that Ramsey told him to give us the files on the Hardiman murder."

"A bold strategy. Damn the torpedoes and all that."

"Right. It's risky. Ramsey would stop cooperating with us entirely when he found out, and we might still need him later." She considered. "Let me see if I can find another way in."

"This other way," Reed said as they began walking for the main door, "it's not going to get us arrested, will it?"

Ellery smiled and put on her sunglasses as they hit the outside again. "You're the one who wanted trouble."

"I'm just trying to determine if I brought enough bail money."

The SUV chirped as Reed unlocked the doors, but Ellery veered off suddenly as she spied a soda machine near one of the buildings. "I'm going for a caffeine hit," she said, jerking her thumb at the machine. "You want anything?" Reed declined, so she jogged lightly across the near-empty lot on her own.

She inserted the bills and waited for the Coke machine to dispense her drink. It whirred and the soda bottle landed with a thunk. As she leaned down to retrieve it, Ellery saw a flash of movement from the corner of her eye, coming from the direction of the sparsely parked cars. She stood up quickly and took a few steps in the direction of the figure she'd seen. Nothing moved. She scanned the cars but saw no one inside them. Neither did there seem to be anyone walking beyond the lot on the sidewalk. She waited a beat longer to see if the motion would repeat, but the scenery did not change. Eventually, she decided she'd imagined it and returned to the SUV, which Reed had idling as he entered the GPS information for Billy Thorndike's last known address.

Only three blocks later, when she happened to glance in the side mirror, she caught sight of a silver BMW sedan that looked just like one she'd spotted in the LVMPD parking lot. She held her breath as Reed made the next turn. The silver BMW popped up again, two cars behind them. It trailed them all the way down the road, and Reed flipped the signal to follow the signs marked SUMMERLIN. "Reed . . ."

"What?"

"I think—" She looked again, and the BMW had vanished. "Never mind." She kept her eyes on the mirror for the rest of the trip but did not glimpse the silver car again.

Billy Thorndike's black-and-white mugshot dated to 1974, and he looked the part, with his extended sideburns, a slick, receding hairline, and a striped, wide-lapel shirt so loud it screamed. His jowly cheeks were coated in stubble, and he had small, bleary eyes. Ellery knew he had to be twenty-seven years old in the photograph, but he looked like he could've been pushing forty. She did not hold out a lot of hope they would find Thorndike still coherent or even alive.

Reed glided the SUV to a stop in front of a small but unexpectedly nice house the color of concrete, with a teensy yard and a cracked driveway. "This is the place," he said, checking the address slip that the sheriff had given them.

They walked the short path to the front door and Reed rang the bell. Apart from them, the street was deserted and silent. Ellery heard someone moving around on the other side of the door, and eventually it parted about three inches and an old man's face peered out at them. "Yeah?"

"Mr. Thorndike?" Reed ventured.

The crack did not widen. "Who's asking?"

"Reed Markham," he replied, and pulled out his FBI credentials. "I'd like to talk to you about Camilla Flores, if I may."

"Don't know her."

He started to close the door, but Reed blocked it with his

foot. "She was murdered—stabbed in her apartment to death forty-four years ago. Right before she could testify against you in open court."

"Oh, her. Yeah, she's dead. Been that way a long time now. What do you care, anyway? Ain't you government people got better stuff to do? Like terrorism. I seen on the TV just today how we got sleeper cells of them Arabs living right here in Nevada. They could be right next door for all I know. Why don't you go knock over there?"

He moved again to shut the door, but Reed pushed back and even widened the gap. Ellery caught the stench of beer and cigarettes flowing from the inside. "Give us fifteen minutes," Reed said. "If you convince me that Camilla Flores's murder is old news, we won't come back to bother you again."

"You have a warrant? I don't gotta talk to you without a warrant."

"You just got done telling me there's no case," Reed said reasonably. "Why would I need a warrant?"

Thorndike swayed and scowled, as though he knew there was a trick in the logic somewhere but couldn't quite place it. "Fifteen minutes," he groused, backing up so they could enter. "That's all you get. Judge Judy comes on at ten, and I love that bitch. She doesn't take shit from anyone."

Ellery stepped over the threshold and saw Thorndike had now lost almost all his hair, leaving just a gray fringe around his ears. His nose had grown longer and taken on a reddish color, while his cheeks caved in. The stubble remained, as did the curl of chest hair, which peeked out from under his white muscle shirt. In his weakened state, Thorndike didn't seem a threat to anyone. He even used a walker. He leaned heavily on it as he led them back to the living room, where, as advertised, he had a morning court show playing at full volume. He grabbed the remote and stabbed angrily at it to silence the television before collapsing, like a deflating balloon, into a nearby stuffed recliner. He picked up a cigarette and tapped the lengthening ash into the tray. "Tick tick," he reminded them. "You wanna talk? Then talk."

Ellery and Reed took a seat on an overstuffed floral sofa. "Camilla Flores," Reed began, but Thorndike cut them off with a wave of his hand.

"The cops have been trying to pin that bitch's murder on me for decades. It never stuck. You know why? Because I didn't do it."

"She was going to testify against you," Reed reminded him. "But that never happened."

"Yeah," Thorndike said before taking a drag on his cigarette. "Shame about that."

"Tell me about the afternoon she was killed," Reed said.

Thorndike looked them over with dead eyes. "I don't know. I wasn't there."

"You must have heard about it."

"Sure, everyone heard about it. The story was that some guy broke into her place, maybe to steal some of her piddly shit. But then she turned out to be home and caught him piling up her stuff. So he gutted her like a fish."

He made a slicing motion to underscore his point, and

122

Ellery's stomach tightened. Something about the way his face brightened with the pantomime reminded her of Coben and Willett, and she remembered that this dissembling wretch of a man had no doubt killed someone, even if he happened to be innocent of the Flores murder. "Where were you when all this was going on?" Reed asked.

"Home with Ma," he replied coolly, blowing smoke. "She wasn't feeling so good and I brought her some groceries. Cooked her an early supper."

"What did you make?"

"Fried sausage and potatoes. Her favorite." He added a cheeky smile after this answer, like he'd had it ready in his back pocket. "I stayed and watched her programs with her while she ate it. So you see? I couldn't have done it. My ma, she swore on the Holy Bible to the cops that I was with her when that bitch got popped."

"And of course your mother would never lie for you," Reed said, and Thorndike replied with a wide smile that showed off a row of yellowed teeth.

"Course she would've. Wouldn't your mama take a bullet for you if it came to that?" He coughed and then grinned at his own remark. "Maybe she wouldn't. Maybe you cops all have tight-ass, pussy mamas who don't care about you. But it don't make no difference, not after all this time. Ma's been gone twenty years now—you want to dig her up and ask her again?"

"I don't think that will be necessary," Reed replied.

Ellery could feel the window closing. "What about

123

Giselle Hardiman?" she blurted out, and both Reed and Thorndike turned to look at her.

Thorndike puffed away on his cigarette for a moment. "Who?" he asked pointedly, and Ellery could tell it was for show. He knew the Hardiman name straightaway. He just wanted her to work for the information. She practically rolled up her sleeves, relishing the job. *I've got your number now, you little creep,* she thought. Forget his grand proclamations about how they had to be leaving in fifteen minutes—this man would let them sit here and grill him all day. Hell, he would probably try to block the door if they left too soon. He'd been rotting in that recliner so long it'd taken on his shape, and then along came two investigators to ask about the time when he might have been big and bad enough to murder someone. No TV program would give him that.

"I'm sorry," Ellery said as she leaned forward, feigning innocence. "Are you hard of hearing? I can speak up if you need."

"I heard you the first time," Thorndike snarled in return. "Hardiman, right? I just don't know the name."

"Giselle Hardiman, that's right," Ellery repeated for him. "She was another young woman killed the year before Camilla Flores. She was also—how did you put it?—gutted like a fish."

Thorndike's chuckle devolved into a wheeze. He reached for an inhaler and sucked on that for a couple of breaths. "Giselle, okay. Yeah, I remember her now. Working girl, and she could work it. Pretty little bow-tie mouth. Big tits."

"So you were a client."

"Honey, I didn't have to pay for it."

124

"Yeah, that's what they all say," Ellery replied, sounding bored. "But the working girls—the smart ones, like you say— they don't just give it away. Maybe you don't pay in cash. But you pay. Am I right?"

He laughed and wheezed again. "I like this one," he told Reed, pointing at Ellery. "She's got spunk. And nice tits, too. Back in my day, the cop shop was always full of dicks. We didn't get anything near this tasty."

"Back to Giselle Hardiman," Ellery said.

Thorndike licked his lips. "Like I said, tasty. Why you asking me about her? You think I killed that one, too?"

"Did you?" Ellery asked, just to stroke his ego a little.

"Fuck no. I got no beef with Giselle."

"Any idea who did?"

Thorndike waved both hands in their direction, dismissing them. "What do I care?"

"Maybe the person who killed Giselle also killed Camilla Flores," Ellery said. "If that person isn't you, it means you're off the hook."

"I look like I'm on some sort of hook to you?" He spread his arms. "You cops got jack shit on me."

Ellery waited a moment and then slapped her hands on her knees. "I guess you're right," she said, rising from the sofa. Reed glanced up in surprise but scrambled to follow her lead. "We should be moving along then, and leaving you to your daytime television."

"Wait just a damn second."

Ellery turned around again, showing impatience. "What

125

is it, Mr. Thorndike? We don't have all day. We have other leads to investigate, you know. We can't be wasting time with dead ends."

Anger flared in his cheeks. "Hey, honey, you rang my bell, remember?"

"And what a bore that turned out to be." She practically yawned as she said it. "We should go."

"Wait. Just wait." She could see his mind spinning. "You guys are FBI, you said."

She let Reed take that one. "That's right."

"What're the Feds doing with a forty-year-old case?"

Reed and Ellery exchanged a glance. "We have some new information that's taken the case in a different direction," Reed answered carefully.

"What new information?"

"I'm afraid I can't say."

"It's corrupt cops, isn't it? It's gotta be. Those cocksuckers think they can get away with anything."

"What makes you say that?" Reed asked, and Thorndike's thin lips curled into a frown as he pointed a shaky finger at Ellery.

"She said it. She brought up Giselle Hardiman."

"What about her?" Reed said.

"Come off it, man. I saw what was going down with her. We all knew the score—which cops would bust your balls and which would look the other way if you made it worth their while. Giselle knew it better than anyone."

"You're saying Giselle bought off police officers."

Thorndike gasped and coughed again at the humor of it all. "Yeah, she bought 'em off, all right—with her pussy. She'd give it up anytime, anywhere, for the boys in blue."

"Can you prove that?" Reed asked quickly.

Thorndike looked offended. "What, you think I got pictures or something? What sort of sick freak do you think I am? I don't gotta prove it. We all knew it. Just no one wants to talk about it, especially after Giselle got whacked. Bet she had some familiar names in her little black book."

He shot Ellery a sly look and winked at her. Ellery repressed a shudder.

Reed was a terrier with a rat in his teeth. "There was a book? What happened to it?"

"Hell if I know. Maybe there ain't any book. Like I told you—I wasn't a client. I just know the cops were boffing her and it got real awkward when she turned up dead."

Ellery and Reed regarded each other silently, and she gave the tiniest shrug. It didn't seem like Thorndike would be of much additional use at this stage. "Okay," Reed said, taking a breath. "Thank you for answering our questions. We can show ourselves out."

"That's it?" Thorndike sounded wounded. "You don't want to take me downtown or something?"

"We don't have a downtown," Reed reminded him. "FBI, remember?" Then he paused and withdrew the picture he'd shown to Sheriff Ramsey earlier. "But maybe there is one more thing you can help us with. Do you recognize the blond woman in this picture?"

Thorndike snatched up the photograph with eager fingers. "That one is the lying bitch, Cammie. That's her friend, Angie something. Always screeching at each other in Spanish, those two."

"Yes, but what about the woman on the end?"

"I recognize her. She hung around with these two *putas*— *stuck* out like a sore thumb. Her name was, uh . . ." He seemed to be searching back through the ages for a memory. "Wendy. No, Wanda. Yeah, that was it. Wanda. My boy Jeff, he had a real hard-on for her, you know what I'm saying? Used to yell out after her sometimes, 'I Wanda fuck you.'"

"Wanda," Reed repeated. So the name on the back of the photo was genuine. "Got it." He took back the picture. "You know her last name?"

Thorndike adopted a philosophical expression. "I'm trying to think about a time I cared about some chick's last name. Nope. Never."

Ellery rolled her eyes. "Good day, Mr. Thorndike," she said, heading for the exit.

From his chair, Thorndike yelled after them, "I'll make an exception for you, honey. Come sit on Daddy's lap for a minute and I'll call you anything you want!"

Reed stepped out with her into the sunshine. "Would you care to do the honors?" he asked, looking amused.

"With pleasure." She reached back and slammed the door behind them. "Gah. I think I need another shower after being in the presence of that creature."

"Good thing we're heading back to the hotel then."

"We are? Why?"

"The name Wanda must be in the case file somewhere. I just have to find the context."

At the hotel, Reed sat down at the long table to start poring over the files, looking for Wanda. Ellery decided to look in a different place, going further back even than Reed dared to venture. "You mind if I borrow the car for a bit?" she asked him, and he tossed her the keys without even looking at her, so focused as he was on the murder book in front of him.

"Knock yourself out."

Ellery ventured to the UNLV library, which she had looked up online, to determine that this was the home for the *Las Vegas Review-Journal* newspaper archives. The newspaper's records had been digitized and were searchable back to 1970, so it didn't take her long to find the articles pertaining to Giselle Hardiman's murder, scant as they were. Her search returned just five items, which seemed to Ellery to be a low total, given the brutality of the crime. She clicked on the first and longest story, which was dated November 12, 1974. Giselle Hardiman, age twenty-four, had been found stabbed in the bedroom of her apartment sometime past nine o'clock at night. A neighbor reported hearing screaming, but by the time the cops arrived on the scene there was no trace of Giselle's attacker. She had been taken to the hospital, where she was pronounced dead shortly thereafter. No witnesses came forward to report any clues that might have led to Giselle's killer.

Ellery read the disappointing text, which offered not much else in terms of new information. The next article mentioned Giselle's history of prostitution and drug use. Apparently, she'd been arrested for possession of cocaine two years prior to her death but was released with time served. The cops said they were looking into the drug angle, but they did not sound optimistic. The other three articles were more of the same, each one shorter than the next, until Giselle Hardiman vanished from the official history altogether. Ellery made copies of each story just in case they might prove useful later, but they had not proven to be any sort of gold mine so far.

When she returned to the hotel, she didn't see Reed at the table where she'd left him, so she wandered the suite until she located him out on the balcony. He squinted at her in the mild sunshine and held up the legal pad he'd been writing on when she appeared. "I've found it," he said. "Wanda Evans worked with Camilla Flores at the Howard Johnson's. She's on the list of coworkers interviewed during the initial investigation. But get this—she says she didn't know Camilla well at all and couldn't offer any insight into who might have killed her."

"So she lied," Ellery said, thinking of the picture of the women with their arms around each other.

"She definitely lied. The question is why she lied."

"I don't suppose we can just drive on over to the Howard Johnson's and ask her."

"Pretty sure they tore down the place years ago," Reed

said. "But there's a Wanda Evans, age sixty-seven, living over on Lakeview Street. That's got to be her, don't you think?"

"Great, let's go try to talk to her." Her stomach grumbled at the idea, and Ellery touched her middle. Back in Boston, it was way past lunchtime. "Maybe after we get something to eat?"

Reed's reply got lost in the buzzing of her cell phone. Reluctantly, Ellery pulled out the phone to check the ID, and her heart seized up when she saw the same number as earlier that morning. She punched the phone emphatically with her thumb to end the call before it could go to voice mail.

Reed lifted his eyebrows at her. "Another wrong number?" he asked lightly.

She let out a shaky breath as she tucked away the phone. "It's my father," she admitted as she lowered herself into the other lounge chair. "He's been trying to reach me."

"What?" Reed dragged his lounge chair closer and swung his legs over the side so that their knees were nearly touching. "What does he want?"

"I don't know. He wrote to the Woodbury PD looking for me, and they forwarded me the letter. I didn't read it and I didn't answer. I hoped that would be the end of it, that he'd get the message I didn't want to talk to him. But somehow, he's got my phone number. Maybe my mom gave it to him, I don't know." Her mother had no love for John Hathaway, but she had a price and the price was low.

Reed was quiet for a long moment. "Are you going to talk to him?"

Ellery looked away toward the shiny casinos, glinting in the high midday sun. "I'm afraid I may have to talk to him long enough to tell him to leave me the hell alone," she said finally.

"You've never really said much about him."

She shrugged. "There's not much to say." John Hathaway had loved eighties music and the 1985 Chicago Bears—she'd laughed 'til she fell over whenever he did the Super Bowl Shuffle—and when he'd set her on his shoulders she'd felt like she was on top of the world. He drove a truck when he wanted to, but mostly he liked to sit around and think up quicker ways to get rich. Selling vitamins. Selling T-shirts. Selling fancy coffee packets that sat rotting in their storage closet years after John hit the road for good. He'd blow through a bunch of money on his schemes, then work overtime for a year to pay them off. The children he'd bribed with candy, always enough to cover the tears and the arguments.

Ellery felt her eyes watering. He'd brought her Reese's Pieces because they were her favorite. Daniel had preferred Mike and Ike. Once her father had left, there'd been no money for candy. "When I was little, he used to sing me this stupid song at bedtime," she told Reed, struggling to talk around the lump in her throat. "It was about these bears all sleeping in the same bed. Only the little one would say, 'I'm crowded; roll over.' But when the bears rolled over, one fell out. At the end of the song, the littlest one is there all by himself, and he says, 'I'm lonely,' and I hated it. I used to make him stop before he got to the end—'Don't sing the lonely part, Daddy!'—and so instead he made up a verse where all the bears come bouncing back into the bed. He knew I couldn't stand for that tiniest bear to be all alone."

She blinked her eyes rapidly, but she couldn't make them clear. She felt Reed reach out and take her hand. "He knew I couldn't stand it," she whispered brokenly. "He knew, and he left anyway. So no, I don't care what he has to say now."

7

"Maybe your father wants to apologize," Reed suggested to Ellery as he drove them toward Wanda Evans's house.

Ellery slowly slung her head around to look at him. "Exactly what words do you think he should use? Because I'm trying to figure out what explanation might excuse walking out on your two kids and not looking back, not even bothering to show your face when one of them died. Maybe he's been in witness protection. Maybe he hit his head and had a terrible case of amnesia. Hey, maybe someone's held him prisoner in a closet all these years—then we'd really have something to talk about."

She hunched deeper into the car seat and glowered out the window. From her closed, angry posture, Reed knew better than to press his point. He didn't know why he was bothering to try to defend John Hathaway, anyway, except possibly for the memory of his own daughter's tear-stained face a year ago when Reed had packed his suitcases and left the family home. He'd seen Tula the very next day and many days after, but he couldn't pretend his split from Sarit hadn't hurt their daughter in ways that no words would ever mend.

From nowhere came a memory: Reed was about Tula's age, six or seven, and he'd fallen off the jungle gym at school, possibly breaking his arm. For some reason his mother had not responded to the phone call from school, so Senator Markham himself arrived to rescue Reed from the nurse's office and take him to the doctor. Reed's arm turned out to be sprained, not broken, and Angus rewarded his boy for his bravery with an ice-cream cone in the park. Reed remembered playing at the edge of the pond with his father, throwing crackers in for the ducks and basking in the glow of Angus's rare undivided attention, when a woman had appeared alongside them. She had long blond hair and big red lips and he could see down her flowing low-cut shirt when she'd leaned over to say to him, "Aren't you the cutest thing? You're going to be a heartbreaker when you get big, just like your daddy." Reed normally puffed with pride whenever someone compared him to his father, but this time he just crouched down and scratched in the dirt with a stick while Angus laughed too loud and long, as though this lady had made some terrifically funny joke. When at last Reed stood up again, he saw his father had wandered off to talk to the woman, the two of them standing close together in the shade of an old oak tree. Reed had resented her intrusion on his sunny afternoon and wished she would just go away. Instead, she'd hung around until they left the park, at one point disappearing entirely with his father into the public restroom for what had seemed like an eternity to Reed. Reed sulked the whole way home, not just because this strange lady took his father away, but because he'd sensed she was the whole reason they had gone to the park in the first place.

"This looks like the house." Reed killed the engine, and they walked up the path to a small ranch-style home with yellow shutters and a sleepy-looking cat lying in the front window. Reed rang the bell while Ellery stretched across the bushes to tap her fingers near the cat. It rolled over and patted its paw against her hand, but no one came to answer the door. Reed tried again, only to have someone yell at them from across the lawn.

"If you're looking for Wanda, she isn't here. She's working today!"

Reed turned to see an older woman wearing a flowered sun hat over a bunch of raucous gray curls. She held a small watering can in her hands and was watching the activity on Wanda's stoop with obvious curiosity. "Thank you," Reed called back to her. "Do you know where we can find her?"

The woman put one hand on her fleshy hip. "Depends on who's asking."

Reed took out his FBI credentials and walked over to the driveway so the woman could see them. "We need to speak with her as soon as possible," he said gravely.

"FBI? What's the FBI want with Wanda?"

Reed couldn't discern whether she was intrigued or

jealous. "I'm afraid that's classified. You mentioned that Wanda is at work now. Can you tell us where she is?"

"Sure, she's waiting tables at Lucky Lucy's up the street—I love their dinner buffet. If you hurry, you can beat the rush."

"Rush," Reed muttered to Ellery as they walked away. "It's two fifteen."

"This buffet," she replied. "Do you think it's all-you-can-eat?"

Reed had seen Ellery put away a plate of food. "If it is, I sense the establishment is about to lose money."

At Lucky Lucy's, they requested to be seated in Wanda's section and the hostess, a sloe-eyed girl with gold-hoop earrings, hadn't bothered to ask why. Wanda bustled over to their booth a few moments later. Reed knew it had to be her because her age seemed about right—mid-sixties—and because the red lettering on her name tag read: *Wanda*. This white-haired, puffy-faced woman bore little resemblance to the hot blond number in the photograph Reed carried in his breast pocket. "Hi there. I'm Wanda, and I'll be helping y'all today. What can I get y'all to drink?" she asked as she placed plastic menus in front of them.

"Wanda Evans?" Reed asked her.

She stood upright, plainly surprised. "That's right," she said tentatively. "Do I know you?"

"No, but I believe you knew my mother—Camilla Flores."

Her lips thinned and she shook her head. "Sorry, doesn't ring a bell. Would you like to order now or do you

137

want to look over the menu some more? Most folks just go with the buffet."

"You worked with her at Howard Johnson's back in the early seventies," Reed persisted.

"Yeah? Maybe. It was a long time ago and I don't really remember." She took a step back from their table, ready to flee.

"You were friends," Reed told her, and he took out the old Polaroid photograph from his pocket. "You and Cammie and Angie. See?"

He held it out toward her, and she leaned in for a quick peek but did not move any closer. "I don't know what you want from me, Mr. . . . ."

"Markham. Reed Markham." He paused for a moment. "But you may have known me as Joey."

The sound of his first name flipped some sort of switch that made her freeze, then soften. "Joey," she repeated staring at him, bemused. "I'll be damned." She snatched the photograph from him and studied it with hungry eyes. "Ha, would you look at us back then, thinking we had the world on a string. I was a dish, though, wasn't I? Lordy, where did those legs go?"

Reed imagined that four decades of waitressing might take their toll. As he watched Wanda's gaze linger on the old photo, he decided to stick with the more personal angle in questioning her about Camilla's murder. After all, she'd given the cops nothing during the initial investigation. He gestured across the booth to Ellery. "Ms. Evans, this is my friend Ellery Hathaway. We're visiting the city this week because I'm trying to learn more about my mother, and I thought you might be able to help."

Wanda's face closed up again and she shoved the picture back into his hands. "I'm real sorry about what happened to Cammie, but there's nothing I can tell you."

"You knew her. I never got that chance." He ducked his head, trying to meet her eyes. "Please? I'd just like to talk to you for a few minutes."

She turned around as if looking for some invisible surveillance, or perhaps a rescuer, and answered with a sigh. "She was a real nice lady, your mom. Didn't deserve what happened to her. I don't know what you think I can help you with, but my break's in half an hour. If you want to stick around until then, we can talk while I eat."

"Perfect, thank you so much."

Reed and Ellery used the intervening time to avail themselves of the buffet, where Reed was pleased to discover a decent salad bar that included both spinach and arugula. He concocted a leafy bowl filled with garbanzo beans and vegetables of varying sizes and colors, upon which he added a smattering of genuine bacon bits for flavor. When he returned to the booth, he found Wanda had left them large plastic cups of iced tea and a stack of paper napkins. Ellery returned a moment later, walking slowly so as not to tip over the Tetris-like assembly of food she had amassed on her single plate.

"They do allow you to make more than one trip, you know," Reed said as he eyed her enormous lunch.

"Right. I still have to go back for dessert." She picked up a deep-fried drumstick and took a bite from it. "I figure we should eat with enthusiasm—you know, to butter her up."

"That doesn't usually require a literal stick of butter," he replied, pointing with his fork at her plate.

"What? I needed something for the rolls."

Reed's ex-wife, Sarit, ate like a bird, alighting at the table long enough to peck at a few bites, only to fly away again in pursuit of more cerebral activities. She had admired his cooking but lacked the attention span and appetite to endure his carefully planned four-course meals. "Remind me to feed you more often," he said, only half-kidding, and Ellery looked up from her food to meet his gaze.

"Name the time and the place."

"Dinner tonight," he said, surprising himself. "Somewhere that doesn't charge by the pound." He hadn't forgotten what happened the last time he'd taken her out, the heat of his hand on her body—right before she'd shown off her scars and practically dared him to see past them. He wasn't yet sure he could. Maybe he wasn't supposed to.

"Dinner," she mused as she broke off a piece of roll. "Okay," she said after a beat, in the same way you might say, *Challenge accepted*. Reed felt himself start to sweat a little. "Nowhere too nice," she cautioned him. "I didn't bring any fancy clothes."

Intrigued, he tilted his head at her. "Do you own fancy clothes?"

"No. That's why I didn't bring them."

Reed could hand over a credit card and set her loose in any of the dozens of expensive boutiques, but that was just a little too *Pretty Woman* for him. Not to mention Ellery would probably take scissors to the card if he made that sort of offer. "So what kind of restaurant level are we talking about here?" he asked her. "I need a calibration."

She shrugged. "Nowhere where the waiters wear suits."

In Vegas, he could probably find a place where the waiters would show up in their underwear, but he wasn't about to play sartorial chicken with her. "Casually attired waitstaff. Got it."

Wanda Evans, herself wearing a red apron over jeans and a pink polo shirt, reappeared when the half hour was up with another glass of iced tea and a sandwich from home that she'd wrapped in wax paper. "They charge us to eat here," she explained as she took a seat in the booth next to Ellery. "We get a ten percent discount, but that's all. Can you believe it? Cheap-ass bastards."

Ellery, who had been working her way through a stack of varying kinds of cookies, slid a couple over to Wanda, who answered with a smile, "Aren't you a doll, thank you." She glanced at Reed as she took up her sandwich. "I haven't thought about Cammie in years. It's kind of spooky, you wanna know the truth, to be sitting here across from you. It's like her eyes looking back at me."

"How did you know her?" Reed asked.

"Like you said—we worked together at HoJo's. Not always the same shift, but enough times that we got to talking. I liked her. She made me laugh, the way she'd handle some of the difficult or nutty customers. Like we'd get some guy who'd point out a picture on the menu, where it said: 'Fluffiest pancakes ever,' or some such thing, and he'd go, 'What is this?' And Cammie, bless her heart, she'd lean in real close and say, 'Those must be the best pancakes ever.' And then he'd go, 'Do you have these?' and she'd say, 'Yes, sir, they're on the menu, so we have them.' And he'd go, 'Well, what else do you have?' She would stand there and smile as he made her read the whole damn menu to him. Lordy, she had the patience of a saint, that woman."

"And you spent time together outside of work?"

Her face wrinkled up in warm memory. "Yeah, we had some times together, her and me and Angie. We used to go out on the weekends, get some drinks, and hear the local bands. We never had much money, but back then a guy would buy you a beer or two for a nice smile and some conversation. Course that was before Cammie went and got herself knocked up."

Reed saw his opening and took it. "You knew my father?"

"No, Cammie played that one close to the vest. We asked her 'bout it, but she never gave up his name, at least not that I knew of." She gave Reed an apologetic look. "I got the feeling he was married."

"Why? What gave you that idea?"

"Well, because she wouldn't say who he was, for one thing. For another, after she had the baby, she said she was maybe going to get some money for him. I figured, you know, that she was putting the screws to the dad. 'Pay up, buddy.'"

She made a jabbing motion that Reed found uncomfortable, given how Cammie had died.

"What kind of money?" he asked.

A shadow crossed Wanda's face, as though she'd said the wrong thing. She took a long drink of iced tea before answering. "I don't know nothing for sure," she said uneasily. "Just talk that I heard. It's not like Cammie told me the number."

"What talk? What number?"

Still, Wanda was reluctant. She set down the tea and carefully folded her hands in her lap. "I heard it was twenty-five thousand dollars," she said finally.

Ellery looked at Reed in surprise, and he tried not to register his own shock. Twenty-five grand back then would be equivalent to more than one hundred thousand dollars today. That kind of cash wasn't for child support. That was hush money.

"Who told you about the twenty-five thousand dollars?" Ellery wanted to know. "If it wasn't Cammie?"

"I don't know. Could've been any one of the girls at the restaurant—I don't really remember. Like I said, it was just talk. I, uh . . ." She checked her watch. "I should probably be getting back to work."

"You have fifteen more minutes on your break," Reed pointed out.

"But I've told you everything I can."

"I don't think so," Reed replied, and Wanda looked up at him in surprise. "You haven't told us why you pretended to the police that you didn't know Cammie."

Wanda's blue eyes became watery and she twisted in her seat. "What's it even matter now, anyway? I just didn't want to get mixed up in the whole thing. I still don't want any part of it. What happened to Cammie, it was just awful. Horrible. I can't even imagine someone waiting for her with a knife, cutting her up like that—" She broke off with a shudder. "But her and I weren't close no more by the time she got killed. Cammie was busy with her baby. She didn't have time to go out and party with the gals like she used to."

Reed remembered the bone-crushing exhaustion from Tula's early days, when the baby woke every ninety minutes demanding to be fed and changed. He and Sarit had slept in shifts for the first six months, staggering past each other like zombies in the kitchen. He had stopped going for drinks with the guys after work, too, but he felt reasonably confident that his buddies wouldn't suddenly deny their entire relationship just because he'd missed a few bar nights and walked around with spit-up on his tie.

"You and Cammie had a falling-out—an argument," he guessed, and from the guilty flash on Wanda's face he knew he'd hit on the truth.

"Not—not really. We just didn't talk like we used to. She was so wrapped up with the baby, she didn't have time for anyone else."

Reed pondered those words for a moment. "Anyone," he repeated thoughtfully. "You mean like David?"

Wanda looked from Reed to Ellery, her expression beseeching. "He was so young. We all were. David always

144

had this urge to do good—you know that's why he joined up with the police force in the first place. Cammie was pregnant and on her own . . . he wanted to help her any way he could."

"You're saying he didn't love her?" Ellery asked.

Wanda swiveled to look her in the face. "Oh, no, he did. I truly believe that. We all used to make fun of the way he followed her with his eyes when he came in to eat at the restaurant. He was just waiting for her to turn around so they could smile at each other. But then the baby came and it got harder. Diapers, bottles, colic—the whole nine yards. I don't think David was ready for all that stuff."

"I was under the impression David and Cammie were going to get married," Reed said.

Wanda looked acutely uncomfortable. "Yeah, that's what Cammie said."

"What did David say?"

"Uh, I think he talked about it, too."

"You were a sympathetic ear," Reed said, beginning to get the picture. "You listened to his problems."

"Cammie cut back her hours some after the baby came," Wanda explained. "She wasn't working when David dropped in for coffee at the end of his shift. We got to talking some. He said there was no point in rushing home because Cammie would be sleeping by eight o'clock, anyway."

"The pressures of his ready-made family started to get to him," Reed said, his voice neutral.

"Yeah, exactly," Wanda said with relief. "He loved her. He did. He just wasn't sure he was ready for all that. He wanted to go out, have fun—be young while he still could, you know?"

"Like you," Reed said. "You liked to go out and have fun—drinking, music, dancing—isn't that what you said?" He paused meaningfully. "Did David ever go dancing with you?"

Wanda seemed to deflate, suddenly looking every one of her sixty-odd years. "Yeah, okay. We got together, once or twice. It was fun—just a way to blow off steam. It didn't mean anything. He was with Cammie, and we both knew it. Cammie never found out; leastways I don't think she did. But I felt bad about it when I saw her, though. She'd volunteer to take a shift for me, or bring the baby by for a visit, and I'd feel like a worthless slut for being with David behind her back. I told him, no more." She picked up a napkin and began shredding it into a pile of paper snow.

"How did he take the news?" Reed asked.

"He was fine with it," Wanda insisted, but Reed had his doubts. "He knew it wasn't serious with us. He—he even thanked me for helping him get his priorities straight. Then that drug dealer started harassing Cammie, and David was all over that situation, making sure she got home safe, setting up extra police patrols by her apartment building. He quit hanging around me after work and going out at night to the clubs. Every extra second he got, he was with Cammie. But that bastard just waited until David was at work to break in and kill her."

"So you think Billy Thorndike killed Cammie," Reed said, and Wanda widened her eyes.

"Sure, don't you? He said he was gonna kill her, and then she ended up stabbed to death. Doesn't take a rocket scientist to figure that one out. That's why—" She stopped herself in a hurry, but Reed could fill in the rest.

"That's why you pretended you didn't know her when the police asked."

"I didn't have any information that could help them," Wanda insisted. "I wasn't there when he did it. I had my own boyfriend by then, and my job to worry about. If the cops found out I was messing around with David . . . well, it would've just given them the wrong idea."

"It would have looked like motive—for David."

"That's just what I mean. David was the kind of guy who found a baby bird on the sidewalk and took it home to make a nest for it in a shoe box. He wouldn't have hurt a fly, let alone done that awful thing to Cammie. David and I were one hundred percent over and done with by the time Cammie got killed. They were solid again, totally happy and in love. The money was going to come in and fix all their problems. They could move out of that neighborhood, away from that Thorndike character, and Cammie could quit her job and stay home with the baby. And David—he was going to get some fancy motorcycle he had his eye on. A blue Harley, I think it was. Cammie promised to buy it for him as a wedding present."

Reed had another flash of his alternate life, the one that might have been. He imagined himself on David's Harley, holding tight as they flew across the desert. "But the money didn't come through in time," he said to Wanda. "Cammie didn't get a chance to move."

"No," Wanda concluded sadly. "Thorndike fixed her up good, that SOB. I can't believe the cops never locked him up for it. We all knew he was guilty as sin." She poked at the pile of napkin bits and they scattered across the table in front of her. "But as to the money, I always assumed David got it."

"What do you mean?"

"Well, I don't know it for sure, mind you, because we never really talked again after Cammie's funeral. David stopped coming round the restaurant for good. Too many memories, I guess."

"The money," Reed prompted.

"Right. Like I said, David didn't come by no more, but I did happen to see him a couple of weeks after Cammie died. I ran into him one night when he was leaving the Save More liquor store just as I was pulling in, and wouldn't you know it? He took off riding that brand-new blue motorcycle."

"So," Ellery said when they were back in the car, "it seems like David left a lot of important details out of his statement. What do you make of Wanda's story about a twenty-five-thousand-dollar payment?"

Reed steered the SUV back onto a main boulevard and checked his rearview mirror. A silver BMW had pulled out behind them from the parking lot at Lucky Lucy's, and he could still see it several cars back. "My father certainly could have afforded it," he told Ellery. "Of course it contradicts that bleeding-heart story he fed me about how he rushed in, desperate to help me, the minute he found out what had happened to Cammie. To hear Wanda tell it, Angus would have been just as happy to hand over a pile of cash and never think of me again."

"Can you ask him about it?"

"Sure, I can ask him. The answer will probably be just another pile of bull—" Reed broke off as he changed lanes and saw the BMW do the same.

Ellery saw him checking the mirrors and twisted in her seat to look behind them. "What is it?"

"I think we've got company."

"The silver BMW."

He glanced at her in surprise. "You noticed it, too?"

"I thought it might have been following us the other day, but it turned off just as I was about to mention it."

"Did you catch the plate number?"

She shook her head. "No, he hung too far back for me to get a good look."

"So we're talking professional surveillance," Reed muttered. "Great." He drummed his fingers on the wheel as they idled at a red light. There was no way to get a look at either the plates or the driver from this angle.

"It could still be a coincidence—right?"

"Only one way to find out." Reed took a deep breath as the light turned green. "Hang on." He accelerated sharply to increase the distance between them and the BMW, and it took up the chase. Reed wove in and out of traffic for a few blocks until the BMW was safely fifty yards behind them. He signaled and moved to the far-left lane, slowing down as if to turn, but then abruptly squeezed in between a pickup truck and a green Honda. The truck's driver laid on the horn, but Reed didn't slow down. He made a quick right and floored it two blocks until he spotted a strip mall with a busy parking lot. They took the speed hump at 30 mph, jolting them both in the air, and Ellery gripped the side of the car.

Reed slid them neatly into a space facing the street and killed the engine. "Duck," he muttered, and they both slouched down in their seats. Adrenaline pulsed through his veins and Reed held his breath as he watched the passing cars over the rim of the dash. Sure enough, about fifteen seconds later the BMW came creeping along as if hunting for something. Ellery gasped softly at the sight of it.

"For a cold case, this sure feels dangerously hot," she whispered.

The reflection from the bright Nevada sun made it impossible to identify the driver, but Reed jotted down the license plate numbers. "Time to put a name to our tail," he said as the BMW continued on past them. He pulled out his cell phone and quickly ran the plate. "It's a rental," he said to Ellery a few minutes later. She'd kept her eyes on the street, watching intently to see if the BMW returned.

"So what do we do? Head back out there and see if he follows us again?"

Reed slid back into the driver's seat and started the

engine. "I don't think that will be necessary," he told her as she took her seat as well. "If this person has been following us for a couple of days, he or she undoubtedly knows where we're staying. Dollars to donuts they beat us home."

Back at the hotel, Reed circled the block once around to see if the silver BMW was lurking on the street anywhere, but they found no trace of it. He parked in the garage and then stalked the floors methodically, one by one, until he found the car. "Told you," he said to Ellery as he walked the length of the car and back. Ellery craned her neck around to see if they were being watched. Reed no longer cared. He had a growing suspicion he knew who the driver was and why he was here, and now he hungered for a confrontation. He cupped his hands around his face and peered in the driver's side window. The seat sat all the way back. A familiar pair of aviator shades lay atop the dashboard. "I know who this is," he said as he straightened up. "And what's more, I know where we can find him."

He strode into the hotel with Ellery right behind him, so close she almost stepped on his heels when he halted in the lobby to make a sharp pirouette toward the bar. The place was as empty as one might expect for a weekday afternoon, and Reed marched straight to the back booths. There he found his expected target: his father's fix-it man, Rufus Guthrie, sitting there with a gin and tonic in one hand and his cell phone in the other. Reed locked eyes with him, and Rufus didn't register a trace of surprise. "Gotta go," he said, holding Reed's gaze. "I'll call you back."

8

"You've been following us. Reporting everything back to my father, I take it?"

Rufus merely shrugged and gestured at the other side of the booth. "Reed, it's been a while. Take a load off and sit a spell. Maybe have a drink."

"It's three thirty in the afternoon."

Rufus grinned to himself and shook his head. "You know, I've always kind of admired that about you, Reed—you play by the rules even though you don't have to. It's . . . quaint." He looked past Reed and nodded at Ellery. "Ms. Hathaway, we haven't yet had the pleasure. My name is Rufus Guthrie. I work for Senator Markham."

He rose awkwardly behind the table and extended his large hand toward Ellery, who looked at it and said nothing. Reed positioned himself between them.

"Is that what you're doing here—my father's work?"

Guthrie sank back down with a sigh. "If you're not

having a drink, I'll go ahead and order another one myself."
He signaled for the waitress and tapped the table next to his
glass. "Bring me another just like this one, will you, hon?"

Reed slid into the booth across from Guthrie, and Ellery
hesitated just a moment before joining Reed on his side. "If
my father wants to know how the investigation is going, he
can damn well pick up the phone and ask me. He doesn't
need to send some lackey to follow me around."

Guthrie's eyebrows shot up. "Lackey? You wound me,
boy. That's a mighty hurtful word to throw at someone who
used to carry you around on his shoulders."

"Don't pretend like you're my friend."

Guthrie looked annoyed. "I'm trying to be. I'm trying to
prevent you from making a god-awful mess of your whole
family, but you seem hell-bent on making life difficult for
everyone."

"Me? I'm the one making the trouble? I suggest you check
your facts again, maybe have a chat with your boss. He's
been lying to me my whole life."

"Right," Guthrie said with dark irony as he took up his
fresh drink. "I forgot about your whole miserable existence,
brought up in that beautiful mansion with the best schools,
the fanciest clothes, taking trips abroad and tended at home
by household staff that made sure you didn't have to dirty
your little hands cleaning up all the messes you created."

Heat flared in Reed's face. "The money is supposed to
make everything okay then, is that it?"

"It's sure as hell a damn good start." Guthrie crunched

down on an ice cube and regarded Reed with bleary eyes. "He loves you, though. They all do. I think if you stopped to think just a second, you'd realize that's true. You'd quit this fool's errand and go back home where you belong." He glanced appraisingly at Ellery. "Ask her. She'll tell you about the value of what you're trying to throw away."

"What's that supposed to mean?" Ellery demanded.

Guthrie's expression turned pitying. "Darlin', no one should have to go through what happened to you. I can't even begin to imagine what went on in that closet. I know Reed knows. He saw it up close and personal the night he pulled you out of there. He puffed himself up like a peacock, solving this big case, rescuing the girl. He didn't know what he was sending you home to, did he?"

Ellery leaned across the table, furious. "What do you know about it?"

"Honey, that's my whole job, knowing things. I'm paid to find out the details of everything and anyone who crosses Angus's orbit, and as of last year, that includes you. So yeah, I know the whole story now. You must've been half-starved by the time Reed got to that closet, but then you were real scrawny to begin with, weren't you? Mama couldn't keep enough food on the table? All that work she had to miss to look after your sick brother." He shook his head as if in sorrow, peering into his drink. "You see, Reed? Money does solve problems. Or it might have, for your girlfriend here, and if she won't be honest about that, then I will. Having a home, a place to go where people welcome you with open arms, that's nothing to sneeze at, either."

Guthrie tilted his glass back for a big swallow, evidently pleased with his speech, while Reed fumed inside. "My mother was murdered," he said, enunciating every word.

"No." Guthrie banged his glass down with sudden force. "Your mother is back home in Virginia, probably getting ready to put supper on the table. You think she'd be pleased to know you're out here tearing down your father's good name?"

Reed could picture Marianne Markham, her white-blond hair now more white than blond, still slim, always pleasant, humming an invented tune as she chopped up vegetables for the dinner salad. He remembered how she used to pull up the red stool next to the counter so that he could work with her, carefully showing him how to hold the knife. She had trimmed his bangs and held his hand and read him bedtime stories in the old family rocker, his face pressed into her warm, perfumed neck. Even now, when he awoke with a start in the black of night, his first thoughts were for her. "Leave her out of this," he said to Guthrie. "She's got nothing to do with this."

"Oh, no? Angus is her whole life, him and the home they built together. You're running around trying to tear it all down. You think she won't be hurt by that? Come on now."

"Hey, I didn't run around on her and break my marriage vows. That's on him, not me."

"No, you just want to rub her nose in it. That's how you're going to repay her after all these years, after she took you in with no questions."

"She didn't know," Reed shot back. Once the words were out there, he suddenly questioned them. Guthrie coughed and looked away. "She didn't know about me," Reed repeated, less certain this time. "Did she?"

"I can't read minds," Guthrie replied carefully. "I don't know what all Marianne knew and when she knew it, but she's a smart lady. Those girls who hung around your father, they saw his wedding ring. They knew what they were getting into. Your mom, she knew it, too. As long as he wore that ring, as long as he had political aspirations, he'd be coming home to her. She somehow made her peace with the rest of it. What she didn't ask he didn't have to tell her—leastways until now, when you've suddenly got a bee in your bonnet about what happened to Cammie."

"I'm just trying to find out the truth," Reed insisted.

"Sure, right. You want to come out here to the desert and find your origin story, is that it? You think tracing Camilla Flores's life, mucking around in her death, that's going to teach you who you are? Listen up, son—that DNA test you took, that's the truth. Your father is your father, just like he always has been. Is he a perfect man? No, I'm sorry to say he is not. I'm sorry, too, if you got to age forty before learning that fact. Angus Markham is human and he has sins just like the rest of us. But he did not kill that girl, and if you don't understand how close you are to ruining him over some half-cocked, wrongheaded idea—" He broke off in disgust.

"How do you know? How do you know he didn't kill her?"

156

"I'm in the information business, remember? It's my job to know. Besides, I know your father. I've known him since we were knee-high to a grasshopper, and he's worked every day to make life better for the people of Virginia—most especially his family." He shot Reed a withering look. "He screwed up when he bedded that girl, and he was sorry for it. But he's a good man. How do you think he gets his way so often with the teamsters, with the preachers, with the tree huggers and tax lawyers and all that long line of people stretched out the door, all of whom want a bigger slice of the pie? He sits down and lets them feel heard. He listens. For as long as you're in front of him, your problems are his problems, and he makes you feel like he'd move mountains just to clear an itty-bitty path for you. I used to think he was just a good showman, and then somewhere in there I realized it isn't an act—he's sincere, every time. He wants to get you what you need, even when he promised the exact opposite thing to someone else the day before."

"Yeah, yeah, he excels at lying. I get it."

Guthrie scowled. "You aren't listening to me. They aren't lies, because he means it at the time. He always does. Maybe he's promising some councilman that he'll get more dollars for sidewalk repairs, or maybe he's telling some sweet young thing that she's the most beautiful creature he's ever laid eyes on. They always believe him, see, because he really does mean it."

Reed wondered what pretty words his father had used with Camilla. Wondered what darker words might have

157

followed when Camilla turned up pregnant. "Camilla wanted money," he said to Guthrie. "Lots of it."

Guthrie ran a hand over his mouth as if debating whether to reply, but it was all the answer Reed required. "I advised him not to pay," Guthrie said finally. "It set a bad precedent. We couldn't even be sure he was the father."

"He was," Reed broke in evenly.

"Yeah, sure, we know that now. Back then? Who knew how many other men Camilla might have been friendly with? Maybe she had her hand out to all of 'em."

"If you're in the information business, then you know that's not true," Reed said coldly.

"Regardless, what's to say she wouldn't take the money and then turn right around and ask for more? But your father, he wanted to pay her. Said it was the least he could do. Now does that sound like a man who wanted to kill her?"

Reed frowned. "Talk is cheap. Twenty-five thousand dollars, that was a lot of money back then. Maybe he had second thoughts about handing it over—especially if, as you say, it might have been just the start."

"He was committed, the last I talked to him about it. He wouldn't hear reason."

"But you don't know if he made the payment."

"I said I'd do it myself, if he wanted to go through with it. He needed some time to round up the cash. I don't know where he was with the process because then she up and got killed, and suddenly we had a whole new set of problems on our hands."

"He said you're the one who told him about the murder."

Guthrie paused, just for a second. "Maybe. It was a long time ago."

"How did you learn about her death?" Reed asked. "Surely you must remember that."

Guthrie worked his jaw back and forth, contemplating. "I had a buddy at the LVMPD, and he called me after it happened. I'd asked him earlier to find out anything he could for me about Cammie—anything we might use to get her to shut up and go away—but she came back squeaky clean. A model citizen, he said. Crusading against some neighborhood drug dealer. We can see now how that all turned out. She might've done better just to keep her mouth shut and mind her own business."

"So she deserved it," Ellery interrupted, and Guthrie wagged a finger at her.

"I never said that. Those are your words, not mine."

"Her death must have been a relief to you then. Problem solved, money saved."

"Not in this case," Guthrie replied hotly. "We just got a whole shit storm of new trouble because Angus wanted that baby."

Reed sat back, blinking as the truth hit him. "You didn't, though. Did you? You would've left me on my own."

Guthrie's gaze flicked over him. "It's not like it was personal. I didn't even know you. You were a few months old, not even conscious yet. They could've found you a nice home with a new momma and daddy, and you never would've remembered any different. Instead, Angus had me tracking down adoption attorneys willing to take big money and not ask too many questions. 'Just you wait,' I told him. 'This whole thing is going to blow up in your face one day. It's gonna hit like a bomb.'" He narrowed his eyes at Reed. "I just never imagined it'd be his own son throwing the grenade."

Reed stretched out over the table so he could look Guthrie in the eyes. "That's right," he whispered. "Boom."

Outside, Reed thrust the keys toward Ellery. "You drive," he told her. His mind felt jumbled and careening, rolling like an avalanche picking up speed. He had no place behind the wheel.

"Where are we going?" she asked as they climbed into the SUV.

"To see a man about a motorcycle."

They drove to the Owens house, where they found the front door open and a small army of young women dressed in black pants and crisp white shirts carrying food containers from the house to the catering van in the driveway. Amy Owens appeared with a large platter wrapped in cellophane. "Oh, hello there," she said with some surprise. "I'm afraid you caught us at a bad time. We're working the Harris wedding tonight over at the country club, and we can't be late or the bride will throw an absolute conniption fit. You know how it goes."

Reed sidestepped one of the girls as she made another trip back into the house. "Is your husband at home?"

"He's bringing up the rear," Amy replied.

David appeared in the doorway carrying a large cooler. "Agent Markham, Ms. Hathaway. What can we do for you?"

"I just had a few follow-up questions for you," Reed said, and David frowned.

"Can it wait? We have to get going." He didn't hang around for an answer and started walking toward the van.

"It's about Wanda Evans," Reed called after him, and David froze with the cooler in hand. He turned back around slowly, his expression wary.

"Who?"

"She was a friend of Camilla Flores. They worked together at the Howard Johnson's." Reed removed the picture from his breast pocket and held it out for David, but David didn't even glance at it.

"Yeah, I think I remember a Wanda. What about her?"

"We had a long talk with her today about the days leading up to Cammie's murder," Reed said. At the word "murder," one of the girls stopped packing the van and turned to stare. "I, uh . . ." David licked his lips in nervous fashion and shifted the cooler in his hands.

Amy came around the side of the van and put her hands on her hips. "David, honey, we've got to go now or Miranda Harris will have my hide."

"Maybe David can catch up with you later," Reed said, holding David's gaze. "I need to talk to him."

"And I need him to make the hollandaise," Amy replied impatiently. "Can't we do this later?"

"They're talking about a murder," the girl told her in a hushed voice, and Amy pursed her mouth, looking conflicted. "Kayla, honey, you and the girls take the van over to the club and start setting up, okay? David and I will be right behind you."

"But—"

"Make sure to reassure Mrs. Harris that we've altered the recipes to accommodate her black pepper allergy." She crossed from the driveway to join Reed, Ellery, and David near the door to the house, her smile fixed in place but her voice steely as she said, "Now then, what's this all about?"

Reed glanced at Ellery, trying to get her eyes. Maybe she could take Amy off somewhere like last time so Reed could grill David alone. David would be less likely to confess his indiscretions with his wife standing right there. Ellery seemed to understand the look and gamely took up the idea. "Mrs. Owens, maybe we could go inside just for a second—"

"No," Amy interrupted her. "We don't have time for that. What's going on?"

David cleared his throat. "They were asking about Wanda."

Amy looked blank. "Wanda?"

"Wanda Evans," Reed explained, and he tried showing off the picture again. Amy accepted it and took a look. "She was a friend of Camilla Flores."

Amy squinted at the photograph a moment. "Wanda. That's the waitress—the little floozy you were seeing for a

162

time. Right?" She cocked her head at her husband, who looked both pained and oddly relieved not to have to dance around the topic any longer.

"A long time ago," he agreed, nodding. "But I only saw her a few times."

"Saw her a few times without her clothes on," Ellery clarified. "At the same time you were talking about getting married to Camilla. That's what Wanda told us."

Amy handed the picture back to Reed. "He felt horrible about it, if that matters any." She shot her husband a grim look, and he ducked his head from her gaze.

"You didn't mention the affair to the investigating officers," Reed said.

"Why would I have? It was over. It didn't mean anything. And it didn't have anything to do with what happened to Cammie. Billy Thorndike killed her."

"Maybe," Reed said agreeably. "Maybe not. It doesn't seem like the police investigated any other leads."

"Anyone like me, you mean." David's voice took on a hard edge. "They looked. I had an alibi."

Amy raised her hand. "Me," she reminded them. "We were on the job."

"That's right," David said, folding his arms. "Besides, I loved Cammie. I never would've hurt her. Even if—even if she found out about Wanda and me, we would've worked it out. I had no motive to kill her."

"Twenty-five thousand dollars sounds like a lot of motive to me," Reed replied.

David's mouth fell open. "Twenty-five Gs? We didn't have that kind of money."

"Cammie was going to be getting it, though—that was the plan. She was putting pressure on my father to pay up big-time, and you were going to get a motorcycle out of the deal. Maybe that wasn't enough for you. Maybe you figured you'd keep all twenty-five thousand dollars and buy the motorcycle yourself."

"What? No. I mean: yes, Cammie asked the baby's father for the money. I don't know if she ever got it. Someone came along and butchered her, you might remember."

"You're sure you didn't get that money?" Reed asked. "You didn't start driving a brand-new blue Harley in 1975?"

Color rose in David's face. "I had the motorcycle, yes. It was a gift from my wife."

Reed felt like the ground had been yanked out beneath him. "I'm sorry—what?"

"I gave him the bike," Amy said. "Or rather, I loaned him the money for it. He was so torn up after what happened to Cammie, and I wanted to do something nice for him, something to take his mind off it for a while. I had a little inheritance money lying around, so I gave him a loan to get the motorcycle he'd been wanting. Only instead of paying me back, he married me." She smiled at the end and hugged David's arm.

He tried to return her smile, but there was no humor in his eyes. "I think if you have any further questions, you should direct them to my lawyer."

"Why?" Reed asked. "If you have nothing to hide . . ."

David's mouth contorted and he looked out toward the empty, sunny street. "Mr. Markham, I appreciate you want to know what happened to your mother. There was a time when that's all I wanted, too. Maybe you won't believe me, but I assure you the day she died was the worst day of my life. I loved your mother and I wanted to marry her." He turned, and the intensity in his eyes seemed to bore a hole right through Reed. "I loved you, too."

Reed swallowed hard, but he stood his ground. "Then you should help me find the truth."

David shook his head, denying this fanciful notion. "I just told you my truth. I loved her and I lost her. I can't change what happened and what you're asking it's . . . well, it's too much. Reopening all those old wounds with no promise at all of any kind of resolution. And even then, even if we found the guy, what would it solve? What would it change?" He paused to let his words sink in, his expression growing sympathetic as he cut Reed loose. "I'm sorry, but you're on your own. I can't help you anymore."

In the car, Reed leaned his head back against the seat and stared out at the road without really seeing it. Ellery drove them in silence toward the hotel. "Maybe he's right," Reed said after a while. "Maybe I should let it go. What kind of hubris is it to think I can come in here forty-plus years later and solve a case that no one else could?"

Ellery glanced over at him. "Because that's what you do," she said, matter-of-fact. "Solve the hardest cases."

Reed answered her with a wry smile. "You know, I think our initial meeting perhaps gave you an unrealistic picture of my usual duties," he said as he straightened up in his seat. "Normally I either push paper around at my desk or else I fly into some strange city, read a bunch of files, look at a crime scene, and offer my opinion. Half the time that's not worth the paper it's printed on. DNA usually ends up solving the case."

"Maybe it will solve this one, too."

"Maybe." Reed's own DNA test had started him down this rocky path, and so far it had offered up more questions than answers. He thought of all the trials he'd seen over the years, when various mundane murderers were dragged out from hiding into the ordinary light of day by virtue of a fingerprint or errant drop of blood. Science could prove they committed the crimes, but it couldn't explain why. Maybe there would be some proximal cause, like a robbery or a rape, but so far DNA couldn't truly explain why one human being decided to turn on another.

"If you want to stop the search, you can," Ellery said gently. "Whatever happened to your mother, Reed, it's not on you to put it right. You can say enough is enough and leave it alone if you want to. No one would think less of you."

Reed considered this possibility but shook his head. "No. Not yet, at least."

Ellery pulled into the parking garage at the hotel, checking

166

the car's mirrors as she did so. "I don't think we were followed this time."

"Guthrie will be busy reporting today's conversation back to my father. They'll have to regroup and form a new strategy." He held out his hand for the car keys.

"Where are we going?"

"Not we. Me. I'm going to pick up some groceries for dinner."

"Reed, you don't have to go to that kind of trouble," she protested as she dropped the keys in his hands.

"I like to cook. It keeps my hands busy, and I could use the distraction. I do my best thinking when I'm chopping."

Apparently, the idea of him lost in thought while holding a sharp knife did not reassure her. "I'm serious," she said. "We can eat out wherever you like, even if it's fancy. I'll even buy a dress if I have to."

"Wear whatever you like," he said, remembering the body-hugging number she'd rustled up the last time. "Just do me a favor and take it easy on the old man."

A smile tugged at the corner of her mouth. "You're the one who said you wanted a distraction."

9

Ellery walked the two blocks to a dress store, intending it to be a quick errand, but when the door tinkled shut behind her it became apparent she had set foot in another world, one filled with gauzy chiffon and brightly patterned silk and endless twinkling sequins. A saleswoman approached, her heels click-clicking on the shiny white floor, and Ellery took an automatic step backward in retreat. "Hi, and welcome," the saleswoman said as Ellery frowned at the premises. The perfumed air was making her nose itch. "Can I help you find something today?" The woman was maybe Ellery's age but looked like she'd been born into another species, with her red lipstick smile, smooth blond ponytail, and perfectly tailored black-and-white dress.

"I came to buy a dress," Ellery said, mustering her resolve. She didn't mention it would be the first one she'd ever purchased. Her mother had sometimes brought home dresses from the Salvation Army store, pieces that were chosen for price and expediency, not because they happened to match Ellery's taste. By the time she had started buying her own clothes, Ellery had desired only unisex T-shirts and jeans, garments designed to make her disappear. Now she had wandered into the universe of skinny red sheaths and plunging purple tops, each one screaming, *Look at me!*

"You've come to the right place!" the saleswoman answered with enough enthusiasm for both of them. "What sort of occasion are you shopping for?"

Ellery looked at her blankly.

"Something for work? A cocktail party? Maybe a wedding?"

"Dinner."

"Dinner! How lovely. Is it a formal affair?"

"No, it's just the two of us." Ellery frowned as she regarded the nearest offering, a low-cut, high-rise number covered in pink sparkles, like something a slutty Disney princess would wear.

"Gotcha. Something suitable for a night on the town, then, with that special someone."

"We're not going out," Ellery replied, distracted by the sensory overload. "We'll probably just eat at the kitchen counter." The dining table in their suite was filled entirely with murder.

"Oh. Um . . ." The woman's smile faltered and she clasped her hands together. "Perhaps if you could describe the kind of dress you're looking for . . ."

Ellery turned over the dangling price tag on an off-the-shoulder green velvet dress and dropped it immediately when she saw the dress cost four hundred dollars. "Not that one," she said firmly, striding away.

"Okay," the woman called after her, still cheery but less certain now. "Please have a look around and let me know if you have any questions."

What the hell am I doing here? Ellery thought, but she pressed onward, grim but determined. She knew she could turn around and leave if she wanted to—it's not like Reed cared what she wore. They would eat a nice dinner all the same even if she showed up in her usual blue jeans and Doc Martens. This was the thing about Reed, though: the more he accepted her just as she was, the more she wanted to try out a new version. She paused to examine a slim midnight-blue dress, its slippery silk gliding through her fingers, and she imagined the whisper-soft fabric up against her skin. An unusual flush of pleasure went through her, and she dropped the dress in a hurry. She moved with businesslike fashion on to the next dress, an airy, floor-length concoction, pure white except for a shimmering silver belt at the middle. Soon she had felt her way up and down all the racks, drunk on the array of new textures and shapes.

She halted at a cherry-red silk dress with a woven gold-and-white pattern decorating it. Sleeveless and fitted, it hit at the mid-thigh and would leave nothing to the imagination. She fingered the red zipper at the front and resolved not to look at the price until she had at least tried it on. "Maybe this one," she murmured to the saleslady, who materialized out of nowhere and was only too glad to show her to a changing room.

Ellery stripped out of her usual clothes and wriggled into the dress, not making eye contact with the mirror until she'd zipped up and tugged the material into place over her hips. "Oh," she said with pleasant surprise when she felt how well it fit. "Not bad." The red color seemed to warm her skin tone—or maybe she was blushing. She pressed her palms to her face but couldn't stop her smile. She twisted to try to see it from the back, but the narrow mirror in the dressing booth provided only a limited view.

She stepped out into the larger changing area, which was devoid of other customers, and hesitantly approached the three-way mirror near the door. The dress looked even better when she could see the full length of it, hugging the curves at her waist and showing off her long legs. She had been born to wear this dress. *You can afford it,* she cajoled herself. *Just this once.*

"If you're interested, we also have the dress in blue—" The saleslady stopped abruptly when she came around the corner and saw Ellery standing there. "Oh God, I'm sorry!"

Ellery shrank back at the woman's flash of horror. She'd been so wrapped up in the beauty of the dress that she'd forgotten about the brutality of her scars. Coben had left his mark all over Ellery's body—discolored, sometimes-jagged lines that marked like a map along her upper arm, her collarbone, and especially her wrists. She hugged herself, hiding

171

the worst of it as the saleslady looked away, embarrassed as though she'd caught Ellery naked out in public.

"So sorry to interrupt," the woman muttered again, laying a blue version of Ellery's dress on the nearest chair. "Take your time."

The saleslady fled the room without making eye contact. Ellery forced herself to look in the mirror, where she smiled softly with regret, stretching her fingers out to touch her own reflection in a wordless goodbye. She walked to the changing booth and turned back into herself again, the fairy-tale dress sitting neatly on its hanger. She was about to exit when her cell phone rang from inside her jeans. Warily, she dug it out and checked the number, but it wasn't her father dogging her this time. "Liz," she said, forcing a note of cheer into her voice. "How's my boy doing?"

"Hi, Ellery. Bump is doing just great. We love having him here."

Ellery's heart squeezed as she heard the familiar scratching of Bump's nails on the floor. He woofed a greeting and she almost wanted to catch the next plane home to him. "What's up?" she asked. "Is everything okay?"

"Well, I hate to bother you, but something weird just happened, and I thought you should know about it. I was out with the dogs when a man came up to me on the street and asked if Bump was your dog. I asked why he wanted to know, and he said his name was John Hathaway and that he's your father." Liz paused, as though waiting for Ellery to confirm or deny it.

Ellery leaned her head against the cool white wall, her eyes closed. "What did he want?"

"He said he's been trying to get in touch with you," Liz said. "I told him you weren't home. He asked when you might be back, and I said I wasn't sure. That's when he said it was extremely urgent that he talk to you—he said it was a matter of life and death." Liz's normally calm and measured voice took on a thread of worry. "I started to get concerned that something had happened to you, but he said you were fine and he just needed to talk to you. I explained that you were in Las Vegas working and I didn't know when you would be back in Boston. I hope I didn't speak out of turn. He looks very much like you . . ."

"It's okay," Ellery said tightly. "You didn't do anything wrong. Have you seen him since? Is he watching the building?"

Ellery heard Liz cross the floor to look out the window. "Not that I can see. I, ah, I take it you aren't on good terms?"

"We're not on any terms."

"Oh. Again, I'm so sorry . . . I won't say anything at all to him if I see him again."

"It's okay," Ellery assured her, trying to sound normal. "He's not dangerous or anything. We just haven't spoken in a long time."

"Well, he certainly seems eager to talk to you now."

"I'll deal with him, thanks. Since you called, can I say hi to Bump?" Liz obliged her by putting the phone down to Bump's level, and he woofed and snuffled while Ellery cooed out a greeting to him. She assured him she'd be home soon. When she hung up with Liz, she kept her hand clenched around the phone until her knuckles started to ache. A matter of life and death, he'd said, which was rich coming from a man who'd missed his own son's funeral. She wondered if John Hathaway might be dying now himself and out to settle his affairs. She lowered herself onto the tiny tufted bench and regarded the mirror, where her father's gray eyes looked back at her. When she imagined him dead, she felt curiously empty. He'd been gone so long she already considered him a ghost, someone she once knew a long time ago.

Ellery reached out her hand to touch the hem of the beautiful red dress, stroking her fingertips over the silky edge. The sleeve of her jacket pulled up as she made the motion, exposing her scars, but for once, she didn't yank it back down. Instead, she wiped her eyes and got to her feet, carefully taking the dress down so that it did not snag anywhere on her way out. She took the dress to the register, where the saleslady regarded her with mild surprise. "I'm taking this one," Ellery said, pulling out her wallet. She still hadn't checked the price, but she no longer cared.

The woman behind the counter rallied at the prospect of a sale, flashing her white teeth in an even smile. "A perfect choice. I'm sure he's going to love it."

"I'm not buying it for him," Ellery replied as she handed over the credit card. "I'm buying it for me."

* * *

Self-conscious, Ellery walked back to the hotel with her new dress slung over one arm, protected by a hanging black fabric bag. She had no shoes or jewelry to go with it, and she'd be eating PB and J sandwiches for a month to make up the cost of this impulsive splurge. Maybe she would wear it to dinner with Reed. Maybe not. Maybe she would just keep it in the bag forever, peeking in on it only when she needed to remember those few moments they'd been beautiful together.

When she slipped her key card in the door, she could tell immediately that Reed had beaten her home because of the heady aroma of cooking smells that greeted her arrival. She made a beeline for her room, where she hung the dress on a hook in the bathroom, and went back out in search of Reed. "I smell chocolate," she said with approval as she pulled out one of the tall chairs along the granite peninsula.

He looked up from whatever he was stirring in the green bowl. "That's dessert. It should be ready to come out of the oven in twenty minutes."

"Can I help?" she asked, peering over the array of vegetables he had sitting out on the counter.

"Depends. How are you with julienne?"

"Who?"

He rolled his eyes, but his sigh was affectionate. "Go. Take a swim. Read a book. I can handle this."

"You're the chef," she replied with a shrug. She helped herself to a carrot, crunching it as she crossed the room to browse the folders, photos, and notes from Camilla's case. Reed had added to his timeline, jotting down all the various events leading up to Camilla's murder, which now included Cammie's slashed tires, the open threats of violence from a convicted felon, a possible twenty-five-thousand-dollar payoff, and a similar killing across town the year before that might or might not be related. Ellery ran her fingers over Reed's neat, black printing. There was one key event he had not added to the written record. "Reed?"

"Hmm?"

"When were you born?"

"August 8, 1975."

Ellery moved her finger back four months from Cammie's murder in December of 1975. Then after a moment's thought, she slid it back nine months further, and her heart skipped a beat when she saw where she'd landed: Giselle Hardiman's murder in early November. Ellery checked the math again on her hands, but it came out just the same: Reed must have been conceived right around the time Giselle Hardiman was killed—which meant Reed's father might have been in town when it happened.

"Why do you ask?" Reed called back from where he was stirring something at the stove.

"Oh, I'm just curious, you know, looking at the timing of things. Did your father say anything about how he and Camilla met?" Giselle Hardiman had been a prostitute, but Cammie theoretically had worked only as a waitress—at least that was what the official records said. Ellery wondered if Camilla might have moonlighted to make some extra cash, but there didn't seem to be a delicate way to ask Reed if his mother had turned tricks and his father had solicited them.

"I don't know the circumstances," Reed replied. "But my father has never had any trouble meeting women. He just walks out into the street and practically trips over them." He turned and shrugged. "She was young and pretty; he was rich and powerful. Around here, that combination always seems to come up aces."

Ellery hummed a noncommittal reply and opened her laptop, which still featured the *Las Vegas Review-Journal* as the open tab. On a whim, she looked up the obituaries this time to see if there was anything on Giselle Hardiman, but she found nothing. The same for Camilla Flores. Two young women were dead, and no one bothered to tell their stories, what little there was left to tell. Camilla and Giselle had been around the age of Francis Coben's victims, only a few years older than Ellery was when she was taken. What could anyone have written about her at the time? Teenage girls were all the same—grown-up curves on the outside obscuring their still-tender children's hearts, their eyes hungry for a future they couldn't yet see.

The return on Ellery's search, a blank page except for three little words, "no results found," was its own heartbreaking elegy. Out of idle curiosity, she searched by date, December 11, 1975, to see what the major news stories had been the day that Camilla Flores died. A ship had disappeared in Lake Superior, with all twenty-nine of its seamen feared lost. Casinos on the Las Vegas Strip had been picketed and union leaders threatened to close down fifteen resorts over a massive walkout of the culinary and bartenders unions. Elvis Presley was coming to town. Ellery paged through to the obituaries again, which reflected the more usual sorts of deaths. The youngest man listed was Arthur Martinelli, who had died unexpectedly at just forty-eight years old. She squinted at the dark, hard-to-read text. A heart attack, it seemed, had felled Mr. Martinelli, the owner of a popular liquor store. The store was closed, but Mr. Martinelli's wife vowed to reopen soon and carry on his love of fine wine.

A timer dinged in the kitchen and Reed removed the chocolate tart from the oven. Normally, Ellery would go devour it with her eyes, but she remained sitting at the table, frowning because Arthur Martinelli's obituary had bothered her somehow. "Is there anything in here about an Arthur Martinelli?" she asked Reed as she picked up the nearest binder. "He owned a liquor store but died of a heart attack around the time Camilla was murdered."

"Doesn't ring a bell," Reed said before leaning into the refrigerator.

"I've definitely heard the name recently . . ." Ellery sat upright as the connection snapped into place in her brain. "Amy Owens mentioned something about Martinelli Liquors. She said she and David had been over at the store that day, checking out some false alarm." Now Ellery did rise and go over to where Reed was chopping fresh herbs. "Martinelli died," she told him. "The store was closed. Amy and David couldn't have been there checking on the alarm."

Reed halted with the knife in one hand. "Maybe the alarm went off in the store with no one there," he said after thinking it over. "If no one was on the premises to disarm the alarm, that makes it all the more likely the police would have been called in."

"Sure. Maybe." Ellery didn't believe it for a second, because wouldn't Amy have remembered that fact? "Or maybe Amy made the whole thing up to cover for David. She did end up marrying the guy a few months later. It's fair to assume she could've been carrying a torch at the time."

Reed resumed his work on the herbs, rocking the knife back and forth on the cutting board, and Ellery tried not to notice how similar the blade was to the one that had been pulled out of Camilla Flores's chest. "So David Owens takes off from his patrol one Thursday afternoon and goes to lie in wait for his girlfriend in her apartment across town. When she arrives home, he gives her just enough time to put the baby down in the crib before he ambushes Camilla with a kitchen knife. She fights back, creating a monumentally bloody crime scene. On his way out, Owens stages the burglary and takes the time to hit Camilla's head a few times with a nearby bookend, just for good measure. He'd be covered in blood at this point—how does he get around that problem?"

Ellery reflected on this question for a moment as she imagined David standing over Cammie's body, his hands soaked in her blood. His shoes, his shirt—everything would be splattered. "He lived there," she said as the truth hit her. "At least some of the time. Maybe he showered and changed right at the scene and then he got rid of his bloody clothes on his way back to work." It would solve the question of the murder weapon, too. David Owens wouldn't have had to bring the knife with him; he'd have known it was already there.

"You're right; it could work," Reed admitted.

Ellery eyed the half-finished dinner. "Will this stuff keep? We could go sweat David and Amy right now."

"David said to direct further questions to his attorney," Reed reminded her. "And we hardly have concrete proof of anything right now. If you're right that Amy is lying to protect him, she'll likely just say she had the details wrong because it's been forty years since all of this happened. As long as she insists he was with her that day, we won't shake his alibi."

Ellery sank down onto the nearest stool and put her chin in her hand. "What kind of person lies to protect a man who butchered his girlfriend?"

"Maybe she genuinely thinks he didn't do it. She was a cop, remember? The cops were all focused on Billy Thorndike, both at the time and ever since. Amy may believe she's protecting David against unfair insinuations. If that's true, then the way you shake her story is to build the case that he's guilty to her first. If that DNA test from the knife handle comes back to someone other than Cammie, David would be one obvious candidate for a match. That's the kind of hard evidence that might break his wife."

Ellery leaned over the counter and liberated a cherry tomato. "Would it be proof, though? Couldn't he just say that he'd used the knife in the past while cooking dinner and happened to cut himself at the time?"

Reed set down his own knife and frowned at her. "You'd make a disturbingly effective defense attorney."

"Nah. But I've watched a lot of *Law and Order*." Hours and hours of it, actually, along with anything else she could find on the dial. Television had kept her company in the long empty hours after Daniel died, when her mother had to work twice as hard to pay off the bills. Meanwhile, Francis Coben lived inside Ellery's head, screaming her name, so she'd just turned up the volume on the television until she could no longer hear him. Sometimes it was still the only way she could fall asleep at night.

"You watched that stuff?" Reed asked, sounding honestly curious. "I'm not sure I would've had the stomach for it, if I'd been you."

Ellery's childhood shrink had wondered the same thing. *Does it make you feel better,* he'd asked her once, *to see the bad guys get punished at the end?* Ellery hadn't bothered to give him an answer, but if she had, it would have been no. She wasn't in it for the bad guys. She watched crime shows to see the surviving victims, the ones who had been cut up, burned, raped, or otherwise tortured and lived to tell about it. These fictional people were the only ones she knew who were like her, and so to her they always felt entirely real. "I liked the courtroom scenes," she told Reed so he'd have some sort of answer. "They always seemed so civilized."

Reed glanced up from where he was wrapping dates in

prosciutto. "Well, real life, they're civilized enough, but they tend to alternate between heartbreaking and deathly boring."

At age fourteen, Ellery's name had been withheld from the records and she had not needed to testify against Francis Coben because the Feds had amassed mountain of bloody evidence from his broken-down farmhouse. The collection of severed hands alone would have put him away for life. Still, Ellery dreamed about the trial sometimes as if she had been there, as if she'd had the chance to look Coben in the eyes and tell the world: *Him. He's the one.* "What was it like?" she asked Reed softly. "When they put him on trial?"

Reed put aside the food and wiped his hands on a dish towel before coming around the counter to sit next to her. Ellery shifted away, uncomfortable now that she had even brought it up. Reed would've testified to everyone how he had found her on the floor of the closet, half-dead, her hair caked to her skin with her own blood. He would have described in detail what Coben did with the farm tools. "It was very difficult," he said, ducking to try to meet her eyes, but Ellery wouldn't look at him. "Coben pleaded not guilty by mental defect, as you know, and plenty of smart people on our side worried that he might be successful, that the jury might need him to be crazy because it was the only explanation that made any sense."

"He knew exactly what he was doing." Ellery folded her hands between her legs protectively, the way she always did when Coben's name came up.

"I believe you're right. Fortunately, the jury believed it,

too. But the hard part . . . the hardest part you're not ever going to see on TV." She looked at him, questioning, and he dropped his chin to his chest in response. "The other families, the people whose loved ones were not recovered, they came to the courtroom, too. They begged Coben at sentencing to reveal what he had done with their daughters, sisters, cousins, and so forth, but Coben wouldn't even acknowledge them. We found the missing girls' hands in some cases, and in others we have only strong suspicion based on circumstantial evidence that Coben was their abductor. The cases are closed, and yet they're not closed. They probably never will be."

Ellery searched his face, saw the pain reflected there, and she knew he wasn't just talking about Coben anymore. "You've done everything you can," she murmured, and Reed shook his head.

"That's the part that television will never show you," he replied as he slid off the stool and returned to his cooking. "It's not enough."

10

Reed poured himself another glass of wine as he eyed the closed door of Ellery's bedroom. She had been in there a while now, longer than it should take to change for dinner, and he was starting to wonder if he'd been stood up inside his own hotel suite. *Not that this is a date,* he thought, sipping his Merlot. Definitely not. There were no candles or flowers on the table. The most he'd done was clear away the dusty folders and curved, fading photographs so that they didn't have to eat dinner next to his mother's murder. The weight of the evidence had grown as he'd carried it back and forth, ancient grime creeping under his fingernails, and he'd scrubbed until raw when the deed was done. The folders sat in shadow in the living room now, silent as the grave. Reed positioned himself at the table so he wouldn't have to see them. Already the alcohol was loosening the tension in his shoulders and quieting the angry buzz he'd had in his head since this whole thing began. He took another long, bittersweet swallow.

Ellery's door cracked open across the room, and Reed turned in his seat, a quip about her tardiness ready on his tongue, but it died there the instant he saw her standing rooted in her doorway.

"I bought a dress," she announced, somewhat defiantly.

"I see that."

She didn't move from her spot. "It's my first one. The first one I ever bought, I mean."

"You should buy more," he replied solemnly. "You seem to have a knack for it."

"I don't know about that," she said with a sigh. She walked reluctantly across the room, and he saw she'd paired the fancy dress with plain plastic flip-flops. He grinned once but then reined it in quick before she noticed.

"Why not?" he asked as she pulled out her chair.

"I got the impression that the saleslady didn't think I should be showing quite so much skin," Ellery replied darkly, skimming her fingers down her bare arm.

He hadn't even noticed the scars, but now he made himself look. In the low light, they were difficult to see, faded by time and by everything else he knew about her. He never looked at Ellery and saw her scars. Not anymore. "The dress is perfect for you," he said, his gaze lingering, "and you are perfect in it."

She narrowed her eyes at him, but he detected the beginning of a smile. "Smooth. Very smooth. I see how you got your reputation with the ladies, Agent Markham."

"What reputation?" he asked as he poured her a glass of

wine. "What ladies? I haven't been on a date since . . ." He paused to consider. "Well, since that spectacular disaster with you in the middle of the blizzard."

"You told me that wasn't a date," she said as she raised the glass to her lips.

"It wasn't. Not until you made it one."

"Mmm." She tried the wine, and he watched her lick her lips. "'Spectacular disaster,' eh? I suppose it could have been worse."

"It ended with your truck on fire," he reminded her.

"Well, we're in luck this time, then—I didn't bring a truck."

She eyed him with an intent that made his stomach flip over. He'd drunk either too much wine or not enough to make it through this dinner with her. Ellery was young and beautiful, quick thinking, and just a little bit dangerous. Half the time they were together, he'd ended up on the wrong side of a gun, an experience that sometimes made him sit up straight in bed at night, gasping for breath when he realized anew how close he'd come. Ellery, however, stalked death like it owed her something. Like they had unfinished business. Maybe that's why the bullets came flying every time Reed got near her—he was always in the way.

"Dinner looks amazing," Ellery said, interrupting his thoughts as she helped herself to some of the dates, which he'd stuffed with goat cheese and wrapped in the prosciutto. He had cumin-rubbed flank steak waiting in the kitchen, with pomegranate salsa, fiesta rice, and a large leafy salad with homemade vinaigrette dressing. "But you shouldn't have gone to so much trouble."

"It's not trouble," he tried to explain. Cooking grounded him. Certain aromas and flavors, like pork with apples roasting in the oven, took him back to his mother's kitchen. The rainbow colors of the vegetables always pleased his eye. The rhythmic chop, chop of the knife would slow his pulse, calming him. Plus, cooking made sense. Do it the correct way and it always came out right. "I like making a meal and watching someone eat it. It—it helps me feel normal."

"Normal," she said, her smile faltering. "I wouldn't know anything about that."

"But eating," he pointed out, "eating you're great at."

She raised her fork in his direction. "This is true." After a few more bites, she regarded him with interest. "So what about you? Did you grow up watching cops-and-robbers shows on TV and decide to be an FBI agent?"

"No, we didn't watch much television. Mama didn't usually allow it. Later, when I got married, I discovered that Sarit loved the crime shows. I had to explain that reality is nothing like what you see on the screen. She was extremely disappointed when I told her I did not have a private jet on standby, waiting to whisk me off to each new crime scene."

"No plane?" Ellery made a show of pouting. "And here I was thinking we could go for a ride later."

Reed swallowed back his baser reply as he rose from his seat to fetch the next course. "Actually, I was leaning toward political science for a time," he told her. "Maybe law. At one point when I was young I thought I might follow my father into politics."

"Really," she remarked with some surprise.

"I know. I'm not the sort for it, am I? I just liked the way people looked up to him, the way he made them happy. He encouraged me, too, and back then we kids would say almost anything to get his attention. He and I were surrounded by women at home, and he liked to joke about it. 'We Markham men have to stick together,' he'd tell me. I tried to convince myself we were totally alike. It didn't matter if I'd been born to some other father—we were the same where it counted."

"Oh," Ellery said quietly.

Reed set the platter of meat on the table between them. "Then I got older, and I had to admit we aren't anything alike. My father loves a crowd. I can't stand them. He loves generating all sorts of new ideas but leaves the details to others, while I love seeing things through. We both liked the idea of helping people, but my father is willing to lie to them in order to do it—you know, telling people what they want to hear until he can figure out a way to get them maybe half of what they're asking for. He thinks that's just part of the job."

"Whereas your job is about finding the truth," Ellery finished for him.

They ate in silence for a minute, until Ellery abruptly set down her fork.

"Reed . . . I know you're angry, and I know he lied to you. But brutally murdering Camilla like that . . . do you really think he's capable of such a thing?"

"He says he didn't do it," Reed answered, choosing his words carefully. "The problem is that I can no longer be sure if he's telling the truth."

Reed knew the alcohol had worked its miracle when his world shrank to the sofa, a deck of cards, and Ellery's shoulder pressed up against his. He held a red deck in his hands, while her cards were blue, but both of them aimed at the same target: the small chrome trash can sitting ten feet away. Ellery flipped one of her cards through the air, sending it sailing into the can. Indeed, nearly all of her cards had gone into the can. Meanwhile, a litter of red cards lay on the carpet at odd angles, surrounding the can but not inside it. He frowned and leaned forward, narrowing his eyes and lining up the shot. With a flick of his wrist, he pitched the king of hearts high into the air and landed him facedown somewhere near the balcony. "I don't know my own strength," he said, sinking back into the sofa.

"Your aim is terrifying. The FBI lets you carry a gun?"

"They positively insist on it," Reed replied, with a touch of dismay. He regarded her with hazy eyes and waved a hand between them. "That's going to be a problem with your new dress, you know—everyone will see your package. You're packing," he corrected himself quickly, but Ellery was already chortling.

"You're hammered," she said.

"I'm mellow," he informed her loftily as he stretched his

arms out along the back of the couch. He felt like he just might melt into the cushions. Maybe he could just stay here, not forever but long enough to feel human again. Ellery flipped several more cards into the can, one by one, while he admired the athletic grace of her toned arms and the slight bounce of her breasts inside that magnificent dress. It had a narrow red zipper down the front that he imagined leaning over and taking between his teeth.

Ellery nudged him with her elbow, rousing him from his fantasy. "It's your turn."

He sat up with a grumble. "I think you have an unfair advantage," he said as he missed again. "The dress has no sleeves. It gives you a better range of motion."

Amusement flashed in her eyes. "That's your excuse? If you like, we can swap outfits. You can take the dress and I'll take your getup as the wannabe European underwear model."

Reed gave his blue cashmere sweater a clumsy pat at the middle as he assessed his clothing with some confusion: button-down shirt with the tails untucked, sweater, jeans, and loafers. "I'm fully dressed," he protested. "Not modeling underwear."

"Yeah, they always start out that way," Ellery agreed as she flipped her last card into the can. "But by the end of the catalog, they're standing around in some itty-bitty black briefs."

He wasn't going to ask why she was looking at menswear catalogs. "You know nothing about my underwear."

"Not true. I've seen you model it in my living room." She gave him a cheeky smile as she reached for her own wineglass, which was still half-full. "That's how I know: it's European."

"You couldn't possibly know that." When she'd walked in on him that time, he'd been standing all the way across the room. It's not like she could read a label at that distance.

"You're saying I'm wrong?"

"I'm saying you lack concrete proof. As a trained investigator, I know insufficient evidence when I see it. Eyewitness testimony is notoriously unreliable."

Ellery paused and then deliberately set her glass aside. She leaned closer into his space, where he could see the shadowy hollow of her cleavage and smell the shower gel on her skin: ginger and citrus, now mixed with a hint of Merlot. All of a sudden he was thirsty again. "Agent Markham," she said in a low voice, "are you inviting me to investigate your underwear?"

God, was he? Maybe he was. His heart started thumping against his ribs like those nightclub girls in their cages, rocking to the beat. "I, uh . . ."

She shifted so they touched, thigh to thigh, and he could feel the heat of her through his clothes. "I bet they're French," she said, looking him over speculatively. "Right?"

Wrong. Although he knew better than to say that. "You like French?" he asked, trying to sound normal over the rush of the blood coursing through his ears. "I mean France?"

"Don't know," she said with a little shrug. "I've never been." She said it like France might as well have been Mars, and Reed was struck anew at how wide his world had been. He'd had his first passport by the time he was a year old.

"Maybe we can go someday."

Ellery shifted away and regarded him with a measured gaze. "Sure. Right. We'll travel the world in eighty days, just like the book says. Maybe we can take that neon balloon down the road and float away."

She said it with sarcasm, with impossibility, but he'd done so many impossible things with her already that he couldn't imagine what might happen next. He'd lived his whole life doing exactly what everyone expected of him, right up until he'd met Ellery. He felt dizzy, his tongue loosened by wine and the late hour. "Why is it," he murmured, stretching a hand toward her, "whenever I go looking for something, I always seem to find you?"

He took her hand and she let him. He pressed a lingering kiss to her knuckles. Ellery had beautiful hands, with fine bones and tapered fingers and soft, tender palms. They had been Coben's obsession, the reason he'd picked her, and so he'd left her hands untouched—smooth and unmarked by scars. Reed reluctantly broke contact, letting her go, but Ellery didn't move her hand away. She touched her fingertips to his mouth experimentally, reading him, and he forced himself to sit still under her exploration as she cataloged his lips and chin and cheeks. She stroked the curve of his face with her thumb and he set his jaw, rigid and barely controlled.

They were so far from home now, in this anonymous city that practically dared to you to become someone else. Someone you could leave behind at the end. Reed had been forced out of its border long ago, with no choice in the matter. The way he saw it, Las Vegas owed him one.

He turned his face to her palm and opened his mouth, and she gasped as his hot breath exhaled over her skin. She was warm and salty. He moved from her palm to her fingers to the inside of her wrist, where her pulse fluttered against his lips. When he looked up at her again, her gray eyes had turned dark. Slowly, giving her time to object, he moved his hand to the side of her head and leaned in to kiss her mouth.

She inhaled sharply at first contact but did not pull away. He kissed her gently, over and over, until gradually her body relaxed its rigid posture. She tilted slightly so their mouths could meet more fully, kissing him for real now as warmth started to spread across his face. The room faded away and there was nothing but the feel of his hands on her body and his lips moving against hers. Her palm slipped down the front of his shirt, and she opened for him, inviting the touch of his tongue.

Wait, he reminded his burning, alcohol-fueled brain. *You shouldn't.* But Ellery was soft and sweet and everywhere at once, her mouth moving on his, her hair a curtain that hid his flaming face. He felt himself cracking open, like ice across a pond, a slow shatter that might pull him under at any moment. He grabbed on to her for purchase, urging her closer until she was almost in his lap, her skirt crimped up around her thighs. They kissed like two kids in the backseat out after curfew, desperate and a little awkward with the groping.

His hands slid under her skirt to find the edge of her underwear, which he traced back and forth with one eager finger.

She arched to give him better access and he broke the

kiss. "Tell me," he muttered against her throat. "What do you like?" He wasn't so far gone that he didn't care. He wanted it to be good for her.

She held his head with both hands as he pressed fevered kisses along her collarbone. He could feel the live-wire hum of the blood coursing through her veins. "This," she breathed, drawing him up again for more kisses. "You." She said the word against his mouth.

"What else? What else?" He skimmed his hands along the outside of her thighs. He had to find out soon before he lost all rational thought.

"I don't know," she said in a rush, kissing him again.

It took a second for the words to penetrate his muzzy brain, which was lost in a fog of arousal. "What?" he said, drawing back to look at her, his breathing unsteady.

Her lips were wet and shining from their kisses, her long hair tangled and mussed, and it hurt him physically to look at her, he wanted her that much. "I don't know," she repeated, faltering. "I mean . . . I've never been able to find out."

She leaned in to kiss him again, but he stopped her, his hands gentle on her shoulders, holding her just above the scars. He'd wanted to forget, to lose himself in her, but she'd reminded him of who he really was. Reminded him of who she was and what they were together. He ran his hands over her bare arms, savoring the feel of her one last time as he tried to find the right apology. His tongue felt thick and dumb in his mouth; he had no words for this.

Ellery froze under his touch, feeling his regret, and she

pulled away with a sharp jerk. "That was the wrong answer, wasn't it?"

"No, Ellery, wait." The room turned cold as she climbed off his lap. "I can explain."

"No need. I get it. I know what I am to you. What I'll always be."

She grabbed up her flip-flops in her hands and started heading for the door. He half-rolled off the couch, clumsy with wine and residual desire. "You're wonderful," he said, desperate to stop her. "It's just—"

"It's just you remembered what he did to me," she finished hotly as she yanked open the front door. "Don't bother to deny it, because I can read it on your face."

The door slammed behind her, reverberating through the suite, and Reed stood alone in his stocking feet, staring at the space she used to be. He could almost feel the alcoholic high evaporating from his brain. The temperature was close to freezing outside, he realized, and she'd left without her jacket. He retrieved it and his loafers before heading out into the hall. He rode down in the elevator hoping that he'd find the right words to make her come back inside, but he hadn't had a lot of success in that area. Whatever he suggested, Ellery usually did the opposite. This, he told himself darkly, was the whole damn reason he'd needed instructions from her in the first place.

Downstairs, he circled the gleaming hotel lobby but found no trace of her. "Excuse me," he asked the doorman, who tipped his black cap in reply, "did you see a woman leave here a few minutes ago? She was wearing a red dress."

"Yes, she was," the man replied with hearty agreement, his smile a flash of white against his otherwise dark face.

"She left without her jacket." Reed held it up to support his case. "Did you see which way she went?"

The doorman rubbed his chin with one hand. "She was going away from here in a hurry. Maybe she left you and that jacket on purpose, eh? Give her some time. She'll come back." He winked at Reed. "They always do, after a while."

"Thanks," Reed said flatly, and then ignored this piece of free advice. He took the jacket and jogged toward the parking garage, feeling in his pocket for the car keys. He fished them out and pressed the button, listening for the answering chirp, which echoed around the concrete walls. "Finally," he muttered to himself when the SUV came into view at the end of the row. As he got closer, though, he noticed it appeared off—lopsided somehow and smaller than he remembered.

He rounded the bend and stopped short when he saw the damage. Someone had slashed the tires. Someone who might still be watching. Reed turned frantically in place, searching for the perpetrator in the shadowy garage. No one was around. He recalled too well that Camilla Flores had her tires slashed—a warning, apparently, that she'd failed to heed, because a few days later someone carved her up with a kitchen knife. "Ellery," Reed said aloud as fresh terror seized him. He forgot all about the car as he began to run.

11

Ellery stumbled blindly in the direction of the lights, but the path she had jogged earlier was now clogged with tourists, party girls teetering on high heels, and other Friday-night-fun seekers. The winter desert wind came howling down the boulevard on full tilt, whipping her hair into her eyes and raising the gooseflesh on her bare arms. She hugged herself for warmth and to make a slimmer figure as she cut through the crowds, angling between the drunk college kids and the gawkers with their cell phones out at arm's length. "Hey, watch it!" She bumped some guy's elbow and he shoved her back in retaliation for messing up his shot, but she didn't pause or apologize, just kept pushing forward through the mass of people. She was desperate to put as much space as possible between her and the thing that had hurt her, that awful scene at the hotel. Her heart beat like a hammer, painful and hard, drumming out the same word over and over: *Go, go, go*. She'd spent three days trapped in a closet and so now she ran—she ran whenever she could. If you stopped to think, the pain could catch you. *Go.*

Reed's face. She could still see it in her mind's eye, the way his dark eyes shifted, kaleidoscope-like, melting from desire into pity. She had never been intimate with anyone who knew about Coben. Her occasional bed partners got to see her only half-naked in total darkness, handpicked as they were to be the sort who would never stop to ask about the scars. *Bike accident,* she would tell them if they ever raised the issue, and no one thought to question her. No, they didn't ask her anything at all. *What do you like?* Ellery halted with the crowd at an intersection, stuck there with the memory of Reed and his warm hands on her body.

She'd slept with men to prove she could, to show she could give away what Coben took and still come out whole on the other side. If she'd felt anything after these encounters, it was triumphant. *Fuck you, all right.* The light changed and the crowd surged forward, dragging her along with it. Her flip-flops scraped against the pavement as she hurried to keep pace. Reed had been into it, she knew, right up until she'd confessed the truth and reminded him exactly who she was. Coben's victim. The girl from the closet. Hot tears burned her eyes, and she swiped them away with a furious gesture. She should've known. She should've kept her mouth shut. Even when Reed talked to her like she was normal, when he touched her like he enjoyed it, she had to remember—the scars were forever. She would never be able to outrun them.

Winded, she stopped again at the next intersection, bent over slightly as she tried to catch her breath. The cold air burned her lungs. She looked around at the blinking lights, the honking traffic, and the enormous casinos. "Hey, lady. Can you spare a dollar?" A scruffy guy with an oil-stained jacket rattled a cup of coins in her direction. In his other hand, he held a cardboard sign that read: MAKE IT RAIN. Ellery automatically patted her sides and came up empty when she felt only the thin material of her silk dress. No money, no phone. "Sorry," she said, with real regret as she realized the vulnerable situation she'd put herself in.

When the WALK light turned again, people streamed forward, but this time she fought to keep her feet. She wrangled away from the main boulevard to get free of the crush of humanity. A car horn blared at her as she balanced on the curb. A man leaned out of the passenger-side window with a sharklike grin. White teeth against orange skin. "Hey there, hot mama, you looking for a ride?"

She ignored him and slipped herself back into the anonymity of the crowd. *Must think*. She couldn't wander around in the freezing cold forever. Eventually, she would have to go back to the hotel and face Reed. Her mistake. He lived alone like her, and he'd seemed like he needed someone. Someone better than her, apparently. How stupid she'd been to think they were the same.

At the next intersection, she veered off abruptly down the side street, where it was darker and quieter. As she made the turn, she heard the squeal of car tires behind her and she turned to see headlights bearing down on her. She raised her hand to shield her eyes just as the car jerked to a stop in the middle of the road. A large man got out of the driver's side. She didn't recognize his shape, but he knew her, because he hollered her name. "Ellery! Ellery Hathaway."

He started barreling toward her, and Ellery turned to run.

"Wait, stop! I won't hurt you, darlin'!"

The Southern twang. That familiar drawl. Curiosity made her peek back over her shoulder, and this time the streetlamp caught enough of his face that she could see: it was Angus Markham. Cautiously, she took a step toward him. "How do you know me?" Reed had shown her some of Markham's videotaped speeches online, but Ellery had never met the senator in person.

His mouth widened into a self-satisfied grin. "It's part of my job. I never forget a face, and yours was all over the TV last summer, right next to Reed's. He likes you. A whole lot, from what Rufus tells me about your suite arrangement here in town. I just got here myself, and when I saw you walking along I figured I'd take a chance and say hello." He doffed an imaginary cap at her.

"What do you want?" Ellery folded her arms, unmoved by his attempts at charm.

His smile vanished, and he spread his hands. "I want Reed to stop this nonsense before he gets hurt. I need him to listen to reason, but he won't talk to me. I thought maybe he'll hear it from you."

"You lied to him."

"So did you," Angus countered, pointing a finger at her.

Heat flared in her cheeks and she looked away.

"Don't try to deny it," he continued. "I read all the stories. I know everything that happened up there in Woodbury."

Ellery snapped her attention back to him. "Yeah? You can't believe everything you read in the papers. That's politician one-oh-one, isn't it?"

He chuckled, seemingly genuinely amused, and wagged that finger at her. "I can see why he likes you. Look, whatever story you told Reed last summer, I'm sure you had your reasons, the same as me."

"We're not the same," Ellery cut in hotly.

"I love my boy." He looked her over, assessing. "You must care about him, too, or you wouldn't be out here on this fool's errand with him."

Ellery said nothing, and Angus took a deep, frustrated breath.

"I'm burning gas here, and you're not dressed for the weather. Let me buy you a cup of coffee. Hear me out. If you still want to tell me to go to hell after that . . . well, you wouldn't be the first. Nor the last, I'm sure."

Before Ellery could answer, she heard her name again, this time at a distance. She looked beyond the headlights and saw a familiar waving figure. Reed. "Ellery!" He came hurtling down the sidewalk at them and practically crashed into her. "El . . . Ellery . . . are you all right?"

"I'm fine," she said mildly. "I was just talking to your father."

Reed jerked in surprise at her words and turned around to face the senator, noticing him for the first time. Angus greeted his son with a short nod. "Evening, Son."

"What are you doing here?" Reed stood protectively between his father and Ellery, but she shifted so she could see Angus's face. He seemed to be holding back a world of emotions.

"You wouldn't talk sense on the phone," he answered finally. "I had no choice."

"You came out here to feed me more lies, then. Is that it?"

"Whatever you want to know, Reed, I will tell you all of it, okay? The God's honest truth." His father sounded weary. "Whatever will get you back home where you belong."

"This was my home. I was born here, as you very well know. If Camilla hadn't been murdered, we'd be strangers to each other. So how about you don't stand there and try to tell me where I belong?"

This shot landed its mark, as Angus's face twisted in pain. He held up his hands weakly, as if in surrender. "You're right, okay? I deserve your anger. I made a stupid, dumb mistake and I made a worse one trying to correct it. You can hate me forever for that if you want to, but I wish you would stop this crusade before you get hurt."

"What's that supposed to mean?" Reed asked evenly.

"I've seen the pictures," Angus said, his breathing unsteady. "Someone carved up that girl like a country steak. It wasn't me, and I hope—I pray—that when you stop to think about it for two seconds, you know that's the truth. I have a hundred sins to my name, but that's not one of them. She wanted money? Fine. I'd pay her. I'd have kept on paying her, too, whatever it took. I sure as hell never wanted to kill her."

"I've interviewed dozens of murderers over the years," Reed said coldly. "They all say the same thing."

Ellery saw shock flicker over Angus's face, but he recovered quickly. "Believe what you like. I can't stop you. All I can tell you is my side, and that's the part where I got bone chilled when I heard what happened to Cammie. Because whoever did that to her, they looked on my boy. Maybe stood over him with that knife. Maybe thought about killing him, too. I got out here quick as I could to make sure he was safe." A defiant gleam appeared in his eye. "That's why I came the first time, and it's why I'm here now."

Ellery watched as Reed weighed his father's words. "You're saying I'm in danger?"

"Someone killed that girl, Reed. Whoever it was, they let you live once. Maybe this time you won't get so lucky."

Reed's jaw tightened. "This is my job, Dad. It's what I do. I hunt killers."

Angus scoffed. "This ain't a job, Son. This is personal. You're not out here with a fleet of FBI agents with you. You've got a shivering lady out on the streets and some fire in your belly about how you deserve answers. That lady and me . . ." He nodded at Ellery. "We both want to see you make it out of here in one piece."

Reed glanced back at Ellery, and she held his gaze, mute.

"Maybe let's go talk someplace warmer, eh?" Angus said. "'Afore she turns properly blue."

She was freezing, she realized as she tried to move her numb fingers. Reed glanced down at the jacket he had in his hands as if seeing it for the first time. He reached over and draped it gently around Ellery's shoulders. "We can go back to the hotel and talk there," he said, nudging her toward Angus's car.

She looked up, surprised. "You didn't bring the car?"

"Long story," he muttered with a frown.

Reed climbed into the backseat with her as Angus took the wheel again. "I'll get the heat right back at you," he said, cranking it up to a roar. Ellery huddled into the deep leather seat and tried to keep her teeth from chattering.

On the other side, Reed looked at her with worried eyes. "Are you sure you're all right?"

"Yes, I'm fine." She sat up to prove it, hiding her shivers. "You didn't have to come after me."

"Ellery." A note of fondness warmed his voice, and his hand crept across the seat to cover hers. "I don't know how you've failed to realize this yet, but I will always come after you."

Back at the hotel suite, Ellery watched as Angus silently cataloged all the evidence of their unfinished evening, from the dirty dinner plates stacked on the counter to the abandoned wineglasses and the couch cushions lying on the floor. Reed rushed around trying to right everything as

Angus withdrew a pack of cigarettes from his jacket pocket. He slapped the pack on the kitchen countertop, next to the wilted remnants of the salad, and took out one smoke, which he did not light. His gaze landed on Ellery, and he lingered over her body-hugging dress. She felt like she'd been caught red-handed at the scene of a crime.

"I'm going to change," she murmured before fleeing to the safety of her bedroom. She shut and locked the door behind her, leaning back against it in relief. She wished for her own bed back in Boston and the warmth of her snuggly barrel-shaped dog. She peeled off the dress and it seemed to melt away at her feet like the Wicked Witch of the West, no power left at all. She yanked on her usual uniform of charcoal-gray yoga pants and a similarly colored long-sleeve T-shirt. When that didn't feel like enough layers between her and the men beyond the door, she added her faded purple cow sweatshirt from Williams College.

She sat cross-legged on her bed and eyed the door, wondering if she should go back out there. Wondering what the hell she was even doing here in the first place. She had no advice to give Reed about how to handle his father. Her knowledge of her father amounted to a collection of old photographs, worn-out memories, and her mother's angry voice on the phone: *You said you'd send the money last month, John. Where the hell is it?* Ellery had no power over her own family, let alone Reed's. Fathers, in her estimation, did whatever the hell they wanted to, their children's wishes be damned.

A soft knock on the door startled her, and she tiptoed over to listen, unsure about whether she had the energy to deal with whatever waited on the other side. "Ellery?" The muffled voice was Reed's. "I made you some tea."

She bit her lip in hesitation but eventually unlocked the door and let him inside. He wore his wire-rimmed glasses and a slightly dazed expression. "Thank you," she said as she accepted the hot mug with its rising steam—a bitter, earthy scent that tickled her nose. He had closed the door behind him, so she couldn't see what Angus was up to in the living area. "Has he told you anything more?"

Reed shook his head. "He's out on the balcony, smoking. He does that whenever one of his bills falls through or some union guy won't agree right away to new contract terms. We could always tell what kind of day Daddy'd had by how strongly he smelled of tobacco when he walked through the door. Sometimes he'd sit parked out in the driveway, finishing the last one in sight of the house."

Ellery smiled a little as she sipped her tea. "Sounds like you know him well."

"Obviously not well enough."

Ellery recalled the senator's earlier words to her: *I'm sure you had your reasons, same as me.* "He came back to get you after the murder," she said softly. "That must have been a huge risk for him, no? He could have let you stay in foster care, be adopted by someone else. Instead, he came back for you."

Reed paced to the window and looked out over the lights

of the city. "So you're defending him now? Angus Markham always could work a room."

"I'm not defending him." She set the tea on the nightstand and joined Reed by the window. "I'm just saying maybe you should hear him out. You don't have to like or agree with his reasons, but at least you'd know what they were." Reed said nothing, and the silence stretched between them for several long minutes. Ellery picked at the gauze curtain, rubbing it between her thumb and fingers. "There was a guy begging for money on the street tonight," she told Reed after a moment. She felt his gaze turn to her, but she avoided looking at him as she confessed this next part. "I usually give a dollar or something to anyone who asks. You know why? Because once that used to be me." She risked a look at him to see how he was taking this bit of news, and he looked askance.

"Ellery . . ."

She held up her hand to forestall him. "After my father left us, I used to scrounge for money anywhere I could get it. I'd pick out cans and bottles from the trash, wash them in public fountains, and redeem them for pocket change. Other times, I'd ride my bike uptown to the business district and stand on the street corners and beg. 'Please, I'm hungry. Can you give me a dollar?' Sometimes I was hungry. Mom would be at the hospital with Danny and she'd forget to buy groceries. Or we'd run out before her next check came in. Whatever food we had, Danny got to eat first. He needed to keep up his strength, Mom said, and of course I understood that. But other times, it wasn't about

207

food. I just wanted the money. I wanted to reach into my pocket and feel those bills and know I could buy stuff if I had to." She pantomimed the gesture, remembering the delicious feel of the secret wad of cash. "I bought candy and comic books and T-shirts no one wore before me. Mom could've used the money, but I didn't share it with her. Or with Danny. I kept it all to myself."

"You were a kid," Reed said gruffly.

"I knew what I was doing. I knew it was wrong, representing myself as worse off than I was, asking people to hand over their money just so I could go blow it on junk. It's not like I'm proud of it. But I'm not especially sorry, either. Those guys in the expensive suits, I turned their pity into dollars, so they could keep on walking, thinking they'd made some kind of difference." She shrugged, dismissing the memory. "There's ugly parts in all of us is what I'm saying."

Reed stared at her for so long that her face started to warm. "You're not ugly to me."

"Yes."

"No."

She turned her cheek away, furious with him anew. "I was there tonight, Reed. Remember?" His hands had fallen away from her body, his erection vanishing as the whole Coben history came rushing back between them. He could try to tell her she was lovely, but his libido wouldn't cosign the lie. "I have mirrors in my house. I know what I look like. You know what he did. Believe me, I get how that could be off-putting. I'd just appreciate it if you could admit it."

Her heart was in her throat again, her feet itchy to run. It took every ounce of control to stand there and wait for his verdict.

"I think," he said slowly, "I think you're beautiful." He reached out to touch her face, but his hand stopped, trembling slightly, and it dropped away. "I think you're shockingly normal."

She gave a derisive snort. "Right."

"I do," he insisted. "For your reality, Ellery, every action you take, every reaction you have, it all makes sense. In a world where everyone is a little bit crazy, you're doing more than fine. And you're completely correct—I know what happened to you. I know nearly every horrible detail, and what little I don't know I don't even want to imagine."

She swallowed hard, her watery eyes on the door. *Go, go, go.*

"So maybe I'm uniquely qualified to tell you: you're amazing. I marvel each time I look at you. You could have given up inside that closet. You could've ended up dead even after you got free. You might've spent the rest of your days in a haze of booze and pills, trying not to remember, and no one could blame you one tiny bit. People have sunk themselves into oblivion for far less than what you went through. Or worse, maybe you could have taken Coben's anger and put it right back into the world." He grabbed her arm gently and pushed up her sleeve to reveal the scars. "You could have tried to make someone, or everyone, pay for this. Instead, you joined the police to try to help people. You came out here to help me." He gave her arm a fierce squeeze. "You didn't just survive, Ellery. You lived."

"Stop," she said, pulling away. "You're making me cry. I hate it when I cry."

"I know," he said, full of sympathy.

She sniffed but did not stop him when he moved to take her in his arms. She laid her cheek against the soft cashmere of his sweater and listened to the reassuring thumping of his heart. Slow, steady. It did not seem to be urging anyone to run. Cautiously, she closed her eyes and hugged him back.

"I don't know if you've noticed," he said against the top of her head. "But there is a ticking time bomb smoking out there in the living room. I don't know what all he's guilty of, but it's possible my life is about to implode in ways I could never have imagined." He smoothed her hair back and rubbed his thumb at the base of her neck, making her shudder. "I don't want you caught up in the shrapnel," he continued in a low voice. "Not now. Not like this."

She drew back and looked at him. "What's a few more scars at this point? Bring it on."

He smiled and leaned forward to place a lingering, gentle kiss on her forehead. "See? Amazing."

She took a shaky breath and stepped backward, breaking the contact. "You should go talk to him," she said, nodding in the direction of the door. "I'll stay here or come with you, whichever you think would be easiest."

"Come," he said immediately. "It would be good to have a neutral party hear the story."

"I wouldn't say I'm neutral."

"You haven't spent the past few weeks imagining his head on a stick. Around here, that counts for neutral."

They went back out into the living area, where Angus sat on the couch. He'd helped himself to the bar—whiskey, from the looks of it—and had removed his shoes and sport coat. "You two were gone so long I figured maybe you had retired for the night," he said.

Reed and Ellery sat together on the other couch, the one they had nearly christened a few hours earlier. She was grateful to Reed for clearing away all the evidence. "Well," Reed said, leaning back. "Let's hear it. You wanted to talk to me, and here I am."

"I didn't kill Camilla," Angus stated again, leaning forward to compensate for the distance Reed had just created. "If that's what you came out here expecting to prove, you're going to be sorely disappointed."

"I came to find the truth, whatever it might be."

"Ah, yes, the truth with a capital *T*. Must be nice if you can still think in those terms. Find the guilty party, lock him up—that's how it goes."

"Are you saying you have some sort of problem with that? I've seen your voting record, Dad. 'Lock 'em up' has been your rallying cry more than once."

"Gotta be tough on crime," Angus said, squinting at nothing in particular. "We're agreed on that. I meant that sometimes you can dig for the truth but come up with sand. Last week, we voted to fund a new school in District Three.

It's going to involve tearing down a bunch of woods that have been growing there since God was young, and the environmentalists are screaming at us louder than a treeful of hoot owls. Meanwhile, District Two says their elementary school is crumbling at the foundation and we're only granting the money to District Three because they have rich businesses pledging to help offset the cost. You know what? District Two is right. The money does come into play. But Three has more kids coming up through the ranks. They have a real need." He shrugged. "So you tell me, then. What's the truth about that school?"

"This isn't politics, Dad," Reed said evenly. "It's murder."

"I know that." He set the drink aside and rubbed his face with one hand. "It's just from my perspective, I got out of this mess with my boy—the best thing ever to come from a bad situation—and so you'll pardon me if I don't want to go back and poke the hornet's nest again. None of us back then covered ourselves in glory with our behavior, and that includes your birth mother, God rest her soul."

"What's that supposed to mean?"

"She threatened to tell your mother—your mother who raised you—about the affair. She was bound and determined to get that twenty-five thousand dollars out of me one way or another, and she didn't care who got hurt in the process."

"She's not the one who broke her marriage vows," Reed said.

"No, she's not. But she didn't need to make such a stink about it. I intended to pay her. I just needed a little time to come up with the money. It's not like I could just write her a check on the family account."

"So you did give her the money," Ellery said.

"A few days before she got killed, yes." He hesitated and picked up his tumbler again, rolling it around so the ice hit the inside of the glass. "But I'm not the one who made the drop."

"Rufus," Reed guessed instantly, and Angus replied with a short nod.

"He flew out here and gave it to her. We argued some about the best way to handle Camilla, but we both agreed it was best for him to take her the money."

"Argued about what?" Reed wanted to know, and Ellery recalled David's statement that he'd seen Cammie exchanging heated words with someone who matched Rufus's description shortly before she died.

Angus shifted on the sofa, looking uncomfortable. "When Cammie called to say she was pregnant, Rufus wanted me to lean on her to get rid of it. But she was too far gone by then—more than five months. It wasn't ever an option, especially not in my mind. My kid is my kid. So then he wanted me to pay her to give up the baby—make the money contingent on severing any connection. I didn't see how that would solve the problem, and I told him so."

"Solve the problem," Reed repeated, his voice hollow. "I see."

"I didn't know you back then," his father said. "I had a wife, three daughters, and a senate campaign. People's lives were riding on me, don't you see? I screwed up and they were going to pay for it."

"How do you know Camilla got the money?" Ellery asked coolly. Reed had grown up with a father who could hand over twenty-five grand without a backward glance, so he might not appreciate the power it brought to suddenly have that kind of windfall in your pockets.

Angus's face went blank. "Rufus told me so."

"You didn't call to confirm?" Reed asked, and his father looked chagrined.

"No, I'm afraid I didn't. Truth be told, I was relieved not to hear from her. But if you're thinking Rufus took that money for himself, you're dead wrong. I've handed him bigger sums than that over the years, and he's never pinched a nickel of it. Whatever disagreements we might have had about Camilla, he agreed it was my call—and my money."

"Hmm," Ellery said. "Rufus—was he out here with you when you first met Camilla?"

"Why? What does that have to do with anything?"

"Just wondering." She thought of Reed's timeline and the murder of Giselle Hardiman.

"Let's see. That was a fundraising trip—flying our bigger donors out to show them a good time. So yes, Rufus would've been there. I don't see how it matters any. He didn't meet her then."

"Does the name Giselle Hardiman mean anything to you?" Ellery asked.

Angus frowned. "No, never heard of her. Why?"

"She was murdered in a similar fashion to Camilla," Reed explained. "About thirteen months earlier. We don't know if there is any connection between the cases."

"You mean like a serial killer kind of thing? Damn." Angus sat back in surprise. "Never once crossed my mind that might be a possibility."

"Who did you think killed her?" Ellery asked.

Angus shrugged. "Rufus said the police suspected a local drug dealer, someone Camilla was going to testify against at an upcoming trial. That sounded pretty reasonable to me. But I guess they couldn't make the charges stick."

"He had made threats," Reed agreed. "And apparently the cops thought he had slashed Camilla's tires as some sort of warning to back off. When she failed to comply, the police thought, Billy Thorndike murdered her. I'm beginning to have my doubts about that theory, however."

Ellery turned to look at him. "You are? Why?"

"Because someone slashed our tires tonight and I'm having a hard time imagining old Billy Thorndike with his walker getting the job done."

"What? Why didn't you tell me?"

Reed gave her a pointed look. "We've had an eventful evening. Who knows? Maybe we'll get lucky and the security cameras caught the person on tape."

Angus's mouth twisted with grief. "You see? You see why I didn't want you getting mixed up in this? Jesus, we all got away clean. Why can't that be enough for you?"

Reed's cell phone buzzed from inside his pants, and

everyone looked at his lap. It was past midnight. Nothing good ever came from phone calls in the middle of the night. Reed pulled the phone out and regarded the caller ID with a deepening frown. "It's Mom," he announced, and took the call. Ellery watched him openly as he murmured a few words of agreement and then ended the conversation. "She's here in town," he told them as he set the phone aside. "And she wants to meet."

12

Marianne Markham asked Reed to come alone, and he'd always been a boy who followed his mama's wishes. He found her in an all-night diner with red booths and chrome stools, the kind of place his other mother might have worked, and he stood outside on the dark sidewalk for a few moments to watch her through the glass windows. It was the middle of the night, but her frosted-blond bob showed not a hair out of place. Her white dress shirt hung untucked in a way that made her look youthful, not rumpled, accenting her ice-blue eyes and trademark red lipstick. She had a mug of what he presumed to be coffee sitting near her elbow, and she ate her piece of pie with precise, familiar movements that made his heart ache to look at her.

He had not stopped to think about Marianne much since he'd made his discovery. She'd been young when it all happened, just twenty-six, a politician's wife with three girls of her own. What story must Angus have given her to make her agree to take in an orphaned baby boy from half a country away? Reed always knew he was adopted, seeing as how he was a different shade of human from his pearly older sisters, but he hadn't appreciated the crux of the difference until one of his grade-school classmates explained it to him on the playground, with all the honesty of a six-year-old: *It means they didn't have to love you, but they do anyway.*

Reed touched the cold glass with his fingertips. If she hated him now, he couldn't blame her. He steeled himself for her reaction and opened the door to the restaurant. His leaden feet halted him just inside the threshold, standing frozen there on the checkered floor as he locked eyes with his mother. Her impassive face gave nothing away. "Hi," said the cheery waitress from behind the counter. "Sit anywhere you like. I'll get you some coffee, coming right up!"

Reed forced himself forward until he stood at the edge of his mother's table. She gestured at the other side of the red pleather booth. "Sit," she said. "Have some pie. I don't usually eat anything after ten P.M., but this is so far into tomorrow that I think it doesn't count anymore. They have blueberry and cherry, and I chose the cherry. I'm afraid the fruit is canned, but the crust is surprisingly buttery. I think I even detect a hint of cinnamon."

"Mom," Reed said as he slid into the booth. He had yet to remove his coat. "How are you?" If she was here, she must have learned some form of the truth.

"I could use a refill on this coffee," she replied as the waitress appeared with a pot and a mug for Reed.

The woman slid a laminated menu in front of him, but Reed didn't glance at it. "Pie is fine," he muttered. "Whatever she's having." He leaned over the table as his mother resumed eating. "Mom, what are you doing out here?"

"Trying to keep my son from making a terrible mistake." She put her fork, tines down, on the edge of her plate. "Your father didn't kill that girl, Reed, and you'll regret it forever if you suggest to anyone that he did. Words like that—you can never take them back."

Reed sat back, confused. "That girl," he repeated slowly. "Camilla. You—you knew about her?"

She picked up her coffee mug and took a long sip. "Your father," she said, barely repressing a sigh. "Your father is a good man, but he's a weak man in some respects. I knew this when I got into bed with him. Most of the others weren't that lucky." She paused to let that tidbit sink in. "Give Angus a city hospital that needs a million dollars in funding and he'll work the numbers, he'll personally go door-to-door if he has to, just to keep the E.R. open. I think he somehow convinces himself that these girls need him the same way—that they'll perish without his personal attention. He's a sucker for a damsel in distress, even if that distress is no bigger than a broken nail."

The waitress reappeared with Reed's pie, but he couldn't imagine eating it now. There was no room left inside him. The painful lump at his middle took up every stitch of room. "So then you knew he was my father," he said, his voice rough.

"Yes." She inclined her head almost imperceptibly. "I knew. The girl called me up and told me so."

"She . . . what?"

"It was late one night, must've been about September of 1975, because the weather was still unbearably humid. Your father was out smoking on the veranda and he didn't hear the phone ring in his study. I happened to be passing by when it rang, so I thought I could answer and fetch him if it turned out to be urgent. She wasn't expecting me, but the story just came pouring out of her. She didn't want to hurt my family, she said. She didn't want Angus to leave us and marry her. She just wanted money for the baby." She looked at Reed. "For you."

"A lot of money."

"Yes. But he could afford it." She sipped her coffee again, calm as could be. Reed held the edge of the table to stop his shaky fingers.

"Did you tell him then? That Camilla called?"

His mother grimaced and set aside her cup. "No. I didn't say anything at first because I was afraid what might fly out if I opened my mouth on the subject. I was furious with him. He'd risked everything we'd worked so hard to build, just because he couldn't keep his pants zipped up for three straight days. What if this girl went public with the story? He'd have been ruined. The girls would have faced all the whispers and the stares . . ." She shook her head, lips pursed. "I waited to see if he would confess the truth. Clearly it was bothering him. He became forgetful, distracted, and nervous all the time, especially when the phone rang. He smoked two packs a day and sweated through several undershirts to the point that Lulabelle couldn't remove the stains. But he never said a word, and so neither did I."

Reed waited a beat through the silence that followed. "I can't believe you didn't tell him."

"Tell him? He already knew! I was the one who'd been kept in the dark. He'd stepped out of our marriage and betrayed his vows. In return, he got to wonder just how much I knew and when I knew it. It turns out that uncertainty was a marvelous deterrent: no other girls have ever called our home to say they were pregnant with his child."

"But after the m—murder," Reed stammered. "He must have said something to you then."

"He said he wanted to adopt a child, a boy like we had always talked about. He said we had an abundance of love and money and we should open our home and hearts to a baby who needed us. An orphan, he said, and that's when I knew—something must have happened to the girl. We didn't have the internet for snooping in those days, but I made a few calls and was able to locate the story in the papers. I felt sick when I read the details about what he did to her, cutting her up like that with her baby in the next room . . ."

Reed felt a chill go through him, like someone walking over his grave, the way she spoke of the baby as though he were someone else. He closed his eyes and tried, not for the first time, to place himself back in that crib and will a memory to come forth. He'd been right there, just steps away from where his mother died. At some point he must have seen the killer—maybe it was even someone he had known—but whatever sounds or faces he'd absorbed that day had disappeared without a trace, much like the murderer himself.

Across the booth, Marianne continued her story. "Angus arranged the adoption through private attorneys, probably paying them top dollar not to ask too many questions. He gave me a diamond bracelet when the papers came through, the same way he'd gifted me with jewelry when your sisters were born. If he meant it to be a bribe, he needn't have bothered. By that time, I wanted you as much as he did."

Reed, drifting in his own thoughts, looked up in surprise at these last words. She nodded for emphasis.

"I kept picturing you there alone in all that blood. I thought of how scared you must have been during the attack, how you must have been wondering what happened to your mother and why she was no longer there to hold you." Her chin trembled as she spoke, and she clutched her shirt at the middle. "Of course you had a father and your half sisters, the same as you always did, even if you didn't know it yet. But you had lost a mother forever. I wanted so much to step in and fix that, but I didn't know if I was worthy. I—I prayed on it. I felt guilty so often, because I'd hated that girl and had wished for her to disappear."

Reed sat stone still under the weight of her words. All the family birthdays and the lavish holidays and the endless campaign events, smiling until their cheeks hurt, with his two parents waving to the crowds—the whole time they knew what had happened to Camilla and they'd never said a word. He wondered if his parents saw Camilla when they looked at him. If they had ever regretted scooping up her child and running halfway across the country, leaving her story unsolved and unfinished. *We all got away clean,* Angus had said, but Reed felt Camilla's blood in his veins, a persistent burn.

His mother reached across the table to grab his hand, and Reed let her do it, noting with clinical detachment how her slender, pale fingers appeared almost ghostlike when intertwined with his. "I'm sorry for what happened to Camilla," she said, and Reed stiffened as his mother finally said the other woman's name aloud. "I never wanted her harmed; you must believe that. Once it happened, I did the only thing I could think to do to make it right—I vowed to be the best mother I could to her son."

She squeezed him hard, but Reed did not return the gesture. He pulled his hand free from hers. "You kept the truth from Dad to punish him," he said tightly. "Is that why you didn't say anything to me?"

Her red mouth dropped open in shock. "Reed, of course not! You were a baby, then a little boy. By the time you were old enough to know the story, it was so long in the past that it felt like it didn't matter anymore. It felt like . . . well, like you were where you'd always belonged." When she reached for him again, he tucked his hand beneath the table. "Please try to understand. Your father and I were trying to protect you."

"It wasn't about me," he said, more harshly than he'd

intended. "Dad tiptoed back into town and made off with his kid, careful not to attract the attention of anyone investigating Camilla's case. I can assure you the detectives would have wanted to have a long chat with him. You understand that, right? He would have been suspect number one if they'd known about his relationship with Camilla."

His mother fixed him with the same withering stare she'd used when he'd fidgeted in church on Sunday morning. "He didn't do this, and I can't believe you would ever think otherwise. Isn't that your specialty at the FBI—psychological profiling? You ought to know your father's weakness is his incessant need to make other people happy—any love is good love, and he takes all that he can get."

"The operative word is 'takes,'" Reed replied, his voice low and hard. "Camilla held all the cards. Who was she, anyway? Some poor girl waiting tables in the desert, barely scraping by, knocked up from a cheap one-night stand. Only this guy turns out to be loaded and suddenly she's seeing dollar signs. If he pays her off once, what's to stop her from coming back? Money has power, but it can't shut someone up for good. There's only one surefire method to do that, and someone sure as hell took it."

He was breathing hard by the end of his speech, his palms sweaty. Marianne pursed her lips and made a show of ignoring him for a few moments as she retrieved her purse and set out a crisp twenty-dollar bill on the table between them, next to his uneaten pie. "I hope," she said finally, "that your mother couldn't hear you just now, speaking of her like that. She'll be thinking we raised her boy to be an insolent, arrogant jackass."

Reed burned under her rebuke. "Someone in this family has to tell the truth."

She rose, somewhat stiffly, and then leaned down so close he could smell the gardenia scent of her perfume. Her whisper scraped like sandpaper against his face. "Do you believe this effort of yours is making her proud? You think she would admire you for trying to destroy your family? That girl gave up her life for you, and this is your repayment."

She straightened and Reed gazed up at her with wide eyes, the way he used to when he was young and she was larger than life. "What do you mean that she died for me? I wasn't the target."

"It doesn't matter. She wouldn't have thought about that. Every blow she fought off was for you, my son. I can promise you that."

Reed ground his jaw, unforgiving. "You weren't there. You don't know."

"I know," she said with certainty. She stalked off without another word, leaving him with only her familiar red lipstick mark on the white mug.

Reed stared at the empty side of the booth until his vision blurred. His mother's scalding words had peeled back his last protective layer, the one that said he was doing the right thing, no matter what the cost. Somehow, he summoned the energy to get up and walk out of the diner into the chilly night air. He felt naked and exposed, a shell-shocked soldier ready to duck at every turn. The wide boulevards sat almost empty, as everyone with a home had seen fit to go there. Reed wandered aimlessly, bathed in the nictitating neon, until he stumbled upon his hotel. He gazed up at it for a long moment before going inside.

His father sat up groggily from the couch when Reed entered the suite. Reed stood near the threshold, his eyes seeking out Ellery. He didn't see her and noticed that her bedroom door was closed. Angus thrust his chin in the direction of Ellery's room. "She sat here staring at me like I was lower than a dung beetle for an hour or so, then went and holed up in there without so much as a by-your-leave. Something's off about that girl, mark my words."

His father heaved himself off the couch and coughed heartily from the effort. "What did your mother want to see you about?"

Reed hadn't taken a step, hadn't even removed his coat. He watched his father go to the kitchen area and fetch a glass of water, which he drained in one go. Angus looked smaller and older now in the wee small hours of the morning, with his shirt rumpled and gray stubble dotting his chin.

"Well?" he demanded belligerently when Reed failed to respond.

Reed felt curiously light and empty. His mother had been keeping her secret for decades now. Reed didn't feel like he could be the one to tell it. "You'll have to ask her," he said, drifting toward Ellery's door.

"What? Reed, come on, now. Tell me what she said."

Reed ignored him. He didn't have the energy to fight anymore. He raised his hand to knock on her door but hesitated at the last second, swaying on his feet. She had every right to refuse him entry, but he wasn't sure he could stand it right now if she did.

"Reed, listen to me. I need to know what she said! Reed?"

The door flew open with Reed still standing there, his hand poised to knock. Ellery's dark hair was mussed, but her eyes were clear of sleep. "I saw your feet," she said, pointing at the floor. "Come in."

He staggered into her bedroom and shed his coat, throwing it in the direction of the nearest chair. His father was still yelling something outside in the living room, but Ellery had closed the door on him and Reed wasn't paying attention, anyway. He collapsed face-first on her bed without waiting for an invitation. The room whirled around him like he had a head full of booze, but the alcohol had worn off hours ago.

Ellery went around to the other side of the bed and took a cautious perch against the headboard, her knees drawn up to her chest. "Are you okay?" she asked softly.

Reed peeked up at her with one eye. "She knew. She's known the whole time."

"Oh, Reed." Ellery's voice welled with sympathy, and she stretched a hand across the bed, almost but not quite touching him. "I'm sorry."

He closed his eyes. "They act like I'm the murderer," he said into the pillows. "That I'm the one determined to wreck our happy family history. Camilla can't be saved, so we should save ourselves."

"You're not a murderer," she assured him reasonably.

"They said they've been protecting me." The implication, of course, was that he couldn't be bothered to do the same for them.

"Maybe they could say that back then and make someone believe it. Not anymore."

"Not anymore," he repeated, sounding unconvinced even to his own ears. He knew he should be getting back across the way to his own bed, but he couldn't seem to make his eyes open again. "Sorry," he said. "Is it too late?"

He felt the covers come up around him, and Ellery's voice floated somewhere over his head. "No, it's not late at all."

13

Ellery lay on her side with one arm tucked beneath her head, watching Reed sleep in the half-light shining in on them from the open bathroom door. She had not slept in the same bed with anyone since her brother, Daniel, was alive, when she used to crawl under the covers with him because it was the only thing that kept his chills at bay. The cancer and the chemo took turns whittling away at him until Danny was no more than a sack of bones, unable to keep warm no matter how many blankets they piled atop him. Ellie had lent him her body heat for a few hours, happy to be able to grant this small service, while they told each other stories about what they would do when they grew up and Danny was finally not sick anymore.

"I want to go to the African desert and paint the sun," Danny had said. He'd continued sketching as the cancer worsened, but his only access to paints and easels was at school, which he no longer attended. "They have colors there we don't see around here—umber and crimson and toffee brown. I bet it's never cold there. I bet if you sit really still you can hear the elephants walking in the distance, feel the rumble of their feet."

"I want to buy a house in Old Town," Ellery had replied. "Something tall, with big windows and a private roof deck where you can see the lake. Somewhere like where Oprah lives." She didn't want to go to far-off lands to make her fortune; she wanted to prove herself here on her home turf where everyone could see. "We'd have barbecues on the weekend, as much as you could eat, and we'd sit up there stuffing our faces and playing music as loud as we wanted because no one's on the other side of the walls."

Danny's answering scoff was low and raspy: "That'll cost you more than a million dollars. Where are you getting that kind of money?"

"I don't know. I'll find a way. Maybe I'll write my memoir. Or I'll write yours—the heartbreaking but true story of the courageous boy who beat cancer. People love those sappy medical dramas about sick kids, right? They make movies out of 'em, like that one about the boy in the bubble."

"That boy died." Danny's tone was darkly ironic.

"Oh. Guess I'll have to hit the Powerball then," she'd said, and he'd thumped her with a pillow.

Later, after Coben took her and then she came back, she wouldn't climb in bed with Danny anymore. He'd been in the hospital more than he was home, but even when they were back in their old bedroom together she couldn't take the feel of it, the press of flesh up against her body. She couldn't close her eyes with someone breathing that near. She'd huddled in her bed, squeezing herself into the tightest ball possible, while Danny's weakened voice pleaded with her from far across the room: *Abby? Come on. You can tell me what happened. It's okay; I can take it. Just come over here and talk to me . . .*

Tomorrow, Ellery would think as she hid her face in the pillow. Tomorrow in the daylight she'd find the strength to go over there and tell her big brother what Coben had done to her. But she never could get the words out, and then Danny went to the hospital that last time and there were no tomorrows left. She'd had both beds to herself, but neither one would let her sleep. Instead, she'd listened to music through her headphones and watched the night city from her window, how the shadows could swallow up whole buildings and make them disappear.

Once she'd gotten out Danny's sketches and found a pencil drawing that might have been Africa. It showed a gentle sloping plain of wavy sand and a watering hole where several large birds and a zebra had gathered for a drink. Ellery had bought a set of cheap drugstore watercolors and tried to paint it, tried to conjure the vivid hues that he'd described to her, but the result turned into a runny mud-brown mess.

Reed let out a sigh in his sleep and flung one arm above his head. Ellery shrank even farther to her side, a continent of space between them. She could get up and go to his room to sleep, but that meant facing Angus Markham, who sat camped out in their living room. Besides, Reed had sought out her company on purpose. He wanted her there. If she left him now, he might never come back. She drew a shuddering breath and shut her eyes experimentally, only to have them spring back open when Reed shifted and changed the tilt of the bed. She leaped up and escaped to the bathroom, where she splashed water on her face and ignored the thundering cadence of her heart. *You've faced down murderers and survived okay,* she told herself as the water dripped from her chin. *You can spend the night on one side of the mattress with him.*

She felt her way back into the darkened room, hugging the wall. Reed did not move from his place under the covers, blissfully unaware of the war going on inside her head. She approached and receded from the bed several times until she finally made contact again, lightly touching the mattress. Reed didn't stir. Gingerly, she lowered herself to the far edge of the bed, keeping a watchful eye on Reed the entire time. His shoulder rose in a steady, soothing rhythm. Ellery turned her back to him and squeezed her eyes shut. She willed her body to relax, forcing down one muscle group at a time until her own breathing slowed. She would not sleep, but she could float. She could take herself away from here to the hot, sandy African desert with its golden sky and waving sage-colored grasses—a place she could only see in her dreams.

* * *

The trill of the hotel phone startled her, and her entire body seized up, instantly on alert. The phone rang only once before falling silent again, and Ellery sagged back into the pillows. Bright light spilled in from around the curtains, signaling that day had long ago arrived. Reed squinted at her across the bed. "What was that?" he asked about the phone call. His hair stood up on end, making him look like a confused hedgehog.

"Search me. But I guess we could've used the wake-up call." The glowing numbers of the bedside clock read: 9:06. Ellery rose in one smooth motion, easing from beneath the covers so neatly that it was almost like she'd never been there at all. She dug her bare toes into the thick carpet and lingered by the bathroom door, using it as a shield between her and Reed. "Think your father is still out there waiting for us?"

They both paused to listen, and sure enough, the shuffle of slow, heavy footsteps could be heard outside in the living area. "Great," Reed muttered, flopping back into the pillows again.

"You want me to get rid of him?"

Reed stared straight up at the ceiling, glassy eyed and defeated. "How?"

She shrugged. "He's scared shitless or he wouldn't be out here trying to stop you. What's he afraid of? Everyone finding out about the affair and the murder and his role in the whole mess. We could tell him that you'll go to the sheriff with the story, or better yet, the press, unless he goes home and leaves you alone. I bet he'd leave a vapor trail a mile wide, he'd be gone so fast."

Reed pondered her words for a moment and then sat up in bed. "No," he said. "Not yet."

"Suit yourself. I'm going to take a shower." In the polished bathroom, she stood under the rain-head spray with her eyes closed, the way she had after it happened and she couldn't seem to feel clean. Her mother had hectored her about the rising water bill as Ellery showered three or four times a day, always with her eyes shut tight so she wouldn't see the scars. It had taken her years to adjust to this new, cracked version of herself, to forgive her body for what it had endured. Even now she sometimes startled at a glimpse of her arm or collarbone from an unexpected angle.

When she couldn't hide in the bathroom any longer, she slipped on jeans and a navy-blue sweater, towel dried her hair, and reluctantly rejoined the Markham men in the living room. They each had coffee—strong, from the smell of it— but Reed had put the kettle on for tea. He sat at the kitchen island, his back to his father, while Angus poked around in the old murder files.

"Jesus," he said when he got to the pictures. "I can't believe you can sleep at night with this stuff lying out here."

"I've seen worse," Reed said without turning around.

Ellery regarded him as she steeped her tea bag. The men, at least, could put the pictures down if they wanted. They could walk away.

"What's your plan for today?" she asked Reed in a low voice, her gaze still on Angus across the room. Reed's father hadn't been so put off by the pictures that he'd stopped snooping through the files.

"First," Reed began, but he didn't get to finish his thought because someone rapped loudly at their door. He and Ellery exchanged a look that affirmed they had not been expecting anyone, while Angus started charging toward the door. "Wait, I've got it." Reed intercepted his father and checked the peephole. He rocked back on his heels, looking torn, but eventually he pulled open the door. "Mama. How lovely to see you again."

Marianne Markham strode in without a backward glance, followed by Rufus Guthrie, who was looking stooped and vaguely hungover. "I've brought bagels and muffins," she announced, holding out two paper sacks. Her Southern accent was soft, like her son's, rather than pronounced like her husband's. "Reed, could you please rustle us up some plates and napkins?"

Reed just stood holding the door open while Angus sputtered from across the room, waving his arms, "Mary, I—what on God's green earth are you doing out here?"

She tucked a fallen lock of blond hair behind her ear, revealing sizable diamond studs, and pierced her husband with an ice-blue stare. "The same thing you are, I presume—trying to save our son from your mistakes." She turned to Reed. "Is that coffee I smell?"

Reed took this second hint and shut the door. He set about fixing a cup of coffee for his mother while Ellery took out a small stack of white porcelain plates. She kept her head down and willed herself to blend into the background, but Marianne was already on the move. "You must be Ellery," she said, stopping on the other side of the counter directly in front of Ellery.

Ellery raised her eyes and nodded once. "Yes, ma'am."

The woman's smile was forced but bright. "Reed has told me so much about you."

Ellery glanced in Reed's direction, but he was pretending not to notice. "He has?" She wondered if his mother had read Reed's book about the Coben case and concluded she probably had. A mother who would fly across the country to bring baked goods to her errant son would certainly take a couple of hours to read his bestselling book. Ellery forced herself not to yank down her sleeves to hide the scars, but Reed's mother didn't seem to be looking for them.

"He tells me you have a dog. A basset hound?"

Ellery smiled at the thought of Bump and felt a pang at missing him. "Yes, Bump's a hound, through and through— but I'm surprised Reed mentioned him. He can't stand the animal."

"Is that so? Well, you'd never know it from the amount of time he—and you—come up in conversation."

Behind her, Angus and Rufus were sharing some form of argument that was quickly growing in volume. "That doesn't give you the right to go meddling around in my affairs," Angus growled, bringing all other conversation in the room to a halt.

Guthrie's red face matched his thinning hair. "You weren't getting anywhere with him! I figured maybe it was time to give someone else a try. That's what you pay me for, isn't it?—solving your problems."

"This ain't your job, Rufus, and it ain't your business. This is my family."

"Yeah? How's this for size? If I do my job, then you get to keep your family. And maybe your job, too—or have you forgotten about the campaign you have going on back home?"

"Oh, screw the campaign right now! Believe it or not, I get to have a life off the podium."

"A life I've helped make possible, and don't you forget that," Rufus shot back. "Your son is out here trying to ruin all of us, so yeah, I'm gonna do whatever it takes to rein him back in before your whole existence—and mine—turns to shit!"

"And you think you've made things better by dragging her into it?" Angus gestured at his wife, who rolled her eyes and turned around again.

"Please. Rufus didn't drag me anywhere. I've been in it with you since the day I said, 'I do.'" She smiled at Ellery. "Would you be a dear and hand me that butter knife?"

Ellery looked down at the rounded edge of the knife and figured it was safe to hand it over. Marianne accepted the knife and began splitting open a whole wheat bagel as though this were just a normal family breakfast.

"You had no right," Angus said, still fuming. He pointed a long finger at Rufus. "None."

"When you gave me the money to give that girl, it became my right. This is your goddamned mess, Angus. I'm just trying to help you clean it up." He stalked off toward the balcony and leaned his palms against the glass doors, glaring out at the city below like it was somehow responsible.

Angus wilted at his departure, the fight going out of him. He kicked at a throw pillow and muttered a curse before joining the rest of his family at the kitchen island. "How long have you known?" he asked Marianne gruffly as he lowered himself onto a stool.

She barely looked at him. "Our son is out here seeking answers about that girl," she said as she stabbed at her bagel with small, furious swipes. "I suggest you tell him whatever he wants to know so we can all go home."

Angus threw his hands in the air. "He wants to know who killed her! If I knew that, don't you think I would've said something a long time ago?"

She fixed him with a hard look. "I don't know. Would you? Think hard, Angus. You might not get another chance at this—anything you know about that girl and what happened to her, now's the time to tell it."

The senator rubbed his grizzled chin and sighed. "It was one night," he said quietly. "More than forty years ago. I barely knew her. She'd gotten herself into a rough situation in the room next to mine—a bunch of drunk yahoos who wouldn't take no for an answer. I helped 'em see reason, and Camilla and I got to talking. It's not like I planned it."

"The drunk yahoos," Reed interjected. "Did you know their names?"

Angus shook his head. "They went back into the room

238

and I didn't hear another peep. In the morning, I dropped Camilla back at her apartment just as the sun was coming up. I didn't get the sense that anyone was following us, if that's what you're thinking. Those guys from next door were probably still belly-up, sawing logs, at that hour. I watched her go into her apartment building and then I drove away. I didn't see her again, didn't even think much about her until she called to say she was pregnant."

There was a heavy silence, and it felt to Ellery like no one wanted to look in Reed's direction. She shifted fractionally so she stood just a little bit closer to him. "That's it?" Reed said. "She didn't say anything about Billy Thorndike or anyone who might have been threatening her?"

"No, nothing like that. She talked about her mama, who'd passed on from cancer not too long ago. We'd just lost your grandmama the year before, so I kind of understood what she was feeling." He paused, looking guilty at the memory, and Ellery saw Marianne's mouth tighten. "She seemed sweet . . . a little lost, like she'd come here with big plans and when they didn't work out she was having trouble figuring out what to do next. I told her that her mama was watching over her, that she'd help her find her way."

They all sat with those words for a long minute, imagining what Mama Flores might have seen if indeed she'd had some sort of window down from the heavens. Angus took a deep breath and nudged aside a breakfast plate.

"I don't know who killed her," he said to Reed. "I wish I could help you; I sincerely do. All I can tell you is that it wasn't

239

me who hurt Camilla. Whoever did that to her, they were here before I got here, and they stayed behind when I left. I know because Rufus has kept an eye on the case. The police have investigated on and off but could never close it out. If they're calling it over, well then, maybe you should, too."

"It's not over," Reed said in clipped tones. "Someone slashed our tires last night. Someone who clearly doesn't want any fresh investigation. Maybe the same someone who slashed Camilla's tires a few nights before she died."

Marianne glared at her husband. "You see? This is what I'm talking about. Your foolishness is going to get him killed."

"Did you not hear a word I just said? I just told the boy to leave it alone!"

Reed put his hands down on the counter and leaned forward between his parents. "Don't you see? It means we're getting close."

"To someone who did that!" Angus pointed back at the table where the pictures of Camilla's body lay. "If you've got a fresh lead, give it to the sheriff. Let him handle it."

"The sheriff says the case is closed. He won't be investigating further."

"Then maybe that's a sign you shouldn't, either," Marianne said, siding with her husband this time.

Ellery drifted away from the bickering, across the room to where Rufus Guthrie stood frowning over the pile of old evidence. She joined him without saying anything, and they stood like that, staring at the grimy files. "She was a little bit of a thing," Rufus said gruffly. "Only came up about yay high." He indicated the center of his chest. "She must've put up an awful fight to have ended up like this."

"You're the one who made the payoff, then," Ellery said, and he nodded.

"Twenty-five Gs, all in cash. I had it wrapped up inside a small duffel bag, hidden under an old sweatshirt. I stood in that apartment, dripping sweat, while she counted out every dollar." He shook his head as if amazed. "Her kid was sitting there in some baby bouncer, watching us the whole time with these huge dark eyes. I remember thinking he looked like her, not Angus, and wondering again if maybe we were paying for someone else's kid."

"You weren't," Ellery said tartly.

"I know it now. Back then . . ." He shrugged.

He lapsed into silence and Ellery bit her lip, debating whether to push further. "Who do you think killed her?" she asked finally.

Rufus reached down and pulled out one of the old Polaroids from the stack with such surety that he must have already known where it was. He and Ellery regarded the picture of Camilla and Angie, arms around each other, dolled up for a night on the town and smiling for the camera. "I don't know who did it," Rufus said, tapping the picture against his large palm. "But if it were me? I'd talk to this one."

"Angie? Why?"

"She took about one look at the body and split town. Maybe she was spooked by what she found, or maybe she

241

had reason to think she might be in danger, too—on account of she knew who did it."

"If she knew who did it, why wouldn't she just tell the police?"

He shrugged again and put down the picture. "Maybe she was too scared."

"Of the police?" Ellery recalled what Thorndike had told them about Giselle Hardiman's murder. The cops didn't investigate too hard because they knew what they might find—like proof that Giselle had customers in uniform. "We'd like to talk to Angie," she told Guthrie. "But she moved to L.A. and Reed hasn't been able to track her down yet."

"She started up a little dance studio near the Valley," Guthrie replied. "I can give you the address if you want it."

Ellery tried not to let the shock register on her face. "You've been tracking her all this time?"

"I haven't set eyes on the woman in more than forty years," Guthrie answered, looking affronted. "Angus asked me to stay informed on the case, and so that's what I did. No reason to go stirring up trouble where there ain't none." He added this last bit pointedly, but Ellery did not rise to the bait.

"We'll take that address."

Ellery left Reed to his dysfunctional family reunion to escape outside for a quick run. Reed said he would ask the hotel security detail for the surveillance footage from their garage in case the individual who had slashed their tires was visible on the video, but neither of them held out a lot of hope. The garage was filled with cars, and it would be easy for someone to duck down between them and puncture the tires. Reed also wanted to go to Los Angeles to track down Angie Rivera, which meant they would need a new vehicle. For her part, Ellery favored any itinerary that let them be free of Reed's parents and the frosty atmosphere that surrounded them. She had a niggling idea, though, that would require following up on yet another old name, this one a byline from the *Las Vegas Review-Journal*. All the articles about Giselle Hardiman's murder had been written by one journalist, a man named Bruce Carr. If the sheriff didn't care to talk about the case, maybe Bruce would.

Preoccupied by this thought, Ellery burst through the automated sliding front doors, ready to run, only to have a man's voice draw her up short. "Abigail!" After all these years, the sound of that name still made her freeze. She knew even before she turned around what she would find because she'd been hearing that voice in her dreams for twenty years. She balled her hands into fists and held her breath as she turned to face her father.

"Abby," he said with relief. "It's finally you. I've been looking everywhere."

John Hathaway looked surprisingly unchanged. He'd always resembled a mountain man, with his strong shoulders, broad face, and full beard, and the plaid shirt he wore only added to the illusion. He had put on a few pounds around his middle and his beard was half-gray, but he certainly didn't appear to be a man on the edge of death. When he took a step toward her, she took a step back. "What are you doing here? How did you find me?"

"Your friend with the dogs told me you were out here, and so when I got to town I just started calling all the hotels and asking to be put through to Ellery Hathaway's room. This is the only one that rang through."

"You shouldn't have come. I have nothing to say to you." *Go,* her brain ordered her, and so she went. She turned around to run, but he immediately hurried after her.

"You don't have to talk; you only have to listen. Abby, please . . ."

She didn't even slow down. "My name's not Abby."

"I'm sorry. Ellery. I just always think of that as your mother's last name, or your grandparents'."

Stop talking about them! she wanted to yell at him. *Stop acting like you're part of the family!* She trained her gaze straight ahead and picked up her pace. Huffing now, her father tried to keep up with her.

"I only need a few minutes of your time. Just . . . just hear me out. Then you can go back to hating me if that's what you want."

"I don't hate you. I don't think of you at all."

The lie landed its mark, as he abruptly dropped out of the race, stunned by her words. She felt him growing smaller in the distance and lengthened her stride. The hard, mean feeling inside her throbbed with each slap of her footsteps on the pavement.

"Run all you want to!" he hollered after her. "I'll be waiting here when you get back!"

Tears blurred her eyes, but she kept going. Whatever he wanted to say to her, it could never make up for two decades of silence. She ran away from the main boulevard, where the crowds still lingered, and down the side streets that looked more everyday, with their array of fast-food joints, car washes, and souvenir shops. She ran until her calves ached and her lungs felt like fire, until she had to bend over to catch her breath. Reed would be wondering where the hell she got to, so she had to turn back, even if that meant facing her father again. Slowly, she started the return route, taking it at one-quarter speed.

True to his word, John Hathaway stood sentry at the front of the hotel waiting for her. Ellery wiped her brow with the forearm of her sweatshirt and went to stand in front of him. "I could have you arrested for stalking."

"I'm your father, not some stalker."

"I haven't seen my father in twenty years. You might understand if I don't remember quite what he looks like." She went into the hotel and he followed her through the lobby.

"Okay," he said, holding out his hands to her. "Okay, I deserved that. I'm sorry. I really am. I meant to call, I promise you. But—"

"But what?" She whirled on him, furious. "You forgot our phone number? For twenty years?"

"I wanted to wait until I had a place, until I was set up good. I wanted you and Danny to be able to come visit. But it took longer than I thought, getting established. I know it sounds lame and phony now, but I promise I intended to call."

She stared at him. "Twenty years," she said finally, and she walked away again.

He scrambled after her. "I know. There's no excuse. I'm not here to offer any, because I know there's nothing I can say that will make it right again. I'm sorry. I'm sorry for you and for Danny."

"He died!" She halted again, almost yelling the words at him. He cowered back under the force of her anger, and the man and woman at the front desk gave them concerned looks. Ellery no longer cared who heard her. "He died and you didn't even show up for the funeral!"

Her father's gray eyes, so like her own, welled up with tears. He wrung his hands together. "I know. Your mother told me when I called. I—I'm so sorry, honey. I didn't know he was sick."

"That's because you walked out and never looked back! You didn't give a crap about us, so I don't understand why you think I should listen to a damn thing you have to say now. Whatever apologies you have, whatever regrets you want to unload, take them somewhere else. I'm not interested."

She stormed over to the elevators and stabbed at the button. In her peripheral vision, she saw her father shuffle over and stop a few feet away. "You have every right to hate me," he said quietly. "I hate myself sometimes when I think on it, how I left you kids. Like I said, I've got no excuse. So much time passed that I convinced myself the pair of you were better off without me."

Ellery turned to glare at him. "Maybe we were."

The elevator doors slid opened and her father surged forward again, grabbing her arm. "Wait," he said, his voice desperate.

She shook him free. "Never touch me."

"I'm not here because of me," he said in a rush. "I'm here for her." He held up his cell phone, which showed a picture of a blond, smiling girl who appeared to be about fourteen years of age. She had braces on her teeth and freckles across the bridge of her nose, and there was something about her that felt eerily familiar. "Her name is Ashley," he said, still holding the phone toward her. "She's your sister."

The elevator doors slid closed again as Ellery failed to get inside. "What?"

"Please, let me explain. Just for a few minutes?" He held out his arm toward a nearby tufted bench. "If you hear everything I have to say and you want me to go away again, I will."

Ellery felt her body moving before she'd mentally agreed to go with him, but she let herself follow him to the bench and take a seat. Up close, she could see the wrinkles at the corners of his eyes, the kind you get from laughing, and the steam rose up inside her again. "Talk," she commanded darkly. "I don't have all day."

"I'll keep it short, okay? If you have questions, just ask me." He took a breath. "When I left, I headed for Detroit because a buddy of mine said there was a guy there looking for truckers who could help him move a bunch of electronics up over the border into Canada in a hurry. He said he'd taken on a bigger contract than he could deliver with his regular personnel so he needed extra drivers. There was the promise of full-time work if we delivered. Turns out, of course, he didn't exactly have his paperwork in order to ship that stuff across the border. I found that out the hard way and ended up doing six months as a result. It wasn't hard time or nothing, but I got injured working in the boiler room—the thing exploded on us, and the wall caved in on my right side. I was okay, but it messed up my knee pretty good, and that's when I got sent to the VA hospital and I met Shirley. We got to talking, and she told me to look her up when I got out." He smiled faintly. "So I did."

"Fascinating, all of it. What about Ashley?"

"Ashley came along two years later. She's fifteen now, and real sick."

Ellery did the math. This girl had been born fifteen years ago, which was one year after Coben and six months after they'd buried Daniel. "Sick," she repeated. "With what?"

Her father swallowed visibly. "Leukemia," he said, his head bowed. "Sounds like similar to the kind that got Daniel."

Ellery looked beyond him to the people passing through the lobby, smiling and chatting and dragging suitcases. "I'm sorry," she said, but the words felt hollow.

"Maybe, maybe it's my fault, huh? If both of 'em got it. I

got bad genes or something." He shook his head. "I wished I would've known."

"Maybe not. Maybe it's just bad luck."

He didn't argue one way or another, just sat there with his own thoughts. "I wasn't there to help Daniel," he said at length. "And I wasn't there to help you."

Ellery felt her ears burn. Where had he been when she was trapped in the closet? Jail? Screwing some other woman named Shirley? "No," she said harshly. "You weren't there."

He nodded sadly. "I'm sorry for that. I'd go back and change it if I could. Meantime, I'm here for Ashley. She needs bone marrow to cure her cancer, and neither Shirley nor I is a match. I was hoping you might agree to get tested."

"I got tested for Daniel. It didn't work."

"But this is another chance. Maybe you'll be a match this time."

Her blood ran cold at the thought. She remembered the long, silent dinner they'd had the night the test results came back, the three of them trying to choke down the steak and potatoes her mother had bought in hopes of a celebration. Ellery'd still had the bruise on her arm from the blood draw, but it was nothing compared to the growing shadows under Danny's eyes. "No," she blurted out, hopping up from the bench as if it had stung her. "I can't."

Her father looked stricken as he rose, too. "Please just think about it."

"No, I'm sorry. It—it wouldn't work, anyway." How dare he come back now, not to make amends, not to throw himself at her feet and beg forgiveness, but to remind her of her worst failure and then demand she try again.

"Just try. Take the test. That's all I'm asking. I did everything wrong, I know, but Ashley doesn't deserve this. She—she's a great kid—"

"Daniel was a great kid!" Ellery cut in angrily. "It didn't even matter!" Dammit, she was crying again. She fled for the elevator, and mercifully, it was there. She ran inside and the doors slid shut on her father's pleading face.

"Abby, please, honey. I'll do anything . . ."

Alone inside, she covered her face with her hands and slid to the floor, shaking. Her father came back at last, not for her, but for some other daughter, some girl he'd loved enough to raise. Maybe it was his fate to lose this one, too, and now maybe he'd finally understand. The black hole he'd created with his absence never went away. It was devouring them all one by one, and no one could escape.

14

Reed was pacing the length of the hotel suite, alternately checking his phone and the windows, when at last the door clicked open and Ellery slid inside. "Where were you?" he demanded as she slunk toward her bedroom. "I've been calling you for over an hour! Two more minutes of no contact and I'd have been ringing up Sheriff Ramsey to go look for you."

"Sorry, my phone was off."

"Are you okay? Did something happen?" He'd checked with hotel security in her absence, and as he'd expected, there was nothing usable on the black-and-white digital recording from the parking garage. Their SUV was barely visible in the upper right-hand corner, and the video didn't show any other cars loitering near it, nor anyone on foot approaching the vehicle. Whoever had slashed their tires had attacked from the rear, staying low to the ground.

"Nothing happened," Ellery said, but Reed didn't quite

believe her. She looked unharmed on the surface, but her pale face appeared clammy and drawn, not invigorated from a run in the brisk morning air. She marched to her room and shut the door with an authoritative jolt that did not invite further inquiry. Reed stared blankly at the white slab of wood for a few moments and then lowered himself onto the nearest sofa, his eyes drifting shut in fatigue. He'd been trying to reach her for the past hour with no success, and now that she was back, their communication level hadn't improved one iota. Like her phone, Ellery was in "off" mode.

Reed patted his pant pockets until he found a crumpled packet of ibuprofens, and he swallowed one dry. His head felt like it was up against a board. Normally he might go knock on her door and try to cajole her into telling him . . . whatever it was she wasn't telling him. But right then, he simply lacked the wherewithal to engage. Ellery possessed an instinctual reticence, a silent wall behind which she secreted details both large and small, from her favorite foods to her childhood memories to, on occasion, the fact that maybe someone was trying to kill her. Reed understood this as a natural reaction to that nightmarish time when Coben had indeed tried to kill her. Coben took her body and then the hungry press had clamored for everything else. *Give them nothing* had been Ellery's survival strategy, and she'd practiced it without fail ever since.

Reed had traversed the thorny darkness with her enough times that he'd glimpsed the garden behind the wall, seen the flashes of beauty that she kept there, as well as the topiary monsters that swayed and rattled in memory's breeze. The raw power he felt in those rare moments of connection with Ellery always kept him coming back, eager to find his way in, but the path to reach her seemed to change with each approach. *Touch me, but stop. Look, but not too much.* On his best days, Reed found the quicksilver challenge exciting. Times like this, when he looked upon her locked door and felt her forceful silence radiating from behind it, he asked himself: *Is this what you really want?*

When her door opened, he sat up again and saw she was ready to go, with fresh clothes, her hair knotted, and her roller bag all packed. She looked past him to the empty suite, which she surveyed with a small frown, as if seeing it for the first time. "Where are your parents?"

"I asked them to leave," he said, forcing himself to his feet.

She looked surprised. "And they just . . . did that?"

"I used the word 'please,'" he replied, deadpan. He went to the kitchen and retrieved a large paper cup, intent on taking some coffee to go. In reality, he'd had another protracted argument with his parents before they had agreed to depart the premises. Only when he'd insisted that the only way he might one day trust them again was if they stopped trying to interfere with his search for the truth did Angus and Marianne reluctantly leave him alone.

His mother had lingered at the door, cupped his chin in her hand. "You've been gone from this place your whole life," she'd said. "Whatever truth is here, it isn't yours."

Reed had said nothing.

She stretched up and kissed his cheek fiercely, her lipstick on him like a wound. "Come home soon," she'd counseled as she left at last. "Your family needs you."

Instead, Reed planned to travel yet farther away. Meeting Angie, he felt, would be the closest he would get to finding his mother's side of the family. Camilla had no living relatives other than himself. Even if Angie had no clues into Cammie's murder, Reed hoped she would be able to bring the woman back to life for him in a way that no one else could.

Ellery stood at the door, zipping something into her bag, avoiding eye contact with him. She looked slumped and miserable, and he regretted dragging her out here on this fruitless excavation of his past. He grudingly gave her an out. "If you like," Reed said, clearing his throat, "I can drop you at the airport and you can catch a flight back to Boston. You've already given up a bunch of your time, more than I deserve. Of course, if you're willing to come to L.A., I would value an outsider perspective."

"An outsider? That's what I am?" She straightened in a hurry, her mouth a thin line. He'd misstepped again.

"An impartial observer," he clarified. She made an annoyed chuffing sound and pointedly looked away, toward the couch they'd rolled around on the night before. Reed felt his ears warm. "I just thought," he finished lamely, "that maybe you wanted to go home."

"On the contrary." She regarded him with a cool gaze. "I'd prefer to keep moving."

Reed stared back at her. Eventually, the case would end,

one way or another. He'd have to go back to his home and she would go to hers. Whatever future was coming at them, they wouldn't be able to outrun it forever. "Okay then," he said, grabbing his coffee. "Let's go."

The drive out I-15 quickly put civilization in the rearview mirror as the barren landscape of the Mojave Desert took over the scenery. Patches of scrub grass broke up endless stretches of brown dirt, while the mountains carved an uneven profile against the stark blue sky. Miles and miles of asphalt cut an almost straight line through the wind-worn desert. The periodic ditches, nondescript dips in the ground, had been given odd names to break up the monotony: Bird Ditch, Opah Ditch, Midway Ditch. *Midway,* Reed had to wonder, *to what?* They passed a defunct water park, with its fossil-like metal skeleton and desiccated pools. It looked like something from an old Western ghost town or the beginnings of a horror movie. Occasional crooked Joshua trees, with their tufted ends, flashed by as Reed kept pace with the rest of the desert traffic, going 85 mph to get out of nowhere, fast.

Ellery didn't say much during the four-hour journey, just kept her face turned toward the window, her knees drawn up and her gaze focused somewhere far beyond the horizon. Her interest perked up when his cell phone rang over the car's speakers, a number too familiar to Reed, but he hit the button to accept the call. "Kimmy," he said, trying to smile as he said his youngest sister's name. "How are you?"

Her voice, sounding uncertain and tinny, came through the speakers. "Reed? I got an email this morning from the DNA testing service—you know the one we did at Christmas? It wanted to alert me to a new connection."

Reed saw immediately where this was heading and bit back a curse. He'd been so worried about what the DNA results told him that he hadn't stopped to consider his sisters might see the same results. "Yes," he said carefully. "I know."

"It says you're either my uncle or my half brother," Kimmy continued. "Reed, what on earth?"

"I'm your brother," he replied, skimming the wheel with his fingers. "Just—just like always. But yes. It seems that Dad is my biological father."

Ellery slouched farther in her seat, as if trying to disappear from the conversation. On the other end of the line, Kimberly said nothing. After a mile of silence, Reed tried again. "Kimmy? Are you still there?"

"I don't understand. You were born after all of us."

"Yes." The math alone painted Angus as a sinner. He'd slept with Cammie when he had a wife and three daughters waiting for him back home.

"Your mother . . . I thought she was murdered in Las Vegas."

"Yes," he said, taking the freeway exit that would cut them toward L.A. "That's still true. Mama and Dad adopted me after her death."

"So Daddy slept with a hooker? And then knocked her up? My God, what will Mama say when she finds out about this?"

"She wasn't a hooker," Reed said tersely, dodging the increasingly heavier traffic. "She was a waitress. Look, I know it's a shock. I was shocked, too, when I saw the results." He hesitated with the next part of his news. "You don't have to worry about Mama. She knows. Apparently, she always has."

"What!?" Kimmy's shout was so loud that Reed nearly slammed on the brakes in response. Ellery winced and covered her face with her hands. "They both knew this entire time and they never said anything?"

Finally, someone who shared his outrage. Reed allowed himself a mirthless grin. "Look at it this way," he told her. "We would've all gone to our graves none the wiser, if you hadn't asked us to take that DNA test."

"I can't believe this! I can't believe they'd lie like that, every day, straight to our faces. For forty years! Remember the pictures they took of all of us at the courthouse steps, the day your adoption went through? I was scared the judge was going to say no, that he'd take you away. I made Mama get out those papers every damn day for a month. I wanted to make sure they were real, that no one could ever take you away again. What the hell was the point of that charade, anyway?"

"I think you know."

"Daddy's job," she said bitterly. "Always first, never last."

"Mama and Daddy were right about how it would've looked, especially back then. The story would have ruined him. A baby from the wrong side of the sheets—with a brown-skinned teenager from Las Vegas, no less."

"Don't talk like that. That's not who you are."

"It is. It always has been. I just know more of the details now."

"I still can't believe Mama and Daddy did this to us. I can't believe they hid a secret this big, right in the middle of our family."

Reed faltered, feeling the shame of his beginnings. "They believed it didn't matter precisely how the family was forged," he said cautiously. "We're related just the same."

"Of course it matters! It matters because we all have to wonder what else they haven't told us. What else aren't they saying?"

Reed gripped the wheel. He couldn't take any more secrets. "I—I don't know. You'll have to ask them."

"Yeah?" Kimmy's voice was low and threatening. "You can bet I will."

When Reed reached for the button to hang up with Kimmy, he saw his hand was shaking. Ellery must have noticed, too, because she spoke to him for the first time in more than two hundred miles. "You're wrong, you know. You're not just some bastard baby they tried to cover up."

Reed appreciated her efforts to try to make him bigger than he actually was, but he couldn't fight biology. "The DNA doesn't lie," he said finally.

Their SUV rushed across the Los Angeles city limits, hurtling him closer to his past. "No," Ellery said. "But it doesn't tell the whole truth, either."

* * *

A1 Dance Studio was located in the Silver Lake region of L.A., a northeast neighborhood anchored around an old city reservoir. The buildings that lined Hyperion Avenue were a mix of residential and commercial real estate, many of them painted raucous colors like peacock blue or sunny yellow. Squat homes stacked up in layers into the surrounding hills, all with wide windows to take advantage of the view. Tall, skinny palm trees framed the street against the hazy blue sky. Winter, and home back on the East Coast, felt a million miles away. Reed spotted the studio—a nondescript horizontal structure made of brown stucco and glass—and pulled the car to the side of the road. Glad for the cover of relentless sunshine, he put on his dark glasses.

"Well?" Ellery asked when he didn't immediately head for the door. "What are we waiting for?"

Reed had visited Los Angeles numerous times, always for work, focused on the goal of catching whatever predator was in front of him at that moment. His real life awaited him three thousand miles away, and he was always eager to return. He'd never looked at L.A. as anything more than a temporary stopover, not any place he might have belonged. It appeared foreign even now, like something from a hipster movie, but the painted Spanish-lettered signs, blooming vines, and little outside eateries with a decidedly mixed ethnic clientele stirred something in him, a longing he could not name.

Ellery tilted her head impatiently. "Are we going to go talk to her or not?"

Reed squared his jaw and gave a short nod. "Let's do it."

The glass front door gave a merry tinkle as they opened it, although the bell was entirely unnecessary in the small entry area, which boasted an empty coatrack, a water cooler, six blue plastic chairs, and a front desk. The woman behind the desk was clearly not Angie Rivera. She was both younger and Caucasian, freckled, with wide blue eyes and big hoop earrings. "Welcome," she said warmly as they entered. "How can I help you?"

"I'd like to speak to Angela Rivera," Reed said, reluctantly removing his glasses.

Her smile, if possible, grew even brighter. "You've come to the right place! Miss Angie is just finishing up the two o'clock class, if you'd care to wait a few minutes."

Reed and Ellery spent the next six minutes idling in the waiting area, taking turns studying the black-and-white pictures of young ballerinas and tap dancers on the walls. Slow, muffled piano music sounded from the back, and Reed had to smile at the pianist's efforts to emphasize the beat. *One, two, three, four . . . one, two, three, four.* Eventually, the music stopped and was replaced by happy shouts and thundering little feet as miniature ballerinas in leotards streamed into the room. The adults followed more slowly, parents chatting with one another while their daughters alternately shoved one another or took up complicated clapping games. Reed felt a pang of longing for his own small daughter, whom he missed dearly amid the chaos. Ellery meanwhile stood plastered against the wall, looking faintly terrified at the noisy herd of children.

Reed meant to reassure her with some wise parental wisdom, but at that moment Angie Rivera appeared across the room. She looked older than her picture, but no less beautiful, with her long dark hair, tawny skin softened by age, and a trim, dancer's waistline. She stopped stock-still when she saw Reed. The children and parents continued to flow out of the studio between them as they stared at each other. Finally, Reed found his voice. "Ms. Rivera," he said, taking a step forward. "My name is Reed Markham. I'm—"

"I know who you are."

They stared some more, until the last student closed the tinkling door and silence filled the room. The woman at the desk cracked first. "Miss Angie? I had a woman call about private lessons for her twelve-year-old daughter. They just moved to town and—"

"I'll call her back later," Angie said, still looking at Reed. "Thank you, Michacla." She clasped her hands together and shook her head, bemused. "I can't believe it. I can't believe it's you. Please, come back to my office where we can talk."

On the way back to the private area of the studio, Reed introduced Ellery as a friend of his, but Angie seemed to pay her no mind. She hurried to clear off two chairs and dragged the third one from around the back of her desk. They all sat so close their knees nearly touched. The walls of Angie's office were crammed end-to-end with dance pictures of a more personal sort—candid shots of her and her students, sometimes concentrating but mostly smiling—as well as ribbons, certificates, newspaper clippings, and cartoons related to dance.

Angie scooted her chair closer to Reed. She reached out impulsively to grab his hand and then stopped herself. "You were so small the last time I saw you. Look at you now, so tall, so handsome." She beamed and looked to Ellery for confirmation. "Don't you think he's handsome?"

Ellery smiled and ducked her head. Reed felt that pull inside of him again, this longing to know where he began. "Ms. Rivera," he said, but she interrupted.

"Angie. Please call me Angie." Her Spanish accent had not vanished completely with the passing years. Reed wondered if Cammie might have sounded the same, if she would look this good, if she would have been as pleased to see him.

"Angie, I'm here because the Las Vegas police are officially ceasing investigation into Camilla's murder. It will no longer be assigned to active detectives. They agreed to let me take a look at it in my capacity as an FBI investigator."

"A profiler," Angie said, swelling with pride. "I know. See?" She pointed to the wall, and Reed turned around in his seat to follow her gaze. CALLIE ALLENS FOUND ALIVE, the headline read. It was one of Reed's old cases, from around ten years ago, when he'd led the team to an abducted eight-year-old girl. Angie was still smiling at him. "I read your book, too." Her smile faded as she looked uncertainly to Ellery. "I'm sorry for that horrible mess. He was a monster."

"Yes," Ellery agreed simply. "He was."

Reed scanned the wall, noting other bits of his biography here and there, and marveled at the irony: here he'd been trying to figure out how to find Angela Rivera when she'd known exactly where he was the whole time. "You've kept tabs on me awhile," he observed.

She bit her lip, looking contrite. "I'm sorry. I hope it's okay. I worried for you a long time. You were just a baby when it happened."

"How did you find me?" The adoption papers had been sealed. Reed had a guess as to how Angie had discovered the information, but he wanted to hear her say it. Angie didn't seem eager to part with the information, however. She fidgeted with her beaded necklace and looked at the ceiling. Reed sighed and let her off the hook. "You knew my father," he supplied for her. "Didn't you?"

She nodded slowly. "Cammie told me who he was." She smoothed her hands repeatedly over her long, black skirt. "When I first got here, I had no way to know what happened to you. I—I wanted to bring you with me. I went to the hospital where they took you. They had put you in with the sick kids even though you were the picture of health. You got a crib to yourself in the corner, and all the nurses were busy with the other babies who needed them more. No one saw me slip inside." She paused to reach for the tissues on her desk, dragging the box into her lap. She plucked one out to dab at her eyes before continuing. "My heart was beating so fast that someone might catch me. I looked in your crib, and you knew me right away. You started smiling and kicking your legs. I picked you up and you grabbed my hair like you always did." She made the gesture on herself, smiling faintly. "I was thinking, maybe I could take you with me and no one would even notice. What did they care? One less problem for them to deal with."

"Why didn't you?" Reed asked softly. Another alternate reality he would never know.

Angie picked at the edge of her skirt, her eyes lowered beneath dark lashes. "I was afraid. I didn't know if I could keep myself alive, and what if something happened to you? The social worker said a nice family would adopt you." Her eyes welled up again. "She said you wouldn't remember any of it."

"You left town right after the murder," Reed said. "Why?"

"Camilla was my family. Without her, there was nothing left in Las Vegas for me. I saw what was happening. After a day went by and no one arrested Billy Thorndike, I knew they weren't going to. He could do whatever he wanted—to Cammie, to me, to the whole neighborhood. It wasn't safe to stay there."

"You believe Billy Thorndike killed Camilla."

Her dark eyes widened. "Yes. Don't you?"

"Never mind about me right now," Reed said, leaning forward. "I want to know what you saw. I want to know what happened in the days leading up to her murder."

Fear etched into the wrinkles on Angie's face, showing the hard years she'd endured. "I would've stayed if I thought I could help," she whispered. "I left because I didn't know anything. Don't you see? I'm worthless to you. I didn't see the killer. I only saw what he did."

"It must have been awful for you," Reed said solemnly. "Walking in on that."

Angie looked at her lap. "I'd been out shopping for some new clothes, having a little fun in the stores, trying on this and that. Cammie was working the late shift at the restaurant and I was going to watch Joey, so I had to be back in time for her to get changed. I got to the apartment a little after four, and nothing seemed strange until I passed the door to Cammie's apartment—hers came right before mine. The door was standing partway open, and none of us would ever do that, not in that neighborhood. So right away, I knew something was wrong."

She stopped suddenly and clenched her hands in her lap. Reed hated to press her, but he had to know more. "What happened next?" he asked gently.

Angie took a shaky breath. "I—I pushed the door all the way open and called her name. As soon as I stepped inside, I saw the place was a mess. Papers on the floor. Chair upside down, and the couch was crooked. That's why I didn't see her right away. I smelled it, though. The blood." She clutched at her throat with one hand. "I called her again and went further in the apartment, and that's when I saw her lying there with the knife still in. I knew she was dead. I—I grabbed the baby from the bedroom and ran next door to call the police."

"Did you happen to notice if the door had been tampered with?" Ellery asked.

"I don't remember. I wasn't looking too close."

"The police said it hadn't been," Reed said. "Nor the windows."

"The windows were always broken, anyways," Angie said with disgust. "The cops wouldn't know the difference."

"I'm interested in the part of your story about shopping," Reed replied. "Do you mind if I show you a picture?" He pulled out a manila envelope that contained some crime scene photos.

Angie looked wary. "Pictures of what?"

"From the apartment. But don't worry, it doesn't show Camilla."

Angie drew a shaky breath. "I don't need pictures for that. I can still see it. I see it sometimes when I don't want to—I close my eyes and I can see her lying there on the inside of my eyelids, like it's burned in forever. Other times, I've seen someone walking down the street, a woman who moves like her, or who has hair like she did, and I have to stop myself from calling out her name." She looked from Reed to Ellery, her eyes sad. "It's always a young woman, you know, that I see. Then I think: 'Stupid, she's not nineteen anymore! It can't be her.' She'd be old, like me. It's been so long since she's been gone now. I just don't see what difference it makes anymore."

Silence fell between them, and Reed held the envelope awkwardly in his hands, wondering whether to bring forth the pictures. Ellery shifted in her seat and spoke directly to Angie. "If you read Reed's book, then you must know what happened. There were hundreds of law enforcement officers working on the Coben case, some of them for years, but Reed was the one who caught him."

"Yes." Angie's reply was full of tears, but still she smiled. "I know he was a hero."

"It doesn't matter how many years have gone by or how many other officers looked at the case before," Ellery continued. "It's Reed's investigation now, and he doesn't plan to stop until he finds Camilla's killer."

Angie looked Reed over in wonder, and he tried not to shrink under the weight of the mantle Ellery had placed upon him. "Let me see the pictures," Angie said decisively, holding out her hands.

Reed gave her the picture he had in mind. "In police narrative, Camilla had also been out shopping that day. The detectives say she might have come home and surprised a burglar in the apartment. They point to these bags near the door as evidence of their theory. The clothes inside matched Camilla's size."

Angie looked at the picture and shook her head. "No, those are my bags. I dropped them when I saw what had happened to Cammie. We wore the same size, her and me. People used to think we were sisters. Cammie wasn't shopping that day. I was."

"So she didn't surprise the killer," Reed said as he took back the picture. "Maybe then she let him inside."

"No way. No way Cammie opens the door for Billy Thorndike. He'd vandalized her car, spat at her on the streets, cussing and hollering. He even threatened to kill her, but did the cops care about that? 'Nothing we can do to him,' they told us. 'Sorry. Call us if he makes a move.' Well, he made his move, and did they get him? No. They couldn't even touch him then, not when she was lying there with a knife in her. Same old sad song: 'Nothing we can do. So sorry.'"

"Cammie was dating a cop," Ellery said. "That didn't help with police attention?"

"David," Angie recalled. "He tried to help us when Billy made his threats, but we weren't on David's beat. He was just a patrol cop working across town. He did what he could to keep Cammie safe, staying at her apartment sometimes. Maybe an extra patrol car went down our street here and there. It didn't make a difference."

"Tell me about David," Reed suggested.

"Oh, he was okay, I guess. Cammie met him at the restaurant, and they hit it off. She was already pregnant, just starting to show, and that might've scared off most guys. Not David. He seemed to want the same things she did—marriage, kids. To David, Cammie was the whole package. Instant family."

"We heard he might have had a wandering eye," Ellery said.

Angie gave a delicate snort. "Wandering, all right. Wandering to Wanda, you mean?"

"Since you brought it up . . ."

"Yeah, David had a . . . what do you call it . . . a fling with Wanda on the side. I saw it happening before Cammie did, the poor girl. With the baby coming, she had a lot of other things on her mind. She didn't want to believe David would do that to her, not when they were just starting to make plans. Then she saw Wanda kissing on him out in the parking lot behind the restaurant one night, and she had to admit the truth. Well, a kind of truth. She blamed Wanda, one hundred percent. David had been lured into it, according to Cammie. He was plenty happy to go along with that version of the story."

"He wanted to stay with Cammie then?" Reed said. "He wanted to make it work?"

Angie frowned. "Sure, maybe. He said he loved her, and she loved him, and there was the baby to think of."

"And twenty-five thousand dollars," Ellery added.

Angie looked surprised, then concerned, her delicately arched eyebrows drawing together. "You know about that?"

"We know," Reed answered firmly. "What we need now is a list of everyone else who knew about that money."

"You have to understand—Cammie didn't like threatening Angus's family. She just wanted to provide for her son. That money would've meant she could move out of the neighborhood, far away from Billy Thorndike. She could get daycare, good schools."

"We're not here to condemn Cammie for her actions," Reed replied. "We just want to find out about the money."

Angie blinked rapidly, tears in her eyes again. "I spent a lot of years hating Angus Markham. I thought he was a user, one of those people who roll into town, shit all over the place, and then let someone else clean it up. I told Cammie to take him for as much money as she could. 'It's all he cares about,' I told her. 'Hit him where he can feel it.' Then about twenty years ago, I was at the library and the clerk told me they just got internet services. You can look up anything now, she said. So I sat down and tried it out. I typed in 'Angus Markham,' and there he was, with his wife, the three daughters I hadn't cared about, and you." She stopped and gave Reed a wobbly smile. "The picture was bad, but I knew it was you. The article said he'd adopted you, and I had to admit to myself that maybe I'd been wrong about him. Maybe he did care."

She looked hopefully to Reed for confirmation, but Reed pressed onward. "But back then, he made the payment. You saw the money?"

Angie's face showed a guilty flash. "I saw it."

"The shopping spree you went on that afternoon," he said. "Was it financed by Cammie?"

Angie replied with a slow nod. "We hadn't bought new clothes in so long. She said we should treat ourselves, and she gave me some cash—kind of as a thank-you for all the babysitting I was doing."

"Who else saw the money?"

"David." She stopped to think. "Me and Cammie. That's it, unless you count Angus and the man who dropped it off."

"Rufus Guthrie," Reed said.

"Yes, him." Her lips thinned with disapproval. "I didn't like that man. He acted like Cammie got pregnant on purpose, like she'd wanted the money all along. Do you know what he did when he came to drop off the payment? He put his hands on her and said with the high price she ought to toss him a freebie. She gave him a knee between the legs and shoved him out the door, yes, she did."

"Did she see him again after that?" Reed asked.

"I don't think so. There wasn't a lot of time. Three days later, she was dead." Even after all this time, she sounded bewildered at the prospect, at how it came to pass that Camilla Flores had existed and then suddenly did not.

"The money wasn't recovered after Camilla's death," Reed said.

"It wasn't?"

He shook his head. "What do you think happened to it?"

She glanced around the room, as if the money might materialize there. "The apartment was a mess, torn apart. I guess . . . I guess the killer must have found the cash and taken it."

"Or he knew it would be there all along."

Angie looked horrified. "You don't think David did this? If he wanted the money that badly, he could've just taken it. He had a key and he knew her schedule. He wouldn't have had to—" She broke off and swallowed hard. "He wouldn't have hurt her."

Someone knocked at the door before Reed could ask another question. The young woman from earlier, Michaela, stuck her head in. "I'm sorry to interrupt, but the kids are arriving for the next class. What would you like me to do?"

271

"I'll be along in a moment, thank you," Angie replied briskly, setting aside the tissue box. "I told you I wouldn't be much help," she said to Reed.

"On the contrary, you've been very helpful."

"You're just flattering an old lady." She took out a pad of paper from her desk and wrote out an address. "I would like to invite you both for dinner at my house tonight. If you have any remaining questions, we can talk about them then."

"I'd like that," Reed said as he accepted the slip of paper. "Thank you."

"No," she replied with feeling. "Thank you. All these years, I've wondered—" She broke off with a small shake of her head. "I'll see you tonight, hmm? Around seven."

"We'll be there." He tucked the paper into his breast pocket. Outside on the street, he suggested to Ellery that they bide their time at a nearby bar. "We can get a drink and a bite to eat." They hadn't stopped in their race across the desert, except for gas and coffee, leaving him feeling jittery and empty.

"Whatever," Ellery answered, which marked the first time she'd ever shown less than complete enthusiasm for food. The trend continued fifteen minutes later, when they sat under an orange umbrella with two beers and hot, crispy tortilla chips in front of them. Reed devoured the spicy salsa and homemade guacamole while Ellery halfheartedly chewed through a single chip.

"Do you mind if I give Tula a ring to say good night?" he asked.

"Suit yourself."

Reed spent the next ten minutes chatting with his six-year-old, telling her about the tiny ballerinas he had seen earlier.

"I don't want to take dance," Tula insisted. "I want to take trapeze."

"I don't think the YMCA offers classes in trapeze, sweetheart. Besides, you're too young for anything that dangerous. What about gymnastics as a start?"

"I want the trapeze. The girl in the circus we saw was only a little older than me, and she could do it."

"Yes, well, she had her parents to teach her. Your mother and I are not acrobats, I'm afraid."

"Mom has the most boringest job in the world," Tula complained. "All she does is type on her computer all day. At least you get to go places."

"Your mother's job isn't as dull as it looks." Sarit worked as a metro reporter for the *Washington Post*. "You might find you quite enjoy it when you're older."

"Daddy . . . is it true that you can grow up to be anything you want to be?"

Reed hesitated, wondering if six was old enough to handle the ugly truth. He decided not to risk it. "Yes," he declared emphatically. "If you work hard and try your best, you can do anything you put your mind to."

"Mommm!" Reed heard the phone clatter to the floor and then his daughter's whooping in the distance. "Daddy says I should take trapeze lessons!"'

Crap. He'd walked right into that one. Reed quickly clicked off the connection before his ex-wife could pick up the line and then tucked away his phone for good measure. Ellery, he noticed, hadn't touched her phone all day. "Still maintaining radio silence, I see. Afraid the dog is going to start hounding you?"

He smiled at his own pun, but Ellery didn't look amused. "My father," she said.

Reed sobered up in a hurry. "He called you again?"

She took a long time with her answer. "Worse. He showed up outside the hotel this morning. That's what took me so long this morning."

"He followed you out here? Why?"

Ellery traced a random pattern in the condensation on her glass. "Why else? He wants something from me."

"Money," Reed guessed. From the little he knew, John Hathaway was always looking to make a quick buck. He might easily have caught wind of Ellery's fame and believed it somehow transformed into dollars.

"Nothing that easy." She sat back with a sigh. "Turns out he has another kid, a daughter who's fifteen years old. She's got leukemia the same as Daniel. He wants me to get tested to see if I can be a bone marrow donor for her." He waited, and she eventually met his eyes. "I told him no."

Reed felt the horror of this immediately. If Tula were sick, he would go to the ends of the earth to make her well again. John Hathaway, he presumed, was a desperate man.

"Mom looked for him, you know," Ellery said, "when Daniel was first diagnosed. But he'd completely disappeared by then. She phoned everyone in the family and told them we needed Dad to come home. He says he never got the message, but the only way that's true is if he never went looking for the messages in the first place. He left us and he didn't look back, didn't want to have to pay money or feel guilty. Turns out, he was off making some other family. Screw the rest of us."

"You have every right to be furious with him," Reed said quietly.

"I wasn't even a match for Daniel. It probably wouldn't work this time, either."

"Maybe not."

She flicked her gaze over him. "You think I should do it."

"It's not up to me."

"Yes, but that's what you think."

He thought for a moment. "I'd want to meet her. If she's part of him, she's part of you, too."

"She's not anything to me. She's some fifteen-year-old kid living in Michigan. What do I know about fifteen-year-olds? I wasn't anything like them even when we went to school together."

"She's your sister," Reed pointed out gently.

Ellery stiffened, her eyes growing wet. She said nothing for a long time. "All these years, I told myself he left because he didn't want a family. Nothing personal. He just couldn't hack it. Turns out, he wanted a family. He just didn't want us."

Reed got up from his side and went to sit next to her. Whatever work it took to reach her this time, he wanted to do it. Cautiously, he slid his hand over to cover hers. She didn't look at him, but she didn't pull away. She tilted her face toward the sky.

"That's the truth of it," she said, her voice rough with emotion. "He didn't care if we lived or died. Why should I bother with this girl now?"

Reed felt his heart crack open, because he knew the answer to this one. "Because," he said, squeezing her, "you're not him."

15

They used the remaining hours before dinner to find a hotel, with separate rooms this time, and Ellery seemed relieved to have her own space as she disappeared behind the door and shut it with a firm click. Reed took advantage of the silence and flopped out on the center of his king-size bed, staring at the ceiling and letting his mind go blank for a few blessed moments. He felt weightless, unmoored, as though he could close his eyes and float away. Growing up, he had reflexively looked for his birth mother's face in the crowds, even knowing she was dead. He would catch a glimpse of dark hair at one of his father's campaign events or see something familiar in the rhythm of a woman's gait as she walked down the street. It was only as he got older that he realized he was looking for himself, that it was his hair color, his stride, the shape of his face, or the color of his eyes that evoked these pangs of longing inside him. He had never met his mother and wouldn't recognize her at all.

Now he was closer than ever, hot on her trail with his stack of fading pictures as he retraced her footsteps and visited the places she had lived. He'd talked to her friends and lovers, looked in their eyes, these same eyes his mother had once seen, but he had no sense of her looking back. Camilla Flores remained elusive, someone beloved but ineffable, like a character in a novel. He knew her and yet could not bring her to life.

At a quarter to seven, he knocked on Ellery's door and she materialized immediately, the ends of her hair damp from yet another shower. That made at least three today by his count, a sure sign of stress, but the tense set of her jaw told him she did not want to talk about it. He thought she should get tested to see if she might be a bone marrow donor for her half sister, if only because he strongly suspected that Ellery would regret it one day if she didn't. He'd like to give John Hathaway a swift kick in the nuts, though, for his thoughtless approach. The man had vanished from Ellery's life so completely that he had no idea what a difficult thing he was asking of his oldest daughter. He wouldn't know her fear of hospitals, how they had only brought her fear and pain, or how Ellery would be skin-crawling terrified at the prospect of being knocked out so that a stranger could drill holes in her body.

"You don't have to come to this dinner if you don't want to," he said mildly as they stood in the hall. "You can stay here and rest."

"No, I could use the distraction," she said, and started

walking away from him, effectively closing the debate. In the elevator, she watched the lighted numbers descend rather than look at him. "I made some calls to the *Las Vegas Review-Journal*," she said. "They connected me to Bruce Carr, and he's willing to talk to us about the Giselle Hardiman case."

"Bruce Carr?"

"The journalist who covered the case. I figure if the sheriff won't give us the details, maybe Carr can. I'd also like to find out if Angie knew her, or if maybe Camilla did."

"Sure, okay." Reed kept his reply neutral as they left the elevator and walked to the car. He remained unconvinced of a link between his mother's murder and Giselle Hardiman's. The women were similar in age, both slim and dark haired, and they had each been killed in a knife attack in their own apartments. Superficially, it seemed like a strong connection, but Reed's years of training taught him to look deeper at the two cases. Camilla had worked an honest job on one side of the city, while Giselle had been practicing prostitution across town. Camilla was clean. Giselle had a drug habit. Giselle sustained only three stab wounds, whereas Camilla's attacker set out to obliterate her. She had endured a prolonged vicious attack with twenty-plus stab wounds, followed by a beating with the horse head bookend. Giselle's killer appeared to have been practiced and physically strong. There were no defensive wounds. If Camilla had been murdered by the same person, why had he or she become so sloppy in the intervening year between the crimes? It didn't make sense to Reed, but he wasn't about to argue with Ellery over it now.

Outside, a bone-faced moon had risen over the mountain ridge to light their way through the hills of Pasadena. Reed easily found Angie Rivera's green bungalow with its glowing porch light and the stout palm tree standing guard in the short front yard. He loped up the walkway, eager to see her again and hear more about his mother. Ellery trailed him at a distance, lingering in the shadows. He poised to knock, but Angie pulled open the door before he could complete the gesture. "You're here," she declared happily, ushering them both inside her home. "And right on time. I love that. I'm always punctual. I never understood people who always run late—can they not tell time? Do they think when I say come at six that I really mean show up at seven thirty? How would the world work if we all behaved that way?"

"Utter chaos," Reed replied with a smile.

"Please come in and make yourselves comfortable."

Reed looked around the tidy living room, which featured a faux mantel with fat beige candles of varying sizes and an antique mirror above them. A framed Degas reprint, one of the artist's many ballerina portraits, hung on the cream-colored walls. Angie apparently had a green thumb, for the bay window seat held a miniature flowering garden. It was homey and lovely, although missing the usual family pictures one expected to see surrounding a woman Angie's age.

Reed sniffed the air, which smelled like tomatoes, sautéing onions, and roasting chicken. "May we help you with dinner at all?" He realized too late that he should have brought a hostess gift, wine or flowers or some small token, and he hid his empty hands behind his back. His mother, the one who raised him, would be appalled.

"No, thank you," Angie replied over her shoulder as she went to the kitchen. "Everything is just about ready."

"Are you sure? I love to cook."

Angie peeked out again with a broad smile. "Really? Me too. There's something so satisfying about watching a meal come together, testing, tasting, until you get it just right."

"I'm good at the tasting," Ellery volunteered with a smile, and Reed was glad to see her looking somewhat more relaxed. Her shoulders had come down from around her ears. "I can vouch for Reed's skills, though. He can go into my barren kitchen and whip out a three-course meal in under an hour."

"Oh," Angie said as she brought out a heavy Dutch oven and set it on the table. "So you two are . . . together?"

She said it casually, but with a note of hope that struck Reed as sweet and sad. She appeared to live alone, and he wondered if it had always been that way.

"No, no," Ellery replied. "It's not like that."

Reed paused to admire her tight-fitting purple turtleneck sweater and the long legs she had hidden under her dark-wash jeans. "It's a little like that," he answered good-naturedly, smiling when Ellery shot him a look. "It's complicated."

"Oh, I see," said Angie, who plainly didn't see at all. She began serving up plates of chicken legs slathered in a sauce of tomatoes, garlic, and olives. "I was wondering if you had a family."

"I have a daughter named Tula. She's six." Reed pulled out a picture on his phone, and Angie cooed over it.

"Would you look at her precious face? She's a darling."

Reed let her hold his phone a long time, watching this woman drink in the sight of his young daughter. Normally he kept all mention of his private life away from his investigations. He didn't so much as hint to the dangerous men he interviewed that he had a wife and child at home, often removing his wedding ring so no one would think to bring it up, compartmentalizing physically as well as mentally. He didn't bring Tula or Sarit with him to the underworld, and he didn't bring the demons back home when he returned—at least that was what he'd told himself. Sarit had had other interpretations.

Angie handed his phone back slowly, her fingers stroking the edges as she did so. She turned politely to Ellery. "What about you? Do you have children?"

Reed held his breath. Angie didn't know. There was nothing in the books or stories about Ellery that mentioned the lingering aftereffects of her rape: she could not bear children. To her credit, Ellery remained calm. She merely withdrew her own phone and wordlessly showed Angie a picture.

Angie laughed with delight at the image. "A four-footed, furry child. Yes, me too. My kitty cat, Zsa-Zsa, is hiding in the bedroom as we speak. She's shy, you know."

"His name is Speed Bump," Ellery said. "Because that's what he is—a lump in your way, trying to slow you down." She rolled her eyes, but her tone was full of affection.

"Zsa-Zsa is a terror. She wakes me up in the morning by knocking things off my dresser. I have no need for an alarm clock."

"Tell me about it. If Bump's dish isn't filled for supper by six P.M., he's on the phone to the ASPCA."

They chatted and ate up Angie's delicious food, devouring the chicken, the crusty bread, and the salad while the candles grew low. Eventually, Zsa-Zsa crept out from the bedroom and slunk along the wall, sniffing at them. Ellery reached down one hand in greeting and the fluffy white cat stared at the outstretched fingers, tail twitching in contemplation. She gave in and approached at full speed, rubbing furiously back and forth against Ellery's hand as she began to purr loudly. "She likes you," Angie declared, clasping her hands together. "She usually doesn't like anybody."

"Aw, she's sweet," Ellery said, smiling as the cat leaped delicately into her lap.

"Angie, thank you for an absolutely amazing meal," Reed said as he leaned back in his chair, his waistband comfortably snug.

"Oh, I forgot the cake!" She popped out of her seat and bustled back into the kitchen.

Reed groaned, but Ellery was game. "I've still got a clean fork over here," she pointed out.

Angie returned with a Bundt-shaped cake covered in salted caramel sauce. "I've put on water for coffee or tea, as you wish," she said. Reed accepted a thick slice of cake, although he didn't see how he could eat more than a few bites.

"Did Camilla also like to cook?" he asked out of curiosity.

Angie seemed flustered at the question, fumbling the knife. "Cammie? I suppose yes, a little. We didn't have money back then to do proper shopping. It was rice and beans a lot of nights."

"I'm sorry if it's hard to talk about her," Reed said quietly.

Angie lowered herself into her chair and regarded Reed with a sad smile. "It's hard, yes. But it's also good in some ways. I haven't talked about her in years. No one here knew who she was, and of course I couldn't say her name. It would've ruined everything."

"What was she like?" Reed asked.

"Cammie was a lot of fun. We laughed together all the time—about stupid stuff like boys and clothes and songs on the radio. We'd go out dancing and feel all the eyes on us, but we didn't look back. We didn't do it for their attention." She chuckled at herself and held up one finger in correction. "Well, maybe a little for their attention. We were young and pretty and free, like painted birds. We planned to open a dance studio together one day. The name I picked, it was Cammie's idea. She said we should call it A1 Dance Studio because then we'd be first in the phone book. She was smart like that."

Reed smiled, and Angie bit her lip, remembering.

"How silly it sounds now, no? The phone book."

"It's a good idea," Reed assured her. He hesitated before broaching his next question. "The nights out dancing . . . they must have come to an end when Cammie got pregnant."

Angie gave a single nod of assent. "Cammie wanted to work every extra shift she could to pick up extra money. I told her I'd help her, but she was worried about all the coming expenses. The trouble with Billy Thorndike started . . . she just wanted to move out as soon as possible."

"Working those extra shifts," Reed said. "That's when she met David, right?"

"Yes, that's right."

"What did you think of him?"

Angie paused to look from Reed to Ellery and back. "Why? You really don't think David had anything to do with it, do you?"

"I don't know," Reed said. "What do you think?"

She shrugged and poked at her cake with her fork. "David was okay. Like I was telling you earlier, he had troubles keeping his pants zipped. I didn't care for that part. Cammie liked him. She said he made her feel safe. I think she just liked the way he looked in his uniform."

"The police didn't make you feel safe?" Ellery asked.

"The police," Angie repeated, distaste creeping into her tone. "Let me tell you about the police. They put all their people down at The Strip because that's where the money was. Back then, if you had a problem somewhere else, you didn't even know which number you should call for help. There was no 911. There was the city police and the county police, and no one knew where the boundaries were. If you called with a problem, you were lucky to have someone show up at all—especially on our side of town. The cops ceded our block to Billy Thorndike a long time before me and Cammie showed up, and I think both sides were fine with the arrangement. Only when she reported him for attempted murder and wouldn't shut up about it, they had to do their jobs for once."

"They must not have liked that much," Ellery said.

"No, they'd rather have been bellying up at the clubs, watching the dancing girls. I should know. I was one of the girls. The cops were always the worst customers. Cheap, cheap, cheap. Always thinking the rules don't apply to them. They'd say whatever they wanted to you, grab at you even when the manager was looking. One night, I got off late at the club and my whole body was aching. I just wanted to go home, take a hot bath, and crawl into my bed. But one of those cops was outside the back door, waiting for me. He'd been in earlier when I was dancing and asked me out for a drink after, but I told him no. Seems he didn't like that answer, because there he was, anyway, waiting. I was the last one out and the place was deserted except for me and him. He said he'd walk me to my car. I told him no thank you. He blocked my path when I tried to leave and told me I was a tease, that I was being unfriendly, that he just wanted to be nice. I could smell the liquor on his breath. I saw the gun at his belt. What was I supposed to do?"

"What did you do?" Ellery asked softly.

"I told him sure, he could walk me to the car. 'Thank you, Mr. Officer, sir.' When we got there, he pushed me up against it and tried to kiss me. I pushed him off. That's when he said I'd better cooperate or he'd take me downtown and book me. 'For what?' I asked him. He said drugs. I said I didn't take drugs and he said I was lying, that he'd search my car and find some on me. I still remember the look in his eyes when he said it. 'I always find some,' he said. And I knew then he'd just plant them and say they were mine. He saw I got it, and he moved in again, his hands on my body . . ."

She wrapped her cardigan sweater closer around her waist. Reed had to force himself to ask the next obvious question. "What happened?"

Angie gave a thin smile. "Someone fired a gun outside the Golden Nugget. He had to go."

"Did you see him again?"

"No, I quit that job and got a different one as soon as I could. It was pretty easy then because the jobs didn't pay so good and so girls were always leaving them and coming back again."

"Angie," Ellery said, leaning in. "Did you know a young woman named Giselle Hardiman?"

Angie's forehead creased in thought. "Her name sounds familiar."

"She was killed about a year before Camilla."

"Oh, yes, I remember her now. Yes, I met her one time. That club I mentioned, the one with all the cops? Giselle used to dance out of there, sometime before I started. She came by once to talk to the manager, something about money. I was coming out of the bathroom and heard them arguing. He told her to vamoose and walked out on her. I was still standing there when she asked me if she could borrow a cigarette. She told me the manager was a filthy perverted rat-faced, lying piece of shit." She sat up, triumphant at the memory. "I remember because I realized when she said it that he did have a rat face. His two top teeth stuck out like this." She held up her fingers to her mouth to demonstrate.

"When was this?" Ellery wanted to know.

"More than forty years ago," Angie said. "I don't remember the date, I'm sorry. Probably not too long before she got killed. I remember it was on the news briefly, what happened to her. Then the story just seemed to go away."

"Yes," Ellery said, looking pointedly at Reed. "Funny, that. Do you know if Giselle knew Camilla at all?"

"No, I don't think so. But . . ."

"But what?"

"Cammie and me, we looked a lot alike back in those days, especially if you didn't look too close. Same height, same coloring. Sometimes, if I needed to work a side job, or if I wasn't feeling too good, Cammie would fill in for me. With the makeup on and hair up, no one ever knew the difference."

"Did Cammie fill in at the club when Giselle was around?"

Angie strained to remember. "Once or twice, maybe. Why does it matter?"

"Giselle was stabbed to death, the same as Cammie," Ellery explained. "It's possible we're looking for one killer."

Angie looked perplexed. "But Giselle didn't live in our neighborhood, and she was a . . ." She caught herself, but Reed filled in the blanks.

"A working girl."

Angie nodded. "Cammie and me didn't go in for that kind of thing. No way."

"If Giselle was into drugs, it's possible she crossed paths with Billy Thorndike," Ellery said. "If she was working in a club frequented by cops, it's possible she knew David Owens."

"I guess," Angie said, but Reed saw she was not convinced.

"That cop who harassed you," Ellery wanted to know, "do you know his name?"

"He didn't introduce himself," Angie replied darkly.

"Do you remember what he looked like?"

Angie considered. "Big. Hairy arms. He had dark hair, but I don't remember his eyes. He smoked Camel cigarettes. Oh, and he had some sort of tattoo on his upper arm. It was a bull, I think. Something with horns."

Ellery pulled out her phone to make some notes. "This is helpful, thank you."

Angie spread her hands in helpless fashion. "I don't see how. The cop was a bully, but I can't imagine why he'd want to hurt Cammie. The detective asked me the day she got killed who hated Camilla enough to want to do this to her, and there was only one person like that. Billy Thorndike."

"You may be right," Ellery said. "After all these years, he's still the prime suspect."

Reed's phone buzzed inside his pants, and he groped for it, surprised to be fielding any calls at this late hour. His family on the East Coast would have long retired for the night. He saw the number came up as the LVMPD sheriff's office. "Please excuse me," he murmured, ducking down the hall to the bathroom to take the call. "Yes, Markham here."

"Agent Markham, sorry to bother you so late." Brad Ramsey sounded tired but still full of purpose. "It's been a long day and I just had a chance to look at this report on the DNA results you asked for. Figured you'd want to know right away, despite the hour."

"You figured correctly." Reed gripped the phone tight to his ear, his heart picking up speed. After forty years, his mother's case might finally be solved. "What have you got?"

"Well, seems your hunch paid off. There was blood on the hilt of the knife that is not a match to our victim. It could very well be the killer's."

Reed closed his eyes. *Yes, yes,* he thought. This was it. "Did you run a comparison analysis against Thorndike's sample?"

"No need."

Reed's eyes flew open at the surprising answer. He didn't have time to voice his questions because Sheriff Ramsey continued straight on.

"The blood came back as female."

16

Ellery had her own preoccupations, so she didn't notice that Reed was unusually quiet on the way back to the hotel until they stopped in the parking lot and he did not get out of the car. She shifted in her seat to look at him. "Is something wrong? Or did you just put away too much food at dinner?"

Reed hesitated a moment before withdrawing something from his coat pocket. Ellery had difficulty seeing in the low light, but it appeared to be a bunch of folded tissues. "Sheriff Ramsey called me earlier to say that the DNA results came back on the knife. There is a second contributor, someone other than Cammie, and that someone is female." Carefully, he pulled back the tissues, and Ellery saw a small black brush lying among them.

"You took Angie's hairbrush?"

Reed's mouth set in a grim line. "We have to run the test. It's the only way to know."

"Yeah, but . . . you can't believe Angie is the one that killed her. I mean, look at her now—she's still destroyed when it comes to talking about Cammie's death. They were best friends. She loved her. What possible motive could she have had to attack her like that?"

"The money. By her own admission, Angie was one of the few people to know about the twenty-five thousand dollars. She was at the scene. She left town immediately after the murder. As suspects go, you could do a lot worse."

Ellery folded her arms, wounded on Angie's behalf. "You sat at her dining room table and ate her food. You saw her face when she talked about Cammie, how horrible the whole experience was for her, how much she misses her friend. Besides, what's Angie weigh? All of a hundred and ten pounds? How's she supposed to butcher another human being to death?"

"She's haunted by what happened, yes. We don't really know why. As for her size, Cammie was no bigger. They wore the same size, remember? The killer being female goes a long way toward explaining the protracted struggle at the crime scene. The attacker didn't have the physical strength to subdue Cammie immediately."

Ellery tried to envision it, Cammie screaming in fear as she tried to get away from her best friend, who was coming at her with a knife. "It doesn't make sense to me. Say you're right and Angie did want that twenty-five thousand dollars. Why not just take it? She had access to Cammie's apartment and she probably knew where Cammie kept the money. It would've been easy enough to slip in there when Cammie was working, grab the money, and take off for L.A. She could've been three hundred miles away before Cammie even knew what happened."

"You're right," Reed admitted. "That scenario fits better with the woman we met today. She doesn't seem like a cold-blooded murderer. But as you and I both know, murderers can appear startlingly sane in ordinary contexts. Hell, it's practically a cliché—you make the arrest and the friends and neighbors are all lined up ready to give their testimonials. 'He seemed like a nice guy' or 'She always had homemade cookies ready for the school bake sale.'"

He exited the car, and Ellery followed more slowly, catching up with him at the elevators. "There are other possible suspects to consider," she said as they waited for the doors to open. "Wanda slept with David, and Cammie found out about it. We have only Wanda's word that Cammie forgave him so easy, or that Wanda was happy to let him go. Maybe Wanda figured if Cammie was out of the picture, she could have David to herself."

"Maybe." Reed didn't sound like he believed this story.

She trailed him onto the elevator. "Also, there's Amy."

Reed eyed her. "What about her?"

"Remember she got a bunch of money right around the time Cammie was murdered. She said it was an inheritance, but—"

"We can check that out easily enough," Reed said shortly, turning his attention to the lighted numbers as they climbed to the twelfth floor. He had his plastic room key out, tapping it impatiently against his thigh.

Ellery watched him in silence for a moment. "It's almost like you want her to be guilty," she said just before the doors dinged open. "Angie."

"That's ridiculous. Of course I don't." They walked to their rooms, and Reed didn't glance at her as he opened his door. "We should head back to Las Vegas in the morning. I want to talk to Sheriff Ramsey about running the DNA comparison on Angie, and I think he's more likely to agree if I make the request in person."

Ellery didn't reply and he didn't seem to care. She stood in the hall after he had disappeared inside his room. There was one other woman with a motive to get rid of Cammie, a woman who knew about the twenty-five thousand dollars and who was eager to shut down the investigation. She was as adept at secret keeping as anyone Ellery had ever met: Reed's other mother, Marianne Markham.

On the drive back to Las Vegas, Ellery explained her plan to go through with her meeting with retired journalist Bruce Carr. Reed frowned at the road rather than at her, but his tone was reproachful: "We now know Camilla Flores's killer was a female, which means that any connection to Giselle Hardiman's murder goes out the window. They are two separate crimes linked superficially by the weapon of choice, a knife. But they have vastly different victimology, different motives, and different patterns of attack. I think you're wasting your time, and Bruce Carr's."

"It's my time to waste, and I didn't get the impression Bruce Carr had much else going on. Even if the woman who murdered Camilla didn't kill Giselle, someone else did. No one much seems to care who. Maybe Bruce Carr can help with that and maybe he can't, but at least we can spend a couple of hours talking about her. Giselle deserves that much." Ellery figured no one had even bothered to say Giselle Hardiman's name for several decades now. The cops were the only ones in a position to care about the case, and they had buried it deep.

"Suit yourself," Reed answered, his jaw tight.

Ellery belatedly remembered she was supposed to be here to support him. "I'll go with you to talk to Sheriff Ramsey about the DNA test on Angie Rivera if you want."

"No, I can handle it. Now that Ramsay knows your history, it's probably better to keep you out of it."

Ellery turned to look out the window. "My history," she repeated dully. "Right."

"I didn't mean that the way it sounded." Reed was genuinely apologetic. "I mean that you're not currently working in law enforcement. You're here in an unofficial capacity."

"Sure, let's pretend that's the important part." If Ramsey knew one part of her story, then he knew the whole thing.

Reed drove hunched over the wheel, leaning forward as if to make it there quicker. "Just think," he said. "This could all soon be over."

When they reached Las Vegas, they checked into yet another hotel, this one less fancy, with rooms on the same floor. Ellery assured Reed he could take the rental car to the LVMPD and she would call a taxi to take her to Bruce Carr's house for their two o'clock appointment. "Just be careful," she said before they parted.

Reed palmed the keys, impatient to be gone. "What do you mean?"

"Whatever Angie Rivera may have done, she didn't slash our tires. She was two hundred miles away and didn't even know we existed at the time."

For the first time that day, Reed looked at her like she was talking sense. "You raise an excellent point. I'll watch my back. Better yet, I'll have Sheriff Ramsey do it. The car should be fine parked in the LVMPD lot, wouldn't you say?"

Ellery declined to rule one way or another, and she let him go. She asked the doorman to procure a taxi for her and gave the driver Carr's address, which proved to be on the north side of the city. The taxi stopped in front of a beige stucco house that was, like its neighbors, dominated by a wide front garage and a short driveway. The landscaping was tidy but minimal, a patch of green grass and a concrete walkway leading up to a brown front door with no decorations on it. The stoop held various-size pieces of painted pottery in desert-inspired colors. When Ellery rang the bell, she heard excited barking on the other side of the door.

"Bella, hush!" The man who opened the door reminded Ellery of the old guy from the movie *Up*, with his large dark-framed glasses and square-shaped head. His handshake was firm and his eyes lively as he welcomed her inside his home. "Ms. Hathaway, please come in. Ignore the feisty furry security system. I promise she doesn't bite."

A Bichon Frisé, all six pounds of her, rushed at Ellery's legs, looping in and out in excited fashion. Ellery smiled and knelt to greet the dog, who responded by putting her front paws up on Ellery's knee and wagging furiously. "She's adorable."

"Don't think she doesn't know it, too," Carr groused, but his tone was affectionate. "Bella, get down already. She's not here to see you. They're never here to see you."

"My dog always acts like he wants the pizza delivery guy to adopt him."

"Yeah? This one even likes the mailman. She got out one day as I was signing for a package and she ran right up into his little car, like she was going to ride shotgun or something. Here, come this way to my office. Well, it used to be my office. Now it's more like a museum."

He led her through the living room to a sizable open area that might have been a den at one time. It held a desk, a small black leather sofa, and multiple framed newspaper clippings on the walls. "War stories," Carr said gruffly as Ellery moved to check them out. "Old glories. Way old, in some cases."

She saw a headline about the big MGM fire in 1980 and noticed Bruce's byline beneath it. Eighty-seven people were killed when the fire broke out in a restaurant attached to the hotel. Ellery regarded the picture, which showed a firefighter helping a singed young man out of the building.

"Worst disaster in Nevada's history," Carr told her. "Later investigation showed that MGM had declined to update their sprinkler system a few years before the fire, despite advice to do so. What a senseless tragedy that turned out to be."

Ellery moved on to the next clipping, this one from another fire, an arson at the Hilton. "I've heard about this one," she said, pointing. "The busboy set it."

"Yeah, he said he was trying to put the fire out. Everyone thought he was a hero at first. Only he effed up his statement to the cops and told them he threw 'a trash can full of fire' instead of a trash can full of water. They started looking at him funny after that."

"You have an impressive collection here," Ellery said as she circled the room and read the rest of the headlines. Pedestrian deaths in Las Vegas. Casino owners pressuring employees to vote for particular candidates.

"Back then, we had time to work a story, really dig into it, you know? Some of the stuff we wrote, it made a difference. We have pedestrian bridges now so tourists aren't constantly wandering into traffic. These days, though, no one cares about the papers. Forget actual journalism. Everything's online now. Video. Tweet this, chat that. My editors used to get excited when I pitched them a story about a payoff to a Strip mogul or loansharking or what have you. Now all they care about is 'viral videos' like a dog poops on a baby or some

298

woman screams real loud on the roller coaster." He shook his head in disgust. "The last assignment I got was to write about why cats are afraid of cucumbers. I said to him, I said, 'Jimmy, I can't take this horseshit you keep handing me. I'm dying here with these crappy little assignments that mean nothing to nobody. Please, let me take on something real. Something with teeth. Woodward and Bernstein would be rolling over in their graves if they knew what we were putting out there and calling journalism."

Ellery scrunched up her nose. "Are Woodward and Bernstein dead?"

"They would be if they saw today's paper." He gestured at the leather sofa, indicating they should sit. "Never mind my gripes. You came here to talk about Giselle Hardiman. Pretty girl, or at least she once was. Giselle's life started out hard and only stayed that way."

"You knew her?"

"Oh, no, I never met her personally, but I did track down her mother in Texas after Giselle was murdered. That was something we did back then—follow up on stories, even if they took us outside the city limits. Anyway, it was a long, sad conversation that told me nothing and everything about why Giselle ended up the way she did. Her mom was three sheets to the wind when we talked, and I got the feeling she'd lived most of her life like that. She wanted me to know she tried to protect Giselle growing up from the different boyfriends who'd come home drunk and angry, looking for someone to pound on. Her mama would hide Giselle and take the beating herself—

mind you, she was proud telling me this—but it never occurred to her to leave. Giselle, she left when she was fifteen, but she didn't get very far, if you see what I'm saying."

"I do."

The dog came sniffing around their feet, and Carr scooped her into his lap and began absentmindedly petting her. "You asked me on the phone what I knew about the investigation, and the short answer is there wasn't one, not really. The cops knocked on a few doors to see if there were any witnesses, and when no one came forward to identify the killer they just shrugged and moved on."

"I heard rumors that the cops might've been friendly with Giselle before her death."

"I heard exactly the same thing back when it happened. Makes you think the cops did not knock too loud on those doors, doesn't it?"

"What do you make of the rumors—true or not?" Ellery put her hand out and lured the dog in her direction. Bella came across the sofa from Carr's lap, wagging happily, eager for another round of scritching.

"Oh, they were true, all right. As I understood it, the cops back then looked at free sex with the working girls as just another perk of the job. The girls took it as the price of doing business."

"Funny you should mention price. If a chunk of your clientele isn't paying, you might find yourself looking for money in other ways. I heard Giselle might've been leaning on different sources of cash in the weeks before her death."

"That's right." He paused, as if measuring how much to say. "She had a drug habit to support. The cops might've been willing to toss her the occasional dime bag as a payment, but Giselle would have needed more than that. If she was leaning on her connections to get more money, then that surely would've included the boys in blue."

"Blackmail."

He hesitated again. "Maybe. Nothing I could ever prove."

"How long did you work the story?"

"As long as I could, which is to say maybe a few weeks. It seemed red-hot at the start. Sure, the victim was a prostitute, but she was reasonably good looking and her murder was the kind that raises goose bumps, you know? Stabbed in her own apartment. Readers eat that stuff up, and so we all thought it had legs. But the cops didn't seem to have any kind of urgency. I asked 'em questions, they'd give me one-word answers and then change the subject. Maybe I'd like to do a piece on some heist attempt at the Tropicana instead. Eventually, my editor said I had to stop going around the station asking questions that got no answers, that I should find something we could actually print."

"These cops, the ones that stonewalled you. Do you remember their names?"

"Sure do." He didn't miss a beat, didn't consult any notes. "Jeff Highlander was the lead on the case. He's dead now. Heart attack in '93. James Finney, he retired ten years ago. Oh, and there's our very own sheriff, Brad Ramsey. Back then, he worked the beat sometimes in Giselle's neck of the woods. He helped canvass the neighborhood after they found the body, but damned if he would talk to me about anything they found out. 'We're still pursuing leads,' he'd tell me." Carr gave a short, derisive laugh. "I bump into him now and then, and sometimes I'll still ask him about that: 'Still pursuing those leads, eh, Ramsey? How's that working out for you?'"

Ellery had stopped petting the dog at the mention of Ramsey's name, and Bella pawed at her hand, reminding her. "What does he say when you ask about the case?"

"He says, 'When we know something, you'll be the first one we call, Bruce.'" He shrugged and then gave her a sly grin. "I'd always tell him that they must not know too much, seeing as how my phone never rings. He doesn't like that answer."

"Do you know," Ellery began, pausing to think how to phrase her question. "Do you know if he might have been one of Giselle's clients?"

"I guess it's possible, sure. He was single back then. Liked to party with the best of them, or so I'm told."

"What kind of evidence did they collect from the scene?" Ellery asked, changing tactics. "There was the knife, I know."

"The knife, yes. They said it was from Giselle's kitchen, so the killer didn't bring it with him. According to the police, no fingerprints were found on the handle." He raised his eyebrows to indicate what he thought of the official report. "There were no signs of a break-in. No one reported any unusual cars or strangers in the area. Of course, Giselle's neighbors weren't the kind to be actively looking, nor were they likely to want to ask the cops in for tea and conversation. There wasn't much to go on."

"Did she keep a record of her clients?"

"Ah, the million-dollar question," Carr replied with a smile. He pulled the dog back into his lap. "I heard mixed reports. One of her friends, a fellow working girl, said Giselle did keep a little blue day planner that had records of her visitors. The cops said they never found anything like it when they searched the apartment."

"So, someone made it disappear."

"Possibly, yes. Or they've had it all along and never bothered to say. Whoever it was, whatever problems they had with Giselle, all of them disappeared with her death." He made a magician's *poof* gesture with his hands. "Her case went cold about a week after the murder, and no one has even mentioned her name to me in more than twenty years until you called me up. So I've got to ask: What's your game?"

"The FBI is taking another look at a homicide that occurred around the same time as Giselle Hardiman's murder. A woman named Camilla Flores was stabbed to death in her apartment."

"I remember the case," Carr said promptly. "Horrible, horrible death. The inside of that apartment looked like an abattoir."

"We were exploring whether the two deaths might be related." Ellery watched him closely, curious to see what he made of this theory. So far, no one but her seemed to think much of it.

"I've wondered that myself."

"Really," Ellery remarked, surprised. "Why?"

"Her boyfriend, David Owens. He was a cop. The cops were into the Hardiman case up to their eyeballs. I don't know if one of them killed her or not, but they damn sure weren't investigating it with their usual rigor. At the very least, they didn't want to turn over too many rocks, on account of what might come crawling out and bite 'em on the ankles. There was something about the Flores murder that had the same feel to it. I figured it had to do with Owens."

"You think David Owens might have been seeing Giselle Hardiman?" Ellery asked. She didn't see how Carr found a connection.

"I don't know one way or another. I've just seen enough crooked cops to be suspicious of all of them." He eyed her. "No offense. Owens, I maybe talked to him once or twice throughout my career. He had a decent reputation as far as it goes. But like I say: I've wondered. There was a rumor back then that Owens liked to play the field. He sure up and married that other cop in a hurry, practically before Camilla was cold in her grave."

"It seems to have worked out. They're still together, forty years later."

Carr made a face and waved her off.

"What?" she asked.

"They say everyone loves a happy ending," he replied. "But that crap doesn't sell papers."

Ellery leaned over to give the dog a last scratch under her

fluffy white chin. "If it all goes to hell," she said, "I'll give you a call."

"Sure," Carr groused. "That's what they all say."

Ellery took a taxi to the LVMPD, intending to meet up with Reed. When she arrived, however, she discovered he had already gone. "Is the sheriff back there?" she asked the desk sergeant, a buxom woman in uniform with a beautiful Afro, bright red lipstick, and a thousand-yard stare.

"No, ma'am, he's in a meeting. I can take a message for you if you like."

Ellery caught sight of Sergeant Don Price walking away from them down the hall. "No, no, thank you," she said quickly, and took off after Price. She caught up with him easily, and he smiled when he recognized her.

"Officer Hathaway. I think your counterpart was just here visiting with the sheriff."

"That's right. He's off running down a new lead now. I was wondering if you might help me out."

"I'd be happy to try."

"I'd like to see the files and any evidence pertaining to the Giselle Hardiman case from 1974."

Price's blue eyes darkened with his frown. "I thought you were investigating the Flores case."

"We are, but they may be related. Sheriff Ramsey said it was fine if we wanted to take a look." Her heart rate increased with the lie, and she hoped it didn't show on her face.

Price checked his watch. "The sheriff's in a meeting for another hour."

"An hour's all I need," Ellery said, smiling broadly. "Just in and out—okay?"

Price thought it over for another few seconds. "I can't let you take anything off the property," he warned her, and she held up her right hand in a promise.

"I just want to read the murder book and get a look at the evidence."

"I'll have someone bring it up for you. Room 208." He looked at her with curiosity. "Are you looking for anything in particular?"

"No. I'm just hoping to recognize it when I see it. Thanks."

Price excavated the bones of another long-dead case, a cardboard box with a fitted lid covered in the same type of fine layer of dust that coated Camilla Flores's files. "I'll leave you to it then," he said as she reached her eager hands for the lid. When she pulled it off, she saw that Bruce Carr had not been exaggerating the half-baked investigation. Whereas Camilla's case had several binders' worth of notes and files, Giselle Hardiman's murder merited a single folder, an envelope of crime scene photos, and a few pieces of bagged evidence. Ellery started with the pictures, flipping through each of them to familiarize herself with the setting. Giselle Hardiman had died in a tangle of pink satin sheets, wearing just her bra and panties and a pair of four-inch heels. Her pose and the bedroom location did suggest Giselle might have been working at the time of her murder. She lay on her back, her eyes open. She had seen it coming, if only at the last moment.

Ellery froze as she heard footsteps and male voices out in the hall. If Sheriff Ramsey found her here, there was no telling what he might do. At a minimum, he could put her up in a jail cell overnight, as she was technically trespassing on police property. The voices receded and Ellery relaxed again, moving on to sift through the bagged evidence. She found the knife with blood on it and she gave it a good, hard look. It was slimmer than the one that had killed Camilla, more like a boning tool. To credit the Vegas cops, it did seem as though the knife might have been printed back in the day, because the handle still bore traces of powder. She set it aside and looked through the remainder of the evidence: Giselle's negligee and panties, scant as they were; a wineglass that appeared to be the one from the bedside table shown in the crime scene photos; Giselle's jewelry; a paperback romance novel that had what appeared to be dried blood on the cover; a bloody hand towel; and a small blue day planner marked 1974 in gold letters on the front.

Ellery looked over her shoulder, flush with shock. Maybe this wasn't Giselle's record book, if the cops had held on to it. Gingerly, she eased it open with her fingernails, careful not to leave fingerprints of her own. She only had to scan a few pages to determine that yes, this was Giselle's client book. Unfortunately, the records seemed to be in code. "AN50M2D," read one entry from February 12. Another entry that month said: "GGPCP*." Ellery looked through a bunch of Giselle's notes but could not determine any sort of obvious pattern. Some of the letters and numbers repeated, but often in different combinations. Occasionally, there was an obvious indication of what had transpired, such as the time when Giselle scrawled: "No-show," or, more ominously, next to "DC40SNK": "Never again!"

Ellery risked a look at the door and briefly debated smuggling the day planner out of the building with her. But Don Price would surely tell the sheriff what she'd been up to, and he'd no doubt perform an inventory. When the day planner turned up missing, she'd be the clear suspect—not to mention the part where she'd be breaking chain of custody. If the planner had probative value, she couldn't just waltz off with it or she'd render it useless in court.

Inspiration struck her when she remembered passing a copy room at the end of the hall. Grabbing a pair of latex gloves, she took both the murder book and the day planner and poked her head out of the room to check if the coast was clear. She didn't see anyone approaching, so she dashed from the windowless little conference room to the copy machine. The large, lumbering machine had been in low-power mode before she showed up, so it took a few minutes of humming and whirring to prepare for action again. "Come on, come on," she urged it under her breath. Her fingers turned clumsy as she tried to rush through the delicate task of flipping the small pages and copying each one. When she had finished both the day planner and the meager murder book, she checked the hall again. No one.

She hurried back to the room and returned the evidence to the box, keeping the copies for herself. She wound a rubber band around them and tucked them inside her jacket. Outside in the hall, she passed a couple of uniformed officers who didn't seem to pay her any attention, as they were deep in conversation with each other. Even still, she kept her head down and walked as quickly as she dared toward the exit. When she glanced up again, she saw the sheriff in her path. She made an about-face but not fast enough that he hadn't spotted her. Mentally cursing herself for the blunder, Ellery made the only move she could: she ducked into the ladies' room.

The room was empty but also useless, as it had a single exit point. Ellery battled as hard as she could with the lone window, but it only opened about four inches. There was no way for her to squeeze through it. She had an inside pocket in the lining of her leather jacket, but it was shallow and might not hold the papers long enough to fend off the sheriff. Maybe she could just wait him out. Or call Reed. She had her phone out, her thumb poised to hit the button, when she reconsidered. If Reed came to her aid now, they'd both be fried. Reed needed the sheriff to run that DNA test. Ellery cast a baleful glance at the window again, wishing she could shrink down and fly away.

As the seconds ticked past, she realized she had only one course of action. She had to outwit the sheriff just long enough to get off the property with the papers intact.

Resolved, she prepped herself with a hard look in the mirror, made the necessary adjustments with the papers, and squared her shoulders. Maybe she'd get lucky and he'd be gone when she left the bathroom.

"And the house wins again," she muttered to herself when she found him waiting in the hall just outside the door, chewing on a toothpick. He seemed to take up half the air in the hall.

"What's that you said?" he asked, cocking his head at her.

"Nothing." She forced a smile. "I was looking for Agent Markham. Is he here?"

"He left some time ago."

"Oh, thanks. I'll just be going then and catch up with him elsewhere."

He moved to block her path. "Sergeant Price told me he already passed on that information. He told me you were looking into the Hardiman files."

"Just a quick peek," she said, spreading her hands. "Turns out there's nothing much there."

"I told you to leave that case alone. I said that expressly."

"Did you?" She put on her best confused expression.

"I made that crystal clear to Agent Markham. Your access is limited to the Flores case only."

"He must not have passed on the message," she said with a shrug. "Sorry for the mix-up. Anyway, I need to go."

He grabbed her arm. "Not just yet. Let's have a chat, shall we?"

He marched her back down the hall, his fingers biting into

her elbow. When they reached room 208 again, he pushed her inside and then closed the door behind them. "Look, I said I was sorry," she said. "I didn't disturb anything. You can check the box and see everything is all right there."

"Take off your jacket."

Her heart jumped in her ribs. "What?"

"You heard me. Take off the jacket."

"Why?"

"Jimenez says you were in the copy room."

"No, I wasn't." She swallowed hard and hoped he couldn't see it.

"You aren't authorized to make copies of these files. They are state's evidence. Hell, you're a private citizen now, Ms. Hathaway. I could lock you up just for looking at this stuff."

She stuck out her chin. "Go ahead and do it then."

"Lose. The. Jacket."

She glared at him for a few seconds before shrugging out of her jacket. "There," she said, throwing it down on the table. "Are you happy now?"

He picked it up and patted it down thoroughly, watching her with dark eyes the whole time. "Turn around."

"No. I don't have to take this. I don't have to—"

He shoved her roughly up against the wall. "Oh, you have to, all right," he breathed in her ear. He used his foot to spread her legs apart. "You have to do every last thing I say."

Ellery felt her stomach surge to her throat as his hands started pawing over her body. She willed herself not to be sick. "Or what?" she asked, hating how choked she sounded.

"You don't want to know." He pulled her hands up and pressed her palms against the wall. "Keep them there and don't move."

He searched her slowly and purposefully, his hands lingering on her breasts, her hips, her thighs. "Whatever you're looking for, I don't have it."

"You think you're pretty cute, coming in here, giving my men orders like you run the place. You aren't the law here, Ms. Hathaway. You aren't the law anywhere, actually, and you'd do well to remember your place around here."

"And where is that?" She spoke through clenched teeth.

"Here looks pretty good." He leaned up against her, pressing her whole body from behind. She sucked in a breath but forced herself to keep her eyes open. She saw his huge hand, holding hers flat against the wall. Saw his hairy arm with its bulging tendons. Her eyes widened when she caught sight of the tattoo now visible beyond his raised shirtsleeve. A large ram, with angry eyes and huge curled horns. Angie's words about the cop from the parking lot came back to her: he had a tattoo on his arm, something like a bull.

"If you're arresting me, I get to call a lawyer," Ellery told him.

He dropped his hands and stepped back. "Get the hell out of here. I see you back on my property, I will throw your ass in jail. Are we clear?"

Ellery gathered her jacket and looked him in the eyes. Her knees threatened to buckle, and her brain was screaming at her to run. "This isn't your property. It belongs to the city."

Sheriff Ramsey's nostrils flared. "It's my house and I make the rules here." He pointed a long finger at her. "Go," he said. "And don't come back."

Ellery went. She scrambled on shaky legs down the hall to the stairwell, where she half-ran, half-fell down to the ground level and out into the open air. The sky had darkened to angry purple streaks. She bent at the waist and sucked in great gulps of air to steady herself, her skin still crawling from the feel of Ramsey's hands. Then she stood upright and slowly, cautiously worked her way around the building until she reached the shrubbery underneath the second-floor ladies' room. She smiled. There in the dirt lay her bounty, a tube of papers wrapped in a rubber band.

17

Reed swallowed a pair of ibuprofens and looked at his reflection. He noted his gray pallor, his bloodshot eyes, and the two-day stubble dotting his chin. If he were one of the agents he supervised, he would send himself home immediately. As the situation currently stood, he might have little choice, anyway. The conversation with Sheriff Ramsey had not gone as Reed had hoped. The sheriff had been intrigued with the new finding that the blood on the knife was female, but he'd balked at ordering a DNA test on the hair sample Reed had collected from Angie Rivera.

"So what if it matches?" Ramsey had said. "She was practically Camilla's roommate, right? They were in and out of each other's apartments all the time. They shared meals together. If Angie's blood is on that knife, she can easily explain how it got there."

"If it is mixed with Camilla's that provides a stronger argument."

"Not much of one. That blood is all of forty years old by now. No telling when and where each little drop got on the knife."

Reed had been forced to swallow his frustration. "That's it? If Angie did it, she just gets away with it because she and Camilla were friends?"

"Yep, that's it. It just doesn't make sense to me, anyways. Like you say, those girls were close friends. Why would Angie want to kill her? I mean, come on now. You're not some rookie, Agent Markham. You know as well as I do that a jury is going to want more than a couple of drops of blood on the knife. If you can't explain why Angie might have done this, if you can't find anything else to link her to this murder . . . I'm afraid your case is dead in the water."

"What if Cammie had come into some money? Would that be motive enough?"

The sheriff had a new gleam of interest in his eyes. "Did she? This is news to me."

Reed knew he had to tread cautiously. If he mentioned the twenty-five-thousand-dollar payout, then Angus Markham's skeleton would come tumbling straight out of the closet and onto the front-page news. "Let's say hypothetically that she did have a fair amount of cash in the apartment, and that Angie knew about it. Let's further note that no cash was recovered at the scene and that Angie left for Los Angeles only a few days after the murder."

Ramsey had leaned way back in his chair and stared at the ceiling for a long moment. "That's all fascinating information—if it's true. Can you prove that Camilla had this money and that Angie took it?"

"No," Reed admitted reluctantly. He couldn't be sure Angie took the money.

"Well, if you can get that kind of proof—or any other outside corroboration that Angie might have had something to do with this—then we'll consider the DNA test."

Later, Reed had tried to plead his case with his boss, but she gave him basically the same answer: a DNA match to Angie Rivera in and of itself would not be enough evidence to forge a case. Reed needed to find some other substantive link between Angie and Camilla's murder before the director would authorize a DNA test on Angie. This left Reed right where he was now, alone in a dark hotel room with a splitting headache. He'd spent the last two hours studying the crime scene photos and the timeline again, looking for something he'd missed. He felt it when he looked at them—something wasn't quite right—but the answer remained maddeningly vague, refusing to coalesce.

Reed tried looking at the photos from a distance. He tried placing them upside down. He went back and forth between the largely happy snapshots the police had seized from Camilla's home and the clinical photographs taken at the time of the murder. He didn't need to study any of the images anymore. They had been burned into his brain and he could summon any one of them at will just by closing his eyes. All the pieces of the puzzle were there: Angie's shopping bags, abandoned by the door; the smears of blood across the floor and on the walls indicating a brutal struggle; the knife in Camilla's chest, and the horse head bookend lying next to her, half-covered in blood. So much blood. The green diamond pattern on Camilla's blouse nearly disappeared entirely under the spreading stains.

Maybe it was what the pictures didn't show—Reed, as a baby, just offscreen—that made it so difficult for him to see what was missing. Or maybe he'd stared at the images just long enough to make himself go crazy. He sat down on the bed and took out his cell phone. No calls from Ellery. Part of him wished that she would come back so he could push the pictures in front of her again: *What do you see here that I am missing?* The other part still felt piqued that she'd run off chasing an old murder that had nothing to do with him.

Suddenly restless, Reed got up to pace the room. He had exhausted the limits of his own imagination. He needed outside input. David Owens might be able to shed some light on this new angle on the murder. Now that he'd been reasonably ruled out as a suspect, he might provide insight into whether Angie had motive to kill Cammie. Hell, Reed figured there was a fifty-fifty shot Owens had been sleeping with both girls back then. The man apparently spread himself around.

He dialed the Owens household, telling himself it wasn't that late, just a few minutes to nine. He didn't want to have to sit in his hotel room until morning. He felt a stab of relief when Amy Owens picked up the phone. "Mrs. Owens, hello. It's Reed Markham. I'm sorry to be troubling you at this hour, but I wondered if I might stop by to talk to you and your husband about the case."

"Oh? Has there been some news?" He heard the sound of her putting away dishes in the background.

"We got a DNA sample from the knife," Reed told her. "It's raised some new questions." He had ruled Amy out as a suspect this afternoon when the sheriff confirmed her story about an inheritance: Amy's uncle had died and left her a tidy sum of money just prior to Cammie's murder, so her sudden boost in income at the time didn't have anything to do with the missing twenty-five thousand dollars.

"DNA," Amy said, a hint of wonder in her voice. "After all this time. Isn't technology amazing? When I was on the job, we counted ourselves lucky to get a couple of fingerprints. What did the test show?"

"I'd prefer not to get into that on the phone. Would it be all right if I paid you and your husband a quick visit?"

He heard her hesitation. "I don't know . . ."

"I don't suspect him of the murder," he assured her in a rush. "Not anymore. I'd just like your perspective on some new information we've collected."

"Okay, sure," Amy relented after another beat. "We're around. Come on over whenever you like."

Reed paused only to run the razor over his face and comb his hair. He hesitated outside Ellery's empty hotel room, wondering whether he should leave a note, but finally decided against it. She had her leads, and he had his. On his way to the Owens house, he considered all the questions he might ask David about Camilla and Angie's relationship. Cammie sometimes had posed as Angie on the job, Angie had said. Maybe there was money at stake somehow, like Angie figured Cammie owed her something.

The Owenses' residential street was dark and quiet, illuminated only by sparse streetlamps and the distant glow from inside the few large houses. Reed rolled to a stop in front of the Owens house and thought it odd that their house had no lights on at all that he could see. Amy and David were expecting him, so he imagined they would leave the light on by the front door at least. Perhaps they were at the back of the house, he reasoned as he approached the darkened walkway. He rang the bell and heard it chime from inside the house. No one answered his call. Reed rang again, longer this time, but still no one appeared to let him inside. He craned his neck back to look up at the house as a distinct feeling of unease settled in the pit of his stomach. Nothing appeared amiss, not with the house or with the street in general. He was the only person around.

Reed decided to walk around to the rear of the house to check it out. Maybe the Owenses had a pool or gazebo and simply hadn't heard him arrive. He unlatched the gate on the fence and walked around the miniature palm trees and other leafy tropical plants to get to the backyard. He could smell the pool, dark and still. He didn't see any trace of David or Amy Owens. Reed crossed the patio and went up to the sliding glass doors. His foot crunched on something sharp and hard, and Reed realized with alarm that he was standing amid broken glass. He reached out a hand and found the shattered seam of what used to be the door. The gaping hole was big enough for a person to climb through, and so that's what he did. He took out his gun and tried to step around the pieces of glass.

He was in the kitchen. It was difficult to see in the dark, but he took another tentative step forward. "Mr. and Mrs. Owens?" he called out. "It's Agent Markham! Are you here?"

He listened for any answer, dread creeping up his spine when he received only silence. *Get out,* he thought, *and call for backup.* But his feet moved him forward, deeper into the house. Amy or David might be hurt, dying. There wasn't time to waste. "Mr. and Mrs. Owens," he tried again. "It's Reed Markham. Can you hear me?"

He kept his gun in his right hand while he felt along the wall with his left, searching for a light switch. A woman's voice, calm and cold, reached out to him in the dark. "Hello, Mr. Markham."

"Amy," he said, relief coursing through him. "You're all right."

"Yes, I'm fine."

"Your house—I saw the glass. What happened?" He looked in the direction of her voice but couldn't quite make her out. He thought he saw her silhouette on the stairs. "Is everything okay? Where is David?"

"I sent David to the store. You make him nervous."

"I—what? Where are you? I can't see anything." He

groped in vain again for the light. "Who broke your door? What's going on?"

"You broke it," she said, and Reed froze.

"No, I found it like that," he said carefully. "It was broken when I arrived."

"No, you broke in after David and I said we wouldn't talk to you anymore. You were crazy. You pulled out your gun. I was afraid you might kill me."

Reed looked down at the gun in his hand, barely visible in the low light. "I'm not here to kill you. I just want to talk."

"No talking. There's no time. David will be back soon." She moved down the stairs into a patch of light and Reed saw she had a gun, too. "Drop your weapon," she ordered.

"Amy, please—"

"I said drop it!"

Slowly, Reed laid the gun at his feet. He considered his options. David was at the store, due home soon. If Reed could keep Amy talking until then, maybe the situation could be diffused.

"Now kick it away."

Reed kicked his gun to the side, sending it sliding over the tile floor toward the refrigerator. "What's this about, Amy?"

"You know. You must know if you ran that DNA test."

Ah, Reed thought, as the truth hit him too late. "You killed Camilla." Reed kept his tone neutral, careful not to sound judgmental.

"David wouldn't choose," she said, her voice hard. "So I had to help him. Get your hands up where I can see them."

Reed had been inching his hand into his coat pocket for his cell phone. Now he had to back off and put his hands up in front of him. "You can shoot me," he said, "but they'll still pursue the DNA results. They know now it's a woman who killed her."

"No, they won't. They hadn't touched this case in years before you came around. Sheriff Ramsey comes to our summer barbecues. You think he cares about some forty-year-old case? He and David watch football together. I know exactly what he will and will not do, and he'll be perfectly happy to let this whole mess become ancient history again."

Reed knew in his bones this was true; he was the only person keeping Camilla's case alive. "Maybe the sheriff would drop it. But Ellery won't." He knew this in his bones, too.

Amy laughed. "She's suspended! I read the stories online about her—half the world thinks she's crazy. I'm not worried about her." Amy pointed the gun at him from across the room as if taking aim. "Sorry it had to be this way," she said, with a tinge of what sounded like real regret. "It's not your fault your mother was a whore."

"Wait! You can't do this!" He blurted the first desperate thing out of his mouth. His hands trembled. His tongue went dry. He thought of his family, of his daughter, of Ellery, who would probably have to identify his body. Amy hesitated, and in the horrible, tense silence they both heard a car engine roar into the driveway. The garage door began to rumble as it opened. David.

"Help!" Reed shouted, and Amy shot him.

He felt only pressure in his chest, but he knew that he'd been hit. He yelled out again for help, but only a wheeze emerged. The room exploded with the sound of gunfire. He felt dizzy now and he struggled to breathe. His chin struck the floor hard as he went down, face-first into the hard tile floor. He heard footsteps, voices, and then everything went black.

18

Ellery tried Reed's cell phone several times without success before catching her own ride back to the hotel. She knocked on his door and waited, but there was no reply. She dug out her phone again and stared at it as though it would magically produce a message that said where Reed was. She hadn't spoken to him since they went their separate ways much earlier in the day. Her phone produced no answers, and his hotel room remained locked and silent. Reluctantly, Ellery returned to her room, where she dug out the copied pages from Giselle Hardiman's murder file. She had been unsuccessfully trying to break the code for a couple of hours now. Each entry in Giselle's day planner began with two letters that might be initials of her clients. *BR*, for example, could stand for "Brad Ramsey." Or not. She had no proof one way or another. She wished that Reed would show up so that she could get a second opinion.

She ordered a sandwich from room service, but when it

arrived she found she couldn't eat much of it. The tension created from the empty room next door sapped her appetite. She tried calling him again, and then again, but each time his line rang through to voice mail. "It's me," she said. "Where are you? Call me when you get this." When another half hour passed with no word from Reed, she went down to the hotel's bar/restaurant to look for him. It wasn't crowded, but she made a slow circle of each table, anyway, even poking her head into the men's room. She checked the parking garage as well but found no sign of their rental car. Her chest tightened with fear, alarm bells ringing loudly in her head. Something was very wrong. Reed wouldn't take off and leave her here with no explanation.

She jogged back into the hotel, her phone out again, but this time she dialed a different number. "Las Vegas Police Department," said a young male voice on the other end.

"I'm looking for someone—Reed Markham. He's an agent with the FBI."

"This is LVMPD, ma'am."

"I know that," Ellery replied, irritated. "He was there today, meeting with Sheriff Ramsey. That's the last anyone's seen him." She didn't know this was true. In fact, it probably wasn't, but it was her only verified point on Reed's timeline.

"There is no FBI agent here now, ma'am, and the sheriff isn't around. Would you like to leave him a message?"

"No, you don't understand. Agent Markham is missing. It's past midnight and he hasn't shown up yet. He's not answering his phone. Something is wrong."

There was a meaningful pause on the other end. "Ma'am, a grown man out past midnight is hardly remarkable around these parts. I'd suggest you wait 'til morning. They all come crawling back in when the sun comes up."

"No, it's not like that. He's not out on some bender." She paced the floor in front of the elevator, ignoring her reflection in the shiny doors. "He's missing, don't you get that? He was supposed to show up hours ago. Can you at least check to see if there are any reported accidents?"

He sighed, put upon by her requests. "None that I know of, but hold on and I'll check." She waited, her heart thumping, while he poked at some computer keys. "No serious accidents reported for the last twelve hours, ma'am—just an armed home invasion. I'm sure he's just fine."

Ellery seized on the only new piece of information available. "What home invasion? What happened?"

"I'm not at liberty to disclose all the details, ma'am."

"Was anybody hurt?"

A long pause. "Intruder was shot," he said, and the hairs rose on the back of her neck.

"Shot," she repeated steadily. "Where? Can you tell me where?"

He gave a heavy sigh. "Ma'am, I told you . . ." He trailed off and Ellery heard only the sound of the blood rushing in her ears. "Ma'am, what did you say your friend's name was again?"

"Markham. Reed Markham."

She waited through an awful, interminable silence. "I can't

tell you what happened," he said finally, his tone now soft, full of regret. "But I think you'll want to go over to University Medical Center right away."

"Why? What's going on? Is Reed okay?"

"Check the emergency room," he replied. "And good luck to you."

Ellery ran back out into the cold night air. She had no car. "Hey," she said to the sleepy-eyed valet loitering on the outside bench. "Hey, I need a cab."

"Yeah, okay," he said, lumbering to his feet. "Lemme call you one."

"Call? Can't you just wave one over?"

He gestured at the empty street. "You see one out there? Relax. It'll take five minutes, tops."

"Five minutes!" She looked up and down the street. Maybe she could just run. "Where's University Medical Center? Is it close?"

"UMC is a few miles north." He looked her over with fresh concern. "Why? You hurt?"

"Just call the cab," she said, taking out her own phone once more. She dialed Reed's number, urging him mentally to pick up. *Pick up, pick up, pick up.* She would hear his voice and then it wouldn't be true. She closed her eyes when she got his voice mail again. *An armed home invasion that put someone in the emergency room. Reed, playing the hero again,* she thought. *Shit.* She rubbed her eyes with one hand and then glared at the valet. "Where's that taxi?"

"Coming."

When the cab finally showed, Ellery scrambled into the back, only to lean into the front seat and urge the driver to go faster. They seemed to hit every red light. By the time she reached the UMC emergency department, close to a half hour had passed since her phone call to LVMPD. She tossed some money at the driver and ran inside the building, breathless as she collapsed across the front desk. "I'm trying to find Reed Markham," she said to the admitting nurse. Ellery kept one eye on the faces in the waiting area, hoping to spot Reed among them.

"Spell that for me?"

Ellery spelled the name through gritted teeth. "There was a home invasion. Someone was shot."

"Oh," said the nurse. "Yes, he's in surgery. Upstairs. But you can't—"

Ellery didn't stop to hear what she couldn't do. She barreled down the hall, dodging doctors, patients, and gurneys, following the signs for surgery. She knew she had found the right place when she spotted a waiting area that contained Sheriff Ramsey and one other officer she didn't recognize. The alcove was otherwise empty. "Sheriff," she called, and he turned with a frown.

"Ms. Hathaway. What are you doing here?"

She made sure to stand out of his reach. "I'm looking for Reed. Is he here? What happened?"

"Agent Markham's in surgery."

Her heart dropped to her knees. So there was more than one victim and Reed had been hurt, too. "What? How? I

328

heard there was a home invasion. Will Reed be okay?"

"Yes, it happened out at the Owens place."

"Did you get him?"

He regarded her with some surprise. "Get who?"

"The person who broke in. I heard he was shot."

"He was."

"I don't understand. What happened to Reed? Why was he at the Owens place? Who broke in?"

The sheriff narrowed his eyes at her. "That's what we're trying to find out. We responded to a 911 call tonight from David Owens. It seems Agent Markham broke into their home—for what purpose I don't know—and Amy Owens shot him in the dark."

Ellery felt the sands shift beneath her feet, her legs going wobbly. "Reed broke into the house? He must have had a reason. The intruder . . ."

"Ms. Hathaway, Agent Markham was the intruder. According to the homeowners, he threw a rock through their patio door and entered the home with a gun. Amy said they had refused to talk to him anymore about the Flores case. Maybe he went in there intending to make them talk."

"What? No." She shook her head emphatically. "He wouldn't do that, not Reed. He . . ." She trailed off, recalling the time Reed had broken into her house, thinking she was a murderer. She swallowed hard and looked at the sheriff. "Is he all right?"

"Shot twice. Once to the head, once in the chest. The doctors are with him now, and that's all I know."

"Oh my God." She reached blindly for the nearest chair and sank down into it.

The sheriff loomed over her, his gun at eye level. "Maybe you can explain what in the hell he was doing breaking into the Owens home."

Her head felt like it was swimming. "I—I don't know. I haven't seen him since early afternoon, when he went to talk to you about the DNA test." She looked up at him. "If he broke into their home, you can bet he had a good reason. He wasn't out to hurt them."

The sheriff looked grim. "Amy says she saw a gun. That's why she fired on him. We found his weapon out and next to him at the scene. Someone had broken through the patio door with a rock. There was glass everywhere."

"If Reed broke in, it was because he thought they were in danger," Ellery insisted.

"If it was on the up-and-up, why didn't he identify himself? Why go smashing through the patio door?"

He was right that it made no sense. "There's an explanation. I know there is. Reed can explain it when he . . . when he's out of surgery."

The sheriff exchanged a look with his sergeant, a broad-shouldered man with sandy hair and a mustache to match. The sergeant walked away toward the coffee machine, and Sheriff Ramsey looked at his shoes. "We'll await Markham's side of the story," he said. "Assuming he lives to tell it."

* * *

Ellery kept vigil through the wee small hours of the morning, shifting in the uncomfortable chair, dosing herself with caffeine from the soda machine down the hall. She had an ancient women's magazine in her lap, but she hadn't read a word of it. She used it as a prop to force herself to stay awake by turning the pages. The sheriff left after a couple of hours, but his deputy remained, keeping a watchful eye on the doors to the surgical suite, as if Reed would somehow rise from the table and escape.

Her face felt taut and lined with fatigue. She kept disappearing inside herself, searching her brain for any answer that might explain what had happened to Reed. The last she'd spoken to him, his focus had been on Angie Rivera, not David and Amy Owens. What had prompted him to go to their house? Why would he break the door in? The time he had broken into Ellery's house, Reed had picked her front door lock with relative ease. If he threw a rock through the patio door, he must've been in an extreme hurry. He must have been convinced David or Amy was in danger. But that explanation didn't add up, either. If there had been a real intruder, why wouldn't David and Amy just say so?

"What in tarnation is going on here?"

Ellery's eyes flew open at the sound of Reed's voice, her body surging forward out of the seat as the magazine slid to the floor. She blinked in momentary confusion because Reed was nowhere to be seen.

"Ellery." She jerked her head around and saw Angus Markham walking toward her. Not Reed. His father. The senator looked rumpled and unshaven, his blue eyes flecked with red. "What's happening?" he demanded. "Where's Reed? They wouldn't tell us much on the phone."

That's when Ellery noticed his wife, Marianne, standing behind him, pale and afraid. She wished she could offer her words of reassurance. Instead, she glanced at the sheriff's deputy, who was listening openly from across the room. "Reed's in surgery. We don't know anything yet."

"They told us he'd been shot," Angus replied tersely.

Ellery looked again at the deputy. "Come with me," she told them. She led them down the hall to the coffee machine, where she explained as much of the story as she could. Angus Markham's frown grew deeper with each passing word.

"That's it? They think he went crazy and broke into some woman's home?"

"There must be some other explanation," Marianne said, folding her arms.

"I agree, but we're going to need Reed to provide it. Right now, the Owenses are controlling the narrative, and their story is that Reed broke in unannounced, with his gun drawn. Amy's saying she had no choice but to shoot him."

"If that's her story, then she's a liar," Marianne replied tartly.

Ellery recalled again how she'd found Reed uninvited in her bedroom, his gun out, prying loose the nails from her closet. "I don't know," she told him. "None of it makes sense to me right now." There was one other complication, and she knew Angus would grasp the implications immediately.

"Both David and Amy Owens are former cops. They're friends with the sheriff, so you can imagine he's inclined to believe what they say."

Angus's lips thinned as he considered the implications. "Right," he muttered with a tinge of disgust. "It's politics, and all politics is local."

Marianne looked alarmed. "She shot an FBI agent. Surely she'll have to answer for that."

"She's claiming self-defense," Ellery answered. "And it sounds like right now they're buying it."

She looked down the hall toward the waiting area, where the deputy had shifted his watch to keep them all in sight. She knew what he was thinking: If Reed was a criminal, they were all potential accomplices. Anything they said might be used against him. "Sheriff Ramsey will be back here looking to talk to you," she said, "but I'd advise you to keep quiet. Any questions he has will be designed to suit his own agenda, to further the Owens narrative. He's implying Reed was so crazy for answers about Camilla's death that he was prepared to threaten David or Amy at gunpoint."

"Was he?" Angus looked at her sharply. "Tell me if it's true."

Ellery saw Reed standing breathless in her bedroom with a hammer, sweaty and dirty, convinced she was a killer. In return, she'd had a gun pointed right between his eyes. But even then, she hadn't been afraid of him. "No," she said with finality. "It's not true."

They returned together to the waiting area, and after only a few more minutes the surgeon finally appeared to give them an update. He looked as exhausted as they did, with his puffy eyes and the five o'clock shadow he sported at seven in the morning. Reed had been shot twice, he explained. Once to the head, once in the chest, but Reed got lucky, considering the circumstances. The bullet that hit his head didn't penetrate the skull; it merely left a fracture on its way by. The bullet in his chest did more damage. It collapsed his left lung but spared his heart, although it had torn a couple of blood vessels and nicked a kidney in the process. Reed remained on a ventilator and in critical condition, but the doctor was optimistic that he would recover.

Ellery sagged in relief at the news. "Can we see him?" Marianne asked anxiously.

"Not yet," the surgeon replied. "He's still in recovery. He'll be sleeping for a while. I'd say another six hours at a minimum. You could go and get some rest."

"We're staying," Marianne answered, drawing her sweater closer around her.

"Suit yourself. There's a cafeteria downstairs. They make pretty decent ham and eggs." He gave them a tired smile. "I'll make sure the nurses know you're here so that you are informed of any changes."

Angus turned to Ellery. "You should go, get some rest. We can call you if there are any updates."

Ellery looked back at the chair she'd occupied since she'd arrived, the place she'd sat while Reed kept breathing. "No," she said. "I think I'll stay."

The hours ticked by, the sun creeping higher in the sky

outside, and the waiting room slowly filled up with other Markham family members. One by one, Reed's three sisters arrived, in the precise order in which they'd first appeared on earth: Suzanne the oldest, followed by Lynette, and then, finally, Kimmy. They were each as blond and trendy as Ellery had imagined them to be—not showy, but put together in a way that Ellery never managed to pull off herself. Their jewelry was understated but obviously the real thing. Their jeans had an even dark wash, not the mishmash of various blue streaks that Ellery usually wore. They sported fashion boots, not winter boots. Lynette had a beautiful camel-colored duster that Ellery admired even as she recognized she could never own it, as hers would be forever covered in dog fur.

Ellery said hello to them but hung back as the Markham family gathered in a huddle. They rearranged the waiting room chairs to suit themselves, and Suzanne had brought everyone coffee. Ellery listened to them talk and laugh and cry and wondered what Reed would say if he could see them now. It didn't matter what the hell his DNA test said: this was obviously his family. She closed her eyes, drowsing as she took in their stories.

"Remember that time he and Timmy Granger thought they were the Wright brothers? They built that glider thing and tried to fly it off the garage roof." Lynette sounded half-awed, half-horrified, at the memory.

"He broke his left arm in the fall," Marianne replied. "Of course I remember."

"What about the time he started his own detective agency?" Kimmy said. "Remember that one?"

"I'm trying to forget," Angus answered darkly, but Kimmy kept going with her story.

"Robby Bellamy hired Reed for twenty bucks because his mother threatened to fire their housekeeper for stealing her underwear. Robby believed the woman when she said she didn't do it."

"I think it was more that he liked her cooking," Suzanne said drily.

"Whatever. Reed set up a sting at the Bellamy household to catch the thief in the act."

"Yes, yes," Angus said uncomfortably. "And he caught Mr. Bellamy. I think we all remember that one. I still can't look Jeffrey in the eyes at church."

"Really? 'Cause I was always checking to see if he had on a brassiere," Kimmy said, and Marianne hushed her.

They got word that Reed had been removed from the ventilator and was breathing fine on his own, but he had not woken up. Ellery could tell from the way the doctor delivered the news that this was unusual. "Can we see him now?" Marianne asked.

"Family only. One at a time. No more than five minutes."

Family only. Ellery retreated to her chair and tried not to let it bother her as she watched the Markhams take turns going in and out. The parade seemed endless, and Ellery had to ask herself what she was doing here. Reed's family had this crisis more than covered. Her body felt on the brink of collapse, her stomach churning nothing but leftover soda and her eyes so tired that her vision had started to blur. She looked up groggily as Kimmy Markham plopped into the seat next to her. "How's he doing?" Ellery asked, rousing herself one more time.

Kimmy gave a helpless shrug. "The heart monitor thingie is beeping like it should. He seems to be breathing okay. But he won't wake up. That's not normal, right? He should be up by now."

"I don't know."

Kimmy ran a hand down the side of the chair, jangling her thin silver bracelets. "It's all my fault," she confessed in a small voice. "I'm the one who made him get that DNA test. I just thought it would be fun, you know? Find out you're related to Joan of Arc or something."

Ellery's head felt fuzzy. "Did Joan of Arc have any kids?" Right now, she wasn't sure if Joan of Arc had even been a real person.

"Maybe not." Kimmy leaned back in her chair with a defeated sigh. "I just thought it would be a fun project. The commercials for these tests make it sound like a hoot, and scientists are coming out every day saying we're all related anyhow. It's just a matter of degree." She cast a troubled look across the room at her father, who was dozing in a chair. "I didn't realize what a hot mess my family was."

"All families are hot messes." On this point, Ellery was sure.

"Do you have any brothers and sisters?"

Yes and no. Either answer could be true. "One of each," she answered finally, and Kimmy gave her a sad smile.

"Then you know how it is."

Ellery said nothing. The mounted television playing silently in the corner had caught her attention. "That's her," she said, standing up. "That's Amy Owens."

All the Markhams gathered with her as Ellery found the remote and turned up the volume on Amy Owens's press conference. ". . . can't eat or sleep since it happened," she was saying with tears in her eyes. "I feel so terrible. It's all a big mistake, a horrible accident. I didn't know it was Agent Markham who had entered my home. All I knew was someone had broken into my home. It was dark. I couldn't see well. I thought he was going to kill me."

"Bullshit," Lynette said succinctly.

"I'd been upstairs getting ready to take a bath. I—I was naked under my robe. My husband wasn't home. Then I heard a loud crash downstairs in the kitchen, and I knew someone was in the house. I was terrified."

Wouldn't you call 911? Ellery wondered.

"I'm so sorry about all of this." Amy broke down sobbing, and a man identified as her lawyer stepped forward to put his arm around her shoulders.

"Amy Owens was within her rights to defend herself," he said. "A strange man broke into her home late at night, his gun drawn. She was terrified, as any of us would be. Amy deeply regrets the harm done to Agent Markham, but he left her no other choice, as the investigation will show. She expresses her condolences to Agent Markham's family, and she's praying for his recovery. We ask that you please respect her need for privacy at this time as the police conduct their investigations. We're confident that the results will show Amy Owens acted well within the law."

"Screw the law," Lynette said. "I want actual answers."

Ellery watched the screen as the lawyer and David Owens led Amy away from the LVMPD headquarters. *Local Woman Shoots Rogue FBI Agent,* said the crawl at the bottom. The only way to get answers, she thought, was to retrace Reed's steps and figure out what he was doing at the Owens household in the first place. "I'm going to go back to the hotel for a few hours," she said to Kimmy, who was standing next to her. "Will you please be sure to call me if there is any change with Reed?"

Kimmy took out her cell phone to grab Ellery's number. "Of course. Please go get some rest. You've been here longer than any of us."

"I'll be back as soon as I can."

Exhausted, Ellery passed out hard in the back of the cab on her return to the hotel. She awoke to the driver calling, "Lady, lady," in accented English as he tapped her knee. "Are you okay?" He squinted at her with a mixture of suspicion and concern.

"I'm fine," she muttered, although her dry mouth felt stuffed with cotton.

She dragged herself up to her hotel room, where she scrounged around until she located the spare electronic key that Reed had given her when they checked in. She used it to enter his room, which had clearly been tidied by the hotel cleaning staff. The bed was made and Reed's papers and files had been stacked neatly on the desk. She checked the bathroom and found his toiletries sitting next to the sink. She paused to finger the rough-textured handle of his razor, which looked for all the world like Reed would be back any moment to use it. At the desk, she checked Reed's most recent notes and saw that Sheriff Ramsey had denied Reed's request for a DNA test on Angie Rivera. Could this be why he had reverted to his earlier focus on David Owens? Ellery could find no obvious connection.

She took the notes with her back to her own room, where her work sat abandoned on the bedspread. Giselle Hardiman's secret code would have to remain unsolved for the moment, as Ellery had more pressing concerns. She shoved the papers aside and lay down with Reed's notes, determined to see whatever he had seen that prompted him to go to the Owens house. She managed to read only two pages before her eyes drifted shut and she couldn't get them open again.

She awoke more than three hours later, jerking in fear when she realized she'd been sleeping. She groped for her cell phone and hastily checked to see if she had missed any calls from the hospital. Nothing. No news was at least not bad news, and she sank into the pillows with some relief. In her sleep, she'd rolled on top of her purloined papers, wrinkling the reports she'd worked so hard to get. She pulled the sheets out from under her body and looked at the top one. It was the start of the murder book, the typed statement from the responding officer the night Giselle had died. Ellery had read through it once before, but her eyes automatically scanned it again. The information told her nothing new. The uniformed officer was responding to an anonymous tip reporting screaming from inside Giselle's apartment. Giselle did not answer the knock, and the front door was found open. The patrol officer had discovered Giselle mortally wounded in her own bed and immediately called for backup.

Only this time, Ellery read to the end, to the part where the officer had typed and signed her name to the statement: Amy Conway.

Ellery struggled to sit up in bed as she clutched the paper tighter. When she looked again, the name was still there. Officer Amy Conway. That had been her name back then, Ellery recalled, before she'd married David—about three months after Camilla had died. So at a minimum, Amy had been at the scene of Giselle's murder and knew how she died. Knew enough, maybe, to re-create it one year later. After all, the DNA on the knife was female.

Ellery felt with chilling certainty now that Reed's shooting had not been any kind of accident. Amy's story stunk like the inside of a fake leg. Ellery quickly changed her three-day-old clothes and stuffed the copy of Amy's incriminating statement in her back pocket. Then she went to get a cab, and thankfully the valet was ready and alert this time. "Certainly, ma'am," he said as he stuck his arm out to wave for a taxi. "Where are you going to today?"

"Twenty-seven Faulkner Avenue," she said. The place would of course be marked as a crime scene, roped off to the Owens family and the public, but Ellery didn't care. There was only one thing that could prove her theory, and that was a piece of Amy Owens's DNA.

She fidgeted in the car on the drive over, worried about her options if the cops had someone posted at the scene. Her concern proved unfounded when the car stopped in the driveway of the Owens house, which looked as peaceful as it ever had from the outside. "Thanks," Ellery said, handing him a pair of twenties. "Do you mind waiting?"

"Your money." He shut the car off but left the radio on, tuned to some soccer game.

Ellery knew the real action had occurred around to the rear of the house, so she followed the path Reed must have taken to get there—through the gate, past the overgrown landscaping, and into the backyard. Sunlight glinted off the pool. The place was so quiet that Ellery heard only her own footsteps as she walked over the patio. Bits of glass crunched under her feet, and she saw that the broken door had been blocked off with black plastic sheeting. She gave it an experimental push, but it held fast. She would have to rip it apart if she wanted to get inside. With a last look behind her, Ellery took out her pocketknife and slit the side of the plastic.

The scene inside made her stomach flip over. Shattered glass everywhere. The telltale rock. Worst of all, Reed's blood smeared from one end of the kitchen to the other. There were dried, bloody boot prints and discarded paramedics gloves.

The place smelled like decaying body fluids and a faint hint of gunpowder. Ellery edged her way around the mess and went to stand near the base of the stairs. Based on her eyeball estimate, this was approximatcly whcrc Amy must have been standing when she shot Reed—only about fifteen feet away. Even in the low light, she should have recognized him.

Ellery went up the stairs to find the master bedroom and bath, one of which would surely have a personal product of Amy's that she could use to get a DNA sample. The sunny bedroom had a thick carpet, pale green walls, and a cheerful quilt spread across the large bed. A pair of eyeglasses sat on one nightstand, a small stack of romance novels on the other. Framed family pictures watched her from thc walls as Ellery crept toward the en suite bath. The tableau looked so homey, so ordinary, that Ellery had to remind hcrsclf that its designer might have slaughtered another human being to attain all this. In the bathroom, she found the tub still filled with water, a pair of candles set along the edge, presumably from where Amy had been set to take a bath before Reed's intrusion. She had lined up her alibi in advance.

Ellery kicked the lever to drain the tub, taking satisfaction in watching some of Amy's story wash away. She located a vanity with an accompanying tufted chair and large, lighted mirror. Amy took care with her appearance. Ellery felt a renewed rage as she imagined the woman applying makeup ahead of her press conference today. "You'll be crying for real next time," she muttered as she started gathering up objects into the paper bag she'd brought with her to the scene. Hairbrush, comb, lipstick. One of these would be enough to match the DNA.

Ellery fled the scene stairs two at a time and pushed her way back out into the warm afternoon sunshine, only to grind to a halt in the pile of glass. There on the patio standing in front of her stood Amy Owens. "Oh," Ellery said abruptly. "Hi. I didn't know anyone was here."

Amy tilted her head as though confused by what she saw. "The sheriff said it was okay if I stopped by to pick up a few personal items, and I got curious when I saw the cab out front. The driver said you'd come around back here. What are you doing?"

"Just checking something." Ellery glanced beyond Amy in the direction of the gate. It was either run back inside or get past her somehow.

"Checking what?" The split plastic tarp behind Ellery started flapping in the breeze, an angry slapping sound. "What were you doing inside my home without permission?"

"I just had to see where it happened. You know how it is."

"I'm calling the cops," Amy said, taking out her phone. "You shouldn't be here."

"It's too bad you didn't call them last night," Ellery said, and Amy froze.

"What's that supposed to mean?"

Ellery shrugged. "You were awfully quick on the draw is all."

"He broke into my house!" Amy gestured with the phone

at her broken patio door. "He was acting crazy!"

"He told you about the DNA test," Ellery said. She cocked her head at Amy. "Didn't he?"

The color drained from Amy's face like that water from the tub. "I don't know what you're talking about," she said tightly. "Agent Markham didn't say anything to me at all. If he had, I wouldn't have shot him."

"I don't think so." Ellery clutched the paper bag to her middle. With the proof in hand, she was feeling bold. "I think you shot him on purpose. As a matter of fact, I think you staged this whole thing."

"That's preposterous," Amy retorted, but Ellery noticed she had stopped threatening to call the police. "It was an accident, plain and simple."

"You're good at staging crime scenes," Ellery continued. "You set up Camilla Flores's place so good that it took forty years before anyone caught on. But then, you had a good model to work from, didn't you? You saw what Giselle Hardiman's bedroom looked like the night she died. Her killer was still out there on the loose—easy enough to try to make Cammie's murder look like the work of the same guy. Only Camilla turned out to be much harder to kill—after all, she had a baby to protect."

"You're crazy. You don't know what you're talking about. I barely knew Camilla."

"You knew enough. You knew the important part, which was that she was David's intended fiancée. I'm betting he talked about her all the time."

"Sure, he talked about her some. Who cares?"

"You cared," Ellery said, her voice turning hard. "You cared so much it made you crazy. I don't know for sure, but I'm guessing that David slept with you, too. It must've made your blood boil watching him go home to her every night after that, listening to him talk about marrying her. What happened? Did you think he'd leave her and marry you?"

"He did marry me." There it was, the triumph in her eye.

"Yeah, after she was dead," Ellery snorted with ridicule, and Amy's look turned mean.

"You can't prove a thing."

"I can with that DNA test." She held up the bag. "I, too, stopped by for some of your personal items. What do you want to bet they're a match to the sample on that knife, the one that killed Cammie?"

Amy took a step toward her. "You can't take those. You have no right!"

Ellery sidestepped her. "I did it. It's done. What, are you going to shoot me, too?"

"I could. You're trespassing." Amy gripped her purse, one hand sliding toward the pocket, and Ellery felt a flash of fear. "I read up about you after you came to the house the first time," Amy continued. "The story is all over the internet. You're already suspended, under investigation for a possible murder. That makes you dangerous, crazier even than he was. Just look at you here, breaking into someone's house."

"The cops took your gun."

Amy gave her a thin smile. "How many cops do you

346

know with only one gun?" She took out a small pistol and aimed at Ellery, her bag slipping down onto the concrete. "Give me back my stuff."

"No." The cabbie was sitting just around the front. All she had to do was get there.

"I said give it to me!" Amy lunged at her and grabbed for the bag. It ripped between them, scattering her things across the patio.

"You can't shoot me," Ellery said, trying to remain calm. "Once might be an accident. Twice is murder. Even your friend the sheriff is bound to ask questions. Then what happens when Reed wakes up? And there's still that problem of the DNA test."

"If he wakes up," Amy said coldly. "And what about the DNA test? You think Brad Ramsey's going to run that test on your say-so? You think anyone is? I don't have to shoot you. I just have to call the cops and let them see you here, acting like a lunatic, and no one is ever going to believe a word you say. You're that cracked-up victim from the serial killer case. You're not a cop. You're not anything. No one's going to run a DNA test just because you ask for one."

"No, but they damn sure will do it for me." There was a rustling, a waving of the palm tree, and Ellery turned to see Angus Markham step out from around the bushes. He held up his phone. "Those cops you keep talking about—I've already called them."

Amy's face screwed up in frustration and the gun wavered in her hand.

"You can't shoot both of us," Angus said reasonably as he came to stand next to Ellery.

"Well, her track record says she could," Ellery replied, matching his conversational tone. "Except for one thing."

Angus raised bushy eyebrows. "Oh? What's that?"

"This." Ellery kicked as hard as she could in Amy's direction, catching the arm that held the gun. It went sailing from her hand and landed with a splash in the pool. Amy let loose a string of curse words that would make a sailor blush as the sirens began to sound in the distance.

Ellery turned to Angus with surprise. "You have good timing," she said. "But I have to ask—what are you doing here?"

"I went to fetch you at the hotel because I know you're without transportation. The doorman informed me that you'd taken a cab over here."

"You came to fetch me? Why?"

He smiled broadly. "Reed is awake."

19

"The patient has no heartbeat. I think we have to take it out. Can you please give me the scalpel?"

Reed's eyes flew open in alarm, on the off chance Tula had acquired a knife somewhere. "The scalpel's just pretend, right?" He craned his head off the floor of his daughter's bedroom, scanning the assembled medical team of stuffed animals for any signs of a sharp implement.

"It's from the same kit as the stethoscope," Tula explained, waving the plastic end at him. "See?" Then she frowned at him, her huge dark eyes rimmed with concern. "You're supposed to be under anna-seethes-you."

"Anesthesia."

"That's what I said." She pushed his head down again. "Now lie back. This is only going to hurt a little."

"Tula!" Sarit called out from the doorway, a dish towel in her hand. "I think it's time to let your father off the floor, okay? He's still recuperating."

Reed reached over to squeeze Tula's small hand. "You're an excellent doctor, sweetheart. I'm feeling much better." He grimaced as he tried to rise from the floor, and Tula stood to give him a hand. It had been more than a month since his discharge from the hospital, but his mobility remained somewhat limited. He'd awoken with no memory of the shooting and the details had yet to come back to him. Ellery had filled him in on what had happened, and when the DNA test came back as a match to Amy Owens he knew it had to be true. In his head, though, he still had trouble matching sweet, round, cookie-baking Amy to the face of a murderer.

"Imagine how David feels," Ellery had replied. "He's been sleeping next to the woman who murdered his girlfriend for forty years now—and he's the reason she did it."

Reed, who'd grown up in a house full of secrets, could imagine it too well. His parents had overseen the bulk of his care since he'd left the hospital, seeming to relish the opportunity to fuss over him. Reed tolerated it in small doses and feigned sleep whenever he needed them to go away. They had apologized, in their way, for keeping the truth from him, but their contrition only went so far. Reed suspected if they could rewind history they'd make the same choices again. They still saw themselves as protecting him, and his brush with the hereafter only cemented this belief.

Reed took the stairs gingerly, although his feet knew them by feel from all the years he had walked them, baby Tula in his arms. He still admired the stately Southern home, with its sturdy redbrick exterior and intricately carved wooden staircase. Generations had come of age in this place, and he was glad his daughter was safe within its walls. He no longer felt a pang of loss looking at the paint choices and picture hangings he had debated with Sarit. It was time for him to go home, and that was no longer here. He found Sarit wiping down the kitchen counters. "Thank you for letting me come over today," he said. "It was really good to spend time with her."

"Anytime, Reed. I mean it."

They stood with the island between them. He noticed she had switched out the light fixture over the sink, the one they had disagreed about all those years ago. "I was wondering if I could borrow a book from the library," he said at last.

"Of course, please help yourself. Half of them are still yours, anyway. I've got the new Tana French novel if you're looking for something to read."

Reed drifted down the hall to the room they'd called the library, the one lined from floor to ceiling with books. It also contained Tula's playhouse, an old sofa, and a small television, but the books gave the room its presence. The hardwood floors creaked under his feet as he studied the shelves, unsure if he would even find the book he sought. He'd looked up the article online the night before and verified his memory was intact: ten years earlier, Sarit had written a series about the psychological impact of rape on the survivors, and Reed recalled she had done extensive research for the piece. It took him a fair amount of searching, but he located the book he'd remembered.

"Daddy!" Tula came bounding down the stairs and hurled herself at him. He winced as she made contact with his chest, but her enthusiastic embrace was worth the pain. He bent to kiss her head.

"My sweet."

"Do you have to go?"

Sarit materialized in the hall with them. "You're welcome to stay for supper. It's just me and Tula."

"That's a lovely offer, thank you, but I'm afraid I must be going. I have dinner plans of my own tonight. Next week, okay?"

"Okay. Love you, Daddy." She gripped his head with both hands, holding him still for a noisy kiss, and then went skipping back up the stairs to her menagerie.

Sarit eyed the book in his hand as he rose to his feet, and he tucked it against his side self-consciously. "Dinner plans," she said. "Like a date?"

He allowed himself to smile. Ellery's plane would be touching down in an hour. They were having dinner, and for once, it wasn't to discuss any sort of case. He had been looking forward to it for a literal month, and he wasn't about to let Sarit ruin his good mood. "Like a date," he agreed.

Sarit nodded at the book, the one he'd turned to obscure the title: *Living and Loving After Sexual Assault.* "It's Ellery, yes?"

Reed knew Sarit didn't approve, but he no longer gave a damn. "It's just dinner," he said lightly.

"Not if you're reading that it's not."

"I care about her, Sarit. I suggest you get used to the idea, since there is nothing you can actually do about it."

"You care about her; that's great. It's just when the pair of you get together, one or both of you end up in a hospital. That's not healthy, Reed. It's dangerous."

"She had nothing to do with what happened to me this time. She wasn't even there when it happened."

"That's supposed to make me feel better? Look, I'm not trying to tell you how to live your life. You're right: that's not up to me. But it is my job to look after Tula."

He narrowed his eyes at her. "Tula's just fine."

"Sure, now. What if she's with you when you and Ellery decide to go on one of your ill-considered adventures?"

Reed's jaw dropped. "Ill-considered? We arrested my mother's murderer!"

"I'm aware of that. Congratulations all around, yes. You also almost got killed in the bargain. I'm sure she's lovely, Reed. I'm not saying she's not a nice person. But—"

"But what?"

"The two of you seem to bring out the worst in each other. Or at least the danger. So yes, I worry. I worry for you, and I worry for Tula."

"You can be sure I'm not dragging Tula along on any investigation, ill-considered or otherwise. Give me a little credit, at least."

"She loves you. Believe it or not, so do I. I just want what's best for you."

Reed drew himself up stiffly. Here was a lesson he had

learned the hard way. "There's a limit to what love can do," he told her. He held up the book as he went for the door. "Thanks for the book. Tell Tula I'll call her tomorrow."

Reed took his dish of cut-up and seasoned potatoes and placed it in the oven underneath the pork. He had the vegetables ready for steaming, and a chocolate torte purchased from the bakery around the corner. Normally, he'd bake it himself, but his stamina wasn't quite back to normal yet. He'd tidied the living room and made sure the downstairs bathroom was presentable. He didn't have to worry about the closets this time, as Ellery had insisted on staying at a nearby hotel.

His cell phone buzzed on the counter, and he snatched it up, thinking it could be her, but the phone number was a familiar one from Nevada. Jackie Baldwin, the prosecutor charged with handling Amy Owens's case, had called him multiple times over the past few weeks to talk about the upcoming trial. "Jackie," he said, hoping it would be short and sweet this time. "How are you?"

"I'll level with you. I've been better."

"Why? What's going on?" He went to peek out the blinds to see if Ellery's taxi was on its way down the street.

"We've got trouble," Jackie told him. "Amy Owens's team wanted a thorough reanalysis of that bookend—you know, the one used to beat Camilla in the attack? Well, they got a solid index print from the base and it doesn't match Amy Owens."

Reed forced himself to pay attention. Amy was out on bail, he knew. Despite the DNA results, no one could seem to believe the charges were true. Amy was well liked and family oriented. She'd raised three daughters in the community, and so far her family, including David, was standing by her side.

"The print doesn't match Camilla Flores, either. This, combined with that missing twenty-five thousand dollars, leaves the door wide open for the defense. You see what I'm saying?"

"I do, yes." Reed returned to the kitchen and shook up his homemade salad dressing. "I'm just not sure what to tell you. It's her DNA on the knife."

"Maybe there was a second doer," Jackie replied. "A coconspirator. We ran David's prints, and they're not a match, either. Amy's lawyer is claiming it's proof his client is innocent. Some other guy committed the murder."

"Her blood was on the knife."

"She's now saying that she had dinner with David and Cammie at her apartment one time shortly before the murder, and that she helped to cook it. Maybe she cut herself on the knife then. Her husband is backing the story."

Reed frowned, the bottle in his hand. "That's a problem."

"A big one. I can't go to trial like this. She's guaranteed a walk."

"Ellery can testify. Amy practically confessed to her."

"Did she? I've interviewed Ellery at length about that conversation. According to her, all Amy did was deny it."

Reed's doorbell rang. "I've got to go," he said. "We can talk more later."

"I'm not sure there will be a later," Jackie replied darkly.

Reed hung up the phone without saying goodbye. He would worry about this latest complication later. He didn't want to spend the evening talking shop with Ellery. He just wanted to see her. Flush with anticipation, he flung open the door and found her standing on his stoop with her roller bag in hand. She gave him a shy smile. "Hi," she said. "You, uh, you look good." Her face turned pink. "Healthy, I mean."

He raised his eyebrows. "I have a doctor's note and everything. Come on in."

He welcomed her inside the small foyer and tried to kiss her cheek, only she moved one way as he moved the other and they bumped heads instead. "Oops," she said, rubbing her temple. "Sorry."

He was determined to get better about touching her. He just hadn't had time to read the damn book yet. "How was your flight? Here, let me take your bag."

She held fast when he tried to take it from her. "About that," she said, laying her hand on his.

"I know; you're staying at the hotel. I just meant I can put it out of the way while we eat dinner."

"I can't stay."

He halted, confused. "What?"

"I did the HLA test," she said. "The one that checks to see if I can be a bone marrow donor for—for Ashley. I just got the call when I landed." She spread her hands in

356

helpless fashion. "I'm a match."

"Really? That's amazing."

She peeked behind him at the kitchen. "No, dinner smells amazing. I've been thinking about it all day."

"It's almost ready. Can you at least stay to eat?"

"Try to stop me."

He set out the dishes while she washed up, and while they ate she explained about the next steps. "I have to go to Detroit. I've already booked a flight for the morning. They want me to donate some of my own blood ahead of the procedure, and then we wait a few days before the actual transplant. Depending on how it goes, they may keep me overnight, or I could go home even the same day."

"Home? Back to Boston?"

"No, I think I'd have to wait a couple of days for that. I'll have to find a hotel or something. At least I have an excuse to have room service wait on me hand and foot for a few days, right?"

"Right." He searched her face. "Are you okay? You're sure about this?"

"Sure, I guess. This kid, Ashley, it's not her fault that her father is an asshole. Besides, what's a couple more scars at this point?" She nodded to him. "What about you? How are you doing?"

He made a show of sitting up straighter. "I'm fine. Mostly healed now, although I'm not allowed back to work for another couple of weeks yet. Like you said, what's a couple more scars?"

"Your family is something else," she told him. "They laid siege to that waiting area like Grant took Richmond. I think they would've set up camp for months if they'd needed to." She paused and pushed the food around on her plate. "They, uh, they love you a lot."

He smiled at her tenderly, although she had ducked her head, hiding from him, so she couldn't see it. He knew she'd been there, too, because his sisters told him so. "How would you feel about dessert?" he said as he rose to his feet.

"I feel passionately about dessert," she said as she helped him clear the table. "You know that."

"Great. We can eat and then I'll go pack."

She looked surprised. "Pack? Where are you going?"

"Apparently, I'm going to Detroit."

She stopped with a dish in each hand and looked at him askance. "Reed, you don't have to do that."

"I'm going completely crazy sitting around here looking at these four walls, and you promised me a weekend. We'll just have to switch up the venue is all." The mess out in Nevada was not his problem anymore. Let Jackie worry about how to nail Amy. For once, Reed was going to spend more energy thinking about his future than his past. "What's your ticket information?" he asked her, and he pulled out his phone. "I'll see if I can get us booked into first class. I think we've damned well earned it, don't you?"

Ellery searched him over for a moment and then smiled. "You know what?" she said. "I think maybe we have."

20

Ellery encountered her father at the hospital when she was done giving blood. They stood far apart in the hallway, watching each other warily, and she thought about the times she used to ride around on his shoulders, ten feet tall, or how she used to go out with him on delivery in his truck, the two of them cranking the radio and singing John Cougar Mellencamp at the top of their lungs, how sometimes love don't feel like it should. Her memories, even the good ones, hurt too much now because they had not been good enough for him. He looked older, his hair streaked with gray, his belly hanging over his belt like a sack of sunflower seeds.

"Thank you for doing this," he said at last, his voice full of emotion, his eyes wet. "Thank you so much. You have no idea what this means to me." He reached for her with both hands, only to fall back when Ellery stepped out of his reach.

"Actually, I do." She'd died a little when Daniel was sick

and she was found not to be a match for him. The results had only reinforced her hatred for her useless body, but Danny hadn't held it against her. He'd patted her as she'd cried. It had been a long time after that before she could look him in the eyes again.

"Yeah, well, thank you," her father said again.

"I'm not here for you. I'm here for her."

He nodded vigorously, his palms raised. "I get that. You won't be sorry. Ashley's a great kid."

"I want to meet her."

Surprise colored his features, then uncertainty. "Uh, sure, when she's better, yeah. Definitely."

"No, I want to meet her now." Her heart thundered in her chest. She hadn't known until she said the words that they were true.

Her father looked up and down the corridor at the doctors and nurses, as if searching for a way out. "I don't think we can. I mean, she's not allowed visitors."

"You can see her, right?"

"Yeah, her mom and me, but no one else. And we've got to be gowned up and everything. She's got no immune system right now. Even the sniffles could kill her."

"I'm perfectly healthy. I'll wear whatever protection is necessary. I just want to meet her."

Ellery had all the power in this conversation, and her father knew it. She could still back out. He scratched his head, stalling for time. "Tell you what. I'll talk to the doctors. See what they say."

"We can talk to them together," she said, and her father spun on his heel in a circle.

"Aw, hell. Look, Abby—I mean Ellery. The thing is, we haven't told her about you yet. Not the whole story. She only knows that we found a donor. I just don't think she could handle the details right now, you know? She's very sick."

"Ah, I see. You haven't explained to your new daughter how you ran off and left your old one."

He flinched as if slapped. "Yeah," he agreed with a short nod. "That."

They stood in silence as Ellery summoned the last bit of pity she could find for him. "I won't tell her," she said finally. "Not until she's better." She didn't want to dump all her hurt and confusion on some fifteen-year-old kid who was fighting for her life.

"Oh, thanks," John said with obvious relief. "That'd be great. Thank you."

They spoke with the doctors, who reluctantly agreed to let Ellery have a short visit with Ashley Hathaway. Ellery first had to put on a gown, a mask, gloves, and a hair protector. When she looked at herself in the bathroom mirror, she saw only her eyes. They were the same gray-blue color she found on the bald, pale girl lying in room 302.

"Hi," Ashley said softly when the automatic door slid open and Ellery entered. "You must be new here. I know because I've been here so long that I know everyone and you don't look familiar." Ashley was so thin that her veins showed through her skin, giving her a faintly blue tint.

Ellery introduced herself but hovered awkwardly near the door. "I'm not a doctor or a nurse," she said. "I—I just wanted to meet you."

"Yeah? Get a good look in now because I'm going home soon." The girl couldn't contain her grin, and it was contagious, taking up her whole face. Ellery smiled behind her mask.

"Good for you."

"Well, not right away," Ashley corrected. "The transplant has to take hold first. But they found a donor, a hundred-percent match!"

A hot flush went through Ellery, and she was glad now for the cover of her disguise. "That's great," she said stiffly. "I'm glad." She had no idea what she'd expected to find here.

"If you're not a doctor or a nurse, what are you?" Ashley asked.

"I'm a cop." Finally, at last. Again. Back in Boston, they had voted to reinstate her position. In fact, the chief now wanted to send her to detective school as part of some program promoting female officers. Ellery was still deciding on that part, as she'd had enough of being singled out.

"A cop, wow. That's pretty cool. You aren't here to bust me, are you?" Ashley gave her a sly grin. "I swear my four-twenty prescription is medicinal."

"No." Ellery hesitated. "I had a brother named Daniel. He had the same kind of cancer you have. It was a long time ago."

"Oh." Ashley's face turned serious, old beyond her years. She smoothed out the sheet by her hip. "He didn't make it, huh."

"No, we couldn't find him a match." Ellery's throat tightened even now at the memory.

"I'm so sorry. You must miss him a lot. I always wished I could have a brother or a sister, but Mom and Dad have only me." She struggled to sit up against the pillows, her bald head blending in with the white cotton. "What was he like, your brother?"

Ellery turned around and looked at the door. "I think I'm supposed to be going now."

"No, stay." Her voice was thin and pleading. "Tell me. What was he like?"

Ellery hadn't talked much about Daniel in years. Her heart pounded at the thought of saying his name out loud, at letting him be real again, if only for a few minutes. She glanced at the door again, fighting the urge to flee. She remembered how useless she'd been to Daniel in his final days when he'd called out to her from the other bed, but she couldn't make herself speak an answer, not with Coben's marks fresh on her body: *Come on, Abby. Talk to me. Anything!* Ellery let out a slow breath, making her decision. She found a rolling chair and pulled it over next to the bed. "His name was Daniel," she began, feeling her face break into a smile behind the medical mask. "He could draw these amazing pictures like you wouldn't believe. It was like he could see into another world."

* * *

Reed had found them another hotel suite, not quite as grand as the one in Las Vegas but just as comfortable and only a few blocks from the hospital. Ellery had her bedroom on one side and he had his on the other. He kept his polite distance, giving her all the space she desired, and she paced her bedroom suite alone. She felt restless, sparky somehow, like a live wire twisting on the ground. Soon she would have to go back to the hospital, where they would put her to sleep while they harvested part of her body. When she thought about the blackness or the coming pain for too long, her brain told her to run: *Go. Go now.*

She couldn't run, not if she was to help Ashley, and the cold April rain outside meant she couldn't even risk a jog. She went as far as she could, to Reed's room. She knocked softly on his door, just in case he was napping, but he called out immediately, "Come in!"

She found him lying on top of the made-up bed, barefoot but fully dressed in jeans and a chestnut-colored sweater. He had his professor glasses on and some sort of book facedown on his chest. "I thought you might be resting," she said.

"I've done enough of that," he said as he set the book aside. "How are you? How was the hospital?"

"Fine. It went fine." She didn't really want to talk about it. Outside, rain slashed against the windows, the sky an angry gray, but Reed's room had buttery light and a cozy comforter on the bed. She took the side opposite him, sitting cross-legged, and glanced at the book he'd been reading. *Living and Loving After Sexual Assault*. Her face flushed hard, but he saw her notice the title, so she couldn't pretend otherwise. She looked down at her lap for a long time. "Is that about me?" she asked finally, feeling him watching her.

"No," he said, his voice rich with affection. "There's no manual for you. Believe me, I've looked."

"That's what scares you, isn't it? I might not be fixable." For her, it was the opposite: she'd accepted years ago that she couldn't change, that parts of normal life would never be for her. Reed made her afraid to hope it could be otherwise.

"Maybe a little."

She lay down next to him so she mirrored his body. "What does the book say? Am I crazy?"

"No," he said firmly, and she looked at him with surprise. He reached up to stroke her cheek with his thumb. "You're entirely normal for someone who's been through what you have. It's your circumstances that are crazy." He smiled at her, his gaze tender.

She took his hand in hers to study it. He was warm and slightly hairy. Her skin tingled when she rubbed their fingertips together, and she didn't want to stop. Reed let her hold his hand as he shifted to lie on his side facing her. She moved experimentally closer, testing the boundary, dipping into his personal space. She could feel him breathing.

"Tell me," he said after a while.

"Tell you what?"

"Whatever it is you think I should know."

She was quiet for a long time, weighing this. She watched their joined hands so she didn't have to look him in the eyes. Coben had killed sixteen girls before he got to her, and she felt the weight of them in ways that were difficult to verbalize. People who heard the story expected her to be perpetually astonished at her good fortune—*Don't you feel lucky?* What she felt was pressure. She was supposed to live her best life, to be everyone's happy ending, and yet sometimes she couldn't even tolerate being inside her own skin. "Before, when I went to bed with guys," she said at last, "I would pretend it wasn't happening. I would go somewhere in my head and think about other things so I could tolerate them touching me. I was glad when it was over." She paused. "That's why I didn't do it very often."

She checked with him to see how he was taking this, whether he would be confused or appalled, but he regarded her with his full attention, his gaze clear and calm. "That sounds . . . difficult," he murmured at length.

"It wasn't," she said, pulling back with a trace of impatience. "It wasn't anything. It was—a lack of feeling, a void. I assumed that's just how it would always be."

"Ah. But now?" He stretched a hand toward her body and she looked down at his fingers. She imagined them touching her in intimate places and her mouth went dry.

"You make me want to try to be different."

"Funny. I say the same thing about you."

"You have to understand," she said, still looking at his hand. "I don't know how long it would last. How much I could take before I had to close the door again." She'd run enough miles over the years to know she could never outrun Coben.

"Ellery . . ." He touched the edge of her T-shirt with one finger, a tiny caress that made her swallow hard. "I hope you know you don't have to do anything with me. You owe me nothing, certainly not this."

"It's not about you," she said swiftly. She shut her mouth and screwed her eyes shut. "I mean, not this part of it. I just meant—If it feels like I'm being forced to be here, that's not wrong." She swallowed again and made herself look him in the eyes. "It's just I'm the one doing the forcing."

He frowned, concerned. "Then maybe we should wait."

"I have waited. That's what I'm trying to tell you. I don't want to wait anymore." She reached and took his hand again. She put his palm to her chest and pressed it down so he could feel her racing heart. She had told him the truth before, that she didn't know what she liked in bed, but for the first time in her life, she wanted to find out.

"Far be it from me, then, to keep a lady waiting," he said as he leaned down. She kept her eyes closed as the air between them grew warm and thick. He shifted his whole body slightly, until their lips were almost touching. She surged forward and closed the last bit of distance and then rejoiced at the contact.

Reed stroked her face while making love to her mouth,

teasing her gently with his tongue in the same slow rhythm of his thumb against her cheek. She made an incoherent sound of pleasure and he backed off, just a bit. "You, um . . . I . . ."

"Yes," she whispered as she traced his features in the gray light.

He rested his head on hers as she reached around to caress his neck, her fingers reveling in the soft little hairs there. "I'll make you a deal," he said, his voice low and inviting against her ear. "Anything I do to you, you can do to me. And you can call it off at any time."

She grinned and nipped his chin. "Can I go first?"

"I insist on it."

He lay back and let her take the lead, returning her heated kisses, helping her pull the shirttail from the waist of his jeans so that her hand could slide underneath to his bare skin. He felt hot and sleek, his stomach lean and toned. She let her fingers play over his ribs and up until she met the scars from where Amy had shot him and the resulting surgery. She pulled her mouth from his and regarded him with concern. "Is this okay? I don't want to hurt you."

"You're not hurting me. It's okay." He put his hand on hers, his sweater and T-shirt trapped between them, and pressed gently until her palm covered his heart, the way she had done with his hand earlier. They watched each other as she tentatively explored his scars with her fingertips, mapping each ridge and smooth, warm valley. How close they'd come to almost missing this. Gradually, her wonderment gave way to a different sort of exploration. She rubbed the pad of her index finger over his nipple and felt it tighten under her touch. Reed sucked in a sharp breath as she dragged her nail lightly over him. Their eyes met and his had gone dark as night. "Oh," he said, like he'd just had some brilliant insight into a case, "it's going to be so good."

When it was his hand under her shirt, she had to remind her body to relax, that she did want to feel his fingers on her stomach, on her breasts, and then, later, a sweet slide down into her jeans. It took effort to quiet her instincts and tolerate another person this close, but the payoff was a delicious ache that grew and grew to the point where she didn't just want him inside her body; she needed him there. Only at the end, when her muscles drew taut and her breath came panting like a long-distance runner's, did she escape to the bright white place in her head where nothing could reach her. She had spent her life refusing to shatter, no matter what the price or reward.

She curled, still shaking, on one edge of the mattress. Reed, deliciously naked, stretched his hand across the mattress toward her, not quite touching. "All right?"

"Yes. I—I liked that part." She finally understood why people did stupid stuff for this.

A rich smile curved his mouth. "Which part? I may need to make notes."

"The kissing part, and then everything after." It turned out she did know what she liked in bed—him. She cuddled a little closer, suddenly cold.

He slipped an arm around her and kissed the top of her head. "What a coincidence. That was my favorite part, too."

"But I may need to collect more data," she cautioned against his chest. "That was only one time." Her hand began an exploratory journey down between them.

Reed hissed in his breath and his grip tightened around her. "I was wrong before," he said. "You might just kill me yet."

She grinned with delight because she was finally in on the joke. "Yeah," she said before she kissed him. "But what a way to go."

21

Reed woke up alone. Just because he and Ellery had spent the last two days together more naked than not didn't mean she slept with him. When it came time for rest, she retreated to her own room. He smoothed the empty space where she had lain. Ellery might never be one for extended cuddling. Maybe this personality quirk was because of Coben, but maybe not. This was the issue, that they would never know who she would have been without him. But without him, Reed would never have known her, so he was determined to look forward this time, not back.

He rolled out of bed and took a quick shower, intending on making her breakfast, but Ellery was already up and dressed, reading a magazine as she sipped her mug of tea. "You've ruined my suave move," he complained as he prepared coffee in the kitchenette. "I was going to bring you breakfast in bed."

"I'm not allowed to eat anything," she replied from her

place on the sofa. "Not until afterward."

"Oh. Right." He left the coffee and came to sit with her. "How are you feeling?"

She took a steadying breath. "Okay. It will be over soon, at least."

He reached over and took her hand, and they sat like that for a long time, saying nothing. When the time came, he drove their rental car to the hospital and she got checked in. Reed was allowed to hang out in her hospital room during the early part of the preparation. John Hathaway, by her request, stayed away, but a different Hathaway showed up instead. "Mom," Ellery said, her eyes wide with shock as Caroline Hathaway entered the room. She carried a trio of balloons and a stack of magazines. "What are you doing here? When I told you I was doing this, that didn't mean you had to come out here."

"My baby's in the hospital," she replied as she began fussing around the room. She had a rodent-like nervous energy to her, her hands constantly in motion as she adjusted the angle of the blinds and tugged at the sheets on the bed. "Where else would I be?"

Reed kept his mouth shut on this one. He knew Ellery had not seen her mother in quite some time because her mother still lived in Chicago at the scene of Ellery's attack. He had spoken to the woman only once, by phone years ago when he was doing research for the Coben book. As Caroline smoothed out her blanket, Reed noted with some irony that mother and daughter shared the same beautiful hands. In a different era, Coben might have plucked Caroline from the streets.

Ellery gritted her teeth and kicked off the blanket that Caroline had just added. "Thanks, Mom, but you didn't need to drive all this way. I'm not going to be here that long." She waved a hand to where Reed stood in the corner, trying to blend in with the medical equipment. "Mom, you remember Reed Markham, don't you?"

Reed dutifully stepped forward to extend his hand, and Caroline took it. "Of course I remember. The man from the FBI."

Reed smiled to himself, dropping his chin to his chest. *The man from the FBI,* he thought. Yes, he was. He was also a father, a brother, an ex-husband, and a son. He'd gone looking to his DNA to figure out who he was but had learned the answer somewhere else. "I'm not here because of the FBI," he told her. "I'm here as the man who loves your daughter."

"Oh! Oh my." Caroline beamed at Ellery, who shrank down under the covers.

A nurse entered, brusque and efficient. "Okay, time to say goodbye for now. You can wait for her down the hall. The whole process should take just a few hours."

"Already?" Caroline looked crushed. "I just got here."

"I'll see you when it's over, Mom."

As Caroline reluctantly left the room, Reed bent down low to kiss Ellery's cheek. "Did you hear what I said?" he asked her, his voice teasing.

"I heard."

"Good luck," he whispered against her skin. "I'm sure you'll do great."

"Mmm." She turned her head away, but when he went to withdraw, her fingers caught at the front of his shirt. "You'll be here the whole time, right?"

He squeezed her. "The whole time."

In the waiting room, he sat with Caroline and listened to her natter on about some disagreement with her neighbors over where the garbage cans should be stored, the bunion on her left foot that wouldn't go away, and some complicated story involving a cousin who'd gone AWOL from rehab. Only when the woman went to get herself a snack did Reed get to enjoy the blessed silence. He leaned his head against the wall, his thoughts drifting from Ellery's mother back to his own. He pictured the crime scene in his head, the puzzle that had failed so long to give up its secrets. After Amy's arrest, he'd let it be, figuring there was nothing left to find there. He probed himself to see how he would feel if Amy ended up getting away with it. Sad, he decided. Sad. But maybe that would always be. There was no way to look at those pictures, to see a young woman murdered like that, and feel anything but regret.

His mind turned to the happier pictures, Cammie's snapshots of her life before and after he was born. Cammie and Angie, dressed up to hit the town, smiling for the camera. Cammie sitting on the steps, holding him in her lap. The three women, Cammie, Angie, and Wanda, friends with their whole lives ahead of them. He recalled the snapshot in which Cammie was dressed in the blouse she'd been murdered in, the one with the green diamonds. Reed could picture it as it was later, soaked with blood. He saw in his mind's eye Cammie's writing on the back of the photo: *Angie, Wanda, and me.*

Reed sat up. "'Angie, Wanda, and me,'" he repeated, ticking them off on his fingers. Then the other way, so the order was mirrored. "'Me, Wanda, and Angie.'" How many times had he looked at that picture? He said the names again inside his head. Jesus, if he was right . . . well, he couldn't allow himself to think that far. He got to his feet and rushed for the door, nearly knocking Caroline over in his haste to get out the door.

"Where are you going? She's not done yet!"

"I'm not leaving the hospital," he called back over his shoulder. "I'll be right back." As he sprinted down the corridor, he called up his boss. "It's me," he said, breathless when she answered. "I need to run one more DNA test."

"Okay, but why won't you at least give me a hint?" Ellery needled him again from the other side of the car. He'd gone total California with the rental this time: they had a red convertible, and he was enjoying the way the wind played with her hair as they drove. At least until the hound shoved his snout in from the back. "Bump, let Reed drive, okay?" Ellery pushed him rearward, and the fur beast put his paws up on the door, ears in the wind.

"He could have stayed home, you know," Reed groused at her without any rancor. "We're going to have to hose down the whole car to get the slobber off."

"He's with me, which means he is home," she replied, reaching back to give the animal an affectionate pat. She'd come through the bone marrow procedure with no complications other than a lingering fatigue that had required her to spend more time in bed. For his part, Reed had been entirely too happy to join her. "I don't think you're in any position to be dictating rules, considering I agreed to come all the way out here without knowing where exactly you're taking me and why."

"We're almost there," he told her as he took the exit for Pasadena. His hands tightened on the wheel. "Just hang on a little longer."

He wasn't sure if he was talking to her or himself. All these years of waiting, of wondering, and now he was just a few minutes away. He navigated through the hilly streets with no help from the GPS, while Ellery watched the scenery with keen interest, trying to discern any clues.

"This is Angie Rivera's neighborhood," she said, turning to him.

"Yes, it is." He rounded the last corner and glided the car to a stop in front of the little green house.

Ellery stared at it and then back at him. "That's Angie Rivera's house."

"Right again," he told her cheerfully. He got out of the

car and went around to open the door for her. Moving up and down still was a bit painful for Ellery, so he reached out to help her.

She took his hand and eased to her feet, reaching back afterward to clip on Bump's leash. "Then I don't understand. Who is it that you want me to meet?"

"All will be explained shortly," he said, keeping her hand in his. "Come with me."

His pulse quickened as they went up the walk, but he felt time slowing down, stretching like taffy as he zeroed in on her front door. Forty years packed into a last few steps. He'd told Angie they were coming, but he had not explained why. She'd apparently been watching and waiting for them, because the front door flung open before he could knock. "Reed," she said, smiling hard enough to crinkle her eyes. "It's wonderful to see you again. And you brought Ellery, too. Oh, and the Speed Bump!"

Bump surged forward, wagging and woofing at the new person in front of him. "I can stay outside with him," Ellery said. "I know Zsa-Zsa probably wouldn't approve of a guest."

"Oh, he's darling." Angie crouched to greet Bump, who wriggled his sturdy body as close as possible to her. "Zsa-Zsa's napping in the bedroom, so I'll just go shut the door." She returned a moment later, still smiling. "Please, come inside. I had no idea you'd be back so soon, but I'm glad you're here. Has there been a development on the case?"

"Yes," Reed said. "A big one."

Both women turned to him in surprise. Reed took a deep breath and a strange calm came over him. "Ellery," he said, watching Angie's face. "I'd like you to meet my mother, Camilla Flores."

Angie/Camilla let out a soft cry of shock, and Ellery's hands flew to her mouth. Reed stood between the two women, awkward now that the truth was out. Camilla had tears in her eyes. She stretched out one hand to his face, her fingers trembling, but she dropped away before she made contact. "So many times," she whispered. "So many times, I wanted to tell you. First, when I found out where you were, that your father had taken you . . . I thought I could go to where you lived and tell you the truth. Then when you came here and found me, I thought it was a sign. But you had come to ask me about Angie's murder, and I . . ." She stopped and closed her eyes. "It had been so long. I couldn't find the words."

"Maybe we should sit down?" Reed asked. They were still standing in the entryway.

"Of course," she said, stepping back out of the way. "Let me get the cake." She stopped and wiped her eyes with the corner of her apron.

Camilla cut them all a slice of pound cake, which sat untouched on pretty flowered plates as they stared at each other in the living room. Looking at her, he wasn't sure how he had missed it the first time—they had the same-shaped brown eyes, the same pointed chin. "How did you learn the truth?" she asked him finally. "At the beginning, I worried so much that someone would figure out the switch, but after forty-four years passed, I didn't think this day would ever come."

Reed took out the picture, the one with the three friends, and showed it to her. "You labeled the back," he explained. "I just read the names in the wrong order. You're the one on the left, and Angie is the one wearing the blouse with the diamonds on it, the same one she wore the day of the attack. That was my first real clue, but once I realized it, other things that had been bothering me started to make sense. Like the shopping bags."

"What about them?" Camilla asked, holding the picture like it was a rare treasure.

"You can correct me if I'm wrong," he said, "but I figure the story you told the police was basically true. You used the windfall from my father's money to go out shopping. Angie stayed home to babysit in your apartment. When you returned, you found her murdered in your living room. You grabbed me and ran next door to her place to call for help."

Camilla nodded slowly. "Yes, that's right. That's exactly what happened."

"I thought it was unusual that you would send Angie out on a shopping spree before you'd spent any money on yourself."

"I would have," Camilla whispered, her gaze falling on the picture. "I would have shared the money with her. I didn't get the chance."

"Once I developed the theory of what had really happened that day, I had my DNA tested against the sample

recorded as Camilla Flores. Needless to say, it didn't match."
He paused and waited a few moments. This was the ugly
part, the part she probably didn't want him to say. "It was
you who used the horse head to hit Angie's face, wasn't it?"
He said it as gently as he could. "You wanted the police and
everyone else to think it was you who had died."

Tears leaked out of Camilla's eyes and she nodded
mutely.

"And you took the money," Reed continued.

Her chin rose. "It was mine to take."

"I know it was."

She swiped at her cheeks with both hands. "She was
already dead. You have to believe me."

Reed had seen the awful violence in the pictures. "I know
she was."

"I—I didn't know what to think. Either someone killed
her thinking she was me or someone killed Angie on purpose
and I could be next."

"Someone," Reed repeated. "You mean Billy Thorndike."

"Him or one of his buddies, yes. He used to get me and
Angie confused all the time. Lots of people did. We were
mistaken for sisters. I thought he would realize soon that he
killed the wrong girl and come after me again. I did the only
thing I could think of—I ran. If Billy thought Camilla was
dead, maybe he wouldn't come after me. Maybe then he
wouldn't come after you." She gave him a mournful look. "It
was the worst part, leaving you. I cried and cried. The social
worker told me how you'd be adopted by a nice family, how

you wouldn't even remember what had happened." She sniffed several times. "And look, it came true."

Reed tried to smile for her. "It did."

"I saw in the paper what happened. You arrested that woman, that cop. The story said that she killed Angie. Is that really true?"

"I believe it is," Reed answered.

"But why? We didn't even know her, Angie or me. Why would she want to do that?"

"You never met her?" Reed asked carefully. "You're sure?"

"Not once," Camilla replied resolutely. "I would remember. Everything from those days, it's like it doesn't go away. I've got it all right here." She tapped the side of her head.

"Amy Owens says she came to dinner at your apartment, her and David. That she helped cook, and that's how her blood got on your knife."

"Never happened," Camilla said flatly. "She's lying."

"If you'd be willing to testify to that, then she goes to prison," Reed told her.

Camilla looked from Reed to Ellery and back again. "Testify? That means everything comes out, right? The whole story?"

"Well, yes," Reed conceded. "But Angie would have her rightful name again, and you would have yours. Your involvement would explain the newfound fingerprint on the horse head, which means Amy would finally pay for what she did."

"I don't know." She twisted her hands together in her lap. "I'd have to say about hitting Angie. I'd have to say where I got that money. Your father . . ."

"Will live with the consequences," Reed said firmly. "Whatever they are. He'll be fine; I promise you. So will I." He reached over and took her hand. "So will you." He looked from her uncertain eyes to the home she'd built around her, overflowing with plants and paintings and pictures of tiny ballerinas. The kitchen beyond held the air of fresh-baked cake and strong coffee. Here, at last, was his answer to what might have been—another warm, loving home, different with its joys and pains but built on the same sense of family, and he knew he could have been happy here. And yet. Whatever twinge of hurt, whatever longing he felt for the years lost with her, he could also admit he wouldn't trade the outcome. Cammie had given him his father back, and with Angus he'd also received a second mother and three sisters. Love, it seemed, really did multiply.

Cammie squeezed his hand almost painfully. "I—I'll think about it." She patted him. "You grew up so good. I guess I have your father to thank for that." She hesitated and then let him go. "And your mother. What you must think of me now, huh? A coward who ran away and left you."

"I'm not angry," he said, and meant it. His near death and resurrection had caused him to shift his thinking. His heart had much work left to do. He didn't want to weigh it down with anger—not for her, nor any of his family.

"You should be angry," she said, her eyebrows drawn

together in pain. "I left you. I've been angry about it all these years, what I did. I was scared. I'd screwed up everything. The only thing I did right was you, and then you were stuck with me, a lousy mother. I did nothing to deserve you."

Reed thought of all the times when he was a child that he'd wished his absent mother were someone famous or extraordinary, someone who made him special just by her very existence. His origin was instead sad and desperate, filled with rash decisions and poor choices. But he no longer felt like this ugliness had to define him, so maybe it was time to tell his mother: it didn't define her, either.

He took her hand. "What a world it would be," he said, "if we all got what we deserved." She sniffed and looked up at him with wet brown eyes.

"I never stopped loving you."

He squeezed her. "Nor I you."

Later, when they said their goodbyes at the door, Camilla stretched up on her tiptoes to hug him tight. "My big strong boy. I dreamed so long for this day. Please come back to see me again."

"I will," he promised her.

Outside, the sun dazzled in a bright blue sky. In the car, Ellery turned to him, her eyebrows raised. "That's a hell of a secret."

"I wanted to surprise you."

"Hers, not yours."

"Ah," he agreed. "Yes." The hot sun beat down on them, but Reed didn't start the car. For the first time in a long time, he had nowhere in particular to go. "My guess is she'll testify," he said as he glanced at Camilla's house. "She'll do it for Angie."

"Or for you," Ellery said softly. She graced him with one of her rare, slow smiles, the kind that made him want to lean over and bite her neck.

His own smile faded as he sighed. "I guess that's it then. It's finally over."

"Not quite. There's still Giselle Hardiman's murder."

"Oh, that's right. You were working on that code from her day planner. Did you ever crack it?"

"Nope." She took out her sunglasses and put them on. "But I found someone who's eager to take on the case. Someone who loves a good crime story and knows the Las Vegas scene inside and out. Someone who's always hungry for the next big scoop."

"Don't tell me—your reporter buddy."

"Bruce Carr. He's on it like a dog on a free leg."

On cue, Bump stuck his head between them, long tongue hanging out one side of his enormous mouth. He licked Reed's face and Reed howled his protest, wiping off the slobber with his sleeve. "Thanks to a plethora of medical bills, my leg is now damned expensive, so tell the hound to back off."

Ellery giggled as he started the engine. "So where are we going now?" she asked as the breeze picked up, swirling her hair.

"I don't know. Home, I guess."

"My home or your home?"

She kept the question casual, but he felt the weight of it nonetheless—his place, her place, and the six hundred miles that separated them. She had a job again in Boston. He had a daughter in Virginia. Eventually, they were going to have to go back to their separate lives. He merged onto the freeway, where they blended in with a dizzying number of other cars streaming along. The City of Angels had 4 million people in it, too many even to contemplate. He pointed the car to the south where the Pacific Ocean waited, cold and blue and endless. "Right now," he said as Ellery tilted her face to the sun, "we're going to the beach."

About the Author

Joanna Schaffhausen is a scientific editor who previously worked as an editorial producer for ABC News, where she advised and wrote for programs such as *World News Tonight*, *Good Morning America* and *20/20*. She lives in the Boston area with her husband and daughter. She is also the author of *The Vanishing Season* and *No Mercy*.

THE VANISHING SEASON
JOANNA SCHAFFHAUSEN

Fourteen years ago, teenager Ellery Hathaway was victim number seventeen in the grisly murder spree of serial killer Francis Michael Coben. She was the only one who lived.

Now Coben is safely behind bars, and Ellery has a new identity in a sleepy town where bike theft makes the newspapers. But each July for the last three years, locals have been disappearing. Then Ellery receives strange messages hinting that the culprit knows exactly what happened to her all those years ago. When she tries to raise the alarm, no one will listen, and terrified she may be next, Ellery must turn to the one person who might believe her story...

"A chilling, breathless dive into fear"
Carol Goodman

"A twisted story with an unforgettable protagonist"
Shannon Kirk

"A gripping debut"
Hallie Ephron

TITANBOOKS.COM

NO MERCY
JOANNA SCHAFFHAUSEN

Police officer Ellery Hathaway is on involuntary leave from her job because she shot a murderer in cold blood and refuses to apologize. Forced into group therapy for victims of violent crime, Ellery immediately finds higher priorities than "getting in touch with her feelings."

For one, she suspects a fellow group member may have helped to convict the wrong man for a deadly arson incident years ago. For another, Ellery gets entangled in the desperate requests of a woman who survived a brutal rape. He is still out there, this man with the spider-like ability to climb through bedroom windows. Ignoring all warnings, Ellery starts digging around in everyone's past but her own – a move that, at best, could put her out of work permanently, and at worst, could put her in the city morgue.

Praise for the series

"Gripping, compulsively readable. Be prepared to lose sleep."
Elisabeth Elo

"Dark, disturbing, and relentlessly sinister…
Be warned: leave on the light!"
Hank Phillippi Ryan

TITANBOOKS.COM

THE VANISHING YEAR
KATE MORETTI

Zoe Whittaker is living a charmed life: wife to a handsome Wall Street trader, with the perfect penthouse and summer home, she is the new member of Manhattan's social elite. What no one knows is that five years ago, Zoe's life was in danger. Back then, Zoe wasn't Zoe at all. Now her secrets are coming back to haunt her. As the past and present collide, Zoe must decide who she can trust before she—whoever she is—vanishes completely.

"A chilling, powerful tale of nerve-shattering suspense"
Heather Gudenkauf

"Twists and turns you won't see coming"
J.T. Ellison

"Great pacing and true surprises"
Kirkus

TITANBOOKS.COM

RIVER ROAD
CAROL GOODMAN

Driving home in a snowstorm, Nan Lewis hits something
with her car. She's sure it's a deer. What else could it be? Then
one of her students is found dead, the victim of a hit and run.
And there is blood on Nan's tyres. As friends and neighbours turn
on her, and she starts finding disturbing tokens that recall the
killing of her own daughter, Nan begins to suspect that the two
deaths are connected…

"Emotion-charged twists and turns that you won't see coming"
Tess Gerritsen

"An intense psychological thriller"
Publishers Weekly

TITANBOOKS.COM

THE PASSENGER
LISA LUTZ

In case you were wondering, I didn't do it. I don't have an alibi, so you'll have to take my word for it...

With her husband's dead body still warm, Tanya Dubois has only one option: run. When the police figure out that she doesn't officially exist, they'll start asking questions she can't answer.

Desperate to keep the past buried, she adopts and sheds identities as she flees. Along the way she meets a cop with unknown motives and a troubled woman who sees through her disguise—and who may be friend or foe.

But ultimately she is alone, and the past can no longer be ignored...

"Told with enormous verve and at a breakneck pace, the story twists and turns like a corkscrew"
Daily Mail

"A complex web of finely honed characters"
Publishers Weekly

TITANBOOKS.COM

For more fantastic fiction, author events,
exclusive excerpts, competitions, limited editions and more

VISIT OUR WEBSITE
titanbooks.com

LIKE US ON FACEBOOK
facebook.com/titanbooks

FOLLOW US ON TWITTER AND INSTAGRAM
@TitanBooks

EMAIL US
readerfeedback@titanemail.com